LACEY LORRAINE

The Truth About Sunsets
A Coming of Age Story

First published by Lacey Lorraine 2023

Copyright © 2023 by Lacey Lorraine

All rights reserved. No part of this publication may be reproduced, stored or transmitted in any form or by any means, electronic, mechanical, photocopying, recording, scanning, or otherwise without written permission from the publisher. It is illegal to copy this book, post it to a website, or distribute it by any other means without permission.

This novel is entirely a work of fiction. The names, characters and incidents portrayed in it are the work of the author's imagination. Any resemblance to actual persons, living or dead, events or localities is entirely coincidental.

Lacey Lorraine asserts the moral right to be identified as the author of this work.

First edition

ISBN: 979-8-9886972-1-3

This book was professionally typeset on Reedsy. Find out more at reedsy.com

To my brothers and sisters, all nine of you, for inspiring me to write about family. I love you all!

Contents

Playlist for The Truth About Sunsets	v
Author's Note	vii
Cajun French Translations	viii
Prologue	1
Chapter 1	3
Chapter 2	6
Chapter 3	15
Chapter 4	23
Chapter 5	32
Chapter 6	41
Chapter 7	53
Chapter 8	62
Chapter 9	69
Chapter 10	75
Chapter 11	87
Chapter 12	98
Chapter 13	108
Chapter 14	119
Chapter 15	128
Chapter 16	139
Chapter 17	151
Chapter 18	160
Chapter 19	168
Chapter 20	174
Chapter 21	183
Chapter 22	189

Chapter 23	198
Chapter 24	204
Chapter 25	212
Chapter 26	217
Chapter 27	227
Chapter 28	236
Chapter 29	243
Chapter 30	251
Chapter 31	259
Chapter 32	266
Epilogue	272
Sneak Peek: The Thing About Sunrises	275
Prologue	276
Chapter 1	278
Acknowledgments	284
About the Author	286

Playlist for The Truth About Sunsets

Bird Set Free - Sia
Us - James Bay
Drip - Cardi B (feat. Migos)
Yosemite - Travis Scott
Untraveled Road - Thousand Foot Krutch
Wasted on You - Morgan Wallen
The Bones - Maren Morris
:((Sad Face) - Bahari
Purple Hat - Sofi Tukker
Blood // Water - Grandson
Fire Up the Night - New Medicine
Dandelions - Ruth B.
Electric Feel - MGMT
Devil - Niykee Heaton
In My Mind - Alice Ivy, Ecca Vandal
Pretty Head - Transviolet
Sweet Jane - Garrett Kato
11 Minutes - YUNGBLUD, Halsey, Travis Barker
Wine, Beer, Whiskey - Little Big Town
I'm Ready - Niykee Heaton
Fake - The Tech Thieves
Fire In My Head - Two Feet

Billie Eilish - Armani White
Thank God - Kane Brown, Katelyn Brown
I'm Good (Blue) - David Guetta, Bebe Rexha

Listen here.
https://open.spotify.com/playlist/2vzJh8RLf4coFafXRfVTR5

If you'd like to immerse yourself even more in the story, check out the Pinterest board!
https://www.pinterest.com/AuthorLaceyLorraine/the-truth-about-sunsets/

Author's Note

As a proud southern woman, I was excited to write this book for a few reasons. One, I haven't read much about Louisiana heritage in the books I've chosen, and even less about Cajuns. As someone who has traveled to and lived in many parts of the United States, I've always been fascinated by the regional differences I've encountered.

And while I have always been proud of my roots, there are some darker aspects that are still alive in the deep south, as well. I've touched on some of these, such as racism and bigotry. Please know, that while I leaned heavily on my own experiences from growing up in the deep south to write this book, I am not intending anything on these pages to be a blanket statement for the south or the people who live there.

This is first, and foremost, a fiction novel. Any use of a slur by secondary characters is meant to showcase an aspect of people with *that* mindset, and to highlight them in a negative way. In no way would I ever glorify or condone the use of any slur. However, I did feel that it was necessary to spell out just how hateful and bigoted some people can be, whether they're southern or from any corner of the world.

Cajun French Translations

1. Le bon temps - The good times
2. La malade vant - Bad stomach ache
3. Vite, vite - Quick!
4. Allons a Boston - Let's go to Boston
5. Pas bon - Not good / Bad
6. Garçon - Boy, young man
7. Gris gris - A voodoo term, but used as a warning for bad vibes or getting in trouble.
8. Cher/Sha - Dear, love, term of endearment to close loved ones.
9. Commo ça vas / Ca vas? - How are you / Doing okay?
10. Mes chers petite - My little loves
11. How's ya momma and them - How is your family doing?
12. Lagniappe - Something extra, like a gift with purchase or a free side with a meal.
13. S'il vous plais - If you please / Please
14. Mes ami - My friends
15. Je t'aime - I love you
16. Come see - Come over here
17. Dressed - When talking about a sandwich, with all the fixin's (lettuce, onion, tomato, etc.)

The Truth About Sunsets

Prologue

énouement
(n) *the bitterness one feels after realizing how their future has turned out, and not being able to warn their past self*

Fall - Senior Year

There are few moments in life filled with as many possibilities as the first day of college.

I'd been full of dreams when I began freshman year. They say starting college is beginning the rest of your life. That it's where you go to grow into the person you're meant to be.

I fully bought into the mindset, but now if anyone said it to my face, I'd say they were full of shit.

This isn't a story about a girl growing into a woman.

This is a story about the only life that girl had known being snatched away on a dark, rainy night, on some backwoods Louisiana highway. That dream died alone in the dark.

I was so naive, thinking that I could have it all. If you work hard, you'll succeed. That's what the motivational posters say.

What they don't say is that all of your hard work will quite possibly never pay off. There are no "Give it your all and prepare to get nothing in return" posters. Maybe there should be. I could at least say that I'd been warned.

After all of the effort and hard work I put into gymnastics during the years, I'm hard pressed to find a reason to go on. My friends have either abandoned me or aren't speaking to me at the moment. I quite possibly ruined my most important relationship, the one with my twin. And the man I figured out too late that I love is with someone else.

I laid every brick of the lonely path I'm forced to walk now, but I can't bring myself to care anymore.

Babe Ruth said, "It's hard to beat a person who never gives up".

Well Babe, this is me.

Giving up.

Chapter 1

eleutheromania
(n) the intense desire for freedom

September, Senior Year of High School

"What do you mean we can't go? Literally everyone will be on that trip, Daddy. We're almost *eighteen*!" Raven pleads with our father while disappointment settles like lead deep in my gut.

I knew not to get my hopes up and big fat did it anyways.

Most of our graduating class is heading to Galveston, Texas in April to spend Spring Break at the beach. It's a huge deal to coordinate with everyone, so the senior class always starts planning at the beginning of the school year.

"I don't care if you're thirty," he barks, slamming the refrigerator door before sitting back down in his chair. Who knew that a simple request would send him into such an uproar? Me. I did. But Raven can't let it go.

"I don't trust those teenagers, and I don't trust you both to make sound decisions when surrounded by partying and drugs," he continues on a roll. "You think I don't remember being young? *Pas bon!*"

Our dad loves us…maybe just too much at times. His over-protectiveness has gotten worse as we get older. It's like he thinks sex, drugs, and rock-n-roll will corrupt his precious daughters. Never mind that he let my older brothers go on trips. I know better than to bring it up again. "The world is much different for girls than it is for boys" will be his ready-made response, inviting no arguments and serving only to make our blood boil at the gender inequality.

"You're ruining our senior year." Raven says dejectedly as she drops her fork, sending it clanging across the table, and Daddy rears back like he's been slapped. No one says anything, and a hot tear rolls down my cheek. I've never made a fuss. I've missed Friday night football games when Gus or Allan hasn't been able to come. I've missed out on parties, on sleepovers, on going out and being a wild and crazy teenager, even just *once*.

But I really didn't think he'd force us to miss our senior Spring Break.

Raven grabs my arm. "Come on Len. I can't stay in this house." Momma just looks at us and shakes her head as we leave out the backdoor. The door slams behind us and we walk towards the barn a few hundred feet behind the house.

Inside the barn, I sit on a hay bale while Raven throws herself onto the old leather couch in the alcove near the tack room. I have a direct line of sight to the house to make sure our parents don't sneak up on us while we're venting. I've learned the hard way.

"I swear, it's like he wants me to hate him. I can't believe Momma just sat at the table and didn't say anything," Raven says, throwing her arm over her eyes.

Does she really expect her to stick up for us? She's worse than he is, making me raise my arms above my head to show that my shirts won't ride up and show my stomach and being the first to say no anytime we want to go hang out with friends. I take a deep breath. If I let myself mope and think up everything they've done over the years to dim our light, I'll be miserable and moody all night.

I clap my hands once to get her attention. "Okay Rae. Let's be realistic about this. They're not gonna change, and I'm sure it'll be the same with Maddie when she's our age. We can't force them to evolve."

My coaches tell me to focus on one problem at a time. If I'm trying to nail a new skill, I give it my undivided attention until I can stick it in my sleep.

"What we *can* change, is what we do after high school. I don't plan on

Chapter 1

continuing this crap when we're in college."

She sits up. "I'm listening."

"I think I have a plan," I say.

Chapter 2

selcouth
(adj) unfamiliar, rare, strange, and yet - marvelous

YEAR ONE - *May*

Maybe it's because our parents are both university professors that they're so vigilant in holding the reins to our childhoods. They've seen it all with Louisiana State University students and know that once we're out in the real world, we're free to do and act as we please, so why not protect us from *living* for as long as they can?

Movies over PG-13 do not exist at our home, nor do sleepovers at other people's houses, or going to parties or on dates that aren't chaperoned. They demand to know where we are, who we're with, what we're wearing, and when we'll be home at any given moment of the day.

To say that it's suffocating is an understatement. To say that it's confining seems like an oversimplification.

When it came time to choose our college, everyone knew that Raven and I would buddy up. It's just our way. What they didn't know is that we would be light years away from Louisiana.

The decision to apply to Kalon University at Boston was almost a no brainer, considering our shared fascination with New England and our fierce determination to take our freedom of choice from our parents who refused

Chapter 2

to give up control.

I just...I want outside of Louisiana. I know it, I live it, it's in my blood. But America is huge, and in all the times I've been outside of the state it's been planes, buses, convention centers, hotels, and restaurants. Competitions are a time suck, so it's not as if I've ever really experienced any other state I've visited.

And it doesn't hurt that Massachusetts is far, far away from Ascension Parish.

Growing up in near Baton Rouge, the only sport worth watching (if you ask any given Louisianan) is LSU Football. Literally, ask someone off the street what sport they love, and they'll just say "LSU" because it's widely known that the one thing almost everyone who lives in Cajun Country watches is Tigers football. Maybe they'll give some love to the Saints, but they aren't king outside of New Orleans.

And since both of our parents are fully adverse to letting us spread our wings, and hold an understanding, if not slightly intolerable devotion to all things *"Geaux Tigers!"* you can imagine how well they took the news.

The news being that we not only applied to Kalon University at Boston, but that I also got a full-ride scholarship with the gymnastics team and my smarty pants twin got a partial academic scholarship to their undergrad economics department. And that, *oh by the way,* Raven and I plan to attend this fall?

In case you're hanging on for the answer as to how well my parents receive this brand-new information, it's *not well, at all.*

Our dad's face gets redder than I've ever seen it, including that time my older brothers got caught skinny dipping in our pond with some girls from their school. Momma's face morphs into her "not impressed" look, while Daddy starts pacing our living room. Raven and I are sitting side by side on the couch and he turns to us before letting us have it.

"So. Not only are you not even considering going to our alma mater, where both of your brothers attend, and your mother and I have taught for *two decades*, you also both applied to this school without even telling us? How could you even consider this? You've never lived on your own, but now you think you can live fifteen hundred miles away?" He ranted, barely breathing between syllables, his volume increasing with each word.

Fifteen hundred miles away sounds even better after that reaction.

"I don't give a damn about you being offered scholarships. You're not going! Lennie, how were you even recruited without us knowing? That is not how the NCAA works!"

I hold my ground, determined not to break like I usually do. Confrontation and I do not go together. "I sent in a recruiting video, outlining my best level ten skills. They want me to come up in person to meet with them, so they can finalize the offer."

He starts to puff up with indignation, his salt-and-pepper hair contrasting with his now maroon face.

Raven and I look at each other knowingly, feeling chastised even though we expected it. Also, it should be known that while our mom is as tiny as Raven and me, our dad is a bear of a man at over six feet tall. So, his outburst is definitely packing some pucker factor. He decides he's done with me for the moment and turns to my twin.

"And you, Rae? You're wanting to be this far from home with your anxiety? You don't even like being in airplanes or on boats, and yet you want to pack up and leave the only home you've ever known?"

It's true. Raven is the most risk averse member of the family. While she rarely ventures out, Maddie and I travel often. She and mom attend her rodeos in the surrounding states, and I sometimes travel to competitions with my elite gymnastics team.

And Raven, well…Raven prefers to stick to her living room yoga and One Tree Hill reruns routine.

But calling her out and using her anxiety to try and change her mind is uncalled for. I can't believe he's trying to use that against her.

Raven narrows her eyes, and unlike me, she doesn't back down from confrontation, ever. "That's really low of you," she says. I can hear the hurt, and apparently so can Daddy because regret flashes over his face.

Luckily, our mom was far less quick to anger, and usually the voice of reason when Daddy works himself up into a fit. What I did *not* expect was for her to side with us.

"Harry, for God's sake, take it back a step," she says consolingly. Rae and I

Chapter 2

look at each other in shock. "We've always encouraged the kids to speak up when they want something, and to work hard to get it." She flashes him an angry face that has my dad looking sheepish. "Mes filles, this is a lot for us to take in unexpectedly. Let's back up a few steps and start by hearing why you chose Kalon University. Lenore, you go first."

And thank God and all His angels because I came to this discussion fully prepared for that question. Our parents are intellectuals who respect hearing the facts spelled out.

"I knew this would come as a shock, and I'm sorry that it took you by surprise. But Raven and I chose KU together for multiple reasons. Yes, it's far away and that was a factor. I know you both love living here, but I want more. I want to see and experience other places, badly. I want to see the leaves turn orange and the snow fall. I want to meet other people from all over, and to learn about other culture outside of ours. And Kalon has an amazing Communications program. Not to mention, their gymnastics team is a top-ranked Division One team."

I had a really disappointing Nationals last year. Not only did I not qualify for the National team, but I also got injured during my beam routine and didn't even place. I missed my chance at the Olympic trials, and I burned with envy when we watched the summer games.

There are four spots and two alternates on the Olympic team, and although I'll be twenty-one when it's time to compete the summer before my senior year, I know that I have what it takes. Oksana Chusovitin has competed for Uzbekistan *seven times*. She's in her forties, so if she can do it, there's no way I'm letting my age be a factor. Gymnasts don't typically have long careers, but I'll still be in the prime of my life at twenty-one.

I've worked hard all year to improve, and I know that joining the KU team will help me develop even more to prepare me for the summer games in three years. If anything, that entire experience made me realize I need a smart back up plan – I'm majoring in communications to become a sports commentator once I step away from the mat. It will be a good way to stay close to gymnastics after I retire.

I take a breath, ready for the coup de grace. "And this isn't some run-of-the-mill, four-year college. Kalon University is Ivy League, and they only accept about twenty-five percent of applicants each year! Don't you think it's fate that Raven and I both got scholarships?" I reasoned.

Raven begins her pitch. "I've done a lot of research on KU's economics department and I'm sure that it's where I want to be." Raven pauses and looks Daddy directly in the eye, full of that backbone that I envy.

"And yes, I don't like doing things I think can be dangerous and I maintain that certain activities are terrifying, but I can't be protected by you for the rest of my life. I don't want to let my anxiety stop me from living, especially in my golden years, and deep down? I know you two don't want that for me."

My father comes from a place of being overly protective, but our mom's strictness has always seemed to come from a place of fear. Fear of what, I'm not sure. She's a very private person and rarely speaks about her past. Even to her children.

And an incident involving a member of our church and several underage girls a few years ago didn't help matters at all. It just caused my parents to double down, even though none of us were harmed.

I hold my breath and look between my parents. This can only go one of two ways.

Absorbing our statements, Daddy takes a slow deep breath with his eyes closed and lets it out, trying to calm himself. Our mom sits back in her chair, looking lost in thought.

"You two clearly have your hearts set on this." She frowns, looking between the two of us.

"Yes, we do," I say quietly. Inside, I'm exclaiming. Is it possible that Momma finally sees us as adults and isn't going to try and stop this from happening?

"Is this revenge for not letting you two go on the Spring Break trip?" Daddy's sudden question doesn't come as a surprise. During that week, the two of us only spoke or looked at our parents if they directly asked us something. The only form of acting out that wouldn't get us grounded.

"No," I say truthfully. "But it definitely put things into perspective for us."

I don't trust that we will get the full college experience under their eyes, and after barely getting the high school experience, let alone the Senior experience,

Chapter 2

I'm not willing to back down. If they say no, Raven and I will go anyway, and I think they're starting to realize that because they both look at each other uneasily.

Daddy sighs. "Alright cher. Let Momma and I talk this through together and we'll circle back. We love you both very much, but I have some real concerns. I'm not prepared to let this go just because it's something you want. Being a parent means making tough decisions for your kids, sometimes in spite of what they think will be good for them. Let's sleep on it and talk tomorrow about this." He stands up and kisses us both on the forehead.

Momma stands up from her recliner, and being the least demonstrative person in our family, simply says "Lenore, go get Madeline for dinner."

Well, I guess that's that.

That night, when I'm lying in bed, I can't help but let hope bloom.

The next day, after a much calmer round two of discussions and a planned trip to scope out the school before they concede, our parents agree to continue the conversation. One trip to Boston and *several* conversations later, we have their blessing to accept our scholarships.

Allons a Boston!

* * *

August

"I may have been on the fence for a while about following your stubborn butt all the way to Boston, but I have to admit, it's gorgeous here, sissy," Rae drawls. Looking out over the rolling green lawn, dotted with lush green maple and ash trees, I have to agree. It's a completely different world that we're used to. Gone are the looming oak trees, clothed in swaying moss. There are no bayous here, no gators, no oppressive humidity and heat.

And there are no overbearing parents. At least there won't be after they head home tomorrow.

When we walk into our dorm room in Anderson Hall, you could have heard a pin drop.

Woof, I am not impressed. With growing disappointment, I take in the square room with its uninspired white cinder block walls, ugly tile flooring, and the twin pine dressers, desks, and single beds, which are arranged helter-skelter.

"Is this a dorm room or a barracks at Fort Polk?" Daddy said, disgusted. Momma just stares.

"None of that," Raven said, breezing past us and opening the blinds. She turns and gives the room another once over before pivoting back and opening the window as far as it would go. "It just needs some fresh air and the Landry Twins special touch!"

Daddy heaves a sigh which the three of us pointedly ignore, and we get to work unpacking and situating. The air gradually becomes less stale and dusty, and after we rearrange the furniture, we finally have it set up to our satisfaction. I know that once we fully get it decorated, it will be cozy and perfect. *Cozy* is my favorite feeling, after all.

There was a brief battle for the bed near the window. Raven wanted it so that she can set up her easel and line up her stupid crystals, and as usual, she gets her way by being annoying.

"Gimme the window, gimme the window, gimme the window, gimm-"
"ALRIGHT!"

Once we got settled in our room, our parents take off to get an early dinner and mention something about visiting a Waterworks Museum. I'm always down for a history or art museum but looking at old pipes sounds like a hard pass, so Raven and I set out to explore campus.

It's breathtakingly beautiful. Everything in Boston just seems older than the rest of the country. Well, what I've managed to see of the rest of the country. There are a lot of old, historic places in Louisiana, but it's not even in the top ten oldest states, Massachusetts being number six. Yes, I googled that. I can't wait to visit Salem this fall with Raven. It's been on our bucket list ever since we watched Hocus Pocus as children.

Fall foliage is something that we don't have in the Deep South, and it's a thing of beauty. At least it is in pictures and on TV. To think about experiencing it in person sends a thrill up my spine, and I hope the pictures of Boston and Salem do it justice in real life.

Chapter 2

When we came to visit in May, I was immediately happy when we got out of the rental car, and I felt the lack of humidity. Louisiana humidity on a good day will make you feel like you need to wring your clothes out. The weather is even better now, a breezy 80 degrees and, for once, I feel like my hair isn't a big, frizzy mess.

I look over at Raven, taking in her thick hair, straight to my out-of-control waves, noting how shiny it is and hoping mine is, too. We're fraternal twins, so while we look very similar with our slim 5'4" frames, green eyes, and long dark hair, there is no chance of mistaking us for the same person.

I've always half loved that we're our own person and half wanted to be able to play "guess which twin." Alas, like our features, we are very different. Raven is more into math and numbers that I'll ever be, and I would rather read novels than do any kind of schoolwork, *especially math*.

Raven loops her arm through mine, and we meander through the main campus, taking in the Gothic architecture of the towering stone buildings and the rolling green lawns. Here and there, students dot the lawns, lounging around reading or talking. The buildings are truly beautiful, and it almost feels like another world here. Bellus Hall looms over us like something from ancient Europe, catching my eye and stopping me as I stare. All towers and gables and archivolts, with the lower levels covered in ivy, it looks like a cross between a castle and a cathedral. I hope this view never gets old to me.

How horrible it would be to get to a place in life where one can't appreciate the beauty around them.

We walk past a game of frisbee, and I laugh to myself at how every-college-movie clichéd this scene is. I don't care. I'm soaking it all in with a smile on my face and the warm wind in my hair. I'm hit with a sense of rightness. Being here feels like it was supposed to happen all along.

"I feel like we're in a cheesy college movie," Raven laughs as we pass through the quad, saying exactly what's on my mind.

It's a twin thing; happens all the time.

"I was just thinking the same thing. It's like a postcard. I already have a list of places to explore. I researched as much as I could. Did you know there's a secret room with an entrance from tree stairs to one of the buildings on campus? And apparently there's a secret tunnel connecting the Caritas and Lectio chapels? Like catacombs, maybe?"

She stops dead and stares at me, eyes wide. "Dude, you had me at secret tree stairs. What exactly *are* tree stairs?" I shake my head and pull her arm to keep us moving.

"Not one clue, but it sounds magical. Know what else sounds magical? The fact that Quintus Ennius is one of the most beautiful college libraries in the *world* and we get to go there whenever we want! I've never said this in my life, but I can't wait to go there to study."

She laughs, knowing that I have the attention span of a gnat and loath studying, but I fully intend on making the most of the gorgeous libraries on campus. And if I'm reading books instead of study material, who's to know?

We're walking past a group of guys that I'm working hard not to openly stare at, specifically because one guy in particular has his shirt off and let's just say he has no cause for self-consciousness.

Also working not to stare because *I don't have on sunglasses.*

"Hey girl, what that mouth do?" one of the guys yells at us.

I stop dead in my tracks in shock. Who talks like that?

Thankfully Raven is much quicker to respond. "The only thing my mouth will do to you is hurt your feelings!" she shouts while pulling my arm to keep us moving. The jerk's friends all laugh uproariously, and I crack a smile as we walk away, feminism intact.

Raven saves the day again.

Just once, I want to have the guts to stand up for myself like that. I need to catalog some quick comebacks for the future.

Apparently, college boys like to play dirty.

Chapter 3

bibliosmia
(n) the smell or aroma of old or good books

"Be sure to stick together if you go to parties. Watch your drinks at all times, but I'm really hoping you'll stay away from that scene *since drinking underage is highly illegal*," Daddy starts, raising his eyebrow to emphasize his last point. "And no letting boys into your dorms, no matter how much they sweet talk you. And trust me, these little shits will try."

Oh God, not another boy talk. Raven thought it was funny, but The Sex Talk when we were younger made me want to crawl into a hole and disappear.

It's Sunday afternoon and our parents are leaving for the airport. Our older brothers have been watching our little sister, and I know my mom is anxious to get back to her and our horses.

"Et pas de garçons du tout!" Momma adds, redundantly.

And no boys at all.

Lord, give me strength.

"Y'all! We got this. Trust that you raised smart, capable women!" Raven says while hugging Daddy goodbye.

"That's the hope, sha." Our big, tough father sniffs, while kissing our cheeks and giving us bear hugs. "Alright mes chers petite, je t'aime."

He drags Momma to the rental while she calls out "Mes petites choux, je t'aime beaucoup! Pas des garçons!"

Mercy, good thing our fellow students lounging around the entrance of our dorm probably don't understand our parent's sappy, basically shouted goodbyes. It's one thing to hug and kiss your parents goodbye.

It's quite another to have explain why our mother is calling us little cabbages and keeps shouting about *NO BOYS!!!* like we're fourteen again.

We watch them drive away, and butterflies take flight in my chest. We've never been away from our family. Never been alone in another state.

Never not had to answer for what we wear, who we hang out with, and where we go.

I realize the feeling is freedom and possibilities and it's swelling in my chest, foreign to me. I like it, not knowing what comes next but knowing that it's my choice to make.

I turn to Raven, and we share a slow, secret smile, just for us.

We're free.

We go back to Anderson Hall and start decorating our room with bits here and there that have been left for last. I hang up my cork board that I've covered in burlap and plan to adorn with pictures and quotes while Raven is arranging her crystals on her desk and windowsill.

Our door is cracked open slightly and we've got a song by Niykee Heaton playing from our Bose speaker. Raven and I haven't shared a room since we were in middle school, but I'm excited. We both know everything there is to know about each other, so we won't be tempted to murder one another this year. *Hopefully.*

There is a quick knock followed by two heads poking through the doorway.

"Hi! We're your suite mates, sorry we didn't get the chance to stop by yesterday."

"Oh hi, come on in," Raven offers.

"Are you French? I heard one of your parents talking when they walked out of here," the Asian girl speaks, talking a mile a minute. "I'm Cora Jennings. Well, my full name is Coraline, but I go by Cora because if one more person compares me to that demented doll movie, I'm gonna whip them with a fishing pole." I can't help but choke out a laugh at the visual. She's radiant,

Chapter 3

with almond eyes and perfect shiny black hair.

Also, *ouch*. She's terrifying.

"Consider us warned." Raven laughs. "Her parents are my parents, and yep they were blabberin' in French."

"Get. Out. I love your accents! Oh my gosh, tell me everything about you," gushes the other girl, adorably beautiful with blonde hair and big blue eyes. "I'm Gabby Ellis, by the way! You two are sisters? Wait, you're both freshmen. *Oh my gosh* are you twins?" She sounds like she may be from up here, somewhere. "I don't think I've ever quite heard anyone who sounds like you two! I'm from Connecticut." (clears that up) "Everyone there just sounds like me."

"Uh, love your accent right back! And yep, we're fraternal twins. I'm Raven or Rae, but I won't smack you for using my government name."

Gabby and Cora turn to look at me and after a beat of awkward silence, I realize they're waiting for me to speak up.

Deep breaths Lennie, you're here to make friends. Stop being so shy!

"Hey, I'm Lenore and because of *my* name being from the 1800s, I go by Lennie. And we do speak French which is pretty common where we live in Louisiana. We joke that it's Franglish since we mostly speak English." I laugh a little awkwardly, realizing that I'm nervously blabbering. Actually, our father is Cajun and speaks a different dialect than traditional French, but we speak a mix of the two sometimes at home. Our mom speaks perfect Parisian French because her mother was from France.

Not that we ever met her.

"Sweet, I like it! Listen, we're starving and wanted to see if you all want to come with us to get dinner at Boreal Hall? I feel like I haven't eaten in as long as I can remember," Cora says.

"Oh, I've heard good things about Aisling Spice Bag. It's in the Union at Bellus Hall. They sell all kinds of Irish street foods, like curry chips!" Gabby adds.

"Oh, I don't actually think we've ever tried Irish food, but curry chips doesn't sound remotely Irish?" I ask, confused.

"I'm always down to try new foods. Aisling sounds good, right Len? Lead the way," Raven says.

Back at home, my school and gym friends and I just grew up with each other and kind of fell together naturally. Can making new friends really be this easy?

* * *

Later that night after we come back from dinner (turns out curry chips is indeed both Irish and delicious) we're hanging out in Cora and Gabby's room while they finish decorating. Their dorm is set up almost exactly like ours, only their desks aren't pushed together to create a room divider, so we can all see each other.

Note to self, source those twinkle lights and put them everywhere.

"I can't get over how the foyer of Bellus looks like a castle courtyard," I say dreamily.

Raven snorts, like she knows I'm never going to stop talking about it. Because *come on*, who didn't want to go to Hogwarts as a kid…or adult.

As it happens, our suite mates are surprisingly easy to talk to, and we all got to know each other over dinner. Cora was born in Thailand but lost her parents in a tsunami when they were on a solo vacation in the southern part of the country. After that, her grandmother cared for her until she died from old age when Cora was three. She was adopted by a Jewish couple from upstate New York and is majoring in Asian Studies after being encouraged by her two dads to learn more about her heritage. She hopes to teach at the university level.

Also, she's *fabulous*.

Gabby, or Gabrielle, has two older brothers named Gavin and Grant. I think Gabrielle is a lovely name, though she insists it's too stuffy. Gabby sounds more like her personality, though, because she's sunshine, perkiness, and a general breath of fresh air. They moved from her dad's native Connecticut four years ago so that he could open his law firm in his wife's native Boston.

From her description, Connecticut sounds like a lovely place to grow up, so I added the state to my growing list of places to explore.

Chapter 3

"So, you mentioned you're both named after Edgar Allan Poe characters?" Cora asks from her seat on her bed as she untangles (attacks) a hundred jumbled hangers with zero patience or finesse. Gabby is tacking pictures up on a pink cork board on the wall by her desk where Raven sits looking at a magazine.

"Not just us," I start, taking a seat in Cora's desk chair. "We have two older brothers named Allan and Auguste. Allan is obvious. He's twenty, and Auguste, or Gus, is named after Auguste Dupin from *Murders in the Rue Morgue*, which is my favorite story of Poe's. Gus is twenty-one and about to graduate this spring. They both go to LSU where our parents teach."

I startle as Cora snaps a hanger that she's trying to extract from the pile and says "Oops."

I continue on. "Maddie is the baby. She's sixteen and her full name is Madeline. She's named after Madeline Usher from *The Fall of the House of Usher*."

At this point I can spit out these facts in my sleep. You'd be surprised how many people our age put together that Lenore and Raven are from Poe's works and asks about it. I've always been a little protective about my name because it's so old fashioned, but I can acknowledge that all of our names fit us perfectly.

But *man*, kids are jerks when you have unique names.

"That's really cool. A lot better than my mother naming all of us with G names because and I quote 'It's the most distinguished sounding letter in the alphabet.' Really, I think it's because *her* name starts with a G," Gabby says while rolling her eyes.

"Uhhhh, I'm gonna throw down my demonic doll namesake card one more time!"

We all agree that yes, 'Coraline' is a highly creepy movie, and then wince as Cora accidentally breaks yet another hanger.

"That's it," Raven declares, getting up and going to sit next to Cora. "Scooch over, I'm helping you untangle these damn hangers."

* * *

The next morning Raven and I head out to check out more of campus. There are two main libraries, Quintus Ennius and Solis, plus four other specialized libraries for specific degree fields.

But I've got my eye on Quintus Ennius, named after the father of Latin literature. Looking at it, you wouldn't know it's a library. It looks like a miniature cathedral and is designed similar to the Gothic style of Boreal and Lectio Halls. It opened in 1791 and, I kid you not, inside it looks like (yep, you guessed it) Hogwarts, complete with arched cathedral ceilings and stained-glass windows that it's famous for.

Classes don't actually start until Thursday, although I'm meeting up with our team the day after tomorrow to get practice schedules and finish registration.

But I'm not focused on classes and the team right now.

I look over at Raven, who is busy taking pictures, as she always does. She insists that she wants a financial job that pays the bills, but I'm happy that she's going to minor in photography.

We head inside the library and set to exploring. Raven focuses the lens of her Canon Rebel on the multi-colored reflections of the stained glass windows that loom overhead, while I take it all in. The main room is six stories tall and at its center goes all the way to the domed ceiling, which has glass paneling to let in natural light. Every level features rows of bookshelves, and lines the cavernous solarium with carved stone railings.

The main study hall is pretty free from students, not shocking considering classes haven't started. What it is full of currently are tourists, as it's fairly famous and open to the public. It's a challenge to find a quiet spot to sit and take it all in.

We're adrift in a sea of fanny packs and walking shoes, and more and more people walk in front of Raven as she attempts to capture the images, prompting her to huff out "Screw this."

She grabs my hand and steers me around middle-aged tourists towards the main grand staircase. We climb up few winding flights and then sit on the top step of a quiet landing, tucking our knees up to our chests. Looking up, I take in the huge stained-glass windows looming above us. They span

Chapter 3

several stories; colorful depictions of Renaissance nobles and people from the book of Exodus regally look down on us. The morning sun filters through the glass and dots the smooth granite stairs below with colored reflections, twinkling like Christmas lights and moving slightly with the sunbeams. It's quiet and cool up here and, it feels special to be experiencing this without having to share it with anyone else. We don't speak for a while, each soaking it in. Taking what we need from this space and these quiet moments.

The scent of old books is all around us, and I pine for all of my novels left at home, lining my bedroom wall of bookcases that I've collected over the years.

Raven and I left our Jeep Wrangler at home for Mads to use this year since we're staying in the dorms. We plan to try and find a house or apartment to share next year, so we'll be driving back up next August with a lot more of our belongings. Until then I need to find a local bookstore to get my fix.

"You know what I'm most excited about?" Raven asks me quietly.

"I could guess, but I'd come up with about a hundred things."

"That no one here will look at me and say, 'there's the girl who survived.' I didn't realize how much I hated being that girl until Daddy tried to use it against me so I'd stay. Because truthfully, I almost let him."

For a second, I don't know what to say. Raven had a drowning accident when we were twelve that profoundly changed her, and if I'm being honest, changed me a little bit too.

I know that she deals with anxiety about her safety and occasionally still has nightmares after what happened. They're rare these days, but when she wakes up screaming and screaming, I know she feels deep shame over her what she considers to be her weakness, though I would never think her anything less than the strongest of us all.

But Raven…she never talks about what happened. She never acts like anything less than someone who is happy to be alive and full of excitement for everything new and beautiful about our world. Because that *is* who Raven is.

But she also is someone who has refused to deal with her trauma, preferring to keep it in a box, locked away in the recesses of her brain. I know that to speak about it is to re-live it, and I can only imagine how hard that is.

So, I don't push.

"I'm excited for you to experience that, Rae," I say, carefully.

"I know they worry and have their own personal issues about it all, but sometimes I just want to shed that girl. Grow out of it and get away from her and let it be like it never happened."

It will never be like it never happened, but, for now, I can be the Agreeable Twin and pretend along with her.

For now.

I want this to be Raven's chance to shed some of her anxiety and fear, and I hope these four years outside of the safe bubble of our home will help her grow. She's my favorite person on earth, truly my twin flame and spirit animal.

Raven, who would help me stretch through my pain and soreness and sit with me in ice baths out of solidarity, even after she quit gymnastics. She carried me on her back for a mile when we were thirteen after I fell off my horse Duster and bruised my tailbone. She held me while I cried and cried after Nationals and took me to every single rehab session as I recovered. She carries cash on her to give homeless people, and fiercely defends the people she loves, even when they won't speak up for themselves.

She's one of the most selfless people I know, and she deserves to be free of her fears.

I just don't know how to help her get there.

Chapter 4

aubade

(n) a love song sung at dawn

Raven and I had a relaxing Monday, which was much needed after all of the travel and exploration and *newness*.

We searched for the secret "tree stairs" with no luck, really not knowing the first thing to look for, and then Raven and I worked out together before lunch. She decided to take a three-hour nap while I read Grady Hendrix's My Best Friend's Exorcism, which freaked me out so bad that I accidentally-on-purpose woke her up to keep me company.

Then we ubered to a Taqueria for dinner where I had the best burrito of my life while waiters carried plates of sizzling fajitas to nearby tables and a Mariachi band played live music in the corner. While I was eating said best-burrito-ever, Raven proceeded to lecture me on every benefit to vegetarianism while watching me shove carnitas into my face.

"Oh, shut up, I saw you sneak bacon at breakfast," I scoff. I take a pointed bite, moaning a little as the flavors of caramelized pork and avocado burst on my tongue.

"A good twin would have acted like she didn't notice."

"The good twin already let you have the bed by the window so that you could charge your precious crystals."

She rolls her eyes and throws her straw wrapper at me. "Oh my God, eat your dang meat then. Heathen."

Raven is always waffling between being vegan, or a vegetarian, or eating all the meat she can. She feels guilty because she loves animals so much. I can love animals *and* love to eat them. I feel zero guilt.

After dinner, Cora, Raven and I watch a movie in the common room of our dorm, which is really just an open space in the middle of the dorm with sofas, chairs, and a large TV. Gabby bounces into the room and her face is lit up like the Fourth of July. "So, I just heard from my cousin that Beta Sigma Sigma Gamma is hosting the first party of the year tonight!! FIRST. PARTY. OF. THE. YEAR. We gotta go!"

Raven jumps up, knocking over our bowl of popcorn in her haste. "This is the moment I've been training for," she exclaims and runs to our room to get ready. "Come on Len!"

I know I talked a big game about wanting freedom and all that jazz, but I just got *cozy*. And parties mean people I don't know, lots of them. Lots of drunk them. It's starting to dawn on me that I may have been resentful of my parents' strict rules based on principle, not necessarily because I wanted to go out and get crazy. There isn't much free time to relax outside of training and school. I'm sure college won't be different.

Cora looks at me and waits for me to move, eyebrows raised in expectation, and I know I'm not going to be able to stay back.

After getting dressed in a cream knit sweater tucked into my favorite tan corduroy skirt over black tights, I take in the full look from my body mirror after putting on some chunky heeled black ankle boots. It's chilly here at night, and I am not used to the upper sixties at all.

It's been an intentional move to not think about how bad it's going to get in the winter. I've convinced myself that anything is bearable with something as pretty as snow to look at.

I decide that I'm digging the fall-in-the-city look that I've got going on. It's way more sophisticated than something I'd wear in Louisiana.

Where it's currently eighty five degrees with a kick to the face of humidity.

I walk around the tall desks we placed back to back to give us some

Chapter 4

semblance of privacy and we take in each other's outfits.

Raven is way more edgy to my nerdy chic. She's rocking sheer black tights under tight black leather shorts, which she has tucked in a see-through black bodice tank that is dotted with tiny stars all over.

I exclaim "Ohhh I'm so into your look!" right when she cries out "Nooo Lennie, you *cannot* wear that!"

Record scratch.

"You cannot wear that to your, *our*, first party. You look like a little virgin librarian from New-fucking-Hampshire."

I gasp in righteous indignation, but with another glance in my mirror I concede. Dammit. She's right. I can't unsee it now.

"Ugh, I had a feeling you would need me," she says, shaking her head. "Come see."

Raven makes me take off the chunky sweater and replaces it with a thin black v-neck sweater. Then she trades me her over-the-knee black boots with a two-inch chunky heel while she puts on my ankle boots.

We stand together in front of the mirror and take it all in.

Huh. Okay.

She still looks edgy and sexy, but now I'm looking more our age. More sophisticated. I am now University Lenore. Who goes to parties. No big deal!

Gabby and Cora barge into the room to come get us, and we leave in an Uber since most of the freshmen dorms are on Aurora campus and the frat house is across from the main campus. When we pull up to the house, it looks pretty much like every college party depicted on TV.

Minus kids swinging from the dormers, although it's only 10 pm.

It's a giant three-story brick house with cool accent details that are probably lost on the frat guys living there, and there is a huge flag showing their Greek letters.

On second look, those letters suspiciously look like they spell BEER. Or is it BEET?

Music is bumping, people are laughing and yelling, and lots of people are half dressed (are they made of lava? It's cold!) and everyone has some kind of drink in their hand.

Now, Auguste and Allan made it a point to sneak us out of the house a few times to go drink with them behind the barn, which is a few hundred yards from the house, in order to prepare us for our first parties. We always had a readymade excuse in case we got caught.

"We saw some of the horses getting out!"

"Swear to God, we heard a burglar. Strength in numbers and all that."

"We were looking at constellations!"

We actually did do that sometimes; our mom teaches Astrology.

They would start a small fire in the fire pit and let me and Raven tipsy on beer, wine, or liqueur depending on which lesson we were learning or what they had on hand. "Beer before liqueur, never sicker" was not a fun lesson to learn. But I digress.

"Ladies, welcome! You're all looking mighty fine."

We're greeted at the door by some dude bro in a popped collar polo, who hands us all solo cups full of beer. I waffle at accepting it, noticing he's handing them out from a table full of solo cups that someone is pouring and filling the table with, steadily. It doesn't look like anything shady is going on, so I take my cue from the other girls and follow them into the house.

Dozens of people are all around, guys in hoodies, girls in revealing dresses and heels, and all kinds of stages of dress in between. All of a sudden, I'm feeling very buttoned up and out of place. And when I say very, I mean *majorly*.

I take a big gulp of lukewarm beer and follow the girls into a large kitchen where there is every kind of liqueur under the sun stacked all over a large island.

Cora starts pouring things into a solo cup before adding juices and using a spoon to stir it up. Meanwhile I'm looking at the huge kitchen and thinking longingly of how many amazing things Raven and I could cook if we lived here. I doubt this kitchen sees its full potential with a house full of guys, but I could be wrong.

Cora pours four shots into little solo shot cups (*cute!*) and then proposes a toast.

"To new friends, new experiences, and new beginnings!"

We clink to cheers and throw back the fruity shots that taste kinda like

Chapter 4

cough syrup, but in a good way. Cora makes us another round, and then we head off in search of something to do.

Within a few minutes, I'm feeling the pleasant buzz that I actually love, not that I've experienced it much. Allan and Auggie never let Raven and I get hammered, just enough to have us giggling and goofy while they laughed at us. Those are great memories.

I miss them.

I plan to facetime them both tomorrow, and then tear my thoughts away from home because the whole point was to *get away*. We come to a den off the main living room that is set up as a huge beer pong table. A guy standing on top of the table tries to land a shot, and I stop in my tracks, having no idea what version of beer pong this is.

Another guy is standing on the ground, directing him.

"Nate, you're aiming to the left." He slurs. "Try leaning on my, yeah put your right hand on my shoulder and use me for balance…YEAH BABY!!!"

Nate lands the shot, and the entire room erupts in cheers and screams like he just ran the game-winning touchdown at the Superbowl. The girls and I look at each other for a split second and then throw our hands up and shout for him too.

When in Rome.

I turn around to grab another beer from the keg in the corner and someone bumps into me, sending me sprawling into Gabby's arms.

"Shit, sorry about that."

An arm comes around my waist and hauls me back upright. I turn around as he's talking.

"I didn't see yo- *oooh*, hey. I'm Nate."

I wait for the shyness to kick in and render me mute, but it doesn't come this time. I'm feeling too happily buzzed. I like this feeling, something between bold and confident. I get a closer look at him and notice he's really attractive in a laid back, jock kind of way. Wavy black hair, hazel eyes, nice muscles. He has a handsome smile and is about 6 inches taller than me.

"I'm Lennie, hi. Nice shot on the table just now."

"Thanks, it was lucky. I haven't seen you before, are you a freshman?" He looks slightly unsteady on his feet.

"Guilty. I'm guessing you're not?"

"Nah, I'm a sophomore. I love your accent. We don't get many southerners up here. Where're you from?"

I've gotten this a lot already, but I'm actually incredibly drawn to his Boston accent. Something prevents me from blurting that out, thankfully.

A few hours and three more drinks later, Nate and I are sitting around the fire with Cora, Gabby, and Raven and we've been joined by his frat brothers Isaiah, Luca, and his beer pong coach, Ryder. We're laughing hysterically at a story Luca is telling about freshman rush last year. He stands from his folding chair, gesturing wildly, clearly bleary-eyed drunk, and beer spills from his solo cup.

"So, Ryder drew the short straw and had to go steal the Harvard flag out of the Dean of Athletics office, Dean Thompson. I know she's a Harvard alum, but damn, it's disrespectful to have it in her office, ya know? Keep that at home. Anyway, he picks the lock and goes in with his flashlight like 007," he says with a strong New York accent.

"Hang on, you're not gonna tell it right," Ryder jumps in, pushing Luca down into his vacated seat. "*Anyway*, so I close the door and head to get the flag but hear talking in the hallway. I have to think quick and wedge myself in between the cabinet and the wall behind the flag stand, which by the way was like two inches too little of space. I still don't know how I did that. So, two people come in the office, and I know if they look down at the corner I'm in, they'll see me. The flag stand isn't hiding me from the knees down, but they only turn on a lamp, thankfully." He takes a gulp of beer and continues.

"So, they don't say anything, but I hear noises, and I peak around the flag and you guys-it's the fucking head football coach making out with the dean on her couch! And then they start going at it and I kid you not, they were like eighties porn stars with their dirty talk. And he's like twenty years younger than her! So, I'm sitting there sweating, trying not to laugh or make any noise, and I have to sneeze. I couldn't hold it in any longer, but she made some high-pitched like, *shriek*, and I finally let it go. Either they heard me and didn't care, or they didn't hear and I'm the luckiest dude on the planet.

Chapter 4

They finished up and left, and I waited like fifteen minutes before I got out. Never again. I lost like ten years off my life that night."

We all laugh our butts off and I'm fuzzily content and relaxed.

I stand up to go to the bathroom. "Anyone need anything from inside?"

They say they're all good, so I go use the bathroom and wash my hands. As I'm opening the door, Nate walks into the bathroom and shuts the door behind him. At this point I'm pretty buzzed, maybe even drunk. Instead of freezing and being nervous, I just cock my head at him.

"I've been wanting to be alone with you all night." He mutters, right before he brings his lips down on mine. I'm shocked still and then the part of my brain that normally would freak out takes flight and vacates. I wrap my arms around his neck, and he hoists me up on the counter, stepping between my legs.

"You're so hot," he says between kisses. "I've wanted to kiss you all night."

His tongue caresses mine and he tastes like beer and boy, and my head spins from it all. Until he pushes up my skirt and starts to pull down my tights. It's like he dumped ice water over my head, the effect snapping me out of my stupor.

"Wait." I pull back. "Nate. I just met you. I've…never done this before." I end on a whisper, red-faced from my lack of experience.

He rears back, and his eyes grow wide. "Whoa, I'm sorry. I didn't even think to ask."

Which I find annoying, but what do I know? I'm sure hookups are the norm at college parties. But the thing is, even being drunk, I'm not ready for that. I don't even know him!

"Yeah, no…this definitely isn't happening," he says, and I'm relieved that he isn't trying to make me feel embarrassed. I still feel it though. I'm probably the most innocent girl at this party, and I feel naive because of it. I've had a few boyfriends, but the most I've ever done is make out with a guy. Turns out, having minimal free time and controlling parents doesn't equate to me being girlfriend material. Go figure.

I don't know what to say, but I'm saved by pounding on the door.

"Lenore Landry, if you're done sucking face, come gather your twin. She just fell asleep, sitting up in a lawn chair. Luca saved her from falling on her face!" Cora shouts through the door.

Nate looks at me, chuckling. "I'm gonna crash in Ryder's room. He has a couch in there. You girls take my room. I have a king-size bed. I can drive you back to your place in the morning. How's that?"

Maybe gentlemen do exist at frat houses.

* * *

We all pile into Nate's bed, which smells like boy in a good way, and immediately fall asleep. I'm awakened by Raven snoring like a lumberjack at 5:30 am after *three hours of sleep.*

"Someone shut up the human chainsaw," groans Gabby, throwing a pillow at Raven. I roll over and stuff my head under my pillow, but it's no use. When I'm up, I'm up.

"That's it. If I'm not sleeping, nobody sleeps." Cora starts hitting Raven with her pillow. "Wakey, no eggs and bakey for you, you loud ass!!"

"GAAHHHHH, wha? Whereumeye?" Raven sits up and mumbles, eyes still closed.

"Loudness, you woke us all up. We slept at the frat house! Let's head out before we wake anyone up. I don't want to deal with grumpy, hungover strangers first thing in the morning." Gabby chirps. She's seriously peppy for getting half a night's sleep.

I leave Nate a note in the notebook on his desk.

Thanks for letting us crash in your bed, we headed out early. I had a great time last night!
  -Lennie (225-430-0722)

On the way out, Cora snags a quilt from the back of the couch and wraps it around herself, and I make a mental note to get that back to Nate.

We're walking aimlessly as we fully wake up. I'm surprised that I don't have any kind of hangover, thank goodness, but I am exhausted. We come up to

Chapter 4

edge of the big lake in the center of campus, and I stop. Weeping willow trees surround the banks, and the circumference of the lake is dotted with benches every few hundred feet that are normally taken by students.

Right now, though, we're the only ones out here.

Past the lake I can see the cathedral in the distance, surrounded by smaller stone buildings. The lake is covered by a thin layer of fog, and it looks ethereal. I don't hear any sounds of nature, not even crickets.

And the water is still. So, so still.

"Y'all," I whisper. "Spread that blanket out. Let's sit and watch the sunrise."

They situate the blanket, and we all sit huddled together in the morning chill. It dawns on me that I've never actually watched a sunrise before.

None of us says a word as we take in the slow ascent of the sun. The sky starts out dark blue, lightening to light blue, to lavender that eventually, so gradually, gives way to reds and pinks, oranges and yellow by the time the bright sun finally breaks over the trees. It's a special moment, I think.

We don't speak as we get up, gather our belongings, and head to the shuttle stop to get back to our dorm. Sometime between last night and this morning, I feel like I've learned some of the universe's secrets. I think back to the easiness of talking to the guys we met, to the laughter and stories, my extroverted ease thanks to the alcohol, and the new closeness that's forming between the four of us girls.

I smile to myself as we make our way onto the shuttle.

It was the best night of my life.

Chapter 5

sonder
(n) the realization that each passerby has a life as vivid and complex as your own

"Okay, so those of you that are Freshmen, you're all in UNIV at 8:30am on Mondays, and don't get too excited because that's likely the only class that you're all together. We have everyone's schedules, so we've set up blocks for cardio, conditioning drills which are afternoons that everyone has free, weights, beam, vault, bars, and floor." Assistant Coach Dwight says. He's a trim Black man with a bald head and handsome face, and he exudes every bit the former Nationals champion he is.

He continues talking about the scheduling blocks while I tune out a bit. It's still early in the morning, and I'm not quite at one hundred percent. I drift off for a few minutes before someone sneezes, taking me out of my haze. I sit up and shake my head a little to clear it. We're in the training center Fulminare, a new state of the art building that houses the gymnastics and basketball teams, though our spaces are separate. Navy and gold are our school colors, and the room is tastefully decorated with them. Coach continues from his place at the front of the small auditorium we're in.

"Now, NCAA rules allow for four hours of training per day, but Head Coach Akeno has capped everyone at three hours and he's very strict about that hard stop." Coach Dwight continues. "Look at your schedule and note the blocks

Chapter 5

that you've been placed into. I don't care how you organize your schedule, but make sure that you do. It's imperative that you take this year to find your groove between academics and athletics." He grabs a stack of papers from the table next to him and starts passing them out to all of us, on which the Kalon University Athletic Affirmations are typed up neatly.

"When we spoke in the spring, we urged you to consider taking on electives and basic classes required for your degrees to ease you into the life of a student athlete. I hope you took that to heart because ladies, it's about to get real." He raises his eyebrows for emphasis and exudes a no-nonsense attitude that many educators have perfected. "We have a high level of expectations for all Kalon Knights. Honor, Character, and Work Ethic will be your pillars for the years you're at KU. Let's start with reciting our affirmations."

We do as we're told, and then breakup to grab our color-coded schedules, booklets on training sets from the strength coach, and one from our team nutritionist. The Freshman booklet is unique, since we're all in the dorms, so our meal examples are all parsed from ready-to-eat options from Market Basket and Whole Foods, as well as options from all of the meal places around campus. Sadly, curry chips and everything else from Aisling Spice Bag has not made the cut.

There's always cheat day...

I wander into one of the main training rooms and take a seat on the edge of the navy blue felt-covered springboard flooring.

Tomorrow is my last free day before classes start on Thursday, and I'm filled with a mixture of nerves and excitement. Growing up, I was always the girl who was excited for the first day of school. I may hate studying, but I love learning. When I'm in the classroom, I'm great. It's just when I go home to start studying in a quiet space that my mind runs away from me. I'm a big-time daydreamer and tend to struggle when it comes to focus. It's part of the reason why I'm so organized, and that's going to come in handy this year. I get a little sense of unease when I look at my class schedule layered with the six days of training blocks, and my new job, but I force it down.

To help with spending money, I got an easy on campus job. Basically, I sit in a table in our dorm foyer and make any guests sign in and out. It's really just time for me to work on homework and be paid for it and is the only kind of job I have time for.

Balancing a tight schedule is the most important part of being an elite athlete. Training, classes, blocks, and life; fitting all this into a day where others hardly manage only classes is something I am used to. What I'm not used to? Waking up at five am to fit in morning cardio and weightlifting before classes start. That seems like an unavoidable part of being a college athlete. Time management can only get you so far; you have to get up early, dig in, and get the work done regardless of your course load.

I'm majoring in Communications for the sportscasting aspect, but I chose a minor in English because I love reading and writing, and it felt like a good fit for me. My advisor estimated that I'll need one hundred and twenty credits over the next four years, so I set myself up to have five classes each semester, and one virtual class each summer to offset my time in the classroom/studying. I look over my schedule to make sure it's correct.

- UNIV (this is a class that all freshman athletes take)
- Intro to Journalism
- Intro to Communication
- Renaissance Humanities
- Critical Family History: Narratives of Identity and Difference

I was overwhelmed by the list of courses for my focuses, but since a lot of the classes revolved around film, it was a little easier to narrow down once I filtered those out. Breathing in deep, I let out my breath to help myself focus. I'm envisioning notebooks, sharpie pens, and dozens of different colored highlighters. I have a big thing for highlighters, I must have them in every color and shade.

"Earth to Lenore, Lenore can you hear me?"

I slide back into the present and look up at my teammates, Jayla and Savannah. We met this morning when we showed up for the meeting. I try to remember our quick intro we all gave.

Ah yes. Jayla is from Baltimore and Savannah is from Louisville.

Chapter 5

They sit next to me on the floor, and I close my booklet and put it to the side, giving them my attention.

"Hey, sorry, I was daydreaming. What's up, have you looked over your schedule?"

"Yeah, it looks right. Are we in any of the same blocks?" Savannah asks, picking up my calendar and glancing at my line up.

"Looks like we're all three in Cardio, Beam, Conditioning and...let me see yours? And Floor together. And free gym obviously." Jayla says while comparing our schedules.

"UNIV at 8:30 on a *Monday*, though? They weren't kidding about being serious about integrating us, were they? Geez," Savannah gripes. I don't say anything, but I agree. Monday scaries are going to be a real thing, especially since Sundays are our only free days until meets start.

"Girl, you don't talk much do you?" Jayla teases me.

I laugh softly, "I promise I do. I have to come out of my shell a bit. I wish I were more verbose."

"Ver-who?" Savannah asks, looking lost.

"Talkative," I offer. "I will be talking your heads off in no time, trust me. I think maybe at first I'm more of an observer, " I say this lightly, but I feel guilty. With Cora and Gabby, they came into my life like beautiful little wrecking balls, and I always feel more confident when I'm with Raven, so I didn't have any kind of opening-up period with them.

I don't want my teammates to feel like I'm not interested in getting to know them. Now that I'm on my own, I can't keep leaning on Raven to be my bolster. It's really important to build relationships within a team, so know I need to start focusing on being more outgoing.

"I was going to head over to Boreal Hall for something not on the approved nutrition list for lunch if you want to come with?" I want to get one last day of comfort food in before it's all rice or sweet potatoes and veggies with lean proteins.

"Girl, you read my mind. Have you tried Aisling Spice Bag yet?" Jayla asks as we head out towards the main dining hall.

"I had curry chips, but what exactly is a spice bag? I know Cajun food inside and out, but Irish food is new to me." I say.

"Yeah, I'm versed on most American foods, and Jamaican, because that's my mom's heritage, but not Irish," she answers. "Lots of Irish places around Boston though!"

"Let me see…." Savannah scrolls on her phone. "Yes, according to Google, someone named Dooley says 'A spice bag consists of crispy chicken, red and green peppers, chili peppers, and chips, all seasoned in a bag. If it's a fancy curry shop, you get it in a box.' That sounds amazing actually," she says.

"Umm, shall we skip Boreal and go straight to Aisling?" I beg.

The response is unanimous.

I made two new friends in Jayla and Savannah at lunch. They're both down-to-earth girls and easy to talk to, and while there are some big regional differences, they don't make me feel like a freak when they ask a bunch of questions about what it means to be Cajun.

I would hug a cactus before I admitted this to my parents, but once I realized I would be outside of my safety net, the comfort of home, I'd started feeling afraid of the unknown. Would I mesh as well with my KU team as I did with my home team? Would I miss home and realize that I made a terrible mistake?

I don't have all the answers yet, but I'm pleased with my current existence. Hopefully that doesn't change once classes start and I juggle books and gym.

***

Thursday morning is my only day without a morning workout, so I take my time getting ready for my first class. So far this week has been practice, conditioning, and taking in the new team dynamic. This feels different than back home for several reasons, but mostly because I feel like this is my second chance at my dream. It took months to recover my confidence after the Nationals disaster, but now I feel stronger because of it.

Class is not until 10, but I wake up at eight. Raven already leaving for hers.

"Byyyeeeee, I love you, make good choices, have a great first day at school," she shouts, smacking a big kiss on my cheek before she runs out the door. I wish we had classes together, but we have totally different majors.

Chapter 5

I feel like a total basket case, and this is such a first world problem to have, but *I don't know what the heck to wear.* I'm flinging clothes around left and right, having already packed my gym clothes for vault training later, and force myself to stop and take a second to pause.

Deep breaths Lennie. Geez, girl.

I know I'm just projecting anxiety about new classes and new people and all the *new new new,* so I mentally buckle down. This is college, not the Met Gala. I can do this. I grab a long-sleeve, navy blue shirt dress with micro-polka dots and top it with a sage green cardigan, rolling the sleeves up to my elbows in one go. I choose my tan leather backpack and matching ankle booties and call it a day. It shouts casual, modest, and just-leaving-a-coffee-shop-in-Brooklyn, and I hate myself for even caring enough to give it a name.

As I make my way across campus, I take in all the activity around me. It's my first time seeing so many students out on campus at once, and it's actually a very cool feeling. In high school, at least in our town, I knew almost everyone. There were never any surprises.

Here, I know that I'm definitely going to get my wish for change and diversity. Everywhere I turn my head, there are people meandering down the walk, or rushing to class, presumably. Hundreds of different styles of dress, so many different ethnicities...it's as if I've been picked up and placed in the middle of a huge crosswalk, deep downtown in a bustling city. I feel small and insignificant, but also like that is a good thing. No one is focused on me, so I just take it all in as I make my way into Lectio Hall for my first class of university, Intro into Communications. I only have this class twice a week, so it's an hour and fifteen minutes. A nice start to the school year. Since this is a required course, I'm expecting it to be a large class, but there are only about thirty people. The small auditorium is situated with five rows of desks, spanning about eight seats wide.

I'm a little early but the class is already fairly full, so I make a mental note to *never* show up late. Hunting for a seat while everyone watches is a fresh hell I'd like to avoid at all costs.

I walk up a few rows and take a seat in the middle, getting out my laptop and notebook. I'm leaning back down to grab a pen when I hear "Lennie, is that you?"

I glance up and smile, relieved to see a familiar face. Catalina Rodriguez is another gymnast on the team with me, a nice and sassy girl from New Mexico. She has beautiful curly black hair and wide brown eyes that are stunning with her makeup. We're about the same size in clothes, though she's a good five inches taller than me.

"Hi Cat, I didn't know you're a Comm major, too!" She takes the seat to my right and starts unpacking. "I'm not. My major is Journalism. But this is required, so here I am!"

"Well, I'm glad to see a familiar face. I was so nervous this morning." I confess.

"Ugh, same. I know exactly no one here. Well, everyone on the team, my roomie and suite mates, I guess. But my suite mates keep to themselves and I'm worried that my roommate is growing weed in her closest so…"

I choke out a laugh, sincerely hoping that she's kidding about her roommate.

"Well, you know at least one person in this class at least."

We turn our attention to the front as our teacher closes the door. The room is packed, and for the first time I notice another familiar face sitting to my left.

"Hi, Ryder, right?" I ask, although I know the answer. Remembering his coaching skills from the frat party earlier this week, I give him a shy smile.

"Oh hey, yeah. And you're Raven? We met at the party, right?"

"Close, Raven's my twin. I'm Lenore. Lennie."

"Ahhh, right on. Sorry, I was hitting the bong pretty hard that night."

Professor Martin welcomes us to the class, but her intro about the high number of group assignments makes it sound like this is going to put me out of my comfort zone, which both excites and unnerves me.

"Do you have anything after this before we head to Vault at twelve?" I ask Cat when the class ends.

"Just inhaling lunch before heading that way. I mean if you call a salad lunch." Cat grimaces. Yeah. We have to get in a solid breakfast in the AM because eating anything substantial right before we go hurtling our bodies over the vault for hours can only end in bad things. I know this based on

Chapter 5

both personal experience and observation.

We grab a salad and take it to eat in the training center lounge at Libertas Center. I've noticed that all of the buildings have Latin names, which I gather is common for catholic places. This school is non-denominational, but there's no denying the huge catholic influence here. I find it fascinating, myself.

As we're warming up with our soft tissue prep by rolling our leg muscles with a hard foam roller, I give the training center more attention than I did during orientation. I thought I would miss my home gym, but it's downright shabby compared to this state of the art setup.

There's a huge foam pit where we practice new skills that we haven't quite stuck the landing to, the two runways and vaults, a few pairs of uneven parallel bars, three full-height balance beams, and a bunch of beams that sit directly on the mats or closer to the ground. All of the equipment and flooring is the same as your standard gym, but this all smells of newness and quality. It's luxurious.

I watch one of the girls on the bars working through her transitions before turning back to Cat.

"Talk to me about the scoring system," I say. "I've read up on it, but is it really as cut and dry as a 10.0 scale?"

"Yes and no."

In elite, you're given two scores that they combine for your final. One for difficulty and one for your execution.

"So, I know how elite scoring is done, obviously," she starts. Almost all of us were elite, first. "But in NCAA, it's graded as one. Judges want more perfect execution than level of difficulty. The issue is that since we're given one score and there is only a 10 point range, a lot of gymnasts get really similar scores. I watched a Florida vs. Oklahoma championship that was won by two tenths of a point!"

I gape at her, mid-thigh roll. Two. Tenths. Of. A. Point.

Now I understand when Bridget Sloan, who won Olympic silver in 2008, said. *"It is very nerve-wracking. One toe point can be the difference between winning the championship and getting second place."*

Starting in January, we'll compete in fifteen meets until April, almost every single weekend, and a lot of those are traveling. I'm looking forward to it and nervous as well. Like most elites, I've been training for years to learn bigger and more dangerous or difficult skills, but there is a whole lot less emphasis on toe pointing. I need to rework some habits.

After training, I head to Renaissance Humanities, which is the only elective I chose this year. My father teaches World History, and we've always had supper table discussions centered around history. One of the things we all love doing is watching documentaries together, and yes, I'm fully aware that we sound like a family of nerds.

That's because we are.

Out of most stretches of history, I've always been particularly fascinated by the Renaissance period, The Age of Enlightenment. Professor Lanege has been talking for about five minutes and I'm already into this. She lectures for the entire fifty minutes, and I soak it in, hopeful that I've found a class that won't necessitate studying.

By Friday, I'm exhausted. I wake up early for cardio, followed by my first UNIV class with my freshman teammates and the freshmen men's Lacrosse team and end the day with Bars from ten to one. I intentionally left the rest of the day free for studying and homework, but since this is the first week of classes, I'm blissfully free.

Raven still has class, so after I take a two-hour nap. I wake up a bit refreshed from the needed rest and then stare at the ceiling for a while, thinking back on the past week, sifting through the new memories and experiences. I smile to myself, thinking about all of the friends I've made, how easy it's felt to open up to them once I forced myself to pry open my jaw and speak.

And how I still can't believe that I made out with Nate on Monday night after just meeting him. That night was amazing, but at the same time it feels like a blur. I've been so busy this week that I really haven't given it much thought, but now I frown as I realize that he never reached out to me.

Chapter 6

petrichor
(n) the smell of the earth after rain.

The weeks pass by in a blur of routine. Training, schoolwork, and socializing all blend together in a sea of memories.

Before I know it, it's the middle of October and the world around us is on fire.

Figuratively, not literally.

I'm in awe of the beauty that is a New England autumn. The pictures I used to daydream about did not do this justice. Everywhere I look, trees are bursting with vibrant reds, oranges, and yellows. Leaves dot the lawns all around, and it's transformed campus into something out of this world. If I were a poet, Autumn would be the only muse necessary for a lifetime of sonnets.

I'm sitting on my favorite bench in front of the lake, reading a novel from my favorite fantasy series and soaking in the afternoon sun. It's sixty degrees outside, so I'm bundled up and feeling especially cozy and happy. It even smells different in the fall, like distant wood smoke and dried leaves.

Someone flops their body onto the bench beside me, absolutely scaring the crap out of me. I shriek and drop my book, making Raven laugh her stupid butt off.

"Not funny," I grouse as I pick up my book. "You scared the hell out of me! And this is a paperback, the cover can crease!" I raise my voice, removing a wet leaf from my book.

"Oh, curse words. You really *are* mad." She teases.

I roll my eyes, shaking my head as I smile at her. "What's up?"

She combs her hand through her hair, getting strands off her face that the wind moves right back. "Just got off the phone with Momma. I think I finally got them to stop the daily check ins. I said 'Okay, we get it. You miss us, and we miss you. But calling daily is just taking time away from class and studying, and there will be way more to talk about if you taper this down some. You promised to give us space to grow, yes?' She scoffs a little, staring at the water.

"And what did she say?"

"She got all offended and said that she would leave me to my Very Busy and Important Grown Up Life, and basically hung up on me."

I wince. The upside to Raven always speaking for the both of us is that I don't have to suffer the discomfort of doing it myself. The downside is that I feel slimy when she's upset that our mom or dad snaps at her. They never even try to see things from our point of view.

"This is exactly why I was excited to come here," she starts. "I feel like I'm making up for lost time, you know? We should have been going to parties in high school, experimenting with boys, just having normal teenage fun." I say nothing because she knows that I agree.

But Raven is nothing, if not resilient, so I'm not surprised when she shakes it off and turns to me with a bright smile on her face.

"Remember when I said I wanted to go to Salem in October? Well guess what? It's October, and our birthday is this coming weekend. Let's make it special."

I've been looking forward to going there, too.

"Should we go Saturday after I have open gym or wait until Sunday when we'll have all day?" I propose.

"Definitely Sunday. I want to take some pictures, so dress, I don't know, witchy?" She wrinkles her nose, deep in thought. She's getting a faraway look

Chapter 6

in her eyes as she dreams up artsy shots she wants to get. I'm quite familiar with the expression on her pretty face, having witnessed it frequently.

"Should we invite the gals?" I ask, knowing she'll know I'm talking about Cora and Gabby.

"Nah, I want this to be a sister's trip. It's special to us," She states, and I like her thinking. "We can always go back with them. It's only a thirty-minute train ride."

Getting used to the train system in Boston took lots of trial and error. Mostly error. We're better at reading the train schedules now, which confused the life out of me at first. There are subways, commuter one-way trains, ferries, and buses. I've mixed up the subway red, orange, blue, and green lines more times than I'd like to claim.

Having solidified our plans, Raven bounces off to places unknown, and I stay on the bench reading my book, losing myself once more in the world of Sarah J Maas.

***

"Hey Lens, do you have the notes from Tuesday? I think I lost mine." Ryder plops down next to me, looking at me expectantly. He's been asking for my notes for Intro to Communications once a week since we started this class, and at first, I was happy to help.

But now that it's been almost eight weeks, I'm starting to not feel so generous. I just don't know how to say no without coming across as rude. It's not like it's more work for me, but it irks me. Still, it's easier and more comfortable to share with him.

"Sure…I'll email them to you." I say. I see Cat look sharply at me on my right and keep my gaze straightforward. She's made it known how she feels about him "mooching off of you constantly!"

Professor Martin closes the door and walks to the front of the room. She shakes out her short blonde hair before putting on her readers and consulting her iPad.

"Today class, we're going to be breaking up into groups of three to start our 'Critical Thinking in Reactive Communications' projects. Your group will turn in your assignments November eighteenth, before we all head out for Thanksgiving break. This project will count for twenty-five percent of your grade, so I suggest you work out an equal system of responsibilities and tasks."

We all count off as she instructs, and my group ends up being Ryder, myself, and Catalina.

Cat huffs out a breath and opens her laptop to take notes. Ryder looks over at me and says "right on" with a smirk and I just look back up at the professor, resigned.

You can start working on that backbone any day now, Lennie.

After class, Cat and I head to grab a salad before we train vault. It becomes apparent that Cat has had enough of Ryder and his shit.

"I have had enough of Ryder and his shit."

See?

"I've held my tongue this long chica." She fumes.

"I know," I groan. "He started out so innocently, but it's every week now. I've dug myself into a hole. I feel so uncomfortable being mean!"

"Girl, it's not being mean to not be a doormat!" She exclaims, and I can't hide my wince. I don't like that about myself, but when I think about standing up to someone, I can practically feel the hives forming. Her face softens when she sees how her words affect me.

"I'm not trying to hurt your feelings. I just want you to feel confident enough that you're in the right if you tell him to kindly fuck off with his laziness. He's *barely* a friend to you! And to be honest, I don't want him thinking he can treat me the same way. I did not work this hard to get into Kalon just to do some pothead burnout's work."

And I can't disagree with her. I need some time to come up with how I'm going to respond, because one thing is clear, she is not going to beat around the bush with Ryder if he doesn't put in equal work with this project.

And I am not about to let his laziness affect my friendship with Catalina. Or my grades.

Chapter 6

***

Sunday morning Raven and I step off the train in Salem and into an uber, heading immediately for The Salem Witch Museum. It opens at ten, so we have the driver drop us at a cute coffee shop with lots of live plants and a bookshelf full of novels with the sign that says, "Take a book, leave a book!"

We both order the Blue Flower Earl Grey tea and head outside into the crisp air, finding a bench to sit on and enjoy our drinks. We're surrounded by vibrant leaves of the maple, oak, and beech trees all around, and the air is crisp with Autumn. I take the lid off my steaming tea so that I can blow on it.

"So…I slept with someone," Raven declares, and I look over at her in surprise. That was quite the random tidbit. I know she's not a virgin. I went straight to training after school each day, but Raven was free to do as she pleased.

At least until our parents came home from work.

She lost her virginity with her high school boyfriend right around our eighteenth birthday. "Nothing to write home about." She'd offered when I asked how it was. I asked her so many questions, did it hurt, how long did it last, does she feel different? She looked at me sternly and said "virginity is a social construct, Len. Don't make a bigger deal of this than it is." Her green eyes gleamed with intensity, and I considered myself educated on that point.

They broke up shortly after, so no insight on if it would have gotten better with time and experience. It never fails to amaze me, the stark differences between us. We're alike in so many ways. We love the same foods, hate the same flaws in people. Rude to waiters? Pass. Litter? Pass. Chew with your mouth open? PASS.

But Raven has this wild streak to her that I've never mastered. She may be afraid of physical risk, but she is careless with her heart. Or maybe it's just that she doesn't develop feelings as deeply as I do.

"Alright, are you going to make me ask?" I say, raising my eyebrow.

"His name is Diego Karlsson, and he's gorgeous. He's half Hispanic, half Swedish, and he's on the lacrosse team. And it was infinitely better than with David." She sighs dreamily.

"How did you meet him?" I hug my warm mug close to my chest, anticipating the story.

"In Statistics. We paired up on an assignment, and one thing led to another."

"Sure, as one usually does when talking over data points." I joke. "Are you going to date him?"

"Nah, I'm not looking for a boyfriend. I just want to kind of enjoy my time here, you know? Not be tied to anyone but me."

I knew she had that mentality going into college, but I'm a little surprised she's holding steady to it after being naked with the guy. Then again, what do I know? I'm not exactly experienced, and I definitely don't have Raven's laissez faire attitude towards sex. I've never been able to separate feelings of intimacy from, well, *feelings*.

She continues. "I know that I kind of have a complex about feeling held down after four years in high school watching our friends go to parties and bond over bad decisions. I just want the same, now. I feel like a boyfriend or even someone who wants to just date will have expectations that I'm not ready to surrender to when I just got my sea legs."

"Yeah, I get that, Rae."

She makes it to parties much more frequently than I'm able to. I can really only spare Saturday nights. Being tired and hungover in the gym isn't just irresponsible, it's dangerous. And I'm not nearly as tempted to be around a bunch of people as she is.

"So yeah, I think I'm content to just do my own thing, no strings attached." She continues speaking, watching people walk by. Though I try to put myself in her head space, I can't. But I am not called the Agreeable Twin for nothing, so I keep my opinions to myself as we get up to walk to the museum.

There is already a crowd forming in front of the looming stone building. It looks like a cross between a small castle and an old Protestant church, and the history lover in me really appreciates the aesthetic. The building towers at three stories tall and the Gothic-style windows are shaped into pointed arches on all three facets of the front. They're backlit with red lights, and it's a whole vibe.

We walk past the statue of Roger Conant, the founder of Salem, and I get chills. His cloak looks to be billowing in the wind, and it's formidable.

Chapter 6

Apparently, the Witch Trials of 1692 didn't start until after his death. Still, it's a very impressive statue, I think as he towers over us, looking like he's going to condemn our souls to the fiery pits of Hell.

Inside, there are life-size mannequins depicting the nine people who were killed between 1692 and 1693. We listen to a recording that outlines the story of the witch trials and how they came to be, before moving into the other room. There were some other mannequins in here, but what really got my attention was the wall full of Ouija boards. Raven and I share a *"hell naw"* look at each other.

Being from Louisiana, we're well versed on the witches of the bayou. There are voodoo priestesses and hoodoo witches, and whether or not you believe in that sort of thing, Raven and I agree; we don't mess with voodoo or hoodoo (we don't want the Gris Gris) and we don't touch Ouija boards *ever*. Our dad told us that his grandmother taught him to never use a Ouija board or have any kind of ritual that invited the spirits in. There are always bad spirits waiting for an opening to attach themselves to you or your home under the guise of being your long lost loved one.

Allan snuck a ouija board home once and when our mom caught him and Auguste red-handed she freaked out, refusing to go back inside until Raven saged the entire house. With sage *and* palo santo. Momma said if it's good enough for Native Americans it's good enough for her. You can't make this stuff up.

After we're done soaking in the history, we go to our favorite last stop of any place we visit, the gift shop. We load up on souvenirs to keep and send home. I look at our purchases and laugh to myself. If our choices don't highlight our uniqueness, I don't know what does. Book nerd, lover of comfort and coziness, boring me. Metaphysical, yoga and tea loving, fun Raven. My twin rifles through my bag to be nosy and finds the free bookmark the clerk stuck in there. "Ohh, they gave us a little lagniappe!"

Sometime later, Raven and I are meandering down a side road looking for "The Spot" according to little miss Annie Leibovitz. "The Spot" being the quintessential perfect picture backdrop.

I dressed in Raven's over the knee black boots, a dark tweed mini skirt with a tucked-in black leotard and a black wide-brimmed hat. I completed my "witchy vibes" look with a black wool trench that I borrowed from Cora, and I'm feeling very Sanderson Sister Lenore vibes. The weather is crisp and perfect, and the sights and smells of autumn are all around us. We come up to Old Burying Point Cemetery and the Salem Witch Memorial. Raven declares "Oh yeah, this is it." I look down at a memorial carved in rock that says, "Here lies Giles Corey, Pressed to Death, Sept 19, 1692." I can't stop the shiver that snakes down my spine.

Ouch.

Though I know that history is bloody and filled with the macabre, I can't comprehend the barbarianism of that time. I remember learning of the brutality of the French Revolution and force the mental images away. Heading into the graveyard, perusal of the gravestones shows more. "Hanged until dead" and "Died by burning" and so forth.

Glad we're not here at night.

We uber to Ropes Mansion and Gardens, which I'm sure is really gorgeous in Spring, but right now is looking very ominous and darkly beautiful. The gardens look like a graveyard filled with flower skeletons. Raven has me walk toward the front door and does a cool shoot of her holding my hand as I reach back and lead her to the door.

I persuade her to let me take some of her and she reluctantly (whining the whole time) lets me take her baby and snap some pictures.

"Let me check the settings one more time." She needles.

"Raven! Shut up and look pretty. You're dressed cute for this shot." I snap at her while taking another picture of her looking peevish. She hates not being the one in control of the camera.

But the last place we go to is definitely the Salem experience.

The House of Seven Gables is a huge black house, in the style of colonial mansions from the 1600s. It has seven triangular peaks, which we've just learned are called gables, and it's well purported to be haunted. According to the legend, during the Salem Witch Trials from 1962-1963, John Turner, Jr., who was the first owner's son, wanted to protect his sisters from the mass hysteria that ensued during that time. He built a secret, hidden stairwell

Chapter 6

along the fireplace that leads down to the first floor so that he could hide his younger sisters from persecution.

The gorgeous house has views of the harbor as well, which just adds to the experience. All in all, it's a beautiful setup. My favorite is the huge stone fireplace where there are hanging cauldrons and other cast iron cookware. The house is styled with furniture and such from the 1800s, and I find myself imagining living here during that time.

Raven gets creative with some of the shots in the master bedroom, saying she can edit out the barrier ropes, but then she gives me the camera and *ducks under the ropes and sits on the bed*. I stare at her in horror.

"Rae," I hiss, looking over my shoulder as the last of our tour group vanishes through the door. "We're not suppose-"

"Just take my picture, vite, vite," she urges, turning her head away from the camera and gazing out of the window. I mumble under my breath, quickly snapping some shots to appease her. She *just* whined about me taking her picture!

"You're taking this 'no rules' thing to a whole other level," I grit out as I shove her precious camera at her chest.

She just laughs it off, the jerk, and we catch up to our group at the base of a hole in the wall that houses the dark, winding secret staircase.

We look at each other at the same time and say, "Nope."

Once outside, I relax a bit. "Ugh, that was creepy."

"Not just creepy," a woman to our left piped up. "That house is haunted." Raven and I exchange an uneasy look.

"There was a psychic back in the seventies who claimed that she saw the ghost of a small boy in that very window," she points to a small window in the attic. "She even has a photograph of it. I'm sure you can find it online," she says, before walking towards the gardens.

We stare at her back with open mouths, and I turn my head to my sister.

"If you google that photo, I will never speak to you again!" I grit out, turning on my heel and walking towards the road. All in all, very neat experience, and not one I will be repeating.

Ghost Hunters, eat your heart out.

We spent the rest of the day walking around Salem, soaking in the sights. I love all of the old houses. Salem is really a cute, eclectic town. I looked it up before we came and found out that the styles of houses here are mostly Queen Anne, Gothic Revival, Victorian Gothic, and Colonial Revival. I can't tell the difference between the styles, but they're mostly one and two story homes designed in almost perfect rectangles with colorful painted-wood siding and very small front stoops. The residents made them their own with pretty gardens, unique signs, and lots of charm.

We got thanksgiving sandwiches from Red's Sandwich Shop and went outside to eat them. The huge sandwiches are filled with turkey, stuffing, and cranberry sauce with butter grilled bread, and I know I'll have to up my cardio to make up for this feast.

Worth it.

As we sit on a bench under a white and yellow beech tree, I look around the little square and notice another thing that sets this place apart from my hometown. All around Salem, and in Boston, I've seen lots of Pride flags proudly blowing in the breeze.

That's one thing about the south. While it's absolutely not true that *all* southerners or even all conservatives are racist and homophobic, it still exists. As much as my parents tried to shield us from it, it was impossible to ignore, growing up.

The first time I heard a slur was when I was seven and we were at a family reunion. One of my older uncles hired a crew to set up and break down the tables, chairs, and tents in his big yard. My dad told me and my siblings to help pick up the chairs and my uncle looked me dead in the eye and said "No, Lennie, let the niggers do it. That's why they're here."

I had never heard that word, but I immediately knew it was hateful and bad. It was in his tone and the mean sneer on his face.

Daddy got in his face and said something quietly to my uncle that made him pale, then stomp away. Then our dad knelt down to talk to us in the most serious voice he'd used before.

"Kids. There are people in this world that look down on others, that think they're superior to other men and women based on the color of their skin. It

Chapter 6

turns them into hateful, ugly people. I don't ever want to hear you use that word. It's for cruel, unkind people, and we raised you to treat everyone as our brother and sister until their actions give us reason to otherwise. We judge others on how they treat themselves and others, not on their appearance."

"So that's a mean word for a Black person?" Auguste asks. He's the oldest, so he usually got things before the rest of us.

A few years later, Raven and I were playing at a friend's house, and our moms were chatting in the kitchen. The friend's live in grandpa told his grandson to "tie your shoes, we don't dress like niggers in this house!"

Raven immediately stood up to her full height and snapped right back at him. "My daddy says that people who use that word are hateful and ugly! You take that back or I'm telling!"

The grandfather looked shocked and then just walked away, grumbling. We were never asked back to play after that.

After that, I started to notice when people were being racist and homophobic. The amount of times I heard people hatefully talking about "queers and faggots and dikes" over the years sickened me a little bit more every time. A lot of this talk was from people in our church. I once heard the preachers wife laughing to another church goer. "Did you hear that they're making a movie about Liberace? He was such a jumped up faggot!"

I think back to those years and shake my head at the sheer hatefulness and hypocrisy.

Coming from a small town southern high school and going to a more liberal city for college was a huge contrast in realities, and one that Raven, and I embraced with open arms. It's been a breath of fresh air to watch people allowed to be themselves and be comfortable in their own skin.

One of my closest friends, Brian, didn't have it so easy in high school. I was actually his fake girlfriend for a year to get the bullying to stop about him being "too feminine."

It wasn't until he started college at Loyola in New Orleans that he was able to come out to his new group of friends. But never to his family. He actually lives in fear of how his grandparents would react, not to mention, his father.

On the train back home a little later, Raven turns to me. "Thanks for coming today. I'm sure there were other things you had in mind for us to do on this day of all days."

"Honestly? It was awesome. I was scared at the gables house, and you're gonna have to vet those pictures before you show me because if I see a ghost, I will cry, but I had fun." I say.

She laughs. "I won't get on a roller coaster for fear of dying, but you're afraid of something that can't even touch you!"

I notice that she doesn't dispute the belief in ghosts are real.

"I'd never let anything bad happen to you Raven. You're my person."

She smiles over at me, linking our pinkies, our special little hand hold. "Happy birthday, Lennie."

"Happy birthday, Rae."

Chapter 7

bumptious
(n) having a feeling of superiority that shows itself in an overbearing attitude

I didn't have anything to worry about. The pictures are lovely, showcasing the colorful trees, the hauntingly beautiful old buildings, and surroundings. The graveyard pictures in particular were amazing, and Raven is happy to get some diversity for her portfolio.

She swears on my favorite horse, Whisper, that no ghosts made a cameo in our pictures, so there's that.

"I can't believe you didn't tell us it was your birthday last weekend!" Cora yells, after barging into our room, scaring Raven mid-shirt removal.

"*Coraline*, what if I were naked!"

Cora narrows her eyes. "You get one pass to call me that. Nice bra by the way, but next time it will be five lashings, missy."

"Let's all get together this weekend to celebrate the big nineteen!" Gabby sings out as she bounces into the room. "Eta Theta Tau is having a party! Sandrine from my bio class invited me, it's at their house on Saturday!"

She's very loud for such a small person.

"Sounds good to me" I say, looking around for my bag. Maybe I'll see Nate and figure out how to get that quilt back to them. I'm over him not texting me. It was a drunken kiss, and I'm sure he was tanked and doesn't remember it.

It's not like I would have time to hang out with him. I haven't even had much time to *read*, and I'm a lot more bent up about that than a guy.

"Yep, I'm down! I'm in the mood to make-out with someone," Raven says, pulling a new shirt over her head.

When the girls and I get to the Eta Theta Tau house, it's just as alive and rowdy as the first party we went to. After weeks of classes, I'm looking forward to letting go and having fun with our friends. I'm stiff and sore from open gym today. Coach had us doing sliders, quad leans, and mat pushes until I wanted to cry.

I just want to cut back and relax tonight.

As soon as we get to the door, a guy meets us there with a bottle of clear liqueur and Solo Cup shot cups. "Welcome babes. Want a shot?" I assume the question is rhetorical since he's already handing them to us. Is this a *thing* at college parties, drinks before we even get through the door? The girls hold their cups up to cheers, so I clink with them before downing my shot.

Sweet Christmas in Hell!

My throat is on literal fire and I'm pretty sure that my esophagus is burned from top to bottom. I can't stop coughing.

"What the . . . " Raven wheezes. "Was that *battery acid*?!"

"Ohhhh, man. That burns in so many ways!" Gabby rasps, not able to reach her full (considerable) volume.

Pretty sure that I've lost power of speech along with Cora because we're both mute, while coughing and gasping for air.

The stupid shot guy laughs, throwing his head back.

"First time trying 151?" he gleefully asks. Ass.

We just give him varying degrees of Glare and push further into the house. I scope out the kitchen, grabbing Cora and nodding for her to grab Raven and Gabby and I lead us straight for the fridge, praying for cold water.

Thank goodness for small favors. There are about two dozen bottles in the fridge, so I snag one for each of us and chug. I marvel at the alcohol content of "151" because that one shot already has me a little fuzzy around the edges, and now that the burn is wearing off, I feel nice and warmed from the inside.

Chapter 7

Still, that was needlessly painful.

"Never again," I gasp out before finishing my water.

"Ohhhh my gosh, who is that?" Gabby grabs my sleeve, pointing to a good looking guy across the room.

"Dylan Blackrock," offers Cora. "He's in my ethics class and is on the lacrosse team. He seems cool."

"Oh, that's right! He's in my UNIV class." I realize. We just tend to stick with our teams, so I haven't spoken to him.

"Oh wow, I want to go meet him, but I think I need another drink first." Gabby says, looking uncharacteristically shy.

"Come on girl, let's go find the White Claw cooler," Cora grabs her hand, and they wander out of the kitchen while she yells over her shoulder "Come find us when you get drinks!"

Raven and I both head to a keg, pour ourselves beers, and pause to take in the party. Loud Cardi B is pumping though the speakers and it's much the same as the last party we were at, only when I look out the open back door I see that someone backed their car into the backyard and has filled their entire trunk with ice and drinks.

This house is as big as the Beta Sigma Sigma Gamma house, but exponentially better decorated.

Girls verses guys, go figure.

"Hey, isn't that Nate, the guy you made out with at the frat party?" Raven nudges me, throwing her chin up in the direction of…yep, that's Nate with Ryder and I think his name is Isaiah? "Did he ever call or text you?"

"Nope," I take a deep drink of my beer, welcoming the buzz. "But it's for the best, he wasn't exactly begging to take me on a date. And I've decided I don't care to get to know someone who didn't even ask before trying to lift up my skirt."

"Ahhh, one of those. I'm sorry sissy." she clinks beers with me. "Make sure the fam doesn't hear about that. Mom will send Daddy to drag us back kicking and screaming, saying "I told you so!"

"It's all good. I do actually need to give back whoever's quilt we took," I hate hanging onto something I've borrowed. "Let's go ask when we can drop it off. Watch it be from someone's grandma or something."

We walk over to the guys, and I start. "Hi Nate, not sure if you remember me from your party. I was hoping to talk to you."

"Lennie, yeah hey. What are you doing here?"

"Hanging out, same as everyone?" I say, slightly taken aback at the weird question. Is this just for Greeks?

"Ah cool cool…listen doll. Sorry I didn't text you. I was pretty blitzed that night. I hope you're not after a repeat," he says lazily, glancing at his friends. This is not the same Nate that was sweet to me that night. Guess an audience really brings it out in him. "I'm not exactly the kind of guy to break you in if you catch my drift." He takes a drink of his beer, basically dismissing me.

My mouth drops open and body flashes hot and cold in shock and humiliation and…anger. Did he just refer to taking my virginity, which I absolutely never offered in the first place, as *breaking me in?* In front of people who don't even know me?

Raven puffs up next to me, no doubt ready to defend my honor, but I am bolstered by the drinks I've had, and the righteous indignation that he would assume I wanted him after he clearly blew me off. This guy needs to be taken down a peg, like, yesterday.

I am so sick and tired of letting people walk all over me.

"Actually, *doll*, as memorable as you seem to think that sloppy bathroom kiss was, that's not why I came to say hi. We borrowed someone's quilt from your house that night, and I just wanted to know a good time to bring it back. No more, no less. I definitely don't need you to 'break me in', seeing as how one-no part of me was ever on the table for you and two-I'm not a *goddamn horse*." I say this all through my teeth, thoroughly provoked. He looks at me with wide eyes.

"Raven, can you find out from John Wayne here when we can bring the quilt back and then come find me? Looks like I need another drink." I say before stalking off without another glance at that arrogant jerk.

I go find Cora and Gabby, but they're not talking to Gabby's crush. They're at the island with some guys I've never met and a girl I think I recognize from my Critical Family History class. "Hey, it's Lonnie, right?" she asks, and I'm

Chapter 7

relieved she doesn't know my name because I can't remember hers.

"Lennie actually, but close!"

"Ahh, sorry. I'm Celeste, we're in Dubois's class, right?"

"Yes ma'am! Good to see you. What exactly is going on here?"

"You've never played Flip Cup?!" she looks shocked, which of course I don't and that embarrasses me a bit, so I just shrug.

"It's so much fun, let me show you how. So, all of these cups along the side of the island will be filled a little less than halfway with alcohol. I recommend beer because you're going to chug it. The person on the right end starts for each side. Your side is your team. Once the first person chugs their beer, they have to turn it over with the edge of the cup left to hang over the island. Yeah like that, and then they try to flip with their finger, so it lands on the bottom of the cup."

She flips the cup, and it turns over twice in the air, landing on its side. Then she tries again, and it flips once and lands perfectly.

"Once that person flips their cup, the person next to them chugs their drink and then flips their cup. The team who finishes first, wins!"

Okay, that sounds weird, but also fun? Raven comes over just in time, so we tell her the rules and then square off, guys against girls.

I recognize some of the guys from the last party, though thankfully Nate and his friends aren't with us. Celeste kicks us off. She makes her flip on the first try.

"Yay, chug!"

"You got this Lennie!" I make my flip and drink victoriously.

"Go Raven!" Oops, she misses.

"Ahh, try agai-YES!"

In the end, these guys must be serious partiers because they kick our butts the first round. Now that we all have the hang of it, though, it's on. The girls and I win three straight rounds before we cry uncle, not willing to get puking drunk just to stick it to the man.

We finally make it home at three am.

"I'm so proud of you for telling that asshole off," Raven hangs on my shoulder, slurring in my ear. "That was so bad ass! You should have seen his face after you stormed off! You're like a new woman sissy! Hear you roar!"

I giggle, hoping he looked ridiculous, and I hug her back as we drunkenly walk from the uber to our dorm. Cora and Gabby walk behind us, laughing uncontrollably about something, and in this moment, I'm just so thankful that we have each other.

I've never spoken to anyone like that before, but *man* he deserved it. It felt great.

I'm about to suggest that we go watch a movie and make some popcorn, but I'm interrupted mid-thought by Gabby running past Raven and me. She stops in front of the bushes and proceeds to throw her guts up. Cora falls down on the ground, rolling around and laughing. Raven staggers over to hold Gabby's hair, and I heave Cora up by her arm. "Get up, wastey-pants!" I laugh at her, losing my balance and falling down with her. We break down into uncontrollable giggles on the ground. I roll onto my back and just lay there, feeling the buzz reverberate through my body.

It's quiet all of a sudden, as we gaze at the stars. I can see our breath and feel the coldness seeping into my back from the frozen ground.

It was such a great night. Raven and Gabby make it back to us, laying down and looking at the sky as well. "You think we'll stay friends all four years and even after college?" Cora asks, breaking the silence.

"I'll accept nothing less." Raven says firmly, still sounding slightly south of sober. I start shivering, so I get up and start helping them to their feet.

"Alright hooligans, time to take our drunk butts to bed."

* * *

Over the next two weeks, it's apparent that Ryder's streak of not wanting to do his own work has continued. We've tried twice to get together with him to work on this project, but he's blown us off both times. We all have class together twice a week, but we have to work on this project outside of that time, and Cat and I are limited with our time blocks because of training.

Apparently, Ryder is on the lacrosse team (not sure how, with as much weed as he smokes, going off the constant smell hovering around him) and has

Chapter 7

begged off twice now due to "last minute stuff."

Cat and I are in a private study room at the Solis Library, frantically outlining our presentation when Ryder sends me a text.

Ryder: Sorry doll. Coach wants us to view tapes. I'll get u my work next sesh

Lennie: Ryder, we literally have TWO WEEKS to finish this. Cat and I need your portion, have you finished?

Ryder: Almost, get it 2 u soon

And I know, *I just know*, that he's blowing me off. I look at Cat and show her the texts and she starts muttering in rapid Spanish. It's taken Cat and I two weeks just to get less than halfway done with our portion, there is no way that we can pick up his slack if my suspicions are correct and he hasn't done anything.

Cat picks up her phone and starts texting.

"This is the last straw, I cannot take anymore!" she grits out, thumbs flying over the screen like a madwoman.

I groan. "I know, I've been flat out working with literally only taking Sundays off to rest my brain and body. I can't keep going like this."

Last week I barely had time to eat. Between training sessions amping up now that we're putting in the finishing touches on our routines that we plan to use during our meets and finals coming up with apparently lightning speed, it's all I can do to keep up.

Back at home, training happens after school and on the weekend. Here, it's before school, during school, and after school. I really didn't have to study in high school, and I wasn't focused on getting straight As. I knew I'd get a scholarship, so I dedicated my time and energy to the gym. Now, in order to keep my scholarship, I have to keep up training and my grades, which means that I'm actually forced to study.

I can't afford to let this go.

"AH HA!" she shouts, making me jump. She shoves her phone in my face. "I knew that pendejo was full of shit!" I read the text thread.

Cat: Hey Dyl, any chance u have to view tapes w/ ur coach right now?
Dylan: Umm, no... Y?

Cat: Some asshole on your team isn't pulling his weight on our project. He blew us off and I knew he was lying

Dylan: Yeah, no we don't. Who?

Cat: Ryder

Dylan: U didn't hear from me, but check his frat house...

I look up at her, fire in her eyes that I'm sure matches mine and I am done with this dude's BS. "I know where to go."

We stop by my dorm to grab the quilt, which I seriously want to just burn at this point, and take her car to the BSSG house. I pound on the door, only stopping when Nate opens it, letting out a huge cloud of weed smoke.

"Uhh, hi?"

"Ryder here?" I ask, barging past Nate after slamming the stupid quilt into his chest.

"Oh, yeah..." he starts, but Cat and I charge on into the living room. I see Ryder lounging on the couch with his friends like Cleo-freaking-patra playing a video game, and I see red.

I think about all the times he asked for my notes without even a thank you, about how he lied to me and kept blowing us off, expecting us to do his work for him. And then I think about how amazing it felt to put Nate in his place. Nate, who by the way is looking very humbled at the moment.

And I realize that I don't need a drop of alcohol for what I want to say to him.

"Oh, hey Ryder, funny seeing you here, baked out of your mind and clearly *not* reviewing film." I seethe. He looks surprised, just sitting there with his mouth hanging open. Cat goes to the TV and turns it off.

"Hey!" Someone shouts out.

"This will only take a minute," she snaps back.

Ryder rolls his eyes, recouping some of this machismo in front of his friends.

"Look, girls—" But he doesn't get to finish whatever crap he was about to spout for his frat brothers' sake, because I cut him off.

"Listen up, because I'm going to say this once. I am not your little schoolwork slave. I'm done with your laziness, your entitlement, and you mistaking my kindness for weakness. From this point forward, you show up

Chapter 7

to class with your *own damn notes*. You will come to *every single session* that we have to finish our project together, or you can fail *alone*." I'm on a roll now, my chest heaving as I finally verbalize what I've been feeling. The guys are laughing and nudging Rider on the couch, but I have no more patience for dumb boys.

"We are not carrying your lazy butt through this class, and if you think I won't get your stoner ass kicked off this project, then think again. Next session is tomorrow at seven, so I suggest you put down the bong, put on your big boy pants and be there, if you plan on passing." His eyes widen and he once again tries to speak.

Without giving him a chance to respond, I turn around and walk out of his house, leaving him sitting on the couch with his mouth hanging open and his friends "ohhhhhing" and razzing him.

Cat follows me out and slams the door. She turns to me with wide eyes. "Holy crap Len, I didn't even have to say anything. That was perfect!"

I smile because even though my hands are shaking, I know he deserved everything I said.

How's that for being a doormat?

Chapter 8

mizpah
(n) *the deep emotional bond between people, especially those separated by death.*

It's December, and I've finally completed the semester. I walk out of my Intro to Communications class feeling great about my final. After I set Ryder straight, he finally got his act together. He actually apologized to me, which I wasn't expecting. I'm not sure if he had someone helping him on the side, but he managed to pull his weight and finish out the project with us.

After training, I float into Anderson House feeling happy and excited to be officially done. Gabby's usual loud voice carries all the way to the front entrance, but I notice as I get closer that her tone is much different from normal.

"I can't believe you slept with him! Of all the guys, you pick the *one* guy that you knew I like! Why are you such a *slut*, Raven, *god!*"

Whoa, that's Gabby's voice, but those words are very unlike her. And she called my sister a slut?

"What is going on here?" I exclaim as I walk through the door to our suite and walk in on tense scene. Raven and Gabby stand face to face with Cora lingering a little behind the latter, her face scrunched with discomfort. Gabby is red faced and teary-eyed but looking livid. This is totally out of character for her.

Chapter 8

And Raven is standing in front of Gabby looking completely shocked.

"What are you talking about?! What guy?"

"Dylan. Blackrock."

The name rings a bell, but I can't land on a face.

"How was I supposed to know you're into him? I just met him like two weeks ago!" Raven sputters, looking like she's getting angry too.

"I told you at the Eta Theta Tau party, what do you mean? I've liked him since last month, and I've been trying to get to know him and then he tells me that he's not interested in anything right now because he thinks he may have something going on with *you* because of your 'hookup'!"

"Ummm, I don't remember most things about that party, but I definitely didn't know that you were talking to him. You never brought it up again, how was I supposed to know?"

At this point Gabby is crying. The fact that Raven's sleeping around has bit her in the butt isn't lost on me, though, and I'm starting to feel frustrated with both of them.

"Listen, Gab, I'm really sorry that you're hurting. If it makes you feel any better, we didn't actually have sex. I have zero interest in starting anything up with Dylan. But you calling me a slut is not only *extremely fucking uncool*, it's not the way I let my friends speak to me. *Ever.*" Raven grits out.

"Oh please, it's no secret that you'll literally sleep with any guy who gives you attention," she yells at Raven, whose eyes widen in hurt, and I am done.

"Enough." I bark out. "She told you that she didn't know you liked him and that they didn't sleep together, so why are you still being hateful?"

"Oh, that's funny. Now you want to stop acting all meek?" Gabby sneers at me, and as she turns to me I smell the alcohol wafting off her in concentrated waves and notice her unsteady movements. Now I understand the sudden level of venom.

"You know what?" Cora starts as she comes between the three of us. "Let's all take a big cool down. Separately. Gabs, you've been drinking your feelings, and I feel like you're going to regret this in the morning."

"I don't regret shit," she slurs.

Cora pulls Gabby into their dorm, and Raven and I stand together in the ringing silence. I look at her and notice that she's holding back tears, and I know, I just know how she's going to handle this.

"Fuck. Her." Raven spits out, turning back into our dorm.

I follow her and close the door with a sigh.

Raven is extremely sensitive, but she's also prideful. She won't let how much Gabby just hurt her show to anyone, maybe even to me.

I shut our door behind me and sit on her bed where she's staring at her phone, scrolling with her thumb.

"Want to talk about it?" I ask, knowing her answer before she gives it.

"Nope."

"Rae, look at me," I plead.

She huffs a sigh and sits up, pulling her pillow to her chin. She looks at me and a tear rolls down her face. She angrily bats it away like it offends her.

"Look, you and I both know that you didn't know about Dylan. I even forgot about it myself. And you're not a slut. Trying different things with guys is like a college rite of passage, there is no harm as long as you're not doing this because of some misplaced self-esteem issue."

I try to assure her. The words just fall out of my mouth, but I find that I do believe them. I feel bad for being so prudish before now.

"It's not that," she says. She's having a hard time meeting my eyes and I wonder just how many judgmental vibes I've been sending.

"I just wanted to get out of my head a little, you know? Blow off steam, have a little fun, experience things before I'm expected to be more of an adult. I didn't mean to upset anyone, and I do feel bad about Gabby, but she just hurt me. I am *not* a slut. I don't throw myself at guys, and I definitely don't lap up attention and fall into bed with just anyone."

More tears fall. She's doesn't even try to wipe them now, so I help her out.

"I know you don't Rae. It's just that maybe this is a sign to slow down with all of the partying and hookups. Just take a breather and try on some new experiences. We've barely explored Boston, or even Massachusetts for that matter. Maybe we can branch out and try more new things. There is more to college than parties and casual sex." I say gently.

She heaves a sigh and smiles at me, finally.

Chapter 8

"Maybe I did take this whole freedom thing too far. I'm not going to stop having fun and doing me, but I hear you. Let's make some plans for when we get back after break."

"Yes! This will be fun," I say enthusiastically, trying to cheer her up.

"But Len? I am never, ever speaking to Gabby again." She says with finality.

I hang my head. One step at a time.

* * *

"Okay, tell me everything!" Maddie shouts out, jumping onto my bed. I've been home for three days, but she and Mom just got back from a rodeo in Arkansas.

I laugh, pushing her off me. "I just saw you for Thanksgiving, Mad! The only thing you missed since then is the stress of finals and projects."

"Nooo, I was hoping to hear a great love story!"

I snort, thinking of Nate. "Yeah…definitely not. Les gars du collège sont boiteux." *College guys are lame.*

"Well dang," she pouts. "I wanted to hear about the sexy times!"

"Madeline Shae!"

She shrugs. "Maybe Raven has some good stories."

I tense, thinking about Raven's 'stories', but then I remember that Maddie is the only person that Raven can be big-sister protective over, and she takes that seriously. She'll probably never stop thinking of Mads as the baby, so I highly doubt she'll try to corrupt her with tales of her conquests.

"You've been reading too many romance novels little sissy," I say with a laugh.

She smiles wickedly. "Don't tell Momma."

After dinner, I go into Raven's room and sit on her bed to watch her work. She's sitting at her easel and smearing blue paint all over a canvas for the start of what promises to be a moody piece.

"Have you talked to her yet?"

Knowing that I'm talking about Gabby she raises her eyebrow without looking away from her art. "Nope."

"Did she apologize?"

"Yep."

"Oh my gosh, *Raven* stop one-wording me! What did she say?"

She rolls her eyes. "She texted the day after and said she was drunk from a party and very emotional and soooo sorry for calling me a slut. And I don't give a shit."

"You don't think she has the right to be upset, and the right to forgiveness when she wasn't sober and clearly didn't mean it?"

"Would you forgive someone who was becoming a best friend for calling you something so hateful?" Raven asks. "I am sick of slut-shaming. Why is it that guys can sleep around, and it's celebrated. But when a girl wants to, she's shamed and called cruel names? As long as it's safe and consensual, how is it different?"

And honestly, I hadn't looked at it like that. I'd been silently judging her for the past four months, and now I feel like a jerk all over again. Because while douche bag behavior makes me judge a guy, guys sleeping around and being honest about it being casual doesn't really give me pause.

Wow Len, way to set back equality by about twenty years.

"Dang. You're right Rae. I'm sorry. I just don't think that cutting her off is the right thing. It won't make you happy."

She shrugs, rinsing her brush in a cup of water before moving on to a darker blue.

I know that Raven's anger is just her shield, but she's always had to be the one to work things out for herself. Hopefully this doesn't cause a divide with our friends.

***

Christmas with my family was amazing. My mom has the ability to make every holiday cozy and special, and I find myself missing home for the first time since I left in August.

Walking back into the dorms for the first time in January is markedly different than back in August. It doesn't help that it's currently twenty degrees

Chapter 8

outside. It's like my body forgot how to feel cold and is in shock.

It's a relief to get into our room and throw our suitcases down. I immediately take off my coat and boots and throw myself under the covers.

"Holy *crap*, I think my joints are frozen!" Raven gripes, shivering. She forces her way under the covers with me. "I can't believe these people deal with this every single year and aren't wearing arctic gear."

I agree silently, too intent on getting warm to pipe up. There's a soft knock at the door, and I'm guessing it's Cora or Gabby. Raven stiffens next to me, obviously making the same conclusion.

I get up and open the door, then relax in relief.

"Hey, how was your break?" I ask Cora as I give her a hug. She returns it gently, which is very unlike her. She's more of the hug-you-so-hard-you-can't-breath type.

"It was great actually. Much better than Gabby's." She starts, quietly. "She- her um…her oldest brother was killed, about a week before Christmas. Car accident."

"Oh my God!" I look over at Raven. She's slowly rising from the bed with a look of horror on her face. Without saying a word to each other, we walk past Cora and head into their room. Gabby is sitting on the bed, staring at the floor.

"Hi guys." she says meekly, looking every bit the grieving sister.

We both walk over to her and sit on either side, pulling her into a twin hug. She sniffles and lets us just hold her.

"I'm so sorry Gabs," I say.

"You must be so heartbroken," Raven adds.

Gabby just nods her head.

"He was a really, really amazing brother," She whispers before breaking into sobs.

Tears pour down my face in empathy, and I look at Raven, seeing the same. My heart breaks for Gabby, and I know that their stupid fight is completely forgotten on both parts.

People tend to get perspective when watching someone they care about grieve over something this profoundly tragic.

We go get dinner and bring it back with us so that we can all eat in Gabby and Cora's room. We let Gabby talk and then cry with her again. She falls asleep after a few hours. She must be exhausted. I can't imagine burying one of my brothers. It makes my heart ache to think about how she's feeling.

I take it as a sign that it snows that night, for the first time since I've been in Boston. I woke up suddenly at 2am, just feeling that something was different, gasping when I saw the snow falling past the window. I drag Raven out of bed to get bundled up and come outside with me to watch the snow fall.

Outside, we put a blanket on top of the picnic table before laying down, side by side, and looking up at sky, seeing the few twinkling stars that shine through the clouds that are raining down big, fluffy snowflakes.

The first snowfall of our lives.

The night is completely quiet, with only the hushed sound of the falling snow making its way to our ears. It's the most utterly peaceful thing that I've ever experienced. I think about the events of the night, about death, the sudden loss of Gabby's brother, who she loves so much. How her family must be grieving that they never got to say goodbye, how they are going to cope with the loss of Gavin.

When my dad's parents died, within weeks of each other, we were devastated. Still are. They were such special people, and my only set of grandparents that I ever got to know. They lived entire lifetimes and died peacefully of old age, and it was still heartbreaking. To think about losing a brother, a son, in his early twenties without warning…I don't have the ability to imagine how much pain I would feel.

They say time heals all wounds, but I don't believe that to be the case at all. I think time just makes them easier to live with, to carry out your day to day life without letting grief weigh you down. It's such a heavy weight.

Chapter 9

vorfreude
(n) the joyful, intense anticipation that comes from imagining future pleasures

"Break a leg!"

"Cora! You can't say that; it's only good luck in theater. In this sport she could *literally* break her leg." Raven gasps.

"Oh no! I'm sorry, don't break a leg!"

I laugh as I gather up my gym bag from my desk chair and finish drinking my gogi berry juice.

"All good, I'm not superstitious."

"Okay good. Well good luck then, we'll be cheering you on!" Cora says, before moving to our door.

"Wait," Raven calls from her bed. "Is Gabby coming?"

Cora hesitates. "I'm trying to get her to come. She's spent the last two weeks in bed, I think she's gone to maybe half her classes."

Raven sits up. "I'll come talk to her with you."

She gives me a big hug and a kiss on the cheek.

"Good luck with your first meet, sissy. I'll be the one screaming the loudest!"

I'm equal parts nervous and excited. My family isn't able to make this first meet because of some department head meeting at LSU, but they'll be at the one in February against Stanford.

Our coaches have tried to prep us for what to expect, knowing that three of the six of us competing today all come from the elite world and are first timers. They play music when we practice and let the basketball team come watch us a lot since we share the same training center. It helps prepare us for the loud and crazy atmosphere and having spectators. I've watched lots of meets on TV, but I'm sure it's different in person.

Savannah said that her cousin goes to Bowling Green, and they practice beam in the student union, surrounded by people talking and eating. It helps train them to concentrate, because like elite competitions, you have to focus while other people do their routines on beam, floor, vault, and bars. At any given time, someone's floor routine music is blaring while we work on our routines.

Ironically, we're competing against LSU today, and they're a tough team. It's only because of my sheer determination to get out from under my parent's eyes that I didn't go to LSU. I'm a huge fan, not just of the football team, but of the gymnastics team as well. When Daddy took me to their state of the art training center, a teeny part of me was swayed. That's what he was aiming for, anyways.

It's going to be tough to compete against them, but I have something to prove.

I walk into Fulminare and head straight for the dressing room, where we congregate for hair, makeup, and our pre-comp rituals. This looks different for everyone, but for me, I always take time to sit quietly and visualize my routines and concentrating on clearing my mind. Then I tape up my fingers and ankle, and start spot checking my appearance.

Around me, the girls are all quiet, doing their own thing, mentally running through their own routines, and getting in the mindset to compete.

Here's the thing about female gymnastics. The rules on appearance are both archaic and overboard, but they aren't changing anytime soon. We're not allowed to have any visible undergarments showing. During the state and national circuit, we're not even allowed nail polish, and you better believe that judges will take off points for it, but at least in NCAA we can all have matching nails. Only two earrings are allowed, no other jewelry or embellishments,

Chapter 9

that even includes a hair tie around the wrist, though those rules are more for safety than appearances.

So, part of our pre-warm up routine is actually spent helping each other police our appearance. We check to make sure each other's bra straps are hidden, spray hairspray on toothbrushes to help smooth flyaway baby hair, reinforce our buns with ten more hair clips than you think you'll need, touch up our makeup, which is heavier than we'd normally wear for day to day…that kind of thing.

The gymnastics team has our own training facility inside, but we use the basketball court for meets because we need the seats for spectators. We also have basketball court flooring in our training center under the mats so that we aren't thrown off by switching rooms.

Six gymnasts are chosen for each meet, and we're scored on the highest five. Our collective scores, as we move on in meets, will determine our national team ranking. One of the biggest things I've had to get used to was switching from an individual dynamic to that of a team. I'm not competing against these girls for my own ranking. We have to all do our best so that the team succeeds.

Back home, there is much more of a competitive and yes, sometimes very petty dynamic to our gym. We all want the gold; we all strive for the best. We do support each other, but when we're in competition, it's for our own glory.

Today it's me, Jayla, Cat, and Neveah, a sophomore, Isis, a junior, and our only senior on the team, Zipporah. Everyone else on the team will be in our track suits cheering us on.

When we're about thirty minutes out, Head Coach Akeno Satō and Coach Sara Johannes walk into the room, followed by Coach Dwight. Coach Akeno is a muscular Japanese man with thick black hair and a tall stature. His handsome face gives zero indication of his age, and he could be between thirty and fifty for all I know. Us girls on the team have spent hours speculating about it.

Coach Sara is a tiny white woman with light brown hair, stunning blue eyes, and a disposition of steel. She is terrifying at times, but I'm convinced she's a secret softy. Once we got her to warm up to us, she acts like a fussy team mom, always making sure we take water breaks and doctor our blisters.

"Ladies. I've watched you bust your asses for the past four months. You've sweated and bled together. You've pushed your bodies to the limit and pushed further still. Every single one of you has what it takes to get out there and get perfect tens," Coach Akeno preaches. "It wasn't hard deciding who would compete today. You've all shown perseverance, dedication, and drive. You've done the work, now let's show LSU who we are!"

Coach Akeno puts his hand out, followed by Coach Dwight and Coach Sara. We follow, and before we throw our hands in the air, we shout "Jump off the beam, flip off the bars, follow your dreams and reach for the stars!"

"Let's go girls!"

We jog out to the doors of the transformed basketball court and I'm immediately winded from the sheer energy radiating from the packed stands. A voice comes from someone with a microphone inside.

"Ladies and gentlemen, get to your feet and welcome your KALON KNIGHTS TEMPLAR LADIES GYMNASTICS TEAAAAAM!!!!"

We jog out waving at the stands and it's insanely loud. It's sea of navy and gold, and my heart is pounding. Nothing the coaches said could have truly prepared me for this atmosphere.

I. Am. Pumped.

The fans are screaming their support, waving signs, poms poms, and banners. I even hear a freaking cow bell!

We start warming up after LSU comes in with their purple and yellow uniforms, and after The National Anthem, we're off.

My first routine is bars, which is my weakest skill. My routine is actually a downgraded version of my elite routine that I did at a competition last spring.

"Up for the uneven parallel bars is Lenore Landry with Kalon U."

I double check that my grips are buckled and walk up to the chalk bucket, liberally chalking my hands and feet. I think to myself, *for the love of everything good, remember to point your freaking toes, Lennie.*

Coach Dwight is spotting me from the side of the bars. My teammates and people in the stands are cheering me on, and Raven's voice yells out over the rest, "YOU GOT THIS LENNIE!!!!"

Chapter 9

I take a few deep breaths to center myself and clear my mind of anything other than my routine. It's me and the bars. Nothing else registers, anymore.

Standing under the high bar, I grab the lower bar and start with a huge toe shoot to shaposhnikova that connects to a bail to handstand. From there, I fling my body up and backwards, grabbing the high bar and swing around to a shoot over to handstand on the lower bar before flying back up to grab the high bar and doing another handstand at the top. I swing around once, letting go of the bar and kicking my legs into a split while my body is midair, a reverse hecht, before swinging back up to handstand on top of the bars. Taking a breath to prepare myself for a big dismount, I take two giant swings over and under the bar, feeling the power in my momentum, before releasing and dismounting with a full twisting double back.

And I stick the landing, with a huge smile on my face and instant thundering applause. Coach Akeno grabs me into a big hug, lifting me off the mats while I laugh, and then sets me back on the ground. The teammates that aren't running their routines all run up and surround me with hugs, and my relief is palpable. After a few minutes I hear: "Lenore Landry for Kalon U scores 9.925 on bars."

We head over to support Jayla while she's up on beam.

"Let's show 'em, Jayla!" I cup my hands and shout, which is followed with shouts of encouragement from the other girls.

We all stand just beyond the mat to watch as she walks up to the beam and does her start pose, arms up and quickly down, smiling to the judges.

Jayla moves through her transitions, combinations, and leaps beautifully, finally ending with a full twist off the side of the beam. She nailed it, and the smile on her face shows that she knows it.

Our team surrounds her with hugs and praise. I could honestly get addicted to this feeling, it's like an adrenaline high mixed with a huge shot of serotonin and dopamine to the brain.

We're all heading to get water when we hear "Jayla Smyth with Kalon U scores a 9.98 on beam!" We all instantly go insane again and she's jumping up and down.

"I don't believe it!" She yells when I pull her into a hug. "Believe it girl, *you did that!!!"*

The meet goes on and we ended up beating LSU by 1.531 points.

The fans are going crazy, and I finally spot Raven and Cora, jumping up and down and cheering.

The smile on my face grows even more when I see Gabby standing and cheering with them. She may be a shell of her former self, but she's here and she's smiling.

Someone shoots off confetti poppers and blue and yellow rain down all around as Gabby hugs Cora and Raven. The sounds around me fade into the background as I remember the night we came back, watching her break down into tears over the death of her brother.

And it makes me think about how time isn't guaranteed at all. We're given each day at a time, a gift. After experiencing the freedom that we've had for the past few months, I feel like Raven and I are more comfortable in our own skin than we've ever been.

And I don't want to lose that by forgetting that what we do matters. Who we are to each other and to other people matters, and I don't want to spend another minute worrying about what ifs.

I'm going to stand on my own two feet and chase what I want, when I want. I'm going to make sure the people I love know how important they are to me. If anything happens to me, I don't want there to be any doubt as to how much I loved those close to me.

I'm going to train and do well in classes, but I also want to live outside of those responsibilities. I shamed Raven for diving into what she thought made college an experience. What do I think this experience should be? It's definitely not endless weeks of class and training.

From this day forward, I am going to make it my mission to be damn sure that I don't leave college in three and a half years wondering how great it could have been if I had just lived a little.

Chapter 10

abendrot

(n) the color of the sky while the sun is setting

YEAR TWO

My mom collects Willow Tree figurines. My father collects cast iron cookware. Raven collects crystals. As for me, I collect words. I've always been a voracious reader, looking up every word that I didn't know, steadily growing my vocabulary over the years.

Ludic - Full of fun and high spirits.
Solivagant - Wandering alone.
Kymatology - The science of waves.

I can usually find an obscure word for any situation. It's the last day of August, and I'm at the campus pool with Raven, Cora, and Gabby, along with some of the gals from my team.

I spent the summer with my home team in the gym, back up to my forty hours of training. It was definitely a mind-bend switching from NCAA back to Elite. There are certain things that are focused on in NCAA that aren't in Elite and vice versa. I had to unlearn some habits and relearn, and I'll now have to undo and redo.

We came back early enough so that I could meet up with the team and greet the incoming freshman, of which there were two. It's been so great to be back with the girls.

At present, we're soaking in the sun, taking advantage of the last days of summer before the pool closes up.

I'm lying on my lounger thinking about classes starting up next week when I'm jolted out of my musings.

"Lennie! Come back me up!" Tatum Patrick shouts at me. She's one of the new freshmen. I sit up and look over, seeing her standing in front of six guys in lounge chairs, hands on her hips.

Oookay.

I walk over to her, grateful to have on sunglasses so that I'm not caught looking at any guy in particular. They're all built, that's for sure.

"Making new friends?" I ask, as I come up beside her and raise my eyebrow.

"Uh, no. That's my brother Jared, right there." She points to a white guy with auburn hair and I wave a little, confused.

She turns back towards me, fired up.

"So, you've watched hockey, right?"

"Uhh, I've seen the Mighty Ducks." I say, unsure of this line of questioning.

"That's it?" She's incredulous.

"Hold up, you've never seen hockey? Ever?" One of the guys asks, looking shocked. A few of his friends pipe up with the same sentiments.

"I take it y'all are hockey players?" I ask with a laugh.

"Uh yeah. Hockey is king around here, haven't you heard?" This particular guy is blonde, and extremely attractive. He looks familiar.

"Didn't we meet last year at a party? I'm Luca." Ah, right. Nate's frat brother.

"Lennie."

"So, tell me Lennie, how is it that you've never watched hockey? I mean, you do live in Boston."

I hold up my hands. "Okay…well, in my defense, hockey is not a thing where I'm from."

"And where is that?"

"Louisiana."

"Hey, so am I! Where from," asks a Black guy with shoulder length braids and

Chapter 10

gigantic biceps. "I'm Dominic by the way. I'm from Natchitoches originally before we moved to Maine four years ago."

"Near Baton Rouge, in Ascension Parish."

"Holy, who knew girls from Louisiana were so fuckable," one of the guys mutters to another in french, causing my jaw to drop.

Going by his accent, he must be one of those French Canadians I've heard so much about. Awesome.

"You know, another fun thing about us girls from Louisiana," I start in English with a fake sweet smile. "Is that *nous parlons français aussi, couillon!*" *We speak french also, asshole!*

The guy who spoke up hung his head "Ahh, hell," he muttered, shoulders slumped, while his friend throws his head back and laughs at his expense.

"*Anyways*, this jerkoff here," Tatum interrupts, pointing back to Luca. "Apparently thinks that gymnasts aren't real athletes!"

I whip my face towards him, and he's looking a little wary now. "Excuse me?"

He mutters something under his breath, but then appears to buckle down.

"I was just teasing her, but yeah I do think we're the superior athletes."

"In what way?" I ask, crossing my arms.

"I'm just saying that we're more well-rounded. We skate full out while we're maneuvering the puck and checking 200 pound dudes for three periods." He sits back, crossing his arms over his head and grinning.

"So? How can you even compare the sports? And why?" I volley back.

"Honestly I was just giving her a hard time. But now that you mention it, I'm sure I have at least one guy on our team that can do what you girls do. Question is, can you keep up with us?" Luca gives me a shit-eating grin and something in me rises up. This is my high school football taking up all the space in our school all over again. The big guys on campus thinking they're superior to everyone who doesn't put on pads and helmets and bro-out while they sweat their manliness all over.

Tomfoolery - Boys being idiots. (my definition)

Morosis - the stupidest of stupids. (see above)

"Alright, Mr. Hockey. Moving a stick and a puck around doesn't exactly look like rocket science," I start, putting my hands to my hips. "But if we put you out on the mats, you most definitely wouldn't be able to perform at a meet."

He looks at me for a beat, assessing.

"Okay sweetheart. Do your best trick and my guy will do it just as good."

Dominic sits up in his lounger, rubbing his hands together.

"Okay, whatcha got for me? Layout, Full Twist, Double Full?"

Clearly, he was a gymnast at some point in his life, which is going to make this victory so sweet.

"On concrete, in a bikini? Hard pass" I wave him off. Thank goodness I wore a conservative top today or I would not be this blasé.

"Actually, I was thinking about a ring pose." I say sweetly.

"Yes!" Tatum beams.

"A who?" Dominic says, looking confused.

Exactly.

I grab Tatum's scrunchie and hand her my sunglasses, putting my hair in a messy bun while walking over to the ladder rails.

"Take notes, boys." I toss over my shoulder.

I step up on one of the rails, and lower my hands to the other, flipping up into a handstand. Once I'm perfectly vertical, I slowly scissor my legs into a front split.

"Whoa!" One of the guys blurts out.

Once my legs are in the split, I bend my back inward, bringing my front leg down in a full bend to touch my pointed toes to my hands, while my back leg comes up to be vertical again. My leg and back are making a ring, bent at the knee and curved through my spine. It's my best pose and one that took me years of conditioning and training my body to achieve.

Once I've held the pose for five seconds, I flip my legs back to stand on the rail and do a back tuck off to land on my feet.

All six guys are staring at me with their mouths hanging open while Tatum smirks at them.

"The stage is all yours" I say to the guys, beaconing them to the rails with my arms.

Chapter 10

Luca looks a little worried. "Uh, Dominic?"

"Luca, my man, I can't do that!" He squeaks out, making Tatum and I laugh. "Are you crazy?"

Luca drops his head back. "I screwed up boys!" he calls out dramatically, throwing his arm over his face. "I stand corrected by the bendy, beautiful southern belle." He looks over at me and grins, winking.

I shoot them a smug smile and turn back to head to my friends.

* * *

A few days later, we're at home cooking. Cora and Gabby are benefiting from our kitchen because it quickly became apparent that the only thing those two know how to make is microwave mac-n-cheese and top ramen. Enter The Landry Twins.

The hardest part of this dish is the roux. It's the hardest part because "perfect" and "burnt" are only a few seconds apart from each other. I start the roux by melting duck fat in the pot and stirring in flour. It takes forever, but the flour slowly toasts and turns the roux a glossy dark brown as I constantly whisk it, and a scent almost like saltine crackers fills the kitchen. Next, Raven throws in the trinity while I continue to stir. The trinity is chopped onion, celery, and green bell pepper, named after the Holy Trinity, and a staple in Cajun cooking.

We're making a big batch of gumbo and having some friends over to watch the first LSU football game of the season. Due to lack of Louisianan influence in northern stores, we had to bring some stuff with us when we drove up a few weeks ago.

I'd called Cora to see what all she could find in the shops up here because I had a feeling that they wouldn't have certain things that are clutch in Cajun cooking.

"Try to find filé powder in the spice section."

"*What* powder?!"

"Figures. Okay, there is a Creole seasoning in a green and red container, Tony Chachere's."

"Tony *who*?!"

"Ugh. Grits?"

"No, we have cream of wheat."

"Eww, what is cream-you know what? Forget it. Andouille sausage?"

"Are you even speaking English?!"

"Oh my God, Cora! Okra?"

"Okay, now you're just making shit up."

Heavy sigh.

"Kidding, we have okra!"

So yeah, we came armed with spices and a cooler of frozen goods on dry ice. I had Boudin withdrawals all last year, and that is not happening on my watch this year. I didn't tell the girls what was in it before I had them try it. It's basically rice dressed with spices and mixed with cooked pork meat and liver, all encased in a sausage casing. And it's amazing. You boil it and eat it without the casing. (This is a huge point of contention with Cajuns. Some are die hard about eating it casing and all. Others, like me, would *never*.) We serve it all the time at home, and at every holiday as a side.

Gabby was appalled that I fed her pork liver. Cora just shrugged and said "I'm Asian."

Now that we're all renting a house together, which was a whole hugely drawn out discussion with our parents on personal safety and responsibility, Raven and I are breaking in the kitchen by cooking for our friends. It's a cute, two story white Tudor style four bedroom, with a highly pitched roof and black trim and details. It actually looks slightly witchy, and I love it.

It's also close to campus, and nice enough that we probably wouldn't have been able to snag if it weren't for Gabby's family connections.

Money talks, no shock there.

They generously decided to pay half as Gabby's portion, leaving the three of us to split the other half. I quit my freshman job since my scholarship accounts for living expenses, and Cora and Raven each have serving jobs at a restaurant near campus.

Another new development is that Gabby started dating Dylan this summer. Thank goodness it's not weird between him and Raven. He's from Toronto, so

Chapter 10

I guess he and Gabby were able to visit each other this summer and start things up. Which is so nice to see, because she spent all last semester depressed about losing her brother, Gavin. Things didn't start looking up until right before summer break when she started getting inner sunshine back.

Cora invited some friends from class, while Gabby invited Dylan and some of his friends from the lacrosse and hockey teams.

Raven and I move around each other to add chopped okra, seasonings, and chicken stock to the pot before she heads into the living room, leaving me to finish up.

I'm slicing andouille when the guys come in.

"Hey Lennie," I look up to see Luca and one of the other guys from last week at the pool. "Hi Luca."

"This is my buddy, Chase." Chase is the dark to Luca's blonde, with olive toned pale skin, black hair, and brown eyes. Very handsome in a boy-next-door sort of way. He smiles at me, and I immediately smile back.

"I'm actually Gabby's cousin," he says.

"Aww, cool. Nice to meet you! Nicer to meet this time, anyways." I offer, teasing.

"Yeah, I'm never gonna live that down." Luca grimaces, "I swear I was just giving Jared's little sister a hard time and it snowballed."

"And then you couldn't back down, so instead you got your ass handed to you," Chase laughs at him. I actually was really embarrassed after that whole episode. At the time I felt empowered, like I finally showed the guys who write off female athletes that we're just as fierce as them. But later when I was overthinking, I just felt like I should have taken the high road and not called so much attention to myself.

"All good! It was fun, actually. Are y'all ready for the best gumbo you've ever had?"

Chase looks in the pot, curious. "Umm, it will be the only gumbo I've ever had."

"Are you a good cook?" Luca asks. I scoff.

"Of course. I'm southern."

"What's that supposed to mean?"

"It means that all southerners are good cooks when they're taught by another one." I smile at him.

"Well, I've never had any Cajun food, but I'll happily judge on your cooking skills." Chase grins as he winks at me.

I feel a sudden burst of shyness and turn to throw the sausage into the pot, stirring it to give myself a tiny moment. It smells like home, and I smile to myself.

Luca wanders off looking for the bathroom, and Chase walks into the living room.

He's talking to Dylan when I walk behind them a little later to grab something off a shelf. They're on the couch facing away from me, speaking quietly, and I hear snippets without meaning to.

"Do you like either…Lennie?"

"I haven't….I might be into her sister."

"Ah, sweet that's…Raven?"

So, Chase likes Raven. I've only been in his company for a short while, but I'm pegging him as a nice guy, and I know for a fact that Raven chews nice guys up and spits them out, so I doubt that pairing would work out. I file that away and go back to the kitchen to finish the gumbo. Anyone can make gumbo, but you have to know how to perfectly season it. I dash in some more filé, a few liberal splashes of Tabasco and Worcestershire sauce and taste it.

Perfect.

Cajun cooking is often done in big batches to feed a lot of people at once. Gumbo and crawfish boils are typically made at times of celebration, where lots of family and friends come together. It's not crawfish season yet, but we plan to have our parents ship us some once the season opens up so we can host a boil. After first semester last year I put a lot more energy into making new friends and setting more time aside to foster those relationships.

After fluffing the finished rice, I call out to everyone to come grab their bowls. Every set of eyes looked at me and Raven like we declared "Praise Satan and all his demons" when we brought out the potato salad as a lagniappe and showed them how to eat it all together. Some people back home just dump heaps into their gumbo, but Raven and I keep it separate so the potato

Chapter 10

salad stays cool. It's the most basic version. Potatoes, mayonnaise, mustard, onions, and paprika sprinkled on top. We take a half spoonful of potato salad, and then load the rest of the spoon up with gumbo and rice and eat it all together.

Trust me, it's the best way to eat gumbo.

Once Cora and Chase were brave enough to try it and loved it, most everyone else gave in and tried it too. We all head into the living room and settle on couches, chairs, and the floor to eat and watch the game.

Dylan takes a huge bite and swallows, his eyes going wide before closing in pleasure. "Oh my gosh, that tastes like a hug from the Lord," he moans, making me laugh.

"I think that's the biggest compliment I've ever gotten on my cooking," I say, chuckling. Everyone pipes up with their praise, and I'm trying not to preen like an idiot over their compliments. Or blush like a fool.

Once everyone finishes eating (Luca and Chase and Dylan have *three* helpings!) we're laying around watching the end of the game when Raven pops up suddenly, looking outside towards the backyard.

"Holy crap, Lennie, go get your leotard on and grab one for Tatum! Quick, *va vite!*"

"What? Why?" I ask, sitting up from where I was slouched against Gabby, looking at Pinterest together on our phones.

"Look at that sunset. I want to get pictures of you two posing, with it in the background, so move it!"

Instead of a fence, our west facing backyard has a four-foot-tall retaining wall, painted white that's about 8 inches wide. Behind it is a field that used to be a retention pond. When you take photos from the ground, all you see is the wall and the sky behind it. Now I remember Raven explaining her vision last night.

Tatum and I change into black leotards and head out to the back. Everyone came outside to see the action, but I block out the attention, just like at meets. It took some getting used to with all of the screaming and cheering, at least for me, and it wasn't until the fifth or sixth meet that I could fully shut it all out as I competed.

Raven instructs us to hoist ourselves on the wall, and the sunset is absolutely gorgeous. The sky is a kaleidoscope of warm, vibrant colors. I shiver at the cool wind that's kicked up as the sun goes down.

She has me do my ring pose, and Tatum smirks at Chase and Luca. I also do a few others that are fairly difficult but will photograph well. Tatum does some of her own, and then she has us face each other and some of the same ones, mirroring each other.

After about 20 minutes she lets us stop. "Slave driver" I mutter as I hop down. We look at the screen and even unedited, they're edgy. Because of the lighting, the sky is lit up with lavenders and oranges and pinks, while Tatum and I look almost blacked out against the backdrop of the sunset, with very little details in our face and hair showing through.

We basically look like solid shadows lit from behind with the brilliant backdrop. She even got one of me doing a One Legged Wheel pose and the setting sun is directly behind the middle of my body. It's an epic shot.

Luca and Chase are back inside talking to Cora and Tatum's brother Jared, so I put some shorts on in my room and head back out to sit with them, too lazy to change again.

"Okay, I know that we saw you do that last week, but I don't think I told you how seriously impressive that is." Chase said. Luca frowns at him, like he stole his thunder.

Luca turns his attention back to me. "Yeah, crazy cool. How long have you been a gymnast?"

"Fifteen years."

"Yeah, that seems about right. I've been playing hockey since I was five." Luca offers.

"Same here." Chase adds.

"Goodness, hockey must be really popular up here to start kids that early. I knew about the team last year, but it wasn't really on my radar."

"Well, I've got a ticket with your name on it to our first game in October," Luca starts. "Tell me you'll come."

"I'd love to. I'll ask the girls if they want to come too. Is it like the Mighty Ducks portrayed? Seems really violent."

Chapter 10

Chase snorts. "Absolutely not. Those kids didn't play the game right at all, and some of those 'clean hits' that the refs ignored were just straight up assault."

Luca laughs.

"So there really isn't violence in hockey?"

Luca laughs louder this time. "Sweetheart, hockey is the bloodiest sport in the world, maybe second to fighting." And I really notice his New York accent now.

"Seriously?" I ask, wary.

He grabs the TV remote from Cora ("Hey!") and opens the YouTube app, searching for something.

"This is a goalie from the 80s who gets hit with a skate in the crease." He said, while I watch. In the clip, the goalie is in front of the net, and some of the players collide, knocking everyone down. At first, I can't see what's happening, but once they clear, blood starts spraying everywhere from the goalie's neck. Cora makes a shocked sound, covering her mouth.

I stare, horrified. It's so much blood. I can feel my eyes welling up, and I feel nauseated. I look over at the guys, eyes wide. "Am I watching someone die?" I gasp out, trying not to freak out like a…well, like a girl.

Chase's eyes widen and he shakes his head. "Oh crap, *no*. No, he lived, sorry about that. Luca man, you gotta preface stuff like this."

Luca purses his lips and looks regretful. "Sorry Lennie. I should have started with that."

Cora rolls her eyes. "Show us something else Chase, *not* blood and gore."

They queued up some NHL Mic'd Up compilations that were a mixture of funny (chirping is trash talk, apparently, and hilarious), shocking (*holy*, they really let them fight during games!) and cringe worthy (injuries on ice while wearing sharp skates and going at high speeds are on another level.)

Still, it looks like a blast, like no sport I've ever seen.

I'm actually looking forward to watching some of their games now.

Before he leaves, Luca pulls me to the side giving me his undivided attention. I take in his light blue eyes, longish blonde hair, and sharp jawline. He really is incredibly handsome, but some of his confidence is gone. He actually looks a little nervous.

"Can I get your number?"

I freeze. Lennie! Say something!

"Of course!" I say, smiling to cover up my surprise. I didn't date at all last year, and I'm finding now that I wish I would have. I feel completely unprepared on how to handle this.

"I like you, Lennie. I want to get to know you more. Okay?"

Whew. I can do this. I feel my cheeks burning and I just know they're dark pink. Still. I really liked hanging out with him today.

"I'd love that." I say.

He beams at me, and just like that, I let myself get a little crush on Luca.

Chapter 11

pluviophile
(n) a lover of rain; someone who finds joy and peace of mind during rainy days

Monday
    Luca: Tell me about yourself
    Lennie: That's a broad question.
    Luca: Siblings?
    Lennie: Auguste, Allan, Raven, and Madeline. She's the youngest, my older brothers are at LSU where my parents teach. You?
    Luca: Nope, just me and my mom. And Nonna
    Luca: Favorite movie?
    Lennie: Practical Magic.
    Luca: Such a girl
    Lennie: Thanks?
    Luca: Teasing. Mine is Jurassic Park
    Lennie: Such a guy ;)

Tuesday
    Lennie: Where in New York are you from?
    Luca: Brooklyn
    Lennie: Why Boston?

Luca: Hockey, obvi. I actually just found out that I'm Captain this year

Lennie: What? That's amazing!!

Lennie: I still can't believe they let you fight. Wild.

Luca: The fans love it

Lennie: Aren't hockey players supposed to be missing teeth?

Luca: We have to wear cages until we're out of college, then all bets are off

Lennie: Something to look forward to...

Wednesday

Luca: When are you gonna let me take you on that date?

Lennie: When I have a spare minute between training and classes!

Luca: Saturday?

Lennie: We're supposed to get together for Catalina's birthday, sorry.

Luca: Sunday then

Lennie: It's a date!

Walking into my first Media Ethics class on Thursday, I'm looking down at a text from Luca when I bump into a human wall and start to fall backwards.

"Ooof," Chase breaths out, managing to catch me before I knock down the person behind me.

"Gah! Sorry, I wasn't watching where I was going!"

"Kids these days, always with their noses in their phones," he teases, grinning at me as we walk to the rows of desks.

I laugh, taking the seat next to him.

"I was responding to your captain."

"Oh yeah? He didn't mention getting your number."

"Yep! We're going on a date this Sunday."

He looks surprised but shakes it off quickly. "Nice. Make him take you somewhere fancy."

I smile at him in response. "So, what's your major? I didn't see you in any of my classes last year."

Chapter 11

"Sports Kinesiology with a minor in Communications."

"Wow...those are wildly different degrees. Let me guess, you plan to go pro and once you retire, you're hoping to be a sportscaster?"

"Uhh, yeah. Exactly that, actually." He looks at me like I'm a sorcerer and I laugh.

"I'm doing the same. Lucky guess."

"Ah," He laughs lightly. "What are you majoring in?"

"Mass Communications with a minor in English Literature."

"Gotcha, that makes sense. So, how does one go pro in gymnastics? Is there a league I don't know about?"

"No, not like the NHL. Pro gymnasts are at the elite level and maintain a high number of training hours and have certain key skills down pat. They're also part of an elite gym or club. I plan to make the National team and then the Olympic team in two years, and to compete after that until I can't anymore. To go pro basically means to have sponsorships and be paid to compete. If I make the Olympic team, I'll have to sign off from the Kalon team senior year, and take a sabbatical to train, but it'll be worth it."

"Wow, I am completely ignorant to that world. That's really cool, Lennie."

"Thank you! Who do you want to go pro with?"

"If I had a choice, the Bruins. But the draft doesn't work that way, so I won't get a say."

"I wouldn't know how that works, I've only ever paid attention to football and gymnastics."

"Blasphemy!" he gasps, clutching his chest dramatically.

Laughing, I point to myself "Southern, remember?"

"With that accent, it's hard not to." He smiles so I know it's not a dig. Chase is easy to talk to and find myself wondering if he asked Raven for her number.

Our professor walks in and closes the door, putting an end to our conversation.

***

Luca picks me up from my house at noon on Sunday. He only told me to "dress casual," so I'm in skinny jeans, a tank top and long cardigan with ankle boots on. Cute, but comfy. He drives an older model black Audi, and he holds the door open for me to sit in the passenger side. Before shutting the door, he leans down to kiss my cheek and then jogs around to the driver's side. Acoustic rock music plays on low volume from the radio. I'm impressed with how clean his car is. My brother's truck was disgusting until they graduated high school and grew up a little.

"Hey sweetheart." Luca says, relaxing back in the seat with one hand on the wheel as we pull away from the curb.

"Hi," I smile back, liking the pet name. "Am I allowed to know where we're going now?"

"I figured, we're both from other places, and I thought it would be cool to discover some of Boston together. Hit a few places to eat, see some of the sights, take a tour cruise of the harbor. I asked your sister to make sure I'm taking you to places you haven't been to before so we can both be first timers."

I'm stunned quiet for a second and stare at his profile. Not that I have much to compare it to, but this has to be one of the most thoughtful dates ever. It definitely beats going on movie dates with my *older brother* sitting on the other side of me.

"I couldn't love that more if I tried," I say. "What all is on our list?"

"I asked a few of the guys who are local. Apparently, the best place to get clam chowder and lobster rolls is at Union Oyster House, so I thought I'd start there. Wait, do you even like chowder? I should have asked." He glances over hesitantly, afraid he already screwed up.

I widen my eyes, feigning horror. "Luca! Shellfish is my least favorite food!"

"Ah, shit," He looks like I kicked his puppy.

I laugh out loud, "Kidding. I grew up on crawfish and gulf shrimp. Clams are just fine."

He smirks over at me "You're trouble."

"Actually, my least favorite food is tomatoes."

"You *hate tomatoes*?!" He looks horrified, which isn't surprising considering that he's Italian. *Luca Lorenzo Rossi*, I would have figured out his heritage from his name alone, had he not told me himself.

Chapter 11

"I would literally rather eat liver and onions," *Gag*, but true. "I do love marinara, ketchup, those kinds of things though. Just raw and cooked tomatoes make me want to vomit."

"You're like an oxymoron right now." He shakes his head. "Anything else completely contradictory about you?"

"Hmmm. I love the rain, like literally *love* rainy days. But I hate when it rains while sunny. I love having time off from school, but I hate summers. They're so hot and muggy back home."

"People complain about how hot New York gets in the summer, but I have a feeling it's nothing compared to down south."

"I wouldn't know but based on my year of living here so far, I doubt it comes close to Louisiana." I sigh.

"Missing home?" he asks, picking up on my mood swing. When I first spoke to him at the pool, I thought he was a cocky jerk. I couldn't have been more wrong. He's really thoughtful and sweet.

"A little. I absolutely love it here, but it took me a while to get used to not being in the south. The culture is completely different here."

"How so?"

"Well, for starters, people are very forward. Not sure if that's a Boston thing or a northern thing. I feel like there isn't an emphasis on manners, like at all. I heard some guy actually yelling at his grandmother in the store yesterday!"

"Seriously? My Nonna would beat my ass in front of everyone, but she's old school Italian, not American."

"Right? It would never even occur to me to be rude to my elders, forget about yelling at them. I thought Raven was going to punch the guy. It was shocking. I mean, maybe things like that happen in the south, but not where I'm from. And up here, people are always hurrying around and don't do things like hold doors open for you."

I'm still getting used to the pace of things up here. Louisianans aren't quite on "island time," but the pace of life is markedly slower.

"Yeah, that's like New York. When I think about the south, I think about southern hospitality. I always wondered what that really meant until you invited us all into your home and you cooked for me. I mean us." He smiles over at me. "It was amazing by the way; I've never had anything like it."

"Thanks. Glad you liked it. I was worried it would be too spicy since you yankees all hate seasoning." I tease.

He parallel parks on a side street and hops out. I step out onto the curb and look around at the tall buildings. I love downtown, but I try not to drive here because I can't parallel park, and having people wait behind me while I try to figure it out would make me die of stage fright.

He takes my hand, and we walk through the door under the "ye olde UNION OYSTER HOUSE" sign. The smell of food hits me, and I take in the restaurant. Live lobsters sit in a giant tank right in front of us, their long antennae waving. The walls are decorated with all kinds of art and plaques, and it has a very old school Boston vibe to it. We get seated at a little red booth and immediately order the chowder and lobster rolls.

When our waitress brings us our chowder first, I startle.

"Oh! It's white?"

Luca stares at me, confused. "Uhh, yeah. You've never had clam chowder?"

"Nope. I thought it would look like gumbo or jambalaya or something."

"New England clam chowder, sweetheart. You'll love it, take a bite."

I don't love the look of this, and I stare at my bowl, unconvinced. Still. He tried gumbo for me, so I'll return the favor. I pop a few little soup crackers on my spoonful and take the plunge and *ohhhh man*. First impressions don't stick because this chowder is delicious. I've never had anything like this. It's thick and creamy, a little salty, and the clams are perfectly chewy. The word decadent comes to mind.

"Oh my God in Heaven. This is *so good*." I moan. I look up, and he's staring at me with his mouth slightly open, full spoonful frozen near his mouth. "What?" I ask.

"I've never seen such a sexy bite in my life," he says, shaking his head and taking his bite. "But holy shit, you're right. This is amazing." he says with his own groan of appreciation.

"Careful," I say. "You might get that spoon pregnant!"

He throws back his head and laughs. I feel myself relax. I wasn't aware that I was tense, but before today I was really nervous that I'd clam up on this date.

Chapter 11

Pun intended.

Since last winter, I've met many cool people, quickly learned what types *weren't* my people, and got much closer to my roommates and my teammates. I was determined to outgrow the book worm introvert, and I did, at least a little. I learned a lot about myself as a newly social being last semester, and getting out of my comfort zone helped me shed some of my self-consciousness.

It really was a heavy weight.

After we finish the freshest lobster roll that I've ever had in my life, we head to see more sights.

We drive to Trinity Church, which is a beautiful historic church in the middle of downtown. As we walk up to the entrance, I pause to take a picture on my phone. The intricately carved stone details and dozens of columns, arched windows and doorways make it stand out in a sea of steel and glass buildings. We walk past a courtyard garden, and I pause again, closing my eyes and inhaling in the smells of earth and flora. It's very soothing here, this beautiful place where people come to learn about God. Maybe if our Southern Baptist church back home looked like this, I wouldn't mind going as much.

Actually, no. It was never the aesthetics that bothered me.

Shaking off darker thoughts about Pastor Jake and all of the mean-spirited people that marred our church for good in my view, I open my eyes and turn to Luca. "It's beautiful here."

He smiles lightly, tucking my hair behind my ear. "Yeah. It is."

As we walk into the main sanctuary, and I don't even try to stop my jaw from hanging open. It smells like frankincense, reminding me of home during Christmas. Momma burns frankincense and myrrh in a resin burner during the holidays—something I look forward to every year. I take a big whiff and start looking around.

It's quiet here, with a few people seated in pews, praying or reading. Maybe just taking a moment to appreciate the sense of wonder that such scenery can invoke. The air feels more concentrated inside, the presence of God feeling like a tangible thing. A man is playing the organ near the altar, and it's silent otherwise.

We quietly walk around, and I take pictures of everything. The stained-glass windows, the paintings on the wall two stories up, the incredible domed ceiling with all of its intricate details. And the beautiful, beautiful altar space at the front, with its golden walls and carved wood and stone partitions. It's quite literally awe inspiring.

As we walk past the front, there is a woman seated in a front pew, praying aloud to herself in Latin.

The space feels alive.

"This church is almost a hundred and fifty years old," Luca says quietly as we walk to the back. "It has nothing on St. Patrick's in the city though."

"Are you Catholic?" I ask, curious.

"Yep, my mom and Nonna are devout. I wouldn't call *myself* devout, but I do take it somewhat seriously. I gotta admit, I hate confession."

"I've heard of this, just through movies. You basically tell the Priest your sins and then you're forgiven?" It sounds very intimate, in my opinion. Telling a man you look up to about calling your sister a bitch, or stealing gum when you were five? Pass.

"That's somewhat accurate. It's more seeking absolution, through confession and then penance. Like, say I bullied a kid at school and confessed it, the Priest may have me say three Hail Marys and one Our Father."

"Not sure what those are, but I don't plan to confess my deepest darkest sins anytime soon."

"Oh, I'm sure you're a saint." he teases.

"Not even close, but I do try to be a good person. Except when Raven or Cora eats my leftovers, then I just want to go on a crazy murder spree."

"Don't worry, I don't see any confession booths in here. Pretty sure this is an Episcopal church."

Whatever that means.

Next up, across the street, is the Boston Public Library.

I can confidently say that it's the most beautiful public library I've ever seen.

We walk up the stone stairs, and he makes me let him take my picture next to a giant stone lion on the staircase before we head down the hallways, easy chatter between us as we hold hands. We're laughing as we turn into a huge

Chapter 11

open room lined with tables dotted with reading lamps and what has to be a hundred people quietly studying. Someone hisses at us to be quiet, stopping us in our tracks.

"Whoops," I whisper at Luca, pulling him back into the hallway.

"We threw off their concentration!" he whispers back, making me giggle as we head down the stairs, out of the library.

Next, we head to the harbor, bypassing the huge aquarium, and walk towards the water. It's nearing sunset at this point, and we sit at a bench, breathing in briny air. All sorts of boats and catamarans glide lazily around the marina or sit silent at their docks.

He puts his arm behind me, resting on my shoulders and I scoot a little closer. It's been so easy today, being with Luca. Getting to know him, his mannerisms and way of thinking. I like him more than I thought possible after just one date.

The air smells of ocean and sea life, the soft breeze carries the chill of Autumn, and we sit quietly for a moment before he speaks again.

"Last thing for tonight. We're taking a cruise around the harbor on that boat in about fifteen minutes." He points to a huge charter boat down the dock.

"This day has been amazing. I know it's not over, but seriously Luca? Best date ever."

He smiles at me, hugging me closer to him. "I'm glad you're having a good time Lennie."

He stands up, and grabs my hand, steering us over to the boat. He shows our tickets to an attendant, and we're ushered over in front of the boat where a worker takes our photo. I make sure to pop my foot out, date-night-cheesy. We head into the boat, pass the snack bar, and climb up the stairs to the top railing where there are seats lined up.

Once the boat starts moving, we stand at the rails, absorbing the view. It's truly beautiful, so different from the coast at home, the tall glass and steel buildings a juxtaposition backdrop to the smaller historic brick buildings closer to the harbor.

The tour guide starts up, talking about the history of Boston and the harbor.

When we sail next to the USS Constitution, I take a picture of it, making sure to get the Bunker Hill memorial in the background.

"I have to send this to my dad, he'll love it," I say to Luca as I text Daddy.

"Tell me about your parents," he prompts, turning to face me.

"Well, my dad is Cajun, like *straight* Cajun. He teaches World History at LSU. He's like a huge grizzly bear, but he's a great dad. My mom is half French, half Cajun. She teaches Astrology at LSU. They met when they were still students there."

"I heard you speaking French with Raven. You don't hear that much up here."

"It's a Louisiana thing. Most Cajuns speak a dialect of french, but my grandmother was from Paris, so my mom and all of us are fluent. She met my Pa in France when he was in the military and moved to the states with him. They settled in Louisiana and had my mom, but I guess she hated living in America. She moved back to France, and they never heard from her again."

"Damn, that's cold. I almost wish my dad had just left us instead."

"What happened to him?"

"Car accident. He was hit by a drunk driver and died on impact. The fucking guy driving? Not one scratch on him. I was six, so I don't remember him well. But I still miss him."

"I'm so sorry Luca, truly." My hearts softens, and I feel the weight of his loss. I'm thankful to have both of my parents, regardless of their control issues.

"It's all good. My mom is awesome. She treats me like she's both parents, and it's enough for me. My Nonna lives in the same building as us, so I had lots of love growing up." He looks out over the water, smiling softly. I'm glad for him, but still feel a pang when I think of this man growing up without a father.

We watch the sunset, and it truly is beautiful. Luckily, the clouds aren't covering the cotton candy sky too badly, and the evening explodes in a kaleidoscope of colors. I think back to the first sunrise I watched and feel that similar feeling, that awe.

As we head back to the harbor, it starts to rain and we startle, looking up at the sky in surprise. I close my eyes and laugh, letting the rain soak into my hair and skin. "I did tell you that I love the rain." I tease, grinning at him.

He's staring at me intently, and I still.

"That day at your house," he starts. "That sunset? I wanted to kiss you so badly then. I want to kiss you even worse, now." I smile at him lightly while lifting my chin, an invitation.

He holds my face in his palms, leans over, and kisses me lightly at first, the rain on our lips mixing together. It starts out slow and becomes gradually more intense as our tongues learn each other. It's the most intimate moment I've ever shared with a man.

He moves his face back from mine after giving me one last soft kiss.

He smiles softly at me and says, "I might just love the rain, too."

Chapter 12

wonderwall
(adj) someone you find yourself thinking about all the time; a person you are completely infatuated with

"I will find these tree stairs if it's the last thing I freaking do." I declare to Raven. We're walking around campus after I left open gym and showered. After eating lunch, I dragged her with me to explore. It's been one year since we started looking for them, and I'm starting to get annoyed. I know they're called *secret* stairs, but dang.

We already tried Quintus Ennius and Solis libraries, so now we're searching around Lectio Hall. The problem is, all of these buildings are huge and made of stone, and there are trees *everywhere*. All over campus!

"I'm convinced it's something everyone tells freshmen just to laugh at them when they wander around campus looking like lost little idiots. Ya know, kinda like how *we are now?*" Raven grits out, ready to throw in the towel. "I want to go inside and take pictures of the archives."

"*Oh my God* Raven, that's all you do lately!"

"Excuse me little miss, it's for my portfolio. For my *minor*."

"Okay, fine. But I am determined to find those stairs before we graduate."

"Well then unglue yourself from your boyfriend, and you'll free up some time, Columbus." We got into an argument last week about how much Luca

Chapter 12

has been over at the house "hogging the remote and eating all my fucking snacks!"

We've been pretty inseparable for the past three weeks, and I've loved getting closer to him. He asked me to be exclusive last week, and I'm still feeling glowy.

We head into the library and take the stairs to the basement. Now, I'm not in the habit of going into two-hundred-year-old basements, but this one is special. Solis has a collection of first edition books and notebooks in special cases that is fascinating. The centerpiece is a huge open sketchbook from the early 1800s, a detailed blueprint for an invention by Charles Wheatstone. There are notes all over the pages and scribbles about various engineering bits that may as well be Greek to me. Solis is also famous for having a large collection of Emily Brontë first editions in a temperature and humidity controlled room.

But what Raven wants to capture are the art archives in the lowest level basement. I run my hand down the intricate scroll work of the dark, ornate stairs as we descend. The stone walls are painted a deep, dark turquoise, and there are unique artwork and prints in every type of frame imaginable, all painted a dark gold. It looks like old money and history down here.

By the time we get to the bottom the air is about 20 degrees cooler than upstairs. There are display cases lined up near the base of the stairs, but we skirt around those and head to the back. The space is two stories tall, with gigantic display racks that go almost all the way to the ceiling. They're attached to huge poles on each end of the room and swing open to reveal rack after rack of paintings, sketches, poster-size pieces of art from hundreds of artists, and even a few paintings bigger than a van. Some are local, and others went to school here once. There are fantastic replicas of famous paintings and prints of some as well. It's a very eclectic collection and presentation.

Browsing through twenty foot tall racks of art is mesmerizing. I feel very small standing next to such a grand display. It's the middle of the day on a Saturday, and we're the only two down here.

"Are you even allowed to photograph this?" I ask Raven, looking back over my shoulder.

She raises an eyebrow. "Who's gonna stop me?"

She directs me on where to stand, how to move from across the room, where she stays to get the full scale of the archives. She has me touch the rack, looking up "in wonder, like you're in awe."

I stand to the side, doing the same pose but altering my faces and movements slightly to give her some variation. I have years of experience at being Raven's model. The silence between the camera clicks have a quality to them, a quiet ringing.

When we're done, I look over the images with her. The effect reminds me of *Alice in Wonderland*. The sun streams down from small windows at the very top of the ceiling, creating an other-worldly look. I appear small and insignificant, looking up at dozens of beautiful depictions of people, places, and things. Art is supposed to make you feel something, but I can't name the feeling that runs through my body as I glance over the images. So many feels, they're aggregating into one frenzy of emotion. This is what Raven's art does to me.

"I wanted to capture how tiny you are and how vast the art is. To me, it symbolizes us here at Kalon. Small town girl experiencing the world, bigger than she could have imagined. She's seeing things for the first time, experiencing new and different. She's optimistic and brave and excited, and a little scared. The world is much bigger than she thought."

I take a breath, sitting with that for a moment. She just summarized what I was feeling, what I hadn't couldn't articulate.

After Raven goes home to edit the photos, I wander around campus, halfheartedly looking for the hidden wonders of Kalon University and enjoying the beautiful day. The beginnings of Autumn are making themselves evident in the cool breeze and the position of the sun. I buy a hot apple cider from a beverage cart, and turn around to nearly bump into Chase.

"Yikes," I say, holding my drink protectively closer.

"We have to stop meeting like this," he jokes as he pulls me in for a hug before buying his own drink.

"What are you up to?"

"Oh," I smile, "Just engaging in some werifesteria."

Chapter 12

He looks at me with a raised eyebrow as he sips his hot chocolate. "Weri-who?"

"Werifesteria. It's an Old English word that basically means to wander through the trees looking for a mystery."

He grins at me, bemused.

"I've been trying to find these secret-tree stair things for over a year now, and I have no clue what they are or where they may be hiding."

"I can confidently say that I didn't understand any of that."

We sit together on a bench by the lake, and I tell him the whispers I found online about the stairs and the hidden catacombs that connect the chapels.

"That's it. Let's go searching, now I'm intrigued."

"Really," I ask, excitedly. "But I feel like walking around campus looking for trees with stairs is kind of a dead end."

He looks around thoughtfully for a few beats. "Well, I've been in Caritas Chapel plenty of times, so why don't we try to explore Omnis Chapel? Plus, it's closer."

We get up and throw our empty cups away before heading down the sidewalk.

The church is about a ten minute journey, and while we walk there we talk about everything under the sun.

"Tell me your favorite thing about gymnastics."

"Mastering a new skill. It's hard work, but the feeling of sticking it finally is euphoric."

"Do you always use SAT words?"

"Affirmative."

He laughs at me, causing his brown eyes to shine and crinkle at the corners.

"What about you, with hockey?"

"Ah, that's the question, isn't it. There isn't just one thing. It's the feeling of my blades cutting through ice, the sounds echoing around the barn, finally getting that puck and taking the shot. Hearing the sound off the cross bar when I get a bar down shot. Nothing like it."

"I can confidently say that I didn't understand any of that," I joke, mimicking his earlier confusion.

We finally arrive at Omnis, though a bit grander than Caritas, isn't nearly as old. I haven't been inside either one yet, but the outside is markedly less worn. I think I prefer Caritas.

Chase leads us through the front doors but bypasses the main sanctuary to head down a side hall to our right. The walls are stone, but the floor is a newer tile which clashes with otherwise Gothic architecture. We explore for a bit, opening doors and getting scolded on two occasions, before circling back to the entrance.

"Well, crap," I grouse.

"We still have plenty of time to search," he consoles me.

"I know, it just felt like we were on an adventure for a second there."

"Isn't that what life is?"

I scoff. "Not with my family."

"What do you mean," he asks curiously.

"Just that my parents were so strict and controlling when we were growing up. We didn't travel, we didn't get to hang out with friends or go to parties or have any normal experiences as high schoolers. It's mainly why Rae and I chose Boston. By that point in our lives, we would have moved to Alaska if someone offered us a scholarship."

"Hmm," he muses. "Sounds like your parents really care."

He earns a pointed look from me. "Maybe *too* much," he acknowledges.

"Yeah. I love them, but I still get a thrill every time I make a decision for myself and don't have to seek permission."

Chase nods. "I get that. My parents were never really strict with me, but I'm a guy and to be honest, most of my time was devoted to hockey. Plus, I'm an only child."

"God, that's all I wanted for myself at times growing up with four brothers and sisters."

"Seriously? All I wanted were siblings. Being an only child is lonely."

"Aw, I can see that. Now that we're grown, it's like having four best friends for life."

He smiles at me, wistfully. I change the subject.

"So…you've never wanted to just…escape? Leave Boston and go explore

Chapter 12

other places?"

"Never," he says, looking out over the school grounds as the breeze blows both of our dark hair. "But you're here now, and I, for one, am glad you chose Boston."

I look at him in pleasant surprise, and he simply smiles back at me.

* * *

Later that evening, I'm stirring beans and ham in the crockpot when strong arms wrap around my stomach, startling me. Luca puts his face in my hair, kissing my neck and breathing me in as he peers over my shoulder. "That smells amazing, babe."

I smile, looking back at him. "You've asked me no less than ten times to make this for you after I mentioned it *once*, so I sure hope you're liking the smell." I joke with him, taking a fork and fluffing up the rice.

He puts his face back in my neck and squeezes me a little tighter. "Because you're an amazing cook. I always want you to cook for me."

I roll my eyes. "Is that very Italian of you?" I joke.

"Uhh, yeah. My mom and Nonna are literally always in the kitchen cooking."

"Ahh. Well, don't get too used to it. There are many things I'd usually rather be doing than giving you a full tummy."

"Psshh. You love feeding me."

"No, I just love hearing you make your yummy noises," I laugh at him, pushing him back to grab bowls and spoons.

I yell out to Raven that dinner is ready, and we take our steaming bowls of red beans and rice to the living room. Luca turns on a hockey game, and Raven immediately snatches the remote from him.

"Hey! What the hell?"

She glares at him. "Speaking of being rude, you've been hogging *my* couch and *my* remote for weeks, buddy. Time to let the girls who actually live here have their way."

"Geez, you watch a few games on your girlfriend's couch and all of a sudden you're a monster." He mumbles before taking a bite. "Holy...*God* Len, this is so good. Soooo good."

I beam at him as he shovels in food, surely burning his mouth. I love feeding people food from my culture, it makes me proud when they love my cooking.

Raven turns on reruns of "Friends," and we all settle in, eating our dinner. I feel warm and happy as I snuggle under Luca's arm after we finish eating. He kisses my temple, saying he's going to watch the game on my laptop in the bedroom.

Once he's out of the room, I turn to Gabby. "How are you doing? I feel like I haven't caught up with you in forever!" Between practices, classes, my time with Luca and her time with Dylan, we haven't had time to just sit and relax like this. I've seen Cora more because we have Creative Nonfiction together on Wednesdays.

The corners of her mouth turn down. "Classes are on another level this year. "I don't know how you athletes are keeping up. Dylan hasn't even started games yet and he's so busy."

Dylan is on the lacrosse team and proud of it since he's First Nation, the Canadian Native peoples. According to him, lacrosse was invented in the 1100s by Native Americans. I've never actually watched lacrosse, but Gabby already made us promise to go to his games when the season starts this spring. It looks interesting, that's for sure.

"Agreed, the level of course work like, doubled since last year," Cora gripes.

"So, things are good with Dylan?" I ask.

"Uhh, better than good," Raven smirks. "I share a wall with her, so I'd say things are *banging*."

We all laugh as Gabby throws a pillow at her.

"Gross Rae, a little privacy? I know you have headphones!"

"Like it's my fault that you two are louder than fighting cats? Tell your man to find some chill!"

I go quiet while they continue bantering. Luca and I haven't taken that step yet, but he's tried. I'm sure he's a little frustrated about it. "I want to be as close to you as I can, in every way. Don't you want that too? But we can take it slow; you tell me when you're ready." is what he said the last time, earlier this week. I mean I'm turning 20 years old soon; I'm getting frustrated at

Chapter 12

myself at this point. I've just never shared that level of intimacy with anyone, and I feel like maybe I have a block about it. It took me two weeks just to let him put his hand in my panties. I feel comfortable and safe with him, so I'm not sure why I'm still hesitating."

Gabby sighs, the conversation lulling briefly. She picks at her sweater, looking forlorn all of a sudden.

"I've been thinking a lot about Gavin, and how I used to vent to him that first semester in school. He was always such a huge supporter. Grant was, too, but he's pulled away a lot since Gav died. All he does is study and focus on law school." She looks so sad, and her light diminishes a bit.

"I'm sorry, Gabs," I say. "I can only imagine how hard it is. How you must feel each day when you can't text him."

"It's hard. But I can't let the grief keep me down, you know? He wouldn't want that for me. I just worry about my parents and Grant. Having Dylan to lean on helps, but what really helped me last semester was you three."

"We didn't do anything you wouldn't have done for us." Cora says, and Raven nods her head in agreement.

"Promise that we'll always be here for each other, and not just in the hard times." Raven says to us.

"Promise."

"Of course!"

"Always." I say.

Gabby decides to head over to Dylan's place to boost her sad mood, and Cora and Raven leave to check out a party they were invited to.

I head to my room after watching one last episode and find Luca sleeping on my bed with my laptop balanced on his chest. Chuckling, I grab the laptop and put it on my dresser. As I get into bed and snuggle into the covers, I look over at him, pensive. We've never slept over at each other's places, but I don't want to wake him up.

I'm starting to fall asleep when he rolls over and pulls me close, spooning me from behind. Kissing my neck, he says "I didn't mean to fall asleep." Kiss. "But now I don't want to go home." Kiss. "Can I stay?"

I let out a contented sigh "Of course."

I think about choices, about how I pushed him back the few times he tried to take things to the next level, telling him I wasn't sure that I was ready. How he was patient and understanding.

I'm an adult, and serious couples have sex, I know this. It's a healthy part of being in a relationship. Am I afraid of the unknown? Of not being experienced? Self-conscious?

All of the above, maybe.

But I also know that I care about him, and I want him to be happy with me, just like he wants me to be happy with him. He's sweet and attentive and makes me feel things I've never felt before. I don't want to keep holding us back, when it's obvious he wants to take things further. It makes me feel special, chosen.

I roll over and pull him closer, initiating a deeper kiss while he settles in between my thighs. He has one hand in my hair and another on my thigh, pulling me closer and kissing me like I'm the oxygen he needs. It's a special kind of feeling, knowing he wants me this bad, and it makes me want him too. I want to make him happy, to have that level of closeness with him, for him to know me like no one else ever has.

"I want you so bad, sweetheart." He mutters between kisses. I pull back, looking at him, letting him see my eyes as I summon up the courage to answer.

"Then have me."

His breath shudders. "God, babe. Are you sure?"

Am I? Right now, my virginity feels like the last barrier between me and adulthood, and I want finally to be rid of it. It's a crutch, and I don't want our relationship to suffer because I'm holding us back from truly being intimate with each other.

"Yes. It feels right to me, and I want my first time to be with you. Plus, we have the house to ourselves which is a luxury we hardly ever have at either of our places. Just...go slow?"

And he does.

It hurts, more than I thought it would, but it's also special.

Sweet.

He moves over me slowly and helps me get past the initial shock of pain

Chapter 12

with sweet kisses and encouraging words.

And afterward, as he holds me tight and kisses me for a long while.

I feel my relief at getting out of my own way.

I've heard about a lot of first times being pretty bad, but all I can think as I fall asleep against Luca is…this feels perfect.

Chapter 13

dépaysement
(n) when someone is taken out of their own familiar world into a new one

Things with Luca and I progress pretty quickly after that. The feeling of having found your person is indescribable. Raven will always be my person, but that's a twin thing. Luca is my *person*.

We find ourselves spending every minute that we can together between our practices and his games, which I go to whenever I can. He's amazing to watch on the ice, and the chemistry between him and Chase is pretty impressive, now that I know what to look for.

After dinner on my birthday, Luca and I just finished having sex in his bed, when he rolls over and decides to give me a heart attack.

"Come home with me and meet my Ma?"

I shoot straight up to sit. "What?" I yelp, pulling the sheet up over my body. We're still out of breath. Luca pulls the sheet back down and opens his mouth to speak before glancing at my naked torso. He closes his mouth and pulls the sheet back up to cover me.

"Nope, can't concentrate with your perfect boobs out," he says, shaking his head and making me laugh.

I've learned very quickly that when Luca is in, he's all in. He gave himself over completely to this relationship and I love that about him. It's probably

Chapter 13

not even occurring to him that we've only been dating for two months.

"You don't think it's too soon?" I ask, unsure, looking down at my hands. I'm in uncharted waters here.

He puts his finger under my chin and lifts up, making me to look him in the eyes.

"In case you can't tell Lennie, I love you. I'm *in* love with you. And maybe that feels soon to you, but I know how I feel. I want to share you with the other woman I love."

I just gape at him in surprise. I did not think this was where the conversation was going. A rosy, warm feeling swells in my heart and I throw myself at him. He grabs me in a hug and squeezes me tight.

"I love you too, Luca." I say in his ear.

We don't leave his room for the rest of the night.

Best birthday ever.

The next morning, we're getting coffee in his kitchen when he decides to pounce again.

"So can we plan a little getaway to NYC?" he asks, looking at me over the top of his mug. He's leaning back against the sink wearing gray sweatpants and no shirt, which is just about the sluttiest thing a guy could wear, and I just want to spend the rest of the day in bed. I give myself a little mental shake.

"It would have to be super quick, unfortunately," I say. "We could leave after I have open gym on Saturday and come back Sunday evening?"

Luckily the hockey team has a bye week next weekend.

"Sounds good sweetheart. I'll let my mom know. She's been asking me to bring you home to meet her since I told her about you in August."

"You told her about me in August?" I'm surprised. We didn't start dating until the first week in September, and even then it wasn't more serious until a few weeks later.

I haven't even told my family about Luca. I guess I don't want to be subjected to lectures or worry my parents that I'm not being responsible. And I really, really, don't want them questioning my sex life. I plan to tell them at Christmas. We'll have been together for three months by then, so I'm hoping they take my relationship a little more seriously at that point. I told

Luca all about them, and why I wanted to wait.

Thankfully, he understands.

"Of course," he looks at me like I'm crazy. "I had to tell her about the sweet southern belle who made a fool out of me in front of my team."

I laugh as he pulls me into his arm to seal things with a kiss.

This will be my first trip to New York City, which excites me, but I'm bummed we can't stay longer. We spend the rest of the day planning the trip.

Guess I'm meeting Ma and Nonna!

* * *

Walking hand in hand with Luca, I watch my breath fog up as it leaves my body. There are no stars to be seen here because of the light pollution. It's the first Saturday of November and we're heading into his apartment building in Brooklyn. It's almost six at night, but the sun has already set.

I look up, taking in the tall, red brick building. It's mirrored across the street by an identical building.

"You're nervous, aren't you," he says knowingly.

"You don't have to grin about it," I grumble back. "It's not like you're not going to be nervous to meet my parents."

"Nah, parents love me."

"So humble, how can they not," I say sarcastically, hiding my smile.

I'm not so sure that he's right to be confident. My dad has been known to intimidate men a fraction of his age. And they weren't even dating his daughter. They're flying down for my first meet in January, so I guess we'll see then.

"Ma and Nonna are going to love you just as much as I do." He says as we step into the elevator, giving my hand a comforting squeeze. I flash back to last weekend, him telling me that he loved me in his bed. I smile at the memory and give him a side hug, feeling mushy.

We get off the elevator and walk up to a door shortly down the hall, wiping our shoes on the floor mat as he opens the door and lets us in. It's an open space, and I immediately spot his mom and Nonna in the kitchen, cooking

Chapter 13

together. The savory scent of basil, oregano, and tomato sauce fills the entryway and my mouth waters. Southern food tastes amazing, but Italian food takes the gold on yummy smells.

"Hi Ma. Hi Nonna," Luca pulls them each into a big hug, towering over them and looking every bit of his 6 feet. They're shorter than I am, which I don't encounter often. This tiny woman birthed this huge man?

His mom is about two inches shorter than me, curvy with shoulder length light brown hair, and is very pretty. She has very light green eyes and it's clear that Luca's Italian heritage is on his father's side. His Nonna is clearly Italian, with short black hair and lovely olive skin, and can't be over five feet. They look over at me, and I realize Luca didn't introduce me. I hadn't wanted to intrude on their moment.

I smile, trying to hide how nervous I was. "Hi, I'm Lennie. It's so nice to meet you both."

Neither of them makes the move to shake my hand or hug me, they just observe me for a beat.

"Lennie? Lennie. That is a boy name, no?" Nonna asks Luca in a thick Italian accent, and I know my surprise shows on my face.

"Nonna! No, it's not. As you can see, she's gorgeous and all girl." Luca lectures.

"It's short for Lenore," I offer.

"Much prettier name for a pretty, pretty girl," she says, and pats my shoulder, moving past me back to the kitchen.

I guess I passed inspection?

"I'm Valerie, but you may call me Val." Luca's mom states, looking at me with a critical eye.

Then again, maybe not.

"Nice to meet you. Luca's told me so much about you." I offer, feeling out of place. Luca's making no attempt to bridge the gap here, choosing instead to wander into the kitchen and start picking at food.

Traitor.

I look around the apartment for a minute. I've never been in a home like this, with high ceilings and exposed brick walls. It's decorated very cleanly, with white furniture, beautiful throw pillows, a big Persian area rug, and huge windows. The drapes are open, showing off a beautiful view.

Luca's mom summons me over to sit on the couch with her. I look out the window at the view of the sparkling city in the distance, past the water and the bridge, and my jaw goes a bit slack. It's breathtaking. I've never seen a city so vast.

"So, tell me Lenore, are you Catholic?"

My mouth snaps closed. I wasn't expecting *that* sort of question. Is everyone up here so forward?

"Um, no ma'am. I was raised Southern Baptist. I'm from Louisiana."

"Ma'am," she scoffs. "Yes, my son tells me you're from the south. Your accent is thicker than I imagined it to be."

"I find it charming," Nonna pipes up from the kitchen.

At least she likes me.

"Yes, it's quite different up here. This is my first time being in New York, though. It's so beautiful. You must love looking at this view every day and night."

This seems to soften her a bit because she finally smiles at me.

Luca comes to the couch and sits by me, putting his arm over my shoulders. Valerie smiles at him like he hung the moon and stars before looking back to me, assessing.

"Are you feeding my boy? Taking care of him?"

For a second, I don't know how to respond. Am I taking care of this 21-year-old grown man? *Feeding him?* I mean, yes, I feed him frequently. He's always asking me to cook for him and sometimes his friends. It gives me affirmation that I'm wanted and needed. It makes me happy when people like the cooking that I put so much love into.

And after sitting with this woman for five seconds, I'm starting to see why Luca likes to be indulged so much.

He's *used* to being indulged. Taken care of. I get it, I do. With Luca's dad gone, he's all she has to take care of. He must get all of her focus, all that love.

"I like to think that I keep him fed and happy," I start. "I'm not sure that it compares to feasts like this, going by the smells. It's mouthwatering." And

Chapter 13

I've said the right thing because her eyes light up and she smiles at Luca.

"It's Luca's favorite, lasagna with beef spare rib. And now that I see you, *little Lennie*, you can use some meat on your bones!" She pinches my side, making me laugh.

"Come, let's go eat before Nonna starts yelling at us to come sit."

Throughout dinner, both Val and Nonna keep trying to put more on my plate, encouraging me to get seconds, doing the same to Luca. "You need some more weight on that frame, you're so lean. How are you going to fight off the defenders unless you bulk up, *cocco*?" Val says as she literally *cuts his food up*. I have to actively focus on not staring at her in confused shock. Am I the only one that finds this weird? I look around and they're all eating and chatting like this is normal.

Alrighty then.

I throw in the towel when thirds are offered.

"I can't fit another bite, but that is the best lasagna I've ever had!" I say, and it's true. I'm pretty sure licking the plate is as gauche to New Yorkers as it is to southerners, so I manage to restrain myself. Barely.

I phase back into the conversation just as Val turns to me. "Have you seen Luca play yet? He's the best player on any given team, guaranteed." He beams at her, loving the praise.

"Yes, actually, I've been to almost all of his home games and some of the closer away games." I say, flashing back to the first game I saw. Luca was like lightening on his skates, so fast and skilled that it took my breath away. When he was knocked off his feet, I was scared for his safety, but he got up and skated away like it was nothing. And when he repaid the favor to another player, knocking him down and getting the puck, I got up and cheered out loud.

That player was a lot slower to get up than Luca.

"*Almost* all?" She asks, unimpressed. I swallow, feeling like I failed a test.

I've had a few study sessions and project groups come between my time and Luca's games, but dang, I'm a college student athlete. We're kind of known for having a lot on our plates. And I know she doesn't go to the games, either.

Don't be petty, Lenore, Brooklyn is almost five hours from Boston.

Luca finally senses my unease and comes to my rescue.

"Chill, Ma. Lennie is fully supportive of me, just like I plan on being when her meets start up after New Years." He smiles at me, pulling me to him and kissing my temple. I immediately relax.

"Yes, Luca tells us you are a gymnast. It's a very dangerous sport, yes?" Val asks, looking interested.

"It definitely can be, especially when we're not completely focused. When I was first learning my Back-Full on the beam, I *literally* almost broke my neck." I say and they all wince, imagining it.

Yeah. It was terrifying. Just something a gymnast lives with and has to mentally master and get past. Fear is just part of gymnastics, but we learn and train early on to block it out. If you're afraid, you hesitate, and if you hesitate, you don't land right.

And if you don't land right, you can get injured.

"Why you choose such dangerous thing?" Nonna asks in her thick Italian accent, looking mildly scandalized.

I smile lightly, remembering Raven and I starting in gymnastics. We begged our parents for weeks after watching the replays of an old summer Olympics. Our mom wanted us to be in the rodeo circuit like she was growing up, but luckily Maddie was obsessed with horses, and she ended up being Momma's protégé.

"My twin sister and I were five, and we watched a Shannon Miller spotlight on TV. It was her Olympic highlight reel. We had never seen anything like it. All I can remember is that I wanted to be her, as she was defying gravity and moving her body so impressively. Raven stopped when we were twelve, but I've always known that I was meant to be doing this. I plan to work hard and make the Olympic team the summer after my junior year. I got injured during Nationals, so I missed the trials for the last summer Olympics, but I needed this time to become more well-rounded."

It's all I've been working towards, all these years. Nothing less is acceptable.

"I haven't seen her compete, but I've seen her practice and the stuff she can do is incredible. I believe in you, babe." Luca gives me a sweet smile, warming me from the inside.

Chapter 13

His mom looks at me for a beat longer than is comfortable.

"Impressive," she says mildly. Her tone tells me she may feel otherwise, and it must show in my face, because she decides to let me off the hook.

"You have no idea how happy it makes a mother to see her son so happy and in love," she says, smiling at Luca and then miraculously at me.

I didn't realize how tense I was until my shoulders slump in relief.

Maybe she likes me after all.

Later that night in bed, I refuse Luca's attempt at sex. I can't believe I have to say, "Your mother is in the next room. Have you lost your mind?" I was floored that she even let us share a bed, but he just said "Babe. We have a two bedroom apartment, and my mother is not going to make me sleep on the couch. Also, Ma isn't strict like your parents are. Also, also, I'm a twenty one year old man."

It's silent for a few beats while we settle in.

"Your mom doesn't seem to really like me," I say, despondent.

He breathes out a laugh. "Sweetheart, of course she likes you. She's a New Yorker. It takes us a while to warm up to people. She's also protective of me, wants to make sure that you're being good to me like she expects."

"Ah yes, I remember her asking if I'm taking care of *you*. You'd think it would be the other way around?" I tease. He pulls me to him, kissing me hard.

"I think we both know just how well I *take care of you*." he tickles me, making me squeal.

"She just wants to make sure you're being spoiled away from home since you're not being spoiled at home." I tease. He pulls back, looking at my face.

"I don't even care that you think I'm spoiled. I like that my mom takes care of me, it's how she shows her love. It's not like I have two parents to get it from." He says with a bite to his voice, and I immediately feel guilty for being judgmental.

"I'm sorry, I was mostly teasing. My parents are good to me, but I can't say that I've ever had that kind of focused attention from them like you have. Hell, I have to basically beg for scraps of my mom's attention. I'm sure it's wonderful for you. I'm only one of five."

He sighs, laying back down on his side. "My mom is awesome, babe. Just give her a chance to warm up to you. Not everyone is a sweet little southern belle like you are."

I try not to take offense.

But I'm not nice *just* because I'm southern, just like Val isn't lukewarm *just* because she's a New Yorker. Maybe I'm being sensitive because I'm out of my comfort zone. When Luca meets my parents, I'm sure he'll have some of the same feelings that I'm having.

I give him a peck and then roll over to go to sleep.

After a few minutes, he sighs before snuggling behind me and pulling me close.

***

The next morning comes too soon. I feel unsettled, forgetting where I am, until I hear Luca's soft snore and feel the weight of his arm around my stomach. I relax, letting myself stay in that fuzzy space between dreaming and waking. His bedding smells like him and I burrow deeper into the covers, into Luca.

Reality seeps into my brain space and I finally fully wake, frowning. Last night was…interesting. I feel bad that I basically shamed Luca for being a Momma's Boy, especially since I know about his father passing away. That's not who I am. I think I just let his overbearing mother cloud my feelings, but I'm not going to let her get the best of me today.

Especially now that I know how doting she is on her little *cocco*, I think snidely.

Ugh! Lennie! Stop being bitchy, you're better than this, I chastise myself.

Luca stirs next to me, breathing in deep as he wakes up.

"Morning, babe," he says, snuggling closer to me. He kisses my cheek, and I know that I'm forgiven for last night.

"I'm gonna go see if I can help with breakfast," I say, getting out of bed.

"Have fun with that," he snorts. "If those control freaks let you help with anything, I'll eat this pillow."

I frown over at him, pulling on my yoga pants before walking into the

Chapter 13

hallway.

Exactly sixty seconds later, he's proven correct.

"No, no, no, you go sit," Nonna points to the couch. "I bring you coffee, you like cream, sugar?"

"Umm, yes please, are you sure-"

"Nonna and I have it covered in the kitchen Lennie, you just sit and relax. Is my lazy boy awake yet?"

"Your *non*-lazy boy *is* awake," Luca pipes up as he walks into the room. He kisses his mom and Nonna on the cheek before accepting my coffee from Nonna and helping himself to it.

"Heeeey," I gripe at him, claiming my mug. I take a sip and almost spit it out, then I accidentally inhale it and end up coughing up my lungs. *Holy,* that's the strongest cup of coffee I've ever had in my life, and my family drinks Community coffee for God's sake.

"I forgot to tell you, Italians like strong coffee," Val smirks. "You'll get used to it. I sure did."

Ah, it's like that, is it?

I steel myself, taking a big sip (OH MY GAWD) and forcing my features into a serene mask. "No, it's not that. We southerners love strong coffee, it just went down the wrong pipe."

Luca chuckles to himself, knowing that I'm full of it but wisely staying mute.

We sit down to eat, and I'm baffled as I take in the spread. How do these women stay trim? There are pastries, biscotti, some sort of brioche and cheese combo that looks mouthwatering and like the amazing lasagna, most definitely isn't on the nutrition plan that is etched on my brain. Eh, I'll run extra during cardio on Monday.

"This looks amazing, Ma." Luca said, helping himself to one of everything. He's lucky that he burns so many calories playing hockey. The man can eat, as he's demonstrated time and time again in my kitchen.

"I know it's a lot, but it's not every day that my son comes back to his mother," she says, patting his head. I swallow down my annoyance and smile dreamily at Luca, for everyone's benefit. Val's reverence of her son annoys me, but honestly, I want her to like me. I *need* her to like me. Luca coming to her defense last night didn't feel great. I'm not a fan of being the bad guy, and clearly their relationship is very important to Luca. And he's important to me so…

I'm probably projecting my own mommy issues. Seeing such blinding affection makes me uncomfortable because while my family loves me, we're not a family that gushes over each other. If my mother ever pulled me in for a big hug and kiss on the cheek, I'd think she was having a senior moment.

"Yes, this is really, really good. Thank you so much for feeding us so well and opening your home to me. It's nice to see Luca with you and Nonna. It makes me miss my family even more." I'm being sincere when I say the last part. They may not cut my food up or look at me like I'm the best thing since the iPhone was invented, but we're a close family.

I need to face time them when I get home. I haven't talked to them in almost a week, a new record for my parents. To be fair, they've really let up since last year. They seem to finally understand that Raven and I are adults.

After wrapping up breakfast and saying (a long, dramatic) goodbye, we're in the car, driving back to Boston. Soft acoustic music plays on the radio and I'm warm and cozy in my coat and scarf.

"I really liked your mom and Nonna," I say to Luca, interrupting the quiet. "You must have loved living there, growing up. The city is impressive."

"Glad you liked it. When we have a longer break, we'll have to stay again so I can show you around the city. I want to take you to Joe's Pizza. Nothing like it."

He knows pizza is my absolute weakness.

"Well, we've already discovered the best New England Clam Chowder. I want us to take my parents there when they come visit in January."

Smiling to myself, I imagine Luca and my father meeting. I sneak a peek at him, driving with one hand resting on top of the wheel, completely confident in every way.

I hope my parents like him and see what I do. I was joking with him last night, but I'm actually a teeny bit nervous.

Okay, a lot nervous.

Chapter 14

ataraxia
(n) a state of freedom from emotional disturbance and anxiety; tranquility.

"That's it, Lennie," Coach Brown shouts out as I flip over the high bar, the leather grips pulling at my wrists.

I circle the bar, ending in a kip by swinging back around and bringing my legs to the bar, pulling up so my hips are against the bar, and then kick up into a handstand. I move into my overshoot transition to the lower bar, doing a half twist and landing in a handstand on the bar. After doing a complete circulation, I pop out a Shaposhnikova by facing away from the high bar and flinging my body back to grab the high bar.

I end the routine by dismounting into a full twisting double layout. Clean. Perfect. Very unlike the disaster when I attempted this bars routine this summer in St. Louis.

This past June when I competed at Nationals, I took home Gold in Floor, Bronze in Beam and Vault, and came in 8th all around. Bars is my weakest skill set and one I've been busting my butt to improve on. I obviously did not make the National team, yet again. I still have bitter thoughts about it.

Elite gymnastics values skill and difficulty levels, whereas collegiate is more about perfect execution. It's been tough to focus on building skill while only training twenty hours a week, but I've improved each summer with my home team and our trainers.

Coach Dwight whistles, "I thought for sure I'd have to catch you on that last release. Shoulda known better…you've improved a lot since last year."

I beam with pride as Jayla runs over and hugs me, Cat following in her steps. "You are going to kill it at the meet against West Virginia!" She crows.

"Oh, hey kettle," I smirk at her. "Look who's talking? I saw that beam routine on Monday!" She smiles happily. It was beautiful, loaded with skills.

I eat lunch with the girls, and then they wander off to separate classes. I'm in my dorm packing up my bag to head to the library when Luca calls me.

"Hi Luc," I start, as I cram in another textbook. "What's up?"

"Hey sweets. I'm done with class, you're still free to come help me get ready for the party tonight, right?"

Crap. I forgot about Luca and his frat brothers' party. He asked me to come make jello shots and snacks.

"Oh no. I didn't write it on my calendar, so it slipped my mind, but I can run over after I study for a few hours!" I rush out, hoping my chipper voice will keep him happy.

"Please, Len? You can't study tomorrow or Sunday?"

I knew he'd be annoyed. One thing I've learned about Luca is that he hates feeling like he's second to something I need to do or someone I am hanging out with.

I sigh. He's right. The days are running together this close to Christmas Break. Luca's been irritated that we haven't had as much time together, and I can't remember the last time I had quality time with Raven. Or Cora and Gabby, come to think of it. I could use a night off.

"Alright, I'll be over in fifteen," I acquiesce.

Cora and Raven come into the house as I'm grabbing the keys to our Jeep.

"Whoa whoa, where do you think you're going?" Raven asks, looking at me expectantly.

"Over to Luca's to help with party stuff."

"Lenore Elizabeth!"

I look at her, confused. "Raven Lisette! What's the issue?"

She looks furious, narrowing her eyes at me. "I haven't seen you for more

Chapter 14

than ten minutes in over a week, and you're heading out to go be with Luca? As usual?!"

"Raven," I start. Her shoulders hunch and she looks at me with puppy dog eyes.

"I miss you sissy." Hell. What do I say to that?

She's feeling Twinvy. We coined the expression when we were seven and Raven was spending all of her time with Tommy Tobin from down the street. He was a jerk to me that summer and I hated his guts. When Raven wasn't paying attention, he ripped off my barbies' heads and called me Little Lanky Lenore until I cried and ran inside. Raven spent all of that first week in July playing with him and I told her I was jealous of her time with him, so she yelled at me "Stop having twin envy, Lenore! I can spend time with other people besides you!"

But then she caught him pulling my hair and taunting me, so she punched him in the nose and that was that.

I huff out a sigh. This isn't the first time that I've heard I'm spending too much time with Luca.

"Well why don't y'all come help me? I could use jello shot makers."

Two birds one stone, and all that.

We pull up to the house and walk in, breathing in the lingering smell of weed. They must not test the Lacrosse and Hockey teams because I swear, half of those guys are potheads.

I tried it freshman year and hated it. Gabby drove us to the gas station to get snacks, and Raven and I were so paranoid that we convinced ourselves the little old lady pumping gas was in the FBI and knew we were baked. I worried for a month after that team would test me and kick me off. I was never tempted to try it again.

We walk in the kitchen and Luca breezes in and pulls me in for heated a kiss. His hair is still wet from his shower and droplets get all over me. "Yuck, get out of here with that hair," I squeal, earning me a face full of wet as Luca shakes his head like a dog.

"You two are gross," Raven says, rolling her eyes.

"Hey Satan, didn't know you were coming to help," Luca teases before turning to me. "Babe, can you make me a sandwich?"

"Uhh no, I'm here to make shots, not feed you!"

He gives me his big puppy eyes. "Pleeease," he whines. "You make the best sandwiches!"

I *know* I do.

Raven scoffs. "You're kidding me, she's not your Momma. Make your own damn sandwich."

He narrows his eyes at her. "Don't even act like you don't love her sandwiches, too."

I elbow in between them, annoyed at their constant griping.

"Chill, I'll make the sandwich. Cora, Raven, want one?"

"Yeah. Dressed," Raven mutters. I raise my eyebrow at her and she sighs. "S'il vous plais."

"Does a bear shit in the woods?" Cora says, not taking her eyes off her screen. She's been quietly ignoring the exchange, playing what I can guarantee is that candy popping whatever-it's-called-game on her phone. She's addicted to it. Last week, she paid a hundred dollars in one day to buy coins and one of her dads called and yelled at her for thirty minutes about wasteful spending.

I put Luca to work putting bags of chips and chex mix out while I whip up sandwiches and Cora and Raven make jello shots. We're finishing eating when Diego Karlsson walks in.

"Oh hey," he says, blushing when he sees Raven. The boy has no chill about his crush on her. I think that's the reason she friend zoned him *hard* after their tumble in the sheets Freshman year.

"My dad just sent me some Swedish food." His arms are full of colorful tubes that look like giant toothpastes and bags of sweets. I grab a bag with "bilar" written on the front. There are little pastel cars on the inside. I can't read the package, but they're soft like little marshmallows. I put those down and pick up a blue bag that says "Polly" on it with little chocolates printed on the bag.

Luca and Cora are more interested in the tubes. Chase walks in and looks over their shoulders.

"What are these?" he asks, taking the yellow tube from Cora.

Chapter 14

"They're spreads. You eat them on crackers or sandwiches."

"Like Cheez Whiz?" Luca asks, looking at a blue tube with yellow writing on it.

"Kinda."

Luca grabs a box of crackers from Diego. "Hell yeah, we're trying these!"

This dude will eat all day if he was able to.

We start with the yellow tube, spreading in on our crackers. It's a very thick, and light-yellow colored paste. I nervously take a bite, not knowing what to expect. It tastes slightly sweet, and another flavor that I can't place.

"What is this one?" I ask Diego.

"Dunno, I can speak Swedish mostly, but I can't read or write it. It's definitely not a phonetic language. Let me Google. I think my dad is on the plane back to California. He was visiting my grandma." He reads from his phone. "Caramelized cheese flavored."

Oookay, didn't know that was a flavor that existed in the world. I shrug and slather a new cracker from the blue tube that Cora passes me. It smells slightly fishy.

"Is this tuna?" Luca asks after taking a big bite. I eat my cracker. Phew, that is salty, but I kinda like it.

"Hmmmm, that's yummy," Raven says, eating the rest of her cracker with relish.

Diego types on his phone and then looks at the screen. His eyes go wide, and the blood drains out of his face.

"What," Cora asks. "What's in it?"

Diego clears his throat. "Ahh. Well, apparently this is cod roe."

I grab Raven's shoulder, looking at her and then back at Diego with wide eyes. "Oh no, it's fish eggs?" Ewww.

"Nope," he bites out. "Turns out, this particular roe comes from the male fish. So yeah, my own father sent me fucking fish sperm spread."

I gasp, dropping the rest of my cracker on the counter. "Ewww! Why?!" I whine as disgusted groans ring out in the kitchen.

Luca stares at the tube in horror, saying "Aww what the fuck man, I have to go brush my teeth now," before rushing out of the room. Chase turns a delicate shade of green and looks miserably at the half eaten cracker in his hand.

Raven turns to Diego and yells "What the *hell*, we fed you gumbo, and you turn around and feed us Nemo jizz?!"

There's a pregnant pause before Cora and I die laughing. Diego joins in and eventually Raven does too. If I don't laugh, I think I may cry. Chase *looks* like he might cry. Ugh, when I said I wanted new experiences, that really wasn't what I had in mind.

The party starts slowly around us as the night wears on, and by midnight it's safe to say that all of us are *drunk*. I started out not wanting to drink much, but Luca and Raven started going hard, and I don't know. I hold myself to such strict standards sometimes that I don't even feel like a college kid. I feel like I'm trying to rush being grown. I have enough responsibilities and obligations, why put more on myself? I can't believe I almost spent tonight studying. It's so nice to cut loose after weeks of hecticness. That's a word, right?

Have another White Claw, Len.

Chase and I are dancing like idiots, laughing at each other and feeling the effects of the shots. I have to pee, so I leave him and head down the hall to the bathroom. I see Raven half laying on the couch with Cora and Jared, looking completely blitzed.

"Ça-va?" I call out to her. *You good?*

"Oui, sha!"

I shake my head, laughing at her goofy expression.

After doing my business and washing my hands, I walk out of the bathroom and smack into a solid chest.

"Oof! Nate? Geez!" I sputter, catching my balance. Not so easy after four claws and three (or was it four?) jello shots.

"Sorry Lennie," he smirks. "Interesting, catching you in this particular bathroom."

It takes me a second in my state, but I catch his drift and narrow my eyes at him, which helps me go from seeing two of him to just one and a half.

"Not really, considering that my *boyfriend* also lives here. Nothing special

Chapter 14

to report about any occurrences in this *particular* bathroom." I push past him, rolling my eyes. What a creep. I can't believe I let him kiss me.

I will not let jerks steal my buzz; I will not let jerks steal my buzz.

I throw myself down on the love seat across from Raven and Luca appears with another jello shot. I smile at him, instantly forgetting…what now? Something about a bathroom?

I open the jello shot and send it down the hatch.

* * *

Something stirs me from my slumber, I'm not sure what. Perhaps it's that my head is five times too big. Or maybe it's that my mouth feels like a desert and tastes like sand and death. Or maybe the sun shining into the second story window, blinding my now open eyes.

Or it could be the too heavy and too hot body sweating all over me on the bed.

"Uuugh," I groan, pushing Luca off me. He's half laying on top of me, spooning me from behind and his room is like a million degrees. I take in a deep breath and roll him off, finally able to breath.

What happened last night?

How high is the heat set to?

Why is the sun so loud?

I remember shots and shots and sho-*ahhh*, I think I know where I went wrong.

I'm such an idiot. How could I have let myself drink that much? Suddenly I realize what day it is, and I lurch out of bed and looking frantically for my phone while trying to ignore the dizziness. Did I miss Saturday Open Gym?

"Shit! What time is it?" I'm searching for clothes, shoes, keys, my phone when I stop suddenly, feeling even more not-so-hot.

"Oh no," I whimper, right before I lunge to the dresser, grab an empty Lays bag, and promptly puke my guts out.

"Babe?" Luca mumbles sleepily from the bed as I heave into the bag. Thank goodness he's a slob. This all could have very well landed in his laundry hamper.

"You okay?"

"No, I'm not okay," I croak. "I'm hungover and I can't find anything. I can't miss practice; my coaches will murder me this close to our first meet!"

"Your phone was in the living room, last I saw," he manages before rolling over and falling back asleep. How does *he do that?!* Doesn't he see that I'm having a crisis?

Ugh, men.

I stomp into the living room after locating my clothes and disposing of the defiled chip bag and start searching for my phone. Like all college houses, there is not one clock in sight, so it could be seven am or five pm on Monday for all I know. I've never drank that much in my life.

People are laying on every surface, including the dining room table, all passed out and in various stages of dress. Or undress, in one case that I'm unfortunate enough to witness. I grab a blanket and throw it over the random passed-out dude's bare lap and continue looking for my things. I spy my phone under the end table, and stab at it to get the time. 8:47 am.

Thank God. The only person I'm scared of more than Coach Akeno is Coach Sara. She's terrifying. Back in September, Tatum was so hungover from her first college party experience that she was too dizzy to even do a back flip and Johannes made her climb the rope until she had blisters the size of quarters on her hands. Maybe a little harsh as far as gym punishments go, but she definitely never did that again.

I'm so screwed.

I grab two bottles of Gatorade from the fridge and head out the door, praying to God, Jesus, all His angels, and the ghosts of my ancestors that I can make it through practice. Open Gym is always a mystery. It could be drills, skills, conditioning, or a mix of all three. Knowing my luck, we'll be doing drills with our waist weights on.

After heading home to shower, woofing down a collagen protein bar and trying not to throw it back up, I head into Fulminare. It's curiously quiet and I round a corner to pass the video review rooms on the way to the training center and stop short. Am I perhaps God's favorite child today?

Chapter 14

All three coaches are in our room setting things up and chatting as my teammates slowly file towards the door. Savannah walks past me, heading in. "Didn't you get the email?" She asks, noticing my expression. "We're reviewing the tapes from last year of the girls who are still competing on the West Virginia team and then watching tapes of our finished routines to critique."

My knees go weak with relief, and I grab the door handle to steady myself. *Thank you to all above for having my back today.*

Chapter 15

atelophobia
(n) the fear of imperfection. the fear of never being good enough

I somehow made it through finals and the end of first semester intact. I most definitely didn't overdo it at parties again. And skipping studying for that big test ended up continuing on Saturday when I was hungover and went to bed directly after Open Gym. Then I laid in bed reading and eating snacks all day on Sunday to recover from my first forty-eight hour hangover. Spoiler…I got a D+ on that test.

Partying isn't going to get me to my goals.

After spending the holidays in Louisiana with our family, Raven and I are back in Boston, frantically trying to get our parent's attention from across the quad. Our first meet is tomorrow against West Virginia, and my parents flew in with Maddie to see it. They'd been to two of my meets and came up for the regional finals last May, but it's not easy for them to get away during the school year since they're professors. Not to mention Maddie's rodeo schedule.

"Momma! MOM!" I shout, waving wildly. They wanted to meet us here so that we could pop into the student union to review our meal balance and a few other things. *It would have been easier to meet at the house,* I think bitterly. It's freezing outside and supposed to snow tonight.

Chapter 15

I give it one last attempt before Raven rolls her eyes and puts those big country lungs to use, hollering out "LYNNETTE LANDRY!" startling everyone in a twenty-foot radius. That finally gets their attention, and they hurry over to us.

"Good Lord," Daddy says as he gives me a Harry Landry Bear Hug. "It's colder than a brass toilet seat in Alaska!"

I laugh, though the image makes my butt feel even colder. It's thirty degrees and dropping this late in the day. It's the second weekend in January, and we've been anticipating the first snowfall.

"It's supposed to snow tonight," Raven offers, making Maddie squeal with excitement as I move on to hug her.

"Oh my GOSH! Snow! I've never seen snow!" She's hopping up and down like a kid in Disney World. "Simmer down, teapot," Raven says as she brings Mads in for a hug. "It's not all that great. Nothing that cold and wet ever is."

I take Maddie's hand, leading her towards Bellus Hall. "Don't listen to her. When it's dark and quiet outside, and it's snowing…gah. There's just nothing more peaceful. We'll sneak out tonight and watch from the backyard." I whisper to her. Maddie is staying at the house with Raven and I, while our parents got a hotel room because, and I quote, "We're too old and cranky to be around a bunch of noisy college kids."

Momma grabs my arm, and I help steady her as we climb the old stone steps up to Bellus Hall. Maddie's never been inside, so she immediately started gawking at the foyer.

"It's like a castle in here," she says, looking up at the five-story ceiling in awe. I smile, remembering when we came to visit with my parents, knowing just from the atmosphere and scenery on campus that Raven and I had made the right decision to go here.

While our parents wrap up their to-dos with the student union, Raven and I take Maddie to Aisling Spice Bag to introduce her to the wonders of Irish street food.

Afterwards, my dad somewhat grumpily asks, "Are we going to meet the boyfriend tonight?"

I narrow my eyes, not taking his tone well. "His name is *Luca*, and no. He has practice tonight and an away game tomorrow night which is almost a full day schedule, so you'll meet him Sunday at the meet."

I told my parents about Luca when we were home for the holidays. Wondering how well that went?

Picture this; it's the week before Christmas and I'm minding my own business, helping Allan and Maddie make fudge with Momma. Maddie and I are laughing at Allan, who's getting swatted by our mom. "Allan Bryant Landry, keep your hands *out* of the fudge! It's cooling!"

All of a sudden, the back door is thrown open making us all jump a foot in the air as Daddy stomps into the kitchen, throws off his Carhartt, and glowers at me like some B-grade movie villain, followed closely by Auguste who does his best to mimic our dad's aggressive stance.

"*So,*" Daddy seethes, looking at me.

"So?" I ask, totally confused.

"What's this I'm hearing from Raven about a boyfriend and *why* am I just *now* hearing about him? *From Raven?* Apparently, he lays around the house all day and expects you to cook for him like you're *the help*? Who the hell is this yank?!"

Everyone whips their heads towards me with versions of "what the hell?!" looks on their faces.

Oh, *that freaking bitch*, I think, giving her the nastiest look I can muster up when she slinks in the door after Auguste. She has the sense to look sheepish, but she is all the way dead when I get my hands on her.

I raise my eyebrow at her. *Et tu, Brute?*

"Okay, *one*, this isn't the friggin' Cold War, so you can all relax and quit looking at me like I sold national secrets to the enemy. And *two*, this is the last time that I expect to use the argument that I am a fully formed grown woman with self-respect and actual intelligence," I start, not about to take this crap at twenty years old.

"I'm not sure what Raven said, but they don't exactly get along, so keep that in mind. He doesn't lay around all day, she just doesn't like sharing her space with him. His frat house is crowded, and it's nicer and quieter at our house, so we both prefer spending time there. And he doesn't treat me like *'the help'*,

Chapter 15

I enjoy cooking and he knows his way around *zero* aspects of a kitchen."

I pause, looking at everyone, putting my arms out to the sides. "That's it, nothing nefarious. I planned on telling you all about him over dinner actually, and letting you know that you'll be meeting him at my first meet. We've been together for three months, he's Italian, from New York City and was raised by a single mother after his dad was killed in a car accident when he was young, and they're Catholic."

I'm stretching a bit here since he curses like a sailor and hasn't attended church once at college.

"He loves his Momma," (understatement of the year) "and he is a complete sweetheart to me. Isn't that what you should want for your daughter?"

It goes quiet as everyone pauses, looking a little taken aback. That's right! Sweet, quiet Lenore has some gumption now. Who would have thought?

"I may have been venting a little," Raven says apologetically. She's not getting any sympathy from me. In fact, I'm furious. But I save that for later, because *unlike* Raven, I believe in Twin Code.

"He drives me crazy, but he's really sweet to Lennie."

Daddy seems to deflate a little. Actually, he seems disappointed that he can't be all *puffed up in righteous indignation*, which is truly one of his favorite states to be in.

"Alright cher. I'll reserve judgment until we meet him," he says, giving me his famous eyebrow raise. "But I will see right through his bullshit if he's not a good one, and Lenore? I will not allow any child of mine to date someone unworthy, no matter what age they are. *Entendue?*"

I shrink a little under his scrutiny. "Yes Daddy, understood." *Sheesh.*

Everyone goes back to their activities, and I sneak out of the kitchen to go find Raven. *Time to murder Judas.*

Raven and I had it out that night, and she knows how badly I could have blown her out of the water to our parents but didn't. Something tells me that Raven embracing her 'Ho Years' would register a lot worse than me being in a loving, committed relationship. I am now the proud majority owner of our Jeep Wrangler, which we've agreed to a 25% - 75% split ratio for second semester. Me being the 75% and her being the 25%.

Fair, considering her betrayal. Say what you want about twins, we know how to haggle over consequences for injustice.

* * *

"Sweet Jesus, that's your dad? Lennie? Is he part giant?" Luca shrilly hisses at me.

I smile to myself, seeing him knocked down a peg from his cocky stance when I met his mom.

"Probably," I say. "But hey, I thought 'parents love me' and all that?"

He gives me the side eye and I kiss him on the cheek, wrapping my hand around his bicep and pulling him forward with me. "He's a softie, it's gonna be fine. Keep in mind if he's gruff, that I'm his little girl and he's protective."

"Great, I'll remember that when he's using me for target practice. He could be Paul Bunyan's brother. I should just hand him an ax and get it over with." He's looking warier the closer they get to us.

I laugh at him. "Like you've ever held an ax, city boy."

We're standing in front of the Fulminare Center watching my family walk up the steps. I'm in my navy-and-gold leotard with our warm-up pants and jacket over it. They're thin, so I'm shivering and burrowing into Luca for warmth.

They finally make it to us and Luca steps forward to shake Daddy's hand.

"Hey, I'm Luca. It's great to meet you, I feel like I already know you from how much Len talks about you all."

"Nice to meet you, son. I'm Harry and this is Lynn and Madeline." Momma gives him a handshake, while Maddie stands shyly off to the side and waves.

"Lenore's told us a lot about you too. Gotta say, I wasn't expecting a blonde when she told me about her Italian boyfriend."

Luca laughs, "Yeah, I get that a lot. My mom has German and French heritage, but my dad was all Italian. He's actually who I got the blonde hair and blue eyes from. He and I look like my late Nonno."

Maddie's looking at Luca with heart eyes and I smile at her. "Told ya he's gorgeous," I whisper to her. Her eyes go wide and her cheeks flame with color

Chapter 15

all of a sudden. I turn to see Chase walking up. "Hey Len," he says, pulling me into a hug. We've spent a lot of time together with Luca and some of the other guys from the team, and I'm happy to see him.

"Meet my parents," I start, turning to Momma and Daddy. He shakes their hands and looks at Maddie. "You must be Madeline, Lennie talks about you all the time." Pretty sure the poor thing is about to detonate because she turns a deeper shade of red and just nods her head.

Relieved that there's no Spanish Inquisition for Luca, I kiss him, and I leave them all to go meet back up with my team before we head to the floor for warmups.

We have about thirty minutes before the meet starts, but I've already been here for a while going through my routine.

"Let's go ladies, time to head out to warmups! Let's huddle up, you know what to do!" Coach Akeno shouts out, clapping his hands.

We all huddle up, touching hands in the center and reciting the same quote by Nadia Comaneci that we say before each meet. A little superstitious boost.

"Jump off the beam, flip off the bars, follow your dreams and reach for the stars!" We roar.

And with that, we're off, heading into the gym where West Virginia has gathered as well. I look at the filled seats and take it all in. The atmosphere during meets is electric as always. As the girls and I start to warm up, as usual, I'm blown away by the crowd. Last year for the championship we literally had fourteen thousand people in the stands! Just another way that Elite is different from NCAA. It's more of the college sports fanatic scene here. Our families and fans always lose it when we file into the space. Even during warmups they're screaming and cheering for us!

Nothing tops the feeling.

I spy Luca, Chase, and my family in the stands and wave at them. Luca has the entire hockey team here supporting us and that makes my heart swell.

The meet kicks off with West Virginia starting bars and me vault, and while I missed a perfect landing at Nationals with my Yurchenko Full, I stick it today without even the tiniest misstep. I release the breath I was holding and sag in relief as Coach Akeno wraps me in a huge hug. "That was beautiful," he shouts, and the girls all run up to hug me. We break apart, heading back down the runway together past the judges and photographers.

The support we show each other equally is a really special type of love, and it's everything on meet days. I get a 9.950 and after we all go wild again, Cat follows with a 9.872 and Jayla gets a 9.971 and well, this is why my voice is always hoarse after meets. I watch Savannah's beam routine but have to head to my next set before we hear her score.

Floor is my best event and most favorite. NCAA rules allow for *much* more creativity and fun music, and we go all out with our routines.

I take my place at the top corner of the mat and listen to the opening chords of my song, Purple Hat by Sofi Tukker. It's upbeat and unique, and it fills me with energy. This routine is a departure from my normal, and I worked on it all last semester. I start my open tumbling pass, an Arabian double front, launching myself backwards and upwards while turning 180 degrees in the air, then completing two forward somersaults in the air before landing.

For the next two minutes I lose myself in the movements and flips, not seeing the crowd or my teammates, although I know Cat and Jayla are doing my choreography on the sidelines like they always do. I love those dorks.

When I stick my last landing and pose as the closing song notes ring out, my team surrounds me, screaming and jumping up and down. And when my score is announced, Coach Sarah pulls me into a spinning hug, yelling out "That was absolutely perfect!" which I barely hear over the screams and shouts and cheers surrounding me.

For the first time in my life, I've gotten a perfect 10.

My teammates pull me into a screaming, jumping group hug, and I can't tell if I'm laughing, screaming, or crying.

We've won the meet by 2.956 points.

There isn't a word I've found yet that accurately portrays this feeling. Actually…

Alexithymia - inability to describe emotions.

After we win the meet, I shower and change, and head to dinner with my family and Luca. Cora, Gabby, Chase, Dylan, and Jared, who just started dating Cora, are all invited to come, and we get a huge table at Sycamore next

Chapter 15

to the large, exposed brick wall.

Once our entrees reach us, I immediately dig into my bistro steak, ravenously hungry after burning so many calories.

"I know I've said this like twenty times, but you killed it today, Lennie Loo," Cora says to me as I shovel another fork full into my mouth. "And your little sister is a doll baby." Maddie beams at her from across the table.

"Thanks, Cor! Today felt good. And Mads is one of the good ones, I wish she were coming here in the fall." I say a little sadly. She's committed to LSU. Unlike Raven and I, the only adventurous streak Maddie has is tied to her rodeos.

"Well crap. I was looking forward to having a little pseudo-sister."

"You'll have to make do with me then," I laugh at her.

"I miss you, Len. This is the first time we've sat down together in months."

I look at my plate, feeling guilty. I love Cora and Gabby, and of course Raven, but I only have so much free time, and Luca and I spend most of it together. I don't understand why everyone is up in arms about it. Gabby has Dylan, Cora now has Jared, and Raven...well, Raven has her fun. Why am I the one who gets guilt tripped?

I sigh.

"I wish I had more free time, Cor. I miss you, too. Let's plan a girl's day in Salem with Raven and Gabby? We've been meaning to get back, but I was waiting for Spring when we can see all of the gardens. Or maybe we can get a hotel room downtown and do something fun?"

I can get away on a Saturday that Luca has an away game now that those days are free again from open gym.

"Yay! Deal. Actually, why don't we plan a big Spring Break trip with the group?"

"Oh, I like that! Raven and I were talking about how fun it would be to show you all New Orleans. Mardi Gras will be over by then, but I know you all were talking about wanting to see the city."

"Well miss travel guru, let's get to planning," she says as she cheers my water with hers.

After dinner we're standing outside of the restaurant saying goodbye to my family. They're flying out in the morning so that Maddie doesn't miss school, and they're heading back to the hotel.

Daddy pulls me into a big hug.

"Alright cher, Luca seems like a good guy. I didn't understand any of what he tried to explain about hockey, but he seems alright."

"Told ya," I smile up at him.

I hug my mom and breathe in her pretty perfume, her hair tickling my nose.

"Did you like him, Momma?"

She smiles a little tightly, but I know this is just her way. She's never been one hundred percent comfortable with hugs and snuggles unless they come from Daddy. "Were you not hugged as a child?" I joked once. She just looked away and changed the subject.

"He seems nice," she says. "I just want you to be sure about him. Make sure he treats you right. You know your worth."

I try not to be annoyed. She's met him, seen how wonderful he is, and is still this hesitant? I swallow down my resentment and smile at her.

Once they take off, Luca walks over and embraces me from behind, which instantly relaxes me. I smile up at him over my shoulder; he's my happy place.

Then he ruins it.

"Told you parents love me." He boasts.

I groan, rolling my eyes, and elbow him in the stomach.

He huffs a laugh and heads to Maddie, putting his arm around her shoulders, making her blush.

"Alright Baby Landry, let's get you to the house before it starts snowing."

We get Maddie all set up in Raven's room, and Luca leaves for the night. I'm sensing that the girls want time together, and frankly I've gone too long without prioritizing my friendships. I make a note to make sure Luca isn't doing the same.

Gabby and Cora came home without their boyfriends, so we pop some popcorn and settle on the sectional in a big pile of cozy clothes and blankets. Gabby's parents bought the furniture and it's ridiculously big and comfortable.

We settle in to watch Clueless, which then turns into Mean Girls, and before I know it, it's one am and we're all asleep on the couch. I'm not sure what

Chapter 15

wakes me up, but after I look at my phone, I notice movement out of the corner of my eye and have an inner freak out moment, sure that there's a serial killer lurking outside the window. After I startle, I turn to face the window and see huge, fluffy snowflakes. As I walk closer, I see that the ground is blanketed in at least two inches of snow. It's coming down hard, and must have been snowing for a few hours.

I go and wake Maddie up quietly. After the first time I woke Raven up, and she spent the next morning trudging through freezing, dirty snow, she's written it off as an annoyance and nothing more. And if I wake Gabby and Cora up, I'm libel to get death threats.

"Shhhh, wake up. It's snowing!!! Let's grab coats and boots and go out back," I whisper.

"Ohh yes, okay!" She whisper shouts back, giving me a nose full of morning breath.

We tiptoe outside after bundling up. We don't have a picnic table in our back yard, and I don't want to get any of our blankets wet by laying it on the ground, so we just stare up at the sky, quietly watching the peaceful snowfall.

"I can't believe how pretty this is. I feel like I'm in a Christmas movie," she says in wonder. I remember how dazed and awed I'd been on that night last January. That beautiful and awful night when Gabby was so devastated.

"The first time I watched the snowfall, I'd just found out that Gabby's oldest brother died." I don't know what makes me say it.

"Oh no," she gasps. "That's heartbreaking. Did you know him?"

"No, I didn't. It was more horrifying to me because I watched my sweet friend be torn to pieces over losing her brother so suddenly. He was killed in a car crash just before Christmas."

"Gabby must be so sad. She seems so…"

"Sunshiny?" I offer and she nods. "She is. It just took her half a year to get back to herself, and even then she hasn't been fully the same since. It made me question a lot of things in my life, how much I give of myself to others, and what I think matters most in the long run. You know how much I love you, right? Have I always shown it well?"

I'm feeling a little guilty about how much time I've taken away from being with my friends and family lately. It's not even that Luca demands it of me. It just kind of happened naturally, organically. We're drawn to each other.

But I need my girls too. Most of Luca's friends are on the hockey team, and they see each other a ton between morning skates, weightlifting, practices, and games. They're together often for entire days and weekends. I do see the girls when he's at away games more, but they also have boyfriends and work and school.

"Len, of course you have. We text all the time, we face time, I see you when you're home, and you've never made me question that you loved me. Where is this coming from?"

I shrug. "Just feeling pensive. The snow always reminds me of death now. Or at least it reminds me of feeling very sad, even though I still love it and think it's beautiful. It also reminds me that I'm freezing!" I shiver and laugh, trying to lighten the mood that I've just darkened.

"Brrrr. Yes. I think this is literally the coldest I've ever been," she yawns out.

We go inside and get to sleep.

Over the next few months, I make it a point to spend time with the girls one on one and to keep regular face times with Maddie and my brothers, and of course my parents. Though that is a little less frequent.

They've seemed to really accept that Raven and I are adults, even more so after they met Luca. My dad is more into him than my mom, but I'm not surprised. When I told them that Raven and I along with all of the friends they met are planning a Spring Break trip for April, they surprised me by not objecting.

I think "Spring Break" is a poor subject for us all.

Chapter 16

kalopsia
(n) the delusion of things being more beautiful than they really are

"Babe, can you grab me a beer from the cooler," Luca calls from the living room. I roll my eyes and grab a bookmark for the novel I'm reading. The salty air is humid and cool, and I was enjoying a break on the balcony; the rhythmic waves being preferable to the sounds of partying coming from the rooms.

We're all in a hotel suite that Gabby's dad set up for spring break, in Myrtle Beach, South Carolina. Apparently, this is *the* place to do Spring Break on the East Coast, so New Orleans was vetoed.

Frankly, I am not impressed so far. Like, at all.

We came down as a group; me and Luca, Gabby and Dylan, Cora and Jared, along with Chase, Raven, Isaiah from the lacrosse team, and a few other guys and girls from school. The fifteen of us are spread out on the fourth floor of the hotel, and it's been four days of pre-gaming in and out of each other's rooms before we attempt to head out into the night life.

After four nights of drinking with my friends and then drinking away my hangovers every day following, I'm taking it easy today.

Luca, however, is not.

He's been drunk basically since we checked in on Sunday, and now at four pm on Thursday, it's looking like we're on day five of what the girls have dubbed "Frat Boy Fuckery."

Basically, all of the guys will be too drunk to leave the hotel, instead turning to booze-fueled shenanigans in the confines of our rooms. Sounds fun but is more like horrifying. Guys are weird and gross and even more reckless than usual when drunk in each other's company.

These idiots never back down from a dare.

Not to mention they all have sex on the brain 24/7, so it's been…interesting, waiting for the girls to catch up to the guys' level of inebriation. Lots of swatting away groping hands and trying not to gag while our boyfriends make out with us with way more than necessary amounts of saliva.

I heave a sigh, closing my well-used copy of John Green's *Looking for Alaska*, an old comfort read of mine, and resign myself to another night of drinking and trying to bottle feed Luca water between beers. These guys don't party too hard during the season, which just ended for hockey and is still going on for the lacrosse players, so now that they're on break for the week, they're partying harder than ever. If I thought hockey players were wild before, they have nothing on their spring break versions.

I grab Luca a beer, a water bottle, and a white claw for myself because if I have to put up with these crazies, there must be alcohol in my system, or I will lock myself on the roof. Luca is lounging on one of the couches with Chase and Dylan, making grabby hands at me as I walk up and settle in his lap. He's warm and smells like beer and cologne, and I smack a kiss on his cheek.

"Water first, or we'll never make it to the foam party tonight." I kiss him to soften the blow, and surprisingly he listens to me. I look over at Chase and Dylan, taking in the state of them. Chase actually seems fine. I've noticed he paces himself and doesn't get hammered like the rest of them. In fact, he's been trying to police the guys with me and the rest of the girlfriends when it gets too rowdy.

Dylan, however, looks like he's about to keel over. Gabby walks over and tugs on his arm. "Come on lightweight, let's go take a nap before we all head to dinner," she says indulgently, giving me a wink as she leads him to their

Chapter 16

room.

"That's not a bad idea," Luca slurs, nuzzling into my neck. Yep, I see where this is going. Drunk Luca thinks that sober Lennie is going to let him get a little afternoon delight, and that is so not happening. Last night, Luca fell asleep on top of me *in the middle of sex* and started *snoring*. I had to shove him off me so I could breathe.

Talk about a blow to a girl's ego.

I look over at Chase, who is looking out at the ocean through the balcony door, and I feel a little uncomfortable. Luca is very demonstrative, but even more so when he's been drinking, and I don't want to make Chase feel like a third wheel. I'm honestly not a huge fan of PDA in general. Cora, Jared, and Raven are in the kitchen taking shots, and everyone else is presumably in their rooms or taking naps, so it's just the three of us.

"Why don't you go take a nap, I'm not tired," I say. He pouts at me like usual when he doesn't get his way. "Babe," he tries to whine, but I put a finger over his mouth.

"I'll come play with your hair."

That's a sure-fire way to get him to go to sleep and hopefully wake up sober enough for us to go to dinner and the foam party later. And he must have been drunker than I thought because it takes all of five minutes before he's snoring.

I head back into the living room and sit next to Chase, bumping shoulders. He looks over and smiles, but there's something sad about it.

"You doing okay?" I ask him. I've been noticing how quiet he has become over the past few days.

"I'm all good," he says, drinking from his water bottle. "I don't know what I expected out of this trip, but I'm not sure this is it."

"I know the exact feeling," I say, looking over at Raven, Cora, and Jared laughing at something in the kitchen. "This place is so…I don't know…gimmicky and touristy. It feels fake to me. And it's weird to be in a constant party situation when you're not a huge partier. Like, I feel the need to go with the flow, but waking up sick every day is wearing on me."

He nods, looking more open now. "Yeah. I don't drink much, so once everyone starts going hard, I start wanting to be elsewhere," he gives me a knowing smile. "Like you with your books."

"Noticed that, huh? Do you like to read?"

"Nah, not really. My Ma is a huge reader though, you two would probably get along really well."

It gets quiet again, and I have an idea. He looks a little melancholy and I know just how combat that.

"Want to go walk on the beach with me? This room is not exactly stimulating my senses right now," I say, getting off the couch.

"Hell yes I do."

We maneuver around the three drunkos in the kitchen, waving off attempts to join them in "shots shots shots!" and make our way to the beach. Mid-April is not exactly summer temperature yet, but it's a lot warmer than Boston.

We walk quietly for a bit, taking in the sounds of the loud and steady waves and the seagull cries. Once we get away from the hotels, the crowds thin out and we take a seat in the sand, looking out over the sparkling water.

I turn to him, watching him brush his longish, black hair from his face.

"Is this your first time to Myrtle Beach?" I ask.

"Yeah, it is," he says, glancing over at me. "I almost didn't come."

"Why not?"

"Since I was in elementary school, my parents and I always take a big trip to see other parts of the country during my springs breaks. My Ma grew up traveling all over with her parents, since my grandpa was a writer for *National Geographic*.

"Woah, that is seriously cool," I say.

"Yeah, the stories she and my aunt tell me are great. Anyway, she traveled so much and wanted me to have experiences like she did, seeing our country. So we'd go to Yellowstone, to Park City Utah, Key West, that kind of thing. Every April, for the past decade or so, we had the best week-long vacations."

I breath out "Chase. You lived my *exact dream*! That sounds amazing."

He smiles at me, looking back at the water lost in a memory.

"It was. Like I told you before, being an only child gets lonely, but on those trips we all had each other's undivided attention. Last year I skipped the

Chapter 16

group spring break to go with them to Colorado, this little mountain town called Estes Park. We got snowed in and had a wicked time. I remember thinking that I wish I had siblings, or some of my friends to make it an even better experience, so I decided to come with everyone this year. Now that I'm here, it's lost its appeal."

"Oh Chase, I'm sorry. Those trips sound really special, I can see how this would pale in comparison. I thought it would be different too. I underestimated everyone's desire to get wasted and stay there, even my own twin!"

He laughs out loud, "Mario Gate wasn't her finest hour."

Our first night here Raven had one or four too many shots and ordered pizza for the group of us in our suite. She called some place named Mario's Pizza and ended up ranting at the poor guy when he showed up with our food about how Mario is always getting the attention and glory. "Why do we never see Luigi getting repped, huh? HUH? It's always Mario this and Mario that! Where's Luigi's Pizza? Why don't you check your privilege," she stupidly slurred out, slamming the door in the poor kid's face. I had to open the door and pay him, profusely apologizing while I tipped him, hopefully well enough to make up for her ridiculous drunken stupor.

It's funny now, but at the time I wanted to smack her.

Mario privilege? My goodness.

"Yeah, you two could not be more different," he says, chuckling. "I mean, you're similar in your mannerisms, but if I didn't know better, I wouldn't have pegged you as twins."

"I get that a lot. She's loud and proud, and I'm quiet and bookish. I used to feel completely overshadowed by her. Not really in life, but in front of others. She just has this way about her that screams confidence and fun. I never quite figured out how to shine like that, so I stopped trying." I don't know where that came from, but it was honest. I glance over at him, feeling pretty sure that I just tanked the mood.

He's looking at me with his handsome face scrunched, thoughtfully.

"Lennie. Raven is great. She's a friend and I like being around her. But being bold and loud doesn't make a person shine. You're kind, thoughtful, and it's easier to talk to you than anyone I've ever met. You shine extremely bright, just be being you."

I have to sit with that for a second and I'm embarrassed to find that I'm suddenly fighting tears. It's the nicest thing anyone has ever said to me.

Also, I thought Chase had a crush on Raven, but maybe that ran its course. Something stops me from asking him about his feelings for her, though.

I give him a smile and a side hug. "You're a great friend, Chase. Thank you for that."

We spend the next two hours talking about anything and everything. It's the most I've enjoyed myself on this trip, and I'm thankful that Chase is so grounded and easy to be with. As the sun starts to set, we fall quiet and face away from the ocean, letting the changing colors of the sky slowly wash over us.

"I don't think I've ever just sat and watched an entire sunset before," Chase says, breaking the quiet wonderment.

"I highly recommend doing it more often. Sunsets are my favorite thing on earth. It always feels like a gift from Mother Nature, just for me. Well," I amend, "just for us, right now."

We go quiet again, watching the dancing kaleidoscope of warm colors until the sun is lost to the horizon of mismatched hotel rooftops, and then head back to the room.

Now that it's almost eight, everyone is slowly waking up and in varying stages of still half asleep and hungover. Raven and Luca being the most hungover and grumpy.

"Where did you two go?" Luca rasps before grabbing a water bottle and chugging.

"Just to walk on the beach. I needed a break from the smell of stale beer," I say jokingly. But also, one hundred percent honestly. *It smells like a brewery in here.*

After he hops in the shower, I go to Raven's room and smack her butt to wake her up.

"Lushy lushy, time to get up!"

"Shumph imnop"

Chapter 16

"Yeah, not real clear on that. RAVEN! *Maintenant*! I'm starving."

She rolls over and gives me a death stare, which would probably be more intimidating if her hair wasn't stuck to her face with drool.

"My head and stomach are killing me," she grits out.

"Oui sha, 'shots! shots! shots!' will do that," I say sarcastically. "It's time to go to dinner, help get rid of *la malade vant*."

That, and I actually really do want to go to the foam party. I may not be a big partier, but I still have *some* things to check off my list of college experiences.

I should have known that the idea would be so much better than the reality.

* * *

So. Much. Noise.

Inside the club is madness. Pure, unadulterated, high as a kite and drunk as a skunk madness, on a level of eight hundred, since that is about how many college kids are crammed into Fiesta Loca.

It's almost midnight and everyone, including myself and Chase, have been hitting the shots and margaritas. There are bodies everywhere in neon shirts, dresses, swimsuits, and everything in between. The stage at the front of the club is outfitted with a DJ and writhing, half naked dancers. And all around, glow sticks fashioned into body jewelry leave streaks in the night as bodies dance, moving, swaying, or in my case, about to get puked on as I narrowly dodge a guy who just started throwing up into his cupped hands.

I'm walking arm in arm with Cora while Luca leads us through the crowd back to the bar.

"This is so much fun!" Cora screams into my ear. "Craziest party ever!"

The DJ pipes up from the booth, his voice projecting above the partiers and music.

"Get loud get loud, what week is it?"

"Spring Break!" the crowd screams back to him.

"I don't think I heard right, what week is it?"

"Spring Break!"

"Let's fuckin' paarrrrttttttyyyyyyy!!!!" he shouts into the mic.

The beat drops as foam starts shooting out from all directions, driving the crowd wild. We're jumping up and down, shouting and laughing as we're covered in bubbles.

All of a sudden, we're joined by Raven and others from our group, and we all melt into the fray, dancing around and having fun. *So* much fun.

This beats staying in the rooms watching people get drunk, act stupid, puke, and then start all over again.

I'm still soberish, but Luca can barely stand up straight, and the others aren't faring too well. I look around and notice that Gabby isn't with us. I haven't actually seen her for half an hour.

I grab Dylan and yell in his ear "Have you seen Gabby?"

"Yes!" he shouts back. "I left her at the bar to come find you guys!" He stops and looks confused, looking around. "I showed her where you all were when I left her, she should have been here by now!"

Okay, that can't be good. Maybe she's in the bathroom?

I grab Chase, Jared, and Cora since we're the most sober ones and we set out to find her. Did I mention there are hundreds of people here? After about ten minutes, I'm starting to get a little frantic. We're in another state, we've all been drinking, and we're surrounded by strangers. My mind starts going down a dark path, when I see a girl with long blonde hair being led by a tall guy, heading toward the back. Her arm is around his shoulders, and he's kind of propping her up and dragging her along as her head bobs back and forth.

Then I notice the same bright green sandals that I complemented earlier, and I realize that it's Gabby.

"Oh my God, DYLAN!" I grab his arm and point, "That's Gabby!"

Everyone looks over and we all lunge into action. Cora and I run up and grab Gabby from the guy, and it's...it's bad. She's almost completely unconscious. She was stone cold sober when we got here two hours ago, and in the short time I haven't seen her, there's no way she could have gotten to this level of intoxication.

"What the fuck did you do to her?"

"What did you do to my girlfriend?!!"

"Who are you?"

Chapter 16

"What do you think you're doing?"

The guys descend on the stranger and it's mayhem. There's screaming and shoving and punching and I'm scared to get too close. They're raining down blows fueled by pure male fury and fear of the answer to the question we're all asking ourselves.

What would have happened if we didn't find her when we did?

Security shows up to break up the fight and, in the chaos, the guy somehow gets away. There are just too many lights, too much foam, and too many drunk, glowing bodies everywhere. It's disorienting now that I'm standing still and just got a sober shock straight to the brain.

Cora and I are barely holding Gabby upright, because she's completely passed out now. Dylan stomps over and takes her from us, gently picking her up into his arms. He pushes past the security guards where Jared and Chase are frantically telling them what happened.

"We called the police and an ambulance, guys. Calm down and take a deep breath." They escort us while we go grab our friends and head out the exit as the cops pull up, the ambulance following right after.

Dylan gets her situated on the gurney and watches protectively while the EMTs start taking her vitals. The cops start taking statements from the five of us, and the gravity of the situation settles over me like a blanket.

I start crying and Luca walks over to me where I'm huddled with Cora, pulling me into a side embrace. "Jesus, sweetheart, you're shaking." I can't get a reply around the lump in my throat. We're all sweaty and covered in drying soap bubbles, adding to the stickiness of dread that coated my skin when I saw Gabby being led away by that stranger.

One of the officers comes over to all of us, and a stern expression comes over his face.

"Your friend appears to have been drugged. They're going to take her to the ER, and they'll test her blood to determine the drug amounts in her system and monitor until her vitals are good enough to release her. I hate to say this, but we see it all the time at parties like this." He listens to something on his radio briefly before continuing. "I was young once and I get it, I do. Away from home finally, having the time of your life with your friends and boyfriend or girlfriend. The reality is that groups like this make people vulnerable. Your guard is down, you're drinking, doing drugs and having fun…and you're not paying attention."

We're all quiet, shaking slightly as the heaviness of his words sobers us one by one.

"This is the perfect situation for predators. Women are drugged and raped in the bathrooms and behind the dumpsters. They're hauled into vans and smuggled across the Mexican border or shipped out of ports to other continents to be trafficked," he continues as he puts his notepad in his shirt pocket.

"Hear that again; you most likely saved her from being raped or sold as a sex slave. You did good but let this be a lesson to you. These things don't always end this well. Keep your eyes open, be aware of your surroundings, and stick to a buddy system. The world is ugly, and you don't always get to learn from some else's lesson that you alone are responsible for your safety. Alright? Everyone okay? Good. Enjoy the rest of your break kids, and please be safe."

It's dead silent as we all take in his warning. Dylan suddenly sits down on the curb, like his legs gave out, cradling his head in his hands, and I know he's blaming himself for leaving her at the bar.

I think back to so many times that we blindly accepted drinks at parties over the last two years. I'm not ignorant to the threat. I know better than this. It wasn't my drink that was drugged tonight, but it very well could have been. I look around at the girls teary faces and we all make eye contact, and I know they're thinking the same thing I am.

We will do better.

The guys straighten, shoulders squared, and I read the promise in their eyes too.

We will watch better.

* * *

When Gabby comes to at the hospital, she immediately breaks down, thinking

Chapter 16

the worst. She knew she was drugged before the doctor came in with her results and verified; GHB. The date rape drug. She recounts her experience with a female officer who is writing everything down on her notepad while Cora, Raven, Dylan and I give our support.

"I was waiting at the bar for Dylan's water and talking to some girl on my right. I had my drink on the left and I must have looked away. When I turned to grab it there was a guy there. He asked me my name, but I acted like I couldn't hear him. There wasn't much left in my drink, but I chugged it because I wanted to leave the cup there when I took Dylan his water. It tasted really weird, but I don't normally drink tequila, and I was a little buzzed, so I didn't think much of it. It gets fuzzy after that." She pulls her knees to her chest, hugging them.

"My head started swimming and all of the lights got brighter and bigger. My tongue felt like fluff, and I couldn't talk. I think I heard him say "Come with me, I know where to go," but it could be anything similar. I just felt heavy, like I couldn't move my limbs and I was so scared." She cries more, unable to hold it in. "It was terrifying, but I couldn't control my body. I don't remember anything after that." Dylan and Raven are holding each of her hands, while the tears run down her face.

Unfortunately, there are no clues to identify the predator. It was dark and crazy with all the foam, and she was tipsy and not paying attention. Cora and I were so focused on grabbing Gabby that we probably couldn't pick him out of a lineup, and the guys were so worked up that their observations are just as unreliable.

I'm so relieved that we found her in time, but it's the thought of what could have happened. Pure horror, that's what we're feeling. I can't seem to stop trembling, imagining that we never got to see sweet Gabby again, imagining her being violated and broken. It's hard to let relief take over, even looking at her alive and well in the hospital bed.

By the time we're all trudging into the hotel, the sun is peeking over the ocean's horizon. I feel tainted, dirty by proxy. Like I've lost sight of things over the past week, or who knows, maybe even longer. I miss home and the comfort that it brings me. There aren't hangovers and evil strangers who view women as a hole to rape or sell for profit, no dirty bar floors or last night's puke splats littering the sidewalks.

There is nothing here but a good story to tell your friends when you get home, once the sweat and body paint has been showered off and you feel clean and good again. Once the grimy parts start to fade in your memory and the smell of tequila and weed smoke are washing down the drain, you're left with the good, the funny, the kind of carefree bliss that only a college kid on Spring Break can experience. These are the stories that come out of spring break, but now that I have one, I don't want it.

It wasn't worth the cost.

Chapter 17

antiscians
(n) *people who live on opposite sides of the world, "whose shadows at noon are cast in opposite directions"*

After we got back from Spring Break, the weeks took on the kind of speed that only exist between mid-semester and finals. That is to say, they flew by. And then, classes were done, and we were packing up the house to leave for the summer. I have such mixed feelings about going home. On one hand, I get another shot at a national title and being that much closer to landing a spot on the Olympic team next year.

On another, I'll miss my friends so much. Gabby and Cora have been such a source of comfort and happiness this year, and the girls on our team have given me amazing memories.

And most of all, how do I say goodbye to Luca? There hasn't been a day that I haven't seen him since August, aside from Thanksgiving and Christmas, and the distance is already wearing on me. Well, on us, if I'm to be honest.

The closer we've gotten to D-Day (Driving Home Day) the surlier Luca's gotten and the sadder I've become. Every summer Luca works sixty to seventy-hour weeks in the restaurant that his mother and Nonna run together to save money for the school year. I'll be working close to forty hours a week with my home elite team. He's been clingier than usual, and I can't fault him for it, because I'm feeling the dread, too. I wish we could visit each other during the summer, but our schedules are packed.

Gabby pokes her head through my doorway as I'm zipping up another suitcase. We're not fully packing since her parents are keeping the house rented for us, and Gabby is staying here this summer with Dylan.

Gabby had to tell them about Spring Break, since they were going to get the hospital bill, so they were actually okay with Dylan staying for Summer. Plus, she's an adult, but I can't help but think that my parents would pitch a fit.

"When are you two heading out," she asks, bouncing as she flops onto the bed. I heave a sigh and flop down next to her.

"Day after tomorrow," I groan out. "The drive is horrendous, but we're stopping in Tennessee overnight to break it up."

"How long is the total drive?"

"Twenty-four freaking hours." Double groan.

"Good God woman, no wonder you're moping around!" she gasps.

I throw my arm over my face, well aware that I'm being melodramatic and not caring at all. A big Luca shaped part of me doesn't want to go at all.

"No kidding. I would say screw it and let's fly, but I need the jeep this summer."

"Well, maybe you can find some car games to break it up. Twelve hours in the car for two days straight would make me lose my mind."

"I found some audio books that Raven said she would be willing to listen to, so there's that. What are you and Dylan going to do this summer with all of us out of the house?" I ask, nudging her side lasciviously.

She laughs, pushing my shoulder. "Not christening every bed in the house, not that at all," she jokes. At least, I hope.

"Kidding," she says. "I actually got a job at one of the women's shelters downtown, and Dylan is coaching lacrosse at a youth camp that his coach helped set up through the rec center."

She doesn't have to work, so of course she and her heart of gold found a job purely for the sake of helping others. Gabby is a true gem. And if working through the aftermath of her being drugged brought us all even closer, it

Chapter 17

definitely made her and Dylan inseparable.

"Well, I think that's amazing, Gabby Goo."

"Thanks, Lennie Loo."

Cora comes bursting through the door like a rocket, followed by Raven who is tickling her. They both fall on the bed in a pile of giggles.

"How come you bitches have cute nicknames and we don't," Cora asks, smacking Raven on the butt to get her moving over.

"Maybe because Raven Roo and Cora Coo sound ridiculous?" Raven pipes up.

"And Gabby Goo is better?"

"Hey!" I say, smacking Cora's arm. "Gabby Goo is cute, it fits her! She's warm and gooey like a fresh baked cookie!"

A solid three seconds of ringing silence fills the room before we all burst out laughing, a tangle of arms and legs and friendship.

Yeah, I'll miss this.

Later that night, as I untangle myself from Luca, I'm feeling the weight of leaving even more. We haven't said much, just ate dinner and watched a movie in bed before losing ourselves in each other. Light touches turned to tight holds, which turned into intense kissing and almost frantic sex. Part of me feels like we're both being dramatic about the whole thing. I mean, it's two months. There are couples who deal with far more distance for longer periods of time.

"We can do this, Luca. I know it seems like forever, but it's two months. We'll both be so busy that it will fly by, just watch." It's as much a pep talk for me as it is for him.

He's quiet for a bit, playing with my hair while I lay my head on his chest.

"I know babe. It sucks, but I know. I'll just miss this."

"This?" I ask, taken aback. As in, *sex?*

He hears it in my tone because he immediately backtracks.

"Jesus, sweetheart, not *this* this, just being with you. Having you physically here to hold and kiss and just be."

I settle back, calming. I'm more on edge than I thought.

"Well, the good news is that you have me all night and all day tomorrow."

"I'm still staying the night at your house tomorrow night, right?"

Crap. I forgot about that. Cora mentioned that she wanted us to hang out together for our last night, but I'm sure I can turn it into boyfriends included.

"Yes, as long as you're good with waking up at five am to say goodbye to me."

"Of course, babe." He kisses me and that's the last talking we do for the rest of the night.

* * *

"I want you to throw that layout like you're trying to break it," Coach Fatima said to me. "I want clean and tight. We have one more week to shape up routines, and you're on the right track."

I'm back in my home gym Beaux Belles, an all-female gym, including my coaches.

I nod, trying to catch my breath after my third pass at this full twisting double layout. I've been at it for three weeks now, and it feels a lot like cramming for my finals did.

Like last summer, I've gone from an enforced twenty hours a week of training to double that, so I've had some catching up to do in terms of stamina. The first week was *brutal*, but I'm looking and feeling much better now.

Coach Lisa and Coach Jess are with other gymnasts, and like Coach Fatima, they're all highly decorated gymnasts in their own right and they've been invaluable to me over the years. Switching from college to elite and back every year takes some adjustments, but it's all-or-nothing time.

There is a reason most Olympic gymnasts choose college *after* the Olympics. After training as an elite gymnast for years, moving to NCAA is like a rest break. Obviously, I'm not going this route because it's easy. If anything, it's much harder to accomplish than if I were to make the national team and get selected for the Olympic team when I was seventeen. Now, at almost twenty-one years old, I may be in my prime, but I'm wiped out.

I shake it off, because no one ever met their goals by letting hard work keep them from persevering.

Chapter 17

Nationals starts on June 24th in Salt Lake City this year. I've spent almost every waking moment getting new callouses, bigger blisters, sore muscles, and everything in between in preparation for the biggest competition of the summer. Olympic trials are next year, so if I have to endure the pain and exhaustion in order to prepare, then that's what I'll do.

I want to make the National team so badly that I can taste it. It tastes like sweat, pain, and chalk dust…but still.

After a quick water break, I line up at the corner of the mat again. I shut out my inner voice, the one that says I can't do this, that I'll choke on the landing, that I'm not good enough for the national team and for the Olympics. I lock that voice in a box and throw away the key so that it's just me and the mat.

On an inhale, I run full speed until I hit the center of the mat, launching into a round off back handspring. From there I launch my body vertically up, rotating my feet over my head while keeping my body straight in midair, and twist my body 360 degrees for a full rotation, sticking my landing without the previous stumbles.

"That's what I'm talking about!" Coach Lisa shouts and comes over to give me a big slap on the back. "That's how you stick it at Nationals, Len!"

I feel almost supernatural and it's an addicting feeling. When you learn a new skill after weeks and sometimes months of working towards it, to finally nail it and do it perfectly…if I could bottle the feeling, world peace would be ours within days.

A few hours later I walk into my house, floating on my cloud nine, and throw my gym bag in the laundry room to sort through later. Momma and Raven are in the kitchen making something delicious, going by the smell. I've been at the gym for six hours and I am starving.

"How was practice," Raven asks, dumping cooked pasta into the sink strainer.

"Tiring, but good. Finally nailed my Chusovitina!"

"Lord, it was hard watching it on YouTube, I think I'll have to cover my eyes when we're in Utah," Momma says with a little shudder.

"Well, prepare yourself now, because it's a big part of my floor routine," I say. "When's dinner? I could eat a horse."

"*Lenore Elizabeth*," my mom gripes at me, and I laugh. Nothing stirs her like someone talking about her babies.

Allan and Gus are here for dinner tonight, which is a nice treat, since they share an apartment in Baton Rouge, and we all settle around the table and dig in. The number of calories I need to intake almost doubled with my advanced hours in the gym, so pasta with meatballs was a great choice.

After I surface from shoveling the first few bites of food in my mouth, everyone is talking about Maddie starting at LSU this fall.

"I think I'm going to love dorm life," she's saying. "Plus, it's not like the two boneheads are going to be far away."

Our parents made a big push to keep Maddie at home instead of in the dorms, but she stuck to her guns, and they eventually let her have her way. I think they're finally tired after us four eldest pushed back at them for so long.

"It's a huge part of the college experience!" Raven was saying in her defense.

"You mean a bigger part of the college experience than partying?" Allan says teasingly.

"Well, you'd know all about that Allan," Daddy says slyly. "Seeing as how you and your brother got the twins prepared for partying all those nights behind the barn, yeah?"

All of our eating comes to an abrupt halt as we stare at our father with shock, mouths gaping.

"You knew about that?!" Gus stammers out while Momma laughs.

"You're not exactly stealthy, y'all. Of course, we knew about it," she says. "Why do you think I made Maddie practice extra hard last spring when she tried to say she had food poisoning the night after one of y'alls 'secret' bonfires?"

Maddie turns bright red.

Huh. Just when we thought we'd gotten one over on them. I guess they let us get away with a little fun after all.

The next week flies by in a haze of frenzied practicing, and before I know it, I'm at the convention center in Salt Lake City. Nationals is a four-day event, with hundreds of gymnasts in different age and genre groups, and they pack a ton into those days. I have two full days of competition, and on each day,

Chapter 17

we do our routines for vault, then uneven bars, then beam, and finally floor.

Day one I finish fifth, and I am *deeply* disappointed. I lost points for things that should be second nature at this point. I had two breaks in my beam routine where I visibly hesitated, and I'm sure I frowned when I wobbled after a brief dizzy spell mid-twist.

Judges are like vigilantes looking for the barest flinch or mouth twitch. If you think they're scoring just based on your execution and difficulty of skill, oh no. They go so much more granular than that.

Points are taken for routines not looking perfectly polished and seamless. If you pause just a beat too long, points are deducted. If your hair comes loose and gets in your face, if you look less than one hundred percent put together, points are deducted. If you mess up, if you misstep, you better keep that stoic poker face, or yep…you guessed it. Judges deduct points for the misstep *and* for the facial expression. And if your tuf-skin spray gives out and your leotard rides up and gives you a wedgie, don't you dare pull it out mid-routine, or…see where I'm going with this?

Points. Points! POINTS!

"Shake that off," Coach Jess says. She grabs me by the shoulders and looks me in the eye with laser focus. "I know you're gunning for top three and for good reason. You get another chance tomorrow, so give yourself five minutes to wallow, and then pull up your big girl panties and do the thing, Len. Fifth out of twenty-eight gymnasts is fantastic. The top six get a spot on the National team and immediate qualifier for the Olympic trials next summer if you do this well again at Nationals. You. Got. This."

I sag, grateful for her belief in me.

"Thanks Jess. Tomorrow will be better. I needed to hear that."

Tomorrow *will* be better.

And it was.

I took notes from my point deductions and focused inward all night and the next morning. By the time I stepped up to the vault runner, I was in that special part of my head space that I save for meets. The place that's quiet from inner dilemma, from self-doubt and from fear.

I wore my Competition Lennie armor, and I did exactly what Coach Jess told me to do.

I did the thing.

I came in second and waves of joy radiated through me when I stood on the podium while my family and coaches screamed as loud as they could.

Every half-dollar sized blister, every sprain, strain, and pain I've endured for sixteen years has led to this point. All of the hours after school and on weekends, missing football games, parties, lazy pool days. All the sacrifice.

It was all worth it.

Maddie tried to face-time Luca when I was up so that he could see my routines, but reception was spotty in the convention center, so she sent him videos instead. I face-timed him after and we spoke for two hours about everything that went down. He was so happy for me. I let myself cry that night because I missed him, but it quickly morphed into happy tears. I made the freaking NATIONAL TEAM!!!

Things move quickly after that.

The National Gymnastics headquarters is in Texas, so for the month of July, I've lived and trained there with the team. There are twenty-eight of us on the senior women's team, and we're all here for the month training before heading back to home gyms, or in a few of our cases, college. I was surprised to hear that there are five other girls on NCAA teams across the country.

It's thirty-two hours of training over six days, plus my one remote class that I signed up for over the summer. It didn't leave much time to talk to Luca, much to our disappointment. Everything comes to a head the last week of training camp after weeks of frustration over the distance between us. It feels like we're on opposite sides of the world.

"What do you mean we can't talk later?"

"I'm sorry, but this last week is a big push for me. I've worked so hard this summer."

"Len," he says, exasperated. "I know, it's all you talk about. It's all I've heard this summer. News flash, I've been busting my ass, too, but you don't see me shoving facts down your throat every time you give me an ounce of your time. I don't even feel like I have a damn girlfriend anymore!"

My mouth drops, and I don't know what to say. I've been living out my dream, and suddenly I'm a bad girlfriend? He's *never* spoken to me like this before.

"Well thanks for making me sound like I just brag about my accomplishments every time we speak. I didn't realize it was getting in the way of making sure you feel like you still have a girlfriend!"

"I'm just tired of not being a priority to you, it's always been like this at school, and I understood because hockey keeps me busy too, but now that you're on the national team it's like fuck me, right?"

"No, not right! This is completely unfair."

"Yeah. Sure. Have fun tonight, I guess I'll talk to you when you're free from your busy schedule and remember that you have a boyfriend who loves you."

And then he hangs up.

He. Hung. Up. On. Me.

Tears of frustration flow down my face as I sit in stunned silence. Have I seriously talked of nothing else all summer? Of course, I have, I'm driven, not vain. I've made him my only priority other than gymnastics and school.

No. I shake my head to myself and take a calming breath.

This is Luca acting out because he misses me and honestly just does not do well when things aren't going his way. It's a big flaw of his, but that's the thing about love. We love our other half in spite of their shortcomings. We all have them. Loving Luca means staying with him despite his sudden urge to be selfish and well, spoiled. Distance hurts, but things will be better when we're back together.

Everything will be fine.

Chapter 18

retrouvaille
(n) the joy of meeting or finding someone again after a long separation; rediscovery

YEAR THREE

Everything was not fine.

Luca didn't speak to me for five days, unheard of throughout the entirety of our relationship. I was busy wrapping up in Texas so one may think my mind was otherwise occupied, but no… I managed plenty of time to feel the sting.

I questioned everything about this summer. Had I truly made him feel like he didn't matter? Because right now that's exactly how his silence was making me feel, and it hurt.

Badly.

I hate that I made him feel this way, and after thinking things over, I can see where he's coming from. But still.

He finally called me the morning of the sixth day when I was rage packing back at home. I started crying as soon as I picked up and heard his apology.

"I'm sorry," he said quietly.

I sniffled. "Thank you. I'm sorry too. I think I tunnel-visioned myself into thinking we would be fine if we just stayed busy this summer."

Chapter 18

"Yeah, you did. But I could have been less of a fucking baby about it. Or maybe spoke up and made my feelings known sooner instead of blowing up at you."

More sniffles.

"Shit, sweetheart, please don't cry."

"Why did you wait so long to call me?" I ask, my voice breaking. I can't help giving into my feels after forcing myself to move on auto pilot for almost a week to keep from breaking down.

"Babe…I was just working through some things. Okay? You and I are good, this was just a blip." He sounds strained and sad, and I just don't have it in me to stay upset. It takes way too much energy to stay mad.

"Yes, a blip," I say, much calmer now that my tears are out of the way. "Our first fight in almost a year isn't bad, right?"

He huffs out a laugh. "Yeah, I like that. Only a few months until the big one year."

"I love you Luca. Just one week and we'll be together again."

"I love you too, Len."

We talked for over an hour that day, and it was the salve to my wounds. I was able to spend a really great last week with my family before Raven and I loaded the Jeep up and headed back to Boston.

But once on campus for our third year, it became apparent that things hadn't changed much with Luca. I couldn't put my finger on anything super tangible that occurred during the first two months we were back. A quiet, grumpy mood here, an out-of-the blue moment where he needs assurance that I'm here and not pulling away from him, there.

The jealousy is something new, though.

This made itself known after Chase and I were assigned a joint project in our Media Psychology class in September.

"Tell me again why you're spending all evening with Chase? Again?" he griped at me as I packed my bag for the library. We're in my room after watching a movie to relax after class and practices.

"Because we have a month to do our project, and we have only two nights each week that we can get together to work on it," I spell out, trying to stay patient with him.

He lays on the bed, staring at the ceiling, not saying anything. Finally, I throw my bag on the bed, standing over him with my hands on my hips to get his attention.

"Alright, that's it. What has gotten into you?!"

He sits up in bed and grabs my hands.

"Chase is into you Len, how are you this blind?!" He looks a little crazed, and I'm mystified.

"Luca. Chase O'Leary is not into me. Chase is our friend. He's my classmate. He's on your freaking team, and you're his captain. He's literally never done anything even remotely inappropriate towards me! And even if he did, *hello*, why would I stay friends with him, that's not me and you know it. Why are you *acting this way*?" I'm getting to my limits here with his crap.

He looks down, dropping his face in his hands.

"I don't know babe. Fuck! I'm sorry, this is lame, even I can hear how pathetic I sound."

I grab his face and kiss him.

"You're not pathetic, Luca. Just lighten up. I love spending time with you, but I'm a package deal, just like you. Gymnastics and hockey and school and friends. It's okay to have balance. It's not okay to give me a hard time for working on schoolwork with another guy. More specifically, a guy who has been a good friend to both of us."

He hugs me around the middle and that's the end of that. Sweet Jesus, I hope he's done with this crap.

* * *

By the time October rolls around, things are back to normal between me and Luca.

On the date of my first-ever anniversary, I breeze through his front door with ingredients to make Luca's favorite thing—red beans and rice. Well, I'm making it for the house, but it's mostly for him. We're going to see a movie later on, but he requested dinner at the house so we could be alone for a bit.

Chapter 18

"Hi!" I exclaim, giving him a huge smacking kiss.

"You're perky," he laughs out while I hang around his neck.

"I'm just so happy! One year!"

I say hi to Diego and Isaiah in the kitchen where they're doing homework at the bar.

Isaiah rubs his palms together, watching me take out the food and crockpot.

"Hey thanks for asking Lennie out, man," he says to Luca. "It's really working out well for me."

I get beans and ham hock all setup in the crock pot and pull Luca to his bedroom so I can give him his gift.

I got the idea from watching Raven put together her portfolio for her photography class. I created a printed photo book of Luca's life for him, from infancy to now, with his mom and Nonna's help. They scanned in old pictures for me, and I added all of the ones I have of us and our friends together from the past year. It turned out great, and the kicker is that his mom had a ton of Luca and his father before he passed.

He unwraps it while I sit, fidgeting, waiting for him to look through them all.

"Babe," he says softly, his eyes flitting from picture to picture. If he were less manly, I'm sure he'd shed a tear, but I read the emotion in his voice just the same.

"I love it. This is perfect. I don't deserve you."

I smack him on the shoulder and fold myself in his lap. "Hush, yes you do. I love my locket, thank you."

He had given me a tiny heart locket for me to put our picture in.

He squeezes me tight and heaves a huge sigh into my hair.

"I love you, Len."

"I love you too."

I give him one last kiss. "Come on, I need to start the rice."

We head to the kitchen where I have him chopping onion while I brown the uncooked rice grains, a little trick to flavorful rice. Diego heads into the kitchen looking confused and says "Luc? This chick says she knows you?"

A pretty girl with olive skin and black hair walks in behind Dylan.

"Surprise!" she says, showing a little uncertainty. She's beaming and Luca immediately looks up and drops his knife, looking horrified.

"Bianca? What the hell are you doing here," he harshly asks.

Her face drops. I look between the two of them with an ache forming in my stomach.

"I'm in town visiting my cousin."

She's looking a lot less happy than when she walked in. She wrings her hands together. "I haven't seen you since you left and I just thought it would be nice to come see you, to say hi."

He turns to me with the worst look on his face. It's a look that says he knows what's about to happen is going to hurt.

Bianca looks at me. "Am I interrupting something?"

"I'm Lennie," I start, stepping forward. "Luca's girlfriend. We're cooking our anniversary dinner. How do you two know each other?"

My hands start shaking as I notice the change in her. Because right now, she's looking angry. Very angry.

"Girlfriend. Anniversary dinner," she bites out, staring daggers at Luca who has now graduated from looking panicked to terrified. "I'm assuming this is not a one month thing? You were together in July?"

"Yes, we've been together for a year. Luca? What's going on?"

My voice is shaking, and butterflies erupt in my belly, fighting for room with my nerves and the sudden fear that I know exactly what is happening here.

He hangs his head and mutters "Fuck!" He puts is hands on his head, looking at the ceiling. Like there are answers up there for him to read.

"Luca, what is happening?! What did you do?" I yell, getting frantic.

"He slept with me at a party in July. That night and again in the morning. He said that he wasn't in the *head space* for a girlfriend when I tried to see him after. I thought it was just because I lived in New York and he went to school in Boston, but no. Apparently it's because I was only good enough to be a place holder for his *girlfriend*, who he *definitely didn't fucking mention at the time!*" She progresses to yelling, and the silence after she finishes has weight.

If she says anything after that, I don't catch it. Ringing fills my ears as the

Chapter 18

shock reverberates through my body, waves of alternating ice and fire. I fall back against the counter and drop the spatula I was holding, vaguely aware of the tears that are starting to track down my face.

He rushes over to me, grabbing my face in his hands.

"Len, *please*, please babe. I'm so sorry! It was right after our fight, and I was mad and lonely and got wasted at a party with a bunch of coworkers. She was there, paying attention to me. It was a weak moment, and it meant nothing."

I look over at her and she's crying angry tears as she watches us. "I've wanted to be with you since high school Luca, but not like this. You're an absolute *asshole*! I'm so sorry Lennie, I had no idea. I'm so sorry!" She runs out of the house leaving utter silence in her wake. Diego sends a disgusted glare towards Luca and leaves the kitchen, shaking his head.

The smell of burning rice fills the room and I jerkily grab the pan off the burner and throw it in the sink. I take a deep rattling breath, trying to compose myself.

Turning back around to face my cheating boyfriend, I try to make sense of things.

"So let me get this straight. We're separated for *two* whole months while I was in training camp, you throw a fit because I'm busy with things after I warned you that I would be, and so you decide to cheat on me?! For what, revenge? Because I was with teammates in Texas, Luca? Finishing my final for summer class, Luca?"

At this point I'm pacing the kitchen and running my fingers through my wild hair before fisting the strands, clinging to the pinch of pain to help me focus. "And not only did you cheat on me, but the next morning when you woke up, you did it again?! Sober? How is this happening right now," I cry out, giving into the rage and confusion and hurt coursing through my body.

He's crying, too, but I can't find it in me to be moved. I never, ever, would have thought that he'd do something like this.

"It all makes sense to me now. You, being moody, and clingy, acting like I was just going to up and fall out of love with you, or that you had any reason to be *jealous* when I never did *anything to deserve it!*"

I'm cycling through emotions faster than I can handle. Meanwhile, he's just standing there, shame faced.

"Babe," he begs weakly. "It was a mistake. I screwed up and I'm so, so sorry. We can come back from this. Please."

I scoff, settling for a second on wrath. "What did you say to me when you finally called me after five days of silence? Five days of making me sweat when I was missing you and sad that you were upset with me after you hung up on me? This was *just a blip?*"

I shove him away and grab my purse and keys. The rest can rot here for all I care. I move past him towards the door, ready to get out of this house, away from this man who just hurt me worse than I've ever been hurt before.

"It was a mistake," he repeats, grabbing me to stop me as he tried to hug me.

I slap a palm on his chest and move him back from me.

"No Luca. It was a decision. And it cost you me."

I slam the door shut and run to the Jeep. Somehow I make it home, driving exactly the speed limit with no music playing, in a zombie-like trance.

I walk into a scene of domestic bliss. Gabby and Raven are making cookies while Cora and Jared are watching The Office in the living room.

The girls look to me, take in my splotchy face, swollen eyes and mascara tear stains, and immediately come over to me.

"Ohhhh no, what's wrong?"

"Who're we killing, Len?"

"Lennie Loo? Are you okay?"

"No," I sob out. "I'm not *fucking okay!*"

And then I break down in a spectacular display of emotions, leaking my broken heart all over the floor.

Jared pops up from the couch like his ass is on fire, grabs his keys and kisses Cora on the cheek. "I'm out of here, you girls seem like you need privacy. I hope things are okay, Lennie," he says, bolting out of the house.

Yeah, girl tears tend to clear guys out of a room.

We settle on the couch, and I tell them every horrifying detail. Reliving the looks on Bianca and Luca's faces, the feelings of humiliation, despair, the complete devastation. The anger.

At the end of it, Gabby is hugging me, stroking my hair, and crying with

Chapter 18

me while Raven and Cora are prepared to go beat Luca's door down, taking him with it.

"That fucking snakey, cocky, lazy, *no good mother fucker!*" Raven rages, pacing in front of me. "I could literally kill him! I knew he wasn't good enough for you, but goddamn. Was she even pretty?!"

She pauses, looking over to me.

"Don't answer that, it's not the point. Of course, she's not prettier than you," she says to herself, lost in a rage. Like looks matter at this point.

"Let's go Raven, I'm ready to beat his ass," Cora bites out, standing up.

"No one is going anywhere!" Gabby yells, making us all jump. "Lennie is hurting, and the last thing she needs is to add this stress to it. You're not going over there to kill him. Calm down. Lennie needs us tonight, so put aside your anger and let's just be there, alright?"

Not used to any kind of exclamation from calm, sweet Gabby, everyone shuts up, including me.

I spend the rest of the night absolutely wallowing in self-pity. The girls tried so hard to help, vacillating between comforting me and talking shit about Luca, but ultimately nothing made me feel better about anything.

The next morning, I wake up to fifteen text messages, six missed calls, and two voicemails from Luca. I throw my phone on the bed and heave a huge, shaky sigh.

I wish I had known that my first one-year anniversary would turn into one of the absolute worst days of my life.

I would have stayed in bed.

Chapter 19

toska
(n) a dull ache of the soul, a sick pining, a spiritual anguish

Boston explodes into Autumn around me, leaves showing off with their colors of flames, and that familiar smell that is uniquely autumn fills the air.

Not that I'm able to enjoy it.

I see in shades of gray, smells didn't register to me, and if my surroundings are beautiful in any way, well…let's just say I'm less than receptive. For the past week I've skipped classes, emailing my professors that I was sick and ignoring assignments. I called my gymnastics coaches and faked the flu, getting bed rest orders for the next week.

I just wanted to hide.

Disappear.

The thought of facing people, having to slap a fake smile on my face to reassure everyone that I'm okay when I clearly am not…I just can't.

How could I be okay? The person that I gave my heart to betrayed me. I've never had to learn this lesson before, and I felt like it would kill me. I leaned on him, shared so much of myself with him, gave him every part of me, and now that it's over, I don't know what I have left for myself.

So yeah, I hid. I stayed in my room, ignoring the two happy couples as they walked past my door, their peppy voices filtering through. Ignored my

Chapter 19

sister who vacillated from being suffocating or needing to be held back from murdering Luca, and nothing in between.

Ignored every text and phone call and voicemail from my cheating ex-boyfriend. I deleted every last one. It was too painful to read his words and listen to his voice, so I didn't.

Instead, I read every book I could that didn't involve love. Thrillers, murder mysteries, and one absolutely terrifying book called Stolen Tongues which scared me so thoroughly that I had to watch a Disney movie just so I could sleep.

I felt so heavy. It was all I could do to keep up with my stretches.

It wasn't until my advisor called me into her office that I started to wake up from my fog of grief.

Beth Newbury has been my advisor since my freshman year. All student athletes at Kalon meet with their advisors weekly, but I called out of our meeting last week, like everything else. I knew I couldn't avoid it again when she reached out to remind me.

"How are you feeling, Lennie? You're looking very pale, and you've lost weight. Still rundown after the flu?"

I cringe internally, feeling really slimy about lying to everyone. If I'd told the truth though, I doubt I would have gotten any sympathy. How does one properly convey that getting your heart broken feels like dying? A relationship ending so brutally feels like a death. I guess in a way it is. A death of something.

"I'm okay, doing a little better," I say, quietly. My voice is hoarse after a week of disuse.

"I kept track of your grades, and they've fallen a bit in the past week. Were you unable to complete work from home?"

Now is the part that I tell the truth, confess that I've had zero drive or focus or hell, even willingness to peel myself out of bed to shower. All I wanted to do was get lost in other people's stories. It helped me forget mine while I was reading about their lives. But I don't.

"I wasn't able to get out of bed. I'll make up the work after speaking to my professors."

My answer placates her, and we moved on to other topics. I felt uneasy after leaving the meeting, uncomfortable in my skin.

I just want to get back to my bed and my safe space, my quiet room with its fluffy blankets and white twinkle lights.

Instead, as I was looking down and picking at a callous on my hand, I ran smack into a familiar chest, and looked up into haunted eyes.

I managed to avoid Luca for eight days. Not that I was counting.

We stand there for a beat, looking at each other.

"Lennie," he starts, but I'm already moving past him, walking as fast as I can without running to my vehicle.

"Len, wait-God," he huffs, catching up to me. He grabs my arm to stop me. "Please, sweetheart, please stop."

It's the term of endearment that does it.

I stop in my tracks and look at him, really taking him in this time. His blonde hair is a mess, like he's been trying to pull it out by the roots. He looks thinner, and the dark circles under his eyes rival only my own. Seeing him again rips a new fissure in my already broken heart.

He looks like I feel, like I'm sure I look.

Broken.

I sigh, looking at the heavens, and wonder what the right move is. *Do I talk to him. Break open the wound again? Will it give me closure?* I still love him and I'm not sure how much time will go on before that goes away.

But I can never be with him again. Not after what he did. And the funny thing? It isn't even the cheating that's the worst part. It was his reason. He got *mad* that he didn't get his way. He was *angry* that he wasn't one hundred percent my priority. He was *upset* because I, *for once*, didn't put him first.

Yeah. I think talking to him will give me closure after all.

"You can come over at three today," I say. Hope blooms in his eyes, and I shut it down hard. "We can talk, hear each other out, and get the closure that we need. Because Luca? This talk is just that. Closure."

I know everyone will be out of the house then.

Can't have my sister arrested for murder when her life is just beginning.

* * *

Chapter 19

When Luca shows up at my door, he looks even more exhausted than earlier.

We settle on the couch facing each other. I pull my knees up to my chest, rest my chin on top, and look at him. He leans down, putting his elbows on his knees, cradling his head in his hands and we spend a few minutes just existing in the same space for the first time in over a week.

"Lennie," he starts. "I know you're mad and hurt. I am so sorry, babe, so fucking sorry that I can't even put it into words."

"I know that you're sorry," I say sadly. "I'm not sure that I'm at a place to forgive you Luca. Just tell me, why? How can you be so selfish with my time, so selfish as to not support me when I am fighting for my dream. Don't I support you? Haven't I always been understanding of your schedule and your time? Why couldn't you give that to me?"

"Because I always felt like I was going to lose you!" he exploded at me. "You're an amazing gymnast, you're so dedicated and driven, Len. I'm in hockey purely to pay for my scholarship at this point. I can't even say that I love it anymore, and I've been questioning things all year. I'm a senior, and all I've thought on repeat is 'what am I going to do with my life'? I don't know, and you do, and it killed me to think that you'd be doing these big things without me, and I guess I just grew to resent it."

His words stun me, and I flop back on the couch. I had no clue, no inkling that he'd been feeling this way. I shake my head to clear it.

"And I don't know, it was like that voice in my head was telling me that you were moving onto bigger and better things without me, my resentment just kept growing so much over the summer and that night I just snapped. I was so angry at you just for thriving without me, I was pissed off at myself for feeling this way, feeling like a fucking loser that I just…acted out." He cringes, looking ashamed.

"I wanted to forget, to forget who I was, and yeah, I can admit now that I was feeling spiteful. I drank too much, and those voices telling me I wasn't good enough got louder and when Bianca came onto me and showered me with attention, I let it make me feel good. Like a man, and not some loser crying about his girlfriend doing great things, because if I can't be there for her and get out of my own head, then what kind of man am I?"

Tears are falling down his face now and I start to cry too.

"I barely remember sleeping with her. When I woke up, I was still half drunk, but I wanted to stay in that bubble. I knew I had already fucked up so badly, and I wanted to forget that too. And after, I was so horrified with myself that I stayed drunk in my room all those nights after getting home from work. I didn't trust myself to talk to you. I wasn't trying to punish you, I was wallowing and feeling like the worst person on the planet because I cheated on my sweet, beautiful girlfriend. I wished so hard that I could go back and take everything back, and I had to come to terms with what I did."

"And did you?" I ask. He shakes his head and looks at me through swollen, red eyes. I'm sure I look the same.

"No, sweetheart. I didn't. I did anything I could to quiet the noise in my mind, but it just kept playing over again in my mind. Over and over and over until it tortured the absolute shit out of me." He runs his hand through his hair as he inhales shakily.

"Every day that led up to our anniversary, it was in the back of my mind. What I did. How much I fucked up, how I knew I'd ruined it all. And when you gave me that thoughtful gift, I almost cried and begged you to never leave me. Because I was honest when I said I didn't deserve you. I know that now."

Ringing silence fills the space between us. I take a deep, cleansing breath, forcing the tears to stop. My heart is breaking all over again, and I would do just about anything to rid myself of this physical ache. But the pain demands to be felt and so I push on.

"Wow. I wasn't expecting any of that. I'm sorry that you've been feeling this way for so long, I really am. I hate that for you. I can see how things could spiral in your mind like that."

And I *am* sorry. Not that I did anything wrong. I won't allow myself to feel guilt over his feelings, they're his own. But I can see things through his eyes a bit, and knowing what I know now, I see other things too.

Luca feels trapped in his own life. He felt that our happiness was threatened by my dedication to my sport, by my level of availability to him. He has things to work through, and he's waited until the golden hour to figure out what he wants to do with his life and now panic has set in, making him feel cornered.

Chapter 19

And I can see now that he is deeply, deeply insecure.

All things I didn't know but knowing them doesn't make the situation better.

Except maybe it lessens my ability to hate him. Not his actions, however. Those are inexcusable. But I can see the man behind the action, and I can recognize that he hurt himself almost as much as he hurt me.

"I can't move past this for us to be together, Luca. I can't. I'm sorry for how you've been feeling, for beating yourself up, for you feeling so bad. Having felt this kind of pain, I can say that I wouldn't wish this on my worst enemy. But we can't be together anymore. You have some things that you need to work on, and I hope that you can learn to be more secure and more accepting, that you can manage your expectations in your next relationship and allow yourself to be vulnerable and honest. I forgive you, and I hope you can forgive yourself."

He hangs his head on a choked sob before nodding, hearing the conviction in my voice. The finality.

Before he leaves, I let him give me a bone crushing hug. My tears soak his sweater and his fall into my hair.

Then he kisses me on top of my head and just like that, he's gone.

More milestones crossed off the list of life.

First relationship.

First anniversary.

First breakup.

First heartbreak.

All unavoidably painful and changing me forever.

Chapter 20

abscond

(v) to secretly depart and hide oneself

I wish I could say that I was back to my old self after ending things with Luca. But I wasn't. Not even close.

It didn't take me long to tire of the pitying looks everyone gave, and I tired even faster of constantly being asked if I was okay.

Sure, I am, if being okay feels like your shredded heart was ripped out of your chest, messily taped back together, and then shoved back in, off center.

I started to internalize everything I was feeling. I can never go back and see love with innocent eyes, never forget the pain it caused me. Love has the ability to hurt so much more than I ever could have known.

So, I spend my time not thinking about Luca. Easier said than done for a classic over-thinker. The only solution was to keep busy. Which is why I snuck back into the training center after everyone left open gym on a Saturday in November. I need to work through some things for my new bars routine. I'm completely flaunting the strict twenty hours a week rule, but I've been putting in double these hours in elite for years.

I can handle this.

I ignore all other thoughts about this being dangerous. I *need* this. And If I'm going to nail the Olympic Trials this summer, I need to be fully conditioned

Chapter 20

before heading back to Louisiana.

I dig through my bag looking for my grips and groan, realizing that I left them on the sink at home to air dry.

"Crap," I mumble.

Rookie mistake, and I do mean that literally. I have a checklist for my gym bag, and I am regimented on exactly what goes in it, down to the brand.

Weighted vest filled with sandbags, P90X brand. Hair clips, not bobby pins because one fell out once when I was mid-air, and I somehow came down on it and cut my foot. Luco Tape, Icy Hot, KT Tape...on and on.

I heave a sigh, mourning the loss of my grips. *You can do this*, I tell myself. I was one of those weird gymnasts who didn't wear them until I went Elite. They felt stiff and the finger holes were always too small for my hands, and I was too impatient to take sandpaper to them to fix the sizing.

I chalk up my hands, hoping that my callouses will protect from damage, and get to work. The first pass through my routine feels okay, but still not as fluid as I need it to be. The second pass I overshoot myself and land face down on the mat, hard. I get up and shake it off, ignoring the sting from essentially bellyflopping onto the ground.

By the time I make it through my fifth pass, my arms are shaking, and my hands are burning. Being a gymnast means being resilient and fighting through the pain. It's just how it is. We do unthinkable things with our bodies and of course, our bodies protest.

You get used to feeling uncomfortable.

I'm starting to feel way worse than just uncomfortable, but it's better than remembering the good times with Luca and torturing myself about being lonely. And worrying for his heart.

After stopping for a water break, I chalk up some more and then jump onto the lower bar. Once I transition to the high bar, a sudden, sharp pain erupts on my left palm, before burning like fire.

"OWW!" I gasp out, falling onto my butt on the mat. One of the callouses on my hand has ripped open in a one-inch gash and immediately wells with blood. "*Motherfucker*, that hurts!" I cry out to the empty room, tears of pain welling as I grit my teeth.

Breathing through my nose to work through the pain, I rush over to my bag, and grab the Sting spray. With shaking hands, I spray it over the wound liberally, sighing in relief when the wound finally goes completely numb.

It's a grimy rip and blood drips off of my hand. I pat it dry as best I can with paper towels until the bleeding stops. But the show must go on.

I blink away the tears, square my shoulders, and take a deep breath.

And jump back on the bars.

When I get home that night, I assess the damage. I grab my medical kit and take out the little scissors. After spraying more Sting spray and waiting for it to go numb, I cut out the jagged edges of the callous around the rip. I waited too long and let it dry and now it's even harder to doctor. Gritting my teeth, I pore hydrogen peroxide on it, mesmerized as I watch the bubbles bring all the grit and chalk residue to the surface. I dry it off and pack the gash with Handibalm to accelerate the healing process, before covering it with gauze and taping it up.

God, rips are the absolute worst.

* * *

In the end, I made it two weeks before I was caught. It was the day before we were set to fly home for Thanksgiving. As I walk back into the training room on Friday, I look up and freeze when I come face to face with Coach Sarah.

She's standing in front with me with her arms crossed and a look of pure anger on her face.

Oh God.

"Uh, hi," I squeak out. Nerves erupt in my stomach, instantly making me queasy.

"My office. Now." she snaps, turning on her heel, knowing that I'll follow.

I do as told, shaking to my toes, and take a seat in the chair in front of her desk. She stares hard at me, practically daring me to look away. It's hard to meet her eyes right about now.

"So," she starts. "How long?"

My heart rate takes flight and I'm hoping I don't puke all over her desk. It

Chapter 20

definitely wouldn't help her anger.

Figuring it's better to be honest at this point, I stutter out "T-two weeks."

"Thank you for being honest. I knew the answer to that already. Had you lied, things would be much worse for you." She leans back in her chair, narrowing her eyes at me. "Imagine my surprise when one of the janitors pulled me aside today and confided in me that one of my gymnasts was working *by herself, after hours!*"

Her voice picks up as she continues until she's almost shouting at me.

"Lenore! We are in one of the most dangerous sports in the *world* and you think it's smart to train alone? Do you have any idea how bad things would be for you, would be for this organization, if you were hurt? Or God forbid, died?"

I feel about two inches tall right now as I realize how right she is and just how wrong I am. See also; *Nemesism - anger towards oneself and one's actions.*

"And completely shitting all over Coach Akeno's rule not to mention the NCAA? *Twenty hours* Lenore! We spelled it out and you signed a code of conduct set to you by the NCAA itself! Who do you think you are? Are you trying to break your *fucking neck?!*"

Oh man, she threw an f-bomb, she is *furious*. I hang my head, deeply ashamed. Yes, I did know how reckless and dangerous it was. I'm stupid, not ignorant. The difference? Ignorance doesn't know any better, but stupid knows and does it anyway. And worse, I didn't think about the position I'd be putting my coaches and university in if I was injured.

I can't believe I've been so selfish.

"I'm so sorry, Coach," I start, tears falling as the enormity of what I've done settles over me like a net. I think I knew at the time, but I'm good at blocking out what I don't want to see or think about. I always have been.

We can fool ourselves about anything if the proper motivation is there.

"I am so, so sorry. I've been hurting over something personal, and I told myself that if I threw myself into training, if I made the hours that I'd be doing at home with my elite team, I could quiet the noise in my brain and get just that much stronger and better. Two birds, one stone." I take a breath, wiping my eyes uselessly as tears of shame fall like rain. "I wasn't thinking. I know better than this. Please, *please* don't kick me off the team. I will never do anything like this again, I am *so sorry*," I break off, full blown sobbing.

I thought getting better, faster, quicker would make things better for me. I'd be more prepped for Nationals, for training with the National team and Olympic Trials this summer, and that somehow meeting my goals would take away some of this pain. That it would make our breakup all be worth it and allow me some peace with my decision to end things, that I could ease the sting of his betrayal.

I haven't been letting myself miss Luca, but I do, I miss him so much. The proximity, being in a close relationship, having that love and comfort and those loving, physical touches. Having someone to share your life with, the good and bad.

I didn't realize how much until this moment when I just need a hug and for someone to tell me that things will be okay.

Coach Sarah looks at me for a long moment, her face softening gradually.

Clearing her throat, she speaks up. "Here's what is going to happen, Lenore. You're going to wipe your tears and collect yourself. You're going to stand straight and hold your head high. You're better than this, and stronger than you think. Whatever is going on in your life is not insurmountable. You can work through this. Are you hearing me?"

I nod my head profusely, waiting for the other shoe to drop.

"You're benched for the first two meets." My heart drops, but it's better than I deserve. I nod morosely.

"And you're going to spend the entire break writing me a ten thousand word essay on gymnast injuries with real life examples. I want to know what they were, how they occurred, and how they recovered. I want examples of parallelization, of knee replacements, and at least one death. You'll give excruciating, painful, graphic details. I want you to write about every single thing that could have happened to you when no one was here to spot you or help you. And you will never, *ever* put yourself or this organization at risk again, do you understand me young lady?"

"Yes ma'am. Thank you so much."

"Now get out of here and have a good break. We start fresh next Monday."

Chapter 20

I fled the building like something was chasing me.
Maybe it was.

* * *

Thanksgiving with seven people is about as loud and chaotic as you'd think. Especially when everyone is grown and wanting to speak after months of being apart. In our family, when everyone wants to talk at once, it's necessary to shout out "Raven time!" or "Allan time!" and whoever is the loudest and gets people to be quiet, gets to speak. The food is delicious, but I find that I don't have much of an appetite. Researching gruesome injuries every day will do that to you.

After dinner, Daddy and the boys have cleaning duty since they helped with exactly none of the cooking, so I go upstairs to work on my essay.

It's been brutal. But I know exactly why she assigned it, and I deserved way worse.

Do yourself a favor and never Google "worst gymnastics injuries in history."

The most common injury in gymnastics is to the knees or ankles. Having gotten a few myself over the years, I knew that to be the case.

What I did not know was that Melanie Coleman, a college gymnast at Southern Connecticut State died from a spinal cord injury after her hands slipped off the uneven bars during practice.

Or that Samantha Cerio, a college gymnast for Auburn, broke both of her legs in a horrifying accident during her floor routine. She dislocated both knees and had multiple torn ligaments. Seeing the image caused my entire body to start shaking.

Those poor women, one after another that I've studied, paying the price that our sport demands from us all. It says, "Give me one thousand percent, work your hardest, strive for the best and then strive for *better*, train to learn the highest skills, and execute them with precision and a stoic look on your face, while ignoring fear and pain."

Gymnastics gives nothing in return. It just takes. When I was in high school, at Nationals, I had a back fracture after my beam routine ended badly. It's why I missed out on my shot at the Olympics when I was still a teenager.

And I still made the decision to practice alone.

I have spent the last six days drowning in a sea of self-loathing, and every word that I type for my essay makes it worse. Every article I read, every picture I see.

I deserve to wallow in shame. I honestly don't know how I'm going to be able to look my coaches in the eyes after betraying their trust and ignoring the rules. This is not who I am. How did I let this happen? I let the pain of this breakup redraw the shape of me, and I don't like it one bit.

I finish my essay at nine o'clock, and lean back in bed, sighing with relief. Let's hope Coach Sarah is satisfied with my special mixture of facts and begging for forgiveness. I'm full of restless energy after not training this week. I go running every day, but that's been it.

Deciding I'm not ready for bed, I grab a blanket and go outside into our backyard where I lay down and do something that always gives me peace, looking at the stars. I love finding constellations. It's one of the few things my mom and I do together. She's usually working, reading, or with her horses. I always wanted her to be at my meets or come traveling to tournaments out of state, but she rarely made one.

I grew to resent her so much for that, but at least I was allowed to do gymnastics in the first place. I know she's proud of me. She's just a very reserved woman, and that's how she is as a mother too.

But on clear nights, she'd grab her telescope, come get me and my siblings, and we'd go to the back field and learn about the stars together. Those are some of my favorite childhood memories.

It's a rare cold night in November, about forty-five degrees, and I can see my breath. My favorite kind of night to see the stars. I want to go to Alaska or Iceland to see the Northern Lights one day. For now, I'll make do with the winter constellations.

I spy Venus, the easiest planet for me to recognize, and the constellation Cassiopeia. The vain queen, who boasted about her daughter Andromeda's beauty being unrivaled. She angered Poseidon, who felt that his sea nymphs were the truly most beautiful, so he took Cassiopeia, and as punishment, he

Chapter 20

put her in the sky, before putting her husband Cepheus and Andromeda in the sky right beside her.

I find Pieces, Tucana, and Hydrus.

And the Phoenix. According to mythology, the Phoenix was a beautiful bird that would live for five hundred years. When it was time for it die, it would build a nest of twigs and leaves, and then catch fire from the sun. A new phoenix would emerge from the ashes, to grow up with a fresh start and live all over anew.

While lying on the cold, hard ground, all alone in the huge field, I think about new beginnings. I've spent the past six weeks vacillating between just about every negative emotion in the book, with nothing good in between. In truth, I haven't liked seeing who peered back at me from the mirror. She's sad, and miserable, and doing nothing good to change it.

I decide that it all ends tonight. That I am going to be the Phoenix. I can't go back and change the past. I can't undo what I did, or correct mistakes.

But I can give myself a fresh start. I can forgive myself for putting my team and coaches at risk for liability, for breaking rules, and for putting myself in jeopardy by training alone. I can stop isolating myself from my friends, I can find ways to be happy again.

I can find my way back to the old Lennie, before she got her heart broken and started feeling like she wasn't enough. Like she had to do better, be better, be more.

I can, and I will.

And I did.

I became the Phoenix and rose from the ashes. I stopped beating myself up about missing Luca, about past choices and mistakes. I spent all of my free time with Raven and my friends, exploring new places on the weekends, going to new restaurants, or discovering hidden gems throughout Boston.

In January, Cora and I discovered Gourmet Dumplings in Little Saigon, and shared a table with two Chinese exchange students. They taught us how to eat soup dumplings and which sauces to eat them with.

Raven and I explored the Museum of Fine Art in February, going back again and again to take in displays we hadn't seen before. The Ancient Egypt and

Arts of Islamic Cultures were my favorites. Art is so beautiful, and it moved me. Feeling positive emotions again felt like a gift.

In March, Raven, Catalina, and I got lost looking for the Orange Line, and stumbled on a beautiful place called St. Anthony's Shrine. We paid offerings to light electronic candles while we said a private prayer. I took a picture of the Our Lady of Fatima statue and sent it to Coach Fatima. I knew she'd get a kick out of it. I'd sat in the empty confession booth that day, alone for a moment of quiet, and thought back to when Luca took me to Trinity Church. I'd made fun of confession and wondered what a confession booth looked like. These are beautiful, all carved wood and intricate details. I smiled in the dark and realized that it was first time a memory of Luca didn't make me sad, didn't make me feel any pain.

I was healing.

When the weather warmed up in April, Gabby and I posed for Raven's Love is Love project, gazing lovingly into each other's eyes, and breaking into giggles as she took our picture. She yelled a lot that day.

My teammates and I rented swan boats in Public Park in May. We paddled around the lake for hours, laughing and joking, and pointing out all of the ducks. We celebrated our championship win together a week later, bolstering me in my quest for Olympic glory.

And the week before school ended, when Luca introduced his new girlfriend to me after I encountered them on the sidewalk, I was able to look him in the eye and smile.

I'd found the grace inside of me to be happy for him. It made saying goodbye to him after his graduation feel like a positive thing, having closure and hoping the best for him.

I finished my junior year with my head held high, my self-esteem recovered, and my future outlook as bright as the sun.

But you know what they say…

What goes up, must come down.

Chapter 21

dormiveglia
(n) the space that stretches between sleeping and waking

"Blue punch buggy," Raven crows triumphantly while drilling me in the arm with her fist.

"Oww, you ho bag!"

"You're the one who said to play road games," she laughs out at me.

"Not ones that include physical assault! That hurt, Raven!"

"Fine, truce. We'll play another game."

We're on day two of our drive home, having left Tennessee at zero dark thirty this morning. It's always a long drive, and this one feels like it will never end. I'm anxious to get back in the gym. I'm moving back to Texas to train for the Olympic Trials with the National Team. I don't even let the thought of not doing well enter my mind. In my eyes? I'm already an Olympian for Team USA. Nothing less is acceptable. I give in to the daydream of being in the leagues as my most favorite gymnasts in the world.

Nastia Liukin, Shawn Johnson, Simone Biles.

They're the goal. They paved the way for my own dreams just by living theirs.

"Tell me what you plan to do this summer," I say to Raven when we crossover into Mississippi.

"Well, you already know about my internship with Charlie Coyle." She's going to be following the famed photographer all over Louisiana this summer, doing nature photography. "And I've actually been thinking about getting back into riding horses."

I look over at her in shock. Since Raven's near-death experience, she's been too afraid to do anything with risk. She stopped doing gymnastics on a dime, which was the right move for her because having your mind and body conflicting isn't just dangerous in gymnastics. It's deadly. You can't be afraid that you'll fall, or you will.

It's just that simple.

It took her a long time to be able to fly again, six years to be precise, when we flew to Boston that first time with our parents. She never stepped foot in another lake or body of water. Never rode carnival or fair rides.

But of all the things she lost, I know saying goodbye to those horses was the hardest on her. She loved riding horses with our family. But a few months after the accident, I was thrown from my horse, bruising my tailbone, and after she carried me all the way back home, she never went into the barn again. She was afraid of being thrown or worse, and she told me she didn't visit them because the memories were too painful, and she couldn't bear to look at her precious loves.

"Wow, that's a big step Rae," I say. "I'm really proud of you sissy."

She takes a shaky breath in. "Thanks Len."

It starts to rain when we cross the Louisiana border, which surprises me not at all.

The border sign into Louisiana should say "Bienvenue to the Louisiana, where summer is our rainy season. Grab your rain boots and get comfortable in them!"

I'm going on and on about my plans for my career, babbling to keep my nerves at bay for what's to come. The rain picks up harder and it's getting really hard to see now that the sun's gone down.

"Len, hush for a bit, I need to concentrate."

We're about ten miles from home, so I settle back in my seat and grit my teeth, ready to be out of the jeep.

Chapter 21

We're coming up fast to a stop sign that's hard to see and Raven blurts out "shit!" as she slams on the breaks. I feel a sensation of swaying, skidding side to side as the car lurches forward, and I look over at Raven.

"Oh my God, I can't stop. I think we're hydroplaning!"

"Raven, don't panic, just pump the brak-"

I don't get to finish my sentence. A blaring horn pierces the jeep and I look over to my right just in time for headlights to flood my vision.

"LENNIE!"

The crunch of metal.

The smell of gasoline.

Raven sobbing.

Darkness takes over.

* * *

Pain is the first thing I'm aware of. Disorientation. Confusion.

I slowly become aware, waking to sounds and smells that are foreign to me. Antiseptic. Scratchy linens. A bed that's too firm. Sounds of beeping and voices I don't know, growing smaller as the owner moves further from me.

I open my eyes, blinking in the bright light, and hear a loud gasp somewhere off to my left.

My thinking process is slow, and it feels like my brain is filled with muck. How did I get here? I lift my left hand to rub my eyes, stopping when I notice that I have an IV tube taped in my inner elbow.

The hospital room comes into focus as I try to summon the last thing I remember. Raven punching me, yelling "Green punch buggy!" Or was it blue? I remember her telling me that she wants to get back to her horses. Shaking my head, I wince when shooting pain radiates from my right shoulder up my neck, and into my head. I look at my arm and see that it's in a sling strapped to my chest.

"You're awake!" Raven cries out, coming to the side of my bed. I stare dazedly back at her, taking in the cuts to the left side of her face. Her left eye is a bit black and swollen. She grips my hand, saying "I'll get a nurse. Be right back."

She comes back with an older man in blue scrubs, a clipboard in his hands.

"Welcome back, Lenore. You've had your family worried somethin' fierce these past few days," he says.

Days?

"What hospital is this? How long have I been here, what happened?" My voice is hoarse, and my throat is sore and dry.

Raven looks at me in shock. "You don't remember the accident?"

"No," I say, shaking my head as slightly as possible. I try to sit up, but my right leg isn't cooperating. I can't bend it and through the pain it feels like it's bound from the knee down. I use my good arm to pull off the covers and gasp at what I see.

My right knee is wrapped in a bandage that makes it look five times its normal size. And my ankle is encased in a hard cast, from just under my knee to my foot.

"What happened to me?" Panic is starting to flow through me like shards of ice in my veins.

"I'm going to call everyone and let them know you're awake, they're down at the cafeteria." Raven says, backing out of the room.

"She has barely left your side," the nurse said. "I'm John Babineaux, your charge nurse. I'll go grab Dr. Guidry after I take your vitals."

"Can I have water? My throat is really sore."

"That's common after being intubated."

"How long have I been here?"

"You've been here for four days."

My mind goes from racing, to feeling like everything comes to a screaming halt.

"Four days," I rasp out, feeling like I'm having an out of body experience. I try to remember, but all I do is make my headache worse.

After he takes my vitals, he leaves the room. I wait alone for the doctor, trying to force myself to breath normally. I know that if I let the panic take hold of me, I'll never be able to reel it in.

Raven comes back in the room with my parents and siblings, and they all

Chapter 21

welcome me. It's overwhelming, but they finally get comfortable on the futon and chair in the corner. Daddy hovers around me like a protective bull, and it's making me feel simultaneously safe and on edge.

"This is not how I thought we'd be seeing you again, baby girl," he says, hugging me awkwardly as he tries to work with my injuries. He figures out how to sit me up with the bed controls, so I can at least have a more dignified position now that I'm awake.

Finally, there is a knock on the door, and a tall, bearded redhead walks in with his clipboard.

"Welcome back, Lenore. I'm Dr. Guidry, your orthopedic surgeon."

Oh Lord, what surgery did I have?

"Hi Doctor," I manage weakly.

"I'm sure you have questions. We will keep this visit with family very brief today. With the extent of Lenore's injuries, she's going to need lots of rest in order to heal."

He looks around at my family, catching their eyes and garnering nods of confirmation.

"Lenore, let's get the tough part out of the way and then I'll have a nurse top up your pain meds since the dose is almost up. I assume you're hurting?"

I give an affirmative head nod.

"Okay. Your charge nurse filled me in on your memory loss. In cases of traumatic injury, especially the high-impact car accident that you were in, this can be normal. You didn't have any skull fractures or brain bleeding, rather a slight swelling of the brain that we managed by putting you into a short medically induced coma. You suffered several lacerations to your scalp, which we were able to treat with stitches and staples. The rest of the cosmetic damage is bruising and lacerations to the body due to metal and glass."

The more he says, the worse I feel.

"Now for the more complicated injuries. Your right shoulder was dislocated and will be healed enough to remove the sling after a few more days. You should be able to walk with crutches in two weeks. Your patella tendon in your right kneecap was severed in the impact and needed to be repaired in surgery along with a partially lacerated ACL and LCL. And lastly, your right ankle was broken when you were struck. You're now the proud owner of two steel plates and nine screws."

I can only gape at him in horror as a heaviness settles over the room. My mom is crying silently in the corner with my dad's arm around her shoulders. I don't even try to look at my siblings. I'm barely hanging on.

He's not unkind, but he's speaking on autopilot without regard to the fact that every word out of his mouth slices me like razors. The pain I feel from my injuries is nothing compared to what is going on in my heart. I've never felt this kind of desperation. What does this mean for my career?

I can't bring myself to ask.

A nurse comes in and administers some medication through my IV. "That should allow you some sleep to speed along the healing process," she says before Dr. Guidry continues.

"I think that's about enough for today. I'm pleased with your vital signs as much as I can be with your current condition. You're going to feel like you shot gunned about five daiquiris before going to sleep. Sleep is restorative, and it's imperative to regaining the full spectrum of your brain function.…"

My eyelids are already drooping, and I zone out as he keeps talking. Before I know it, I'm drifting off, being carried away from consciousness in a cloud of haze to a dreamless sleep.

Chapter 22

sciamachy
(n) a battle against imaginary enemies; fighting your shadow

The squeal of brakes, the screech of metal and glass crunching and shattering is an aggregated roar that reverberates through my head. Pain and fear erupt from my body in response to being trapped under the pressure of my door that's now pushed in from the grill of the truck that t-boned us, pinning me against the center console and ravaging the left side of my body.

Blinding pain and horror is interrupted by Raven's scream.

"Lennie!"

I cry out in fear and pain, begging someone, anyone for help.

"Lennie, Len, wake up!"

My eyes snap open and I struggle to sit up, breathing like I ran a marathon. Raven is gripping my shoulder and staring at me with wide eyes. I take some deep breaths to try and calm my racing heart and control the adrenaline coursing through me.

"Another nightmare about the crash?" Raven guesses.

Deep breaths, Len, in and out.

"Yeah. Just a dream," I whisper to myself.

For the past few weeks, the nightmares have grown in detail and frequency. It's not just me; Raven has been getting them too. I don't know if she's having her reoccurring childhood nightmare or new ones from the crash.

I don't ask.

I haven't been able to look at pictures of the crash, not that my parents have offered. All I know is that our beloved Jeep sits in a heap of twisted metal in a junkyard somewhere in the town over.

It's the third week in June, and I've been home for the last seven days. These past three weeks have been a waking nightmare—one that I wouldn't wish on my worst enemy.

The first week after I woke from my coma was the hardest. I didn't have use of my right arm while it healed in the sling, so I graduated from a catheter to bedpans. Nothing will humble a person more intensely than being that incapacitated and having someone else wipe you and empty your waste. When I was able to make it to the bathroom on crutches, I cried in relief, alone on the toilet, for a full ten minutes before I could pull myself together. You don't realize how much your mobility, the freedom to move on your own and to be able to care for yourself, can mean for your mental wellbeing until it's snatched away from you.

The second week I was finally more lucid and was able to have visitors. This was both good and bad. It was nice to see my Beaux Belles coaches and some friends and local teammates along with my family, but I was strained and unhappy. I had to announce that I was withdrawing from Nationals that week and I was still processing.

When I looked into my coaches eyes, I saw the ending.

I can't face it.

At that point, Raven had told some of our close friends in Boston. Along with texts from my local and Nationals teammates, I started getting messages from Cora and Gabby and some other friends from school. Chase texted me, and I even got one from Luca wishing me the best. I didn't know how to answer. He resented my devotion to my sport before, and I swallowed the intrusive thought that maybe he felt I deserved to lose it.

My memory had also started coming back, and with that came the nightmares. The first time it happened I woke up alone in my hospital room, screaming incoherently and devolved into a panic attack. I thought I was

Chapter 22

dead or dying. I could actually smell the gasoline and smoke. They had to sedate me to calm me down. I understood what was happening more after that and was able to keep the panic attacks from taking over again, for the most part.

But the same nightmare came night after night.

Once I was settled at home and a bit more mobile, things got a little better. It was comforting to be surrounded by my things, my home, and my family. The downside is that Raven became so clingy and suffocating that I started fake napping or claiming that I was busy working on a summer project for my class. Lie. I chose the easiest class that I could because I thought I'd be in Texas.

I couldn't handle her guilt because it made me feel bad for her. She was also backsliding in her anxiety and having her close felt a lot like we were making each other worse instead of better. Our combined energy was too negative.

I spent most of the next five weeks resting as I healed, reading books to escape, and trying to be as independent as I could. I was still hopeful that I'd be able to recover enough to join the team back when we went back to Boston in two weeks.

Side note: we were flying.

But every single day of living in my broken body threatened the illusion I created for myself; that I'd be going back to normal.

Today I'm meeting with the Orthopedic team at the hospital, a consultant that the Nationals team sent out, and my coaches. I've regained full use of my shoulder and have been able to walk with a walking boot for the past few weeks.

I'm anxious to get out of the walking boot and start PT for my ankle, which will happen once I'm back at Kalon. My knee feels fairly good finally and I've been able to get up and around much easier. Our medical team at the gym set me up with physical therapy for my knee, at least what I could do while wearing the boot.

Another milestone was being able to slowly go up and down the stairs twice a day so that I could get some fresh air and move my body.

As my parents pull into the doctor's office, the butterflies start to kick in. I try not to think too much or have too much hope.

Coach Fatima, Coach Lisa, and Coach Jess all meet us in the front office, where the medical consultant from the Nationals team staff introduces himself as Dr. Finner. He's barely taller than me, and is slight with graying blonde hair, but gives us all a firm handshake and a polite smile as we make introductions.

None of my National team coaches could make it due to the Olympic Trials happening this week.

Don't think about it, Lennie.

Dr. Guidry came into the modified exam room/office and brought in my x-rays and my latest MRI scans on my knee. He put the ankle x-rays up on the light board and like I do every time, I can't hide my flinch when I see the before photo. The after isn't much better and as I take in the plates and screws, I can almost *feel* them, all sharp points and jagged edges under my skin, in my bones.

The MRI scans are harder for me to discern since they're darker, less detailed, and I'm not sure what to look for. I look from doctor to doctor, and neither is giving anything away with their body language.

Luckily, Dr. Guidry doesn't leave me hanging long.

"Thanks everyone for coming in today to support Lenore. Dr. Finner and I reviewed the latest scans and x-rays this morning. I'd like to address the two injuries separately."

He grabs a pointer and walks over to the x-ray of my ankle.

"Your ankle joint consists of your fibula, your tibia, and your talus," he says, pointing out each bone. I can clearly see that the break was the fibula, the smaller bone on the outside of my foot.

"Lenore's break was to the fibula, in three places. The longer plate attached with seven small screws secured the two main breaks, and the smaller, third break is the small plate on the bone below the other plates." He points lower on the x ray "Here, and the two longer screws secure the fibula's position by anchoring it to the tibia. The breaks have knitted together nicely, and I am satisfied that the ankle has healed without any miscorrection of the bone placements."

Chapter 22

Before I can stop it, hope swells.

Dr. Finely steps forward. "Now for the knee. This was the most concerning injury to me, as it impacts every bit of your mobility in the sport. Dr. Guidry is an orthopedic specialist with a concentration in sports injuries, while my area of expertise is connective tissues as it pertains specifically to gymnastics. When the patella tendon, which keeps the knee bone anchored to the shin bone, was severed, they were able to surgically reattach it, but with a four milometer loss to the tendon due to the severity of the damage. The LCL or lateral collateral ligament gives stability to the outer knee. The ACL or anterior cruciate ligament gives stability to the center of the knee. Both were lacerated to varying degrees and were in turn, repaired."

The air in the room starts to come alive as I find it harder and harder to take in breaths. It's too thick to be considered oxygen and I can't seem to work it into my lungs.

Dr. Finner continues, ignorant to the impact his words are having on me. "Lenore, I'm going to be as clear as I can without giving you false hope. In elite gymnasts, your physical tools are your mobility, your strength, and your flexibility. That's it. The rest is conditioning and mentality. You're expected to be able to land hard, planting your feet and sticking the landing without anything to help you stabilize. You have to cycle through your flips and transitions with minimal flex in your knees, hips, and ankles. It's enormously straining on the muscles and connective tissues in your legs, and that's when they're whole and healthy."

The longer he speaks the more I feel like I'm going to throw up. My heart is pounding, my hands are shaking, and my ears are ringing.

"When you have one weak side, it's an uphill battle to even out the disadvantage. But when you have an entire leg that is compromised and sewn back together with less tendon and ligament than you had before, even if a fraction shorter and less strong..." he trails off and the part of my brain that isn't buzzing with panic hears what he isn't saying. "It is the entirety of the injuries we have to consider together. You have to think about quality of life beyond retirement, and you're nearing the common age to step away. If you get hurt again, this time through gymnastics, you may never walk again, at least without the use of a cane or any sort of impediment to the right leg. Your knee is not up to the standard that this sport requires." He spares me an apologetic, but firm glance.

"My assessment as a medical doctor and an expert in the field is that you're not equipped to participate in the sport at an intermediate level, and most certainly not at the elite level. And I can see in your face that you wanted another outcome Miss Landry, and I'm so sorry that I can't give it to you."

Tears started running down my face right around the words "entirety of the injuries" and now that he's done obliterating any hope that was left in my heart, I can only bury my face in my hands and sob as my coaches surround me, rubbing my back and putting their arms around me.

The doctors step out with a discreet "we'll give you a moment." I'm left feeling like everything I've ever wanted and worked for was killed in that crash, and any remaining bit of happiness that I had left died on that rainy highway.

We drive home silently, and I stare out of the rain-pelted window. You'd think that I would be afraid to ride in the rain again, but instead of fear, I just felt numb. We reach home and Daddy turns the car off, but no one makes a move to get out. He turns around regards me sadly.

"I'm so sorry cher, I truly am. I know what it meant to you and how hard you worked for it and baby, I just hate this for you."

I sniffed, nodding my head, unable to meet his eyes. I can't handle the pity in them right now. Momma turns around too.

"Everything happens for a reason, ma fille. We just don't always know what it is until it's right in front of us."

I focus my eyes on the floorboard so that she can't see the rage that fills them at her careless words. What a cop out thing to say when all she has to do is acknowledge that the only dream I ever wanted for myself has been yanked away due to circumstances that were outside of my control.

She may as well have said "hopes and prayers" like all her damn Baptist friends.

But sure, I bet there is a great reason for all of this, just full of rainbows and sunshine, waiting around the corner for me to discover.

Chapter 22

The only thing stopping me from snapping back at her is a lifetime of reinforced good southern manners. I take a steadying breath and force my tone to stay neutral.

"How can you say that to me?" I ask.

Daddy, sensing the brewing storm decides to abandon ship. "I'll give y'all some privacy to talk," he says, hauling ass out of the car.

"What do you mean?" Momma asks, turning fully around to face me.

"I mean you barely supported me in this. I can count the number of times you've come to practices and competitions in the past ten years probably on two hands, Momma. You don't have anything understanding or more supportive to say than it was meant to be, for some unknown reason?"

I try to keep my voice steady, but it's a losing battle because my anger towards her bubbles up at the end. She just stares at me in shock for a few moments before gathering herself.

"Lenore…I'm sorry that I made you feel like I didn't support you. Of course, I did, and I do. When we almost lost Raven . . ." her voice breaks and she has to stop and take a deep breath, taking me by surprise.

Lynnette Landry doesn't do emotions.

"When we almost lost Raven, she wasn't the only one who lived in fear. It was all I could take to keep myself on a horse and even more to let Madeline continue. I was relieved when Raven quit gymnastics, to be honest. Every time I'd see you vault through the air, more than twice your height, every time you ran your layout or flipped over the bars, I was terrified that you'd get hurt. That you'd land on your neck or that you'd break both of your legs."

My anger towards her starts to dissipate. I never knew she felt that way.

"I'd start to panic when you were mid-routine and I'd have to do these breathing exercises to keep hold of myself. It wasn't because I didn't care that I stayed away. I wasn't there because I cared too much, and at times I just couldn't handle watching you put yourself in danger again and again."

I could understand that. And if I were in her shoes, maybe I'd feel the same. But I really don't have it in me to let her off the hook, not with how I'm feeling.

"Well. Turns out, you don't have to be afraid anymore." I deadpan.

I get out and make my way up to my room. There's some PT that I need to do with the workout bands, but instead I lay down on my bed and look at the ceiling. I don't go down for dinner that night and no one comes up to get me.

I think about going to check on Raven. I know she blames herself and is probably beating herself up right now, because she told me she did and begged for my forgiveness.

I told there was nothing to forgive because it was an accident, of course, it was.

But a kernel of anger holds tight, hidden deep in my secret thoughts. I knew if I was driving, we would not have hydroplaned. Because I wouldn't have panicked. Raven cannot handle riding passenger, due to needing to feel in control of her safety. For the first time, I let myself be just a little bit mad at her for that. I knew to pump the breaks, but Raven being Raven, reacted out of fear and slammed on the breaks. I stop that line of thinking immediately, ashamed of myself. It isn't her fault.

It could have happened to anyone.

But it didn't.

It happened to me.

* * *

The night before Raven and I were scheduled to fly back to Boston, I snuck outside with my blanket to look at the stars one last time. I couldn't sleep, and I wasn't sure what I was looking for, but I went anyway, in search of...*something*.

Anything to make this new reality make sense.

Lying back on my blanket, I listen to the whinnying and neighs from the horses in the barn, smelling their oats and hay and unique horse smells, carried on the breeze.

I think back to that night last November where I found the Phoenix constellation and vowed that I would move on from Luca and find my happiness again. Honestly, *to rise from the ashes again*, was what I said to myself. How cheesy.

That girl was so naive.

Chapter 22

I truly thought my little broken heart would be the worst thing to ever happen to me.

Once again looking for answers in the stars, I spy Aquila first, the eagle that carried down Zeus's thunderbolt from the heavens. Like an errand boy delivering death by lightening.

I find Lyra, the lyre of Orpheus the poet. What happened to Orpheus again? Something awful.

Ah yes, he was torn to shreds by the Thrace women because he didn't give them any attention, but not before witnessing his wife die of a snake bite on their wedding day.

I locate Sagitta, the arrow, and Sagittarius, the archer, the dangerous duo.

After a while, I give up and head inside. Looking to the stars was a mistake. There is nothing up there but pain, loss, and death.

Taking one last look at the barn before I close the door, I realize that Raven never did seek out those horses this summer.

Chapter 23

anhedonia
(n) the loss of interest and enjoyment in all activities that you once liked; the feeling of not caring anymore

YEAR FOUR

Raven and I arrived back at our house a week before school started. It gave me seven days of mentally preparing myself to go meet my coaches and team. They knew that I was officially retired from gymnastics. Just thinking that phrase fills my mouth with ash. Every time I relive that last appointment, bitterness takes hold of me, and I don't even try fight it. It's like something many tentacled that grabs on tight, bit by bit and doesn't let go until it drags you down to the abyss.

It's good to see Gabby and Cora, though. We spend a few days getting unpacked and getting situated back in the house and having girl time. Thank goodness we didn't haul everything back in the trailer when we left for home in May, or we wouldn't have any of our things to come back to. I picture all of my books, strewn over the rain-soaked highway, getting run over. Thousands of pages, floating in the wind.

Dylan moved back into his frat house, leaving just us girls again. We watched movies, made meals together and, as usual, just blended back into

Chapter 23

our co-existence. I try to stifle the nightmares, but they still come a few nights a week. Gabby and Cora take turns between soothing me and Raven when we inevitably succumb to them.

I spend a lot of nights reading late when either insomnia takes root because I'm too afraid to wake up screaming, or when I wake up drenched in cold sweat after hearing Raven scream *"LENNIE!"* in my dreams...or in real life, from her room. I start to crave the escape, diving deep into other worlds, other people's lives. Anyone's existence, other than mine.

Three days before school, I finally made it to Libertas to speak with my coaches and team. I'm here on a full athletic scholarship and, now that I can't compete, I'm terrified that I'm going to be kicked out. Or maybe have to fork over a year's worth of tuition, and I know that my parents need the college fund for Maddie since she isn't on scholarship at LSU (they don't exactly give out scholarships for barrel racing) and Raven who only got a partial scholarship.

I inhale deeply as I walk in the door. Someone on the basketball court dribbles a ball, and the scent of new vinyl floors and fresh paint dominates the space. Walking past the open training center doors, the smells, a mixture of chalk, vinyl mats, and foam from the pit, call out to me. It smells like home.

I pause outside of our open meeting room, knowing everyone is there. I've procrastinated coming here for five days, and now that all the gymnasts are checking in and getting schedules set, I know I have to show my face.

Unsure of what to expect, I take a steadying breath and walk into the room.

"Lennie!"

"Len!"

"You're back!"

I'm instantly surrounded by smiling faces and hugging arms. Jayla, Catalina, Savannah, Tatum, they all surround me in a big hug, and I have to blink back tears.

I'll miss this so much.

They take a step back and all start talking at once.

"I'm so sorry about Nationals..."

"How is your knee?"

"Are you recovered after . . . "

"Ladies!" Coach Dwight pushes through the gaggle of my friends. "You all give her space to breathe, I swear y'all are likely to make her go nuts."

I laugh, glad for the breathing room.

"Thanks Coach. It's fine," I say "To answer your questions, I'm okay. Almost fully recovered, but I have to start PT today, actually. It sucked withdrawing from Nationals, but I had no choice." I pause to clear my throat around the lump that's formed. "And I'm sure you heard, but with everything that happened to my knee specifically, I'm um...I'm done. Retired."

I'm met with ringing silence.

"Oh girl," Jayla whispers "I'm so sorry. Coaches didn't tell us too much."

I look to Coach Sarah as she walks up, and she nods in confirmation.

"Ladies, why don't you all head to the tables. The new nutritionist has some things for you all to look over. Go help round up the freshmen."

She puts a hand on my upper back to guide me into her office with Coach Dwight following.

"Coach Akeno is going to handle the first part of orientation," she starts. "So how are you really doing, Lennie?"

"We were really sorry to hear about the accident," Coach D adds.

"Thanks," I say quietly. "I'm hanging in there, still trying to process things. The weeks after the accident were the hardest, but now that I can walk unassisted again, I'm better."

"I know what this Nationals meant to you Lenore; I can't tell you how sad I am that you were forced to miss your shot at the Olympics. I hope you know that we believed you'd make it all the way." She has this earnest look in her eyes that makes it hard to keep mine dry. I'll take scary Coach Sarah Johanssen over this compassionate one.

God, make it to stop, or I'm not going to make it out of here without looking like a blubbering fool.

"Thank you," I say more firmly. "I'm looking forward to starting PT and putting this behind me. It wasn't meant to be, and that's okay. I have some time on my hands to make sense of things."

I wonder if they even believe the lies I tell myself.

Chapter 23

"Understood." At least she knew when to stop. "Also, I know that you're concerned about your scholarship. Your mother called and spoke with me a few days ago about your options."

I barely manage to stifle my anger. *She spent three years detached from my college career, but all of a sudden when it's over, she's worried about it...because of money?!* I brace myself, head held high, in order to hide the fact that I'm shaking like a leaf in my seat. Am I about to be kicked out?

"When an athlete is on full scholarship, it rides not on athletic ability, but on grades. If an athlete is injured, they're not kicked out on the streets. As long as they keep their grades up, they're allowed to keep the scholarship. We've spoken to Mrs. Wheeler about your options and your grades. Surely, you're aware that your grades of A's and B's are perfectly in line with keeping your scholarship. The kicker was the team placement. We conferenced in the Dean of Athletics, who has agreed to work something out. How do you feel about coming onto the team as a Volunteer Coach through the end of season?"

I stare open mouthed in shock at him. Looking to Coach Sarah, I raise my eyebrows in question.

"This would start after December, which I'm told is after you're set to finish physical training for your ankle and knee, and it would be for ten hours a week. You'd be able to participate in the cardio and modified weightlifting sessions, while coaching the freshmen and sophomores levels eight and nine alongside Head Coach in skill."

"I-I...wow, I don't know what..." I'm rendered speechless. I had no expectations coming in here aside from possibly negative ones that I built up in my mind. Never, did I expect this.

"Can I have some time to get back to you on this? I'm honored, I am, and I really appreciate the opportunity."

I just never thought that I'd be faced with either losing the only sport I've ever loved or being part of it from the outside. My mind is reeling.

"Yeah kid, I'd probably want some time too, coming off a big transition like this" Coach D said.

"How about you go to PT and give it your all. Get back to us after the new year, at the start of the season?" Coach Sarah offers. "You wouldn't be starting until then anyways. This will stay between us for now, and we'll let the Dean know that you've accepted in the interim."

I puff out a breath of relief. "Thank you so much, all of you," I say, with a heavy heart and mixed feelings.

Can I handle watching my team succeed without me when I'd give anything to be on the mat with them?

I'm not so sure that I can.

After saying my goodbyes to everyone, I made my way to Solis Occasum, home to the hockey arena and one of the sports medicine centers. I check in and follow the student trainer back to the area where there are several rooms for PT and light rehab.

The trainer introduced me to a large olive-skinned man with a bald head and very toned physique. Well, I guess he would know a lot about working out, considering his profession.

"Hey there Lenore, I'm Dr. Mohammed Amawi, your physical therapist. My student intern will be here shortly."

"Nice to meet you. You can just call me Lennie," I say, shaking his hand.

"Lennie?" I turn around at the sound of the familiar voice. My day just improved significantly.

"Chase!"

He's standing at the door to the room looking surprised, but then quickly walks forward to give me a huge hug. *Man, he's gotten bigger this year*, I think, as I inhale his cologne and feel his strong arms around me.

"So, I guess that saves me from introductions, huh," Dr. Amawi chuckles.

"Yeah, we go way back," Chase grins.

In truth, I didn't see him much last semester. After we came back from Christmas break, I spent my time either with the team or Raven and my friends, and he and I didn't have any classes together again. It's so good to see him, and I'm surprised by the pang in my heart. I haven't hugged a man that wasn't family since Luca, all those months ago.

"Well, I guess we're in this together," I say, forcing my mind on the topic at hand. "I'm sorry that I didn't text you back much this summer. It took

Chapter 23

me while for my brain to work better than scrambled eggs, and I-I just…" I stumble over the words, momentarily flustered and feeling emotional as I try to explain myself. He stops me with a hand on my shoulder.

"Lennie, you don't have to apologize. I'm just glad you're okay. And I hope I can help Dr. Amawi make you better."

I smile at him, relieved.

I hope you can too, Chase.

Chapter 24

eternitarian

(n) one who believes in the eternity of the soul

You know that amazing feeling when everything that you suffered and everything that broke you down all makes sense in the end?

Yeah, me neither.

I have exactly zero clue what I'm going to be doing after I graduate college.

What I do know? Is that I am not killing this physical therapy thing.

Two weeks into school and therapy, I'm already frustrated with my lack of progress.

"Once more." Dr. Amawi instructs.

I grit my teeth and try again. I'm lying flat on my back with my left leg bent up completely. I have a cloth under my right heel, and I'm dragging it back to bend my knee up as far as I can, to match the position of my left. My left heel is touching my butt, but I can't bring my right heel closer than a foot before crying out in pain.

"Slow it down, Lennie. You're still going too fast, which is why it hurts. You're putting too much strain on the ligaments, and that tendon needs conditioning to become more flexible," he says patiently.

Where does all of his stoicism come from? I'd pay good money for it.

I huff a breath and move more slowly this time. It's the most basic of

Chapter 24

movements, and while I remember everything Dr. Finner said about my tendons and ligaments being shorter and more taut than before, it's another thing to have that physical feeling applied over and over during PT.

It doesn't feel good, and it doesn't feel natural.

To be fair, having your connective tissues damaged by the brute force of metal meeting metal at fifty miles per hour isn't natural, either.

Blinking rapidly to dislodge the headlights suddenly appearing in my mind's eye, I try again. And again.

Chase makes notes of my progress.

He helps me up, and I grab some water before the good doctor continues.

"Let's work the ankle a bit. Extend your foot just slightly, yes that's enough. Point your toes as much as you can and try to spell the lower-case ABCs with your foot, using your big toe as the pencil tip."

I look at him like he's crazy while Chase laughs at my confusion.

"Like this," he says, perfectly balancing on one foot and...ahh I get it.

"Show off," I huff at him, while following his act. I wobble and he has me put my hand on his strong shoulder.

I can see how this is effective. It's not my bones that need the PT, it's the ligaments and tendons that were inactive and stationary for the ten weeks I was in the cast. My ankle is pretty tight at first, but then it gradually loosens up.

"I want you to do that before and after bed until I say otherwise," Dr. Amawi says.

A few more drills and we call it a day.

It's the second week of September, a Friday evening, and for once, I don't have anywhere to go. Chase walks out of the office as I'm getting ready to head out.

"What are you up to next?" he asks, heading over to me.

I think about the empty house and stack of books waiting on me and can't seem to muster up any excitement. "Nothing, really. Raven and our roommates are going to the Sigma Tau Alpha Beta party tonight, but honestly the last thing I feel like doing is being around a bunch of drunk people."

I don't add that my knee always throbs after PT.

He regards me closely. "Yeah, I feel you. Do you want to come somewhere with me?"

Yes.

"Where?"

"Somewhere I go when I like to think and seek peace. You seem like you would benefit."

"Don't you have practice?"

"Not until tomorrow morning."

"Alright, lead the way."

I follow him to his truck, and I'm surprised that he only drives about a half mile through campus before stopping at the cathedral that I've never been to. Caritas Chapel, the on-campus Catholic church.

"Normally I'd walk, but I figured you needed the break after working your knee," he says, like the thoughtful guy he is.

"We're going to church service?" I ask surprised. Not because he's religious, or even Catholic, but I wouldn't have pegged a college senior's ideal stop to be church on a Friday night. Sophomore year feels like a lifetime ago when we explored Omnis Chapel in search of the catacombs. We never did find them.

"Catholics call it Mass, and no, we don't have to stay for services." he gets out and runs around the truck as I open my door. He helps me out so that I'm not jumping down with sore leg, and we make our way into the sanctuary.

This church isn't as old or opulent as Trinity, but it's ornate and special in its own way. A singular aisle leads down the center of the dark mahogany benches lined up on either side to a large altar space that peaks at least three stories high. Beautiful, carved wooden confession booths stand silent on each side, waiting for parishioners to shed their sins. The stone walls, like those in all the Gothic buildings on campus are accented with large stained-glass windows.

A peaceful feeling comes over me, which is something that I haven't felt in a while. I look up at Chase finally to see him watching me. I look down and smile, feeling a little bare. He was right about this place being calming.

"Do you come here a lot?" I ask.

Chapter 24

"When I can. I love this place. When I'm feeling sad or lonely or aimless, I come here and find solace. I won't claim to be a virgin until marriage or to being a perfect catholic, but I do have a relationship with God."

"Wow, you speak about this place with such veneration."

"Vener-what?" he asks, laughing.

"I love using unique words, sorry. It just means that you have a deep, reverent love for something." He looks at me for a moment before glancing away.

"I've been coming here since I was a kid, with my parents. They went to school at Kalon and stayed together after. They actually got married here."

"Oh wow, I didn't realize that people could marry on campus. I guess it makes sense, seeing this space though. It's perfect."

"You'd be surprised at where people get married in Boston. I've lost track of how many people get married at the public library."

"Really? It's such a beautiful library, now that you say that I can see it."

He leads us over to one of the tables that lines the back of the last row of seats where there are about seventy-five white candles in clear pillar jars, some lit, some not. There is a jar of skinny wooden sticks, like matches without the flammable end on either side of the table. I saw something like this at the shrine, but those candles were electronic, and I was being more exploratory than spiritual then.

"Do you want to light a candle?" he asks, grabbing two sticks.

"I'm not sure what to do. I've never been to a Catholic church when I was seeking something out other than pictures." I confess.

Will he think less of me?

But no, he just chuckles, and hands me a stick.

"Some people light a candle to help aid their prayers to God, like a physical form of prayer. See the flame and pray to it, like you're looking into God's eyes. That's my vision, anyway. Others light the candle as gratitude to God in general. My Ma lights candles when she's praying for other people, usually the eternal salvation of mine and my Pop's souls," he says, nudging me with a smile. I giggle quietly at the twinkle in his dark eyes.

Clearing my throat, I focus my eyes on the candles.

"Alright, I think I can handle that."

We go quiet for a bit and light our candles, concentrating on our thoughts.

There's a bubble of space between us that fills with something alive, and I stare at my flame, a little mesmerized. Chase touches my arm, breaking the spell, so I blow out the fire and follow him to a bench a few rows up. We move all the way to the end, near the confession booths.

It's between services now, so the church is pretty empty and quiet. There are a few confession booths with a sign that says "In Session" but I can't hear anything from them.

It's quiet for a few minutes before Chase speaks up.

"Anything you want to talk about? I don't know you as well as I want to, but I can tell that you're not the same girl that sat on that beach with me and watched the sunset last year."

I look over at him, a little surprised that he just went for the kill. He just looks back, softly encouraging me to answer with his open expression.

"Ahh. Well, I guess you could say that I'm still adjusting to things. You know, forced retirement before I was ready and all."

"Yeah, I figured that was part of it. I'm not sure how I'd take it if I were in your shoes."

"You're still planning to go pro?"

"Absolutely. I can't sign with an agent yet, NCAA rules, but I plan to declare myself for the draft. It's coming up, in July."

Yes, I like this line of talking. The last thing I want to do is talk about my failed career any more than I already have.

"Tell me how that works? Don't you have to be scouted?"

"Yes and no. Most players who declare themselves for the draft do so when they're eighteen or nineteen," he explains. While he talks about declaring as a free agent and leagues the NHL drafts from, I admire his earnestness. He's excited, and it shows. I just want to bask in it.

"Why did you choose Kalon instead of the draft? I've seen you play, and while I'm not skilled enough to recognize talent enough to speak on it, I can see that you're the fastest by far. And Luca always talked about you being the leading goal scorer. You could already be scoring goals at TD Garden!"

Chapter 24

He smiles at me, too humble to acknowledge the brag.

"I told you that my parents met here. Pops played hockey and was in talks to go pro, but he went out with a career-ending injury senior year and lost his chances. Instead, he married Ma right out of college, they had me, and he went to trade school to be an electrician. He always instilled in me that I need to have a solid backup plan, one that I truly would love, in case professional hockey either doesn't work out, or I get injured down the line. I know myself. I wouldn't want to finish schooling when I'm twenty-five or thirty and done with hockey, be it injury or losing my place on the team."

Wow. Not only is he really mature and levelheaded, but he's also unintentionally making me feel like the most ignorant, naive person alive. I thought my backup goal was brilliant, but in reality, it was completely contingent on my success as a gymnast.

There is a reason that Tara Lipinski is a sports commentator for NBC National Figure Skating. It's because she's a highly decorated gold medal Olympian with beauty and poise, and people *want* to see her because they *know and respect her.*

Feeling about as sharp as a beach ball, I try to steer my thoughts out of the dump.

"I think that your plan is really well thought out, Chase. I admire that, seriously."

"Thanks, Len. I can sense that you don't want to talk about you-know-what, so can I ask a really personal question? Feel free not to answer. What did you pray about when you lit the candle?" He looked so hopeful that I'd answer, so I did.

I've never talked about my problem with the church before. I'm not sure how he'll take it, but my problem isn't with God. It's with man.

"I'll answer that with a story first. I grew up in a Southern Baptist community, and while I don't know much about Catholicism, I know it's very different from the way Baptists view God and Jesus. Y'all are taught that the Son, the Father, and the Holy Spirit are more one than three. We're taught that God is truly the Father of Jesus, and therefore, two different beings. You with me?"

He nods quickly.

"From Sunday School to Summer Bible Camp, and years in the church, Jesus is talked about as if He's our buddy. He wants us to succeed, to do well, and he's cheering us on from Heaven. You need a new job? Pray on it, Jesus died for you, He has your back. You need some guidance in your life? Give it to Jesus. He'll show you the way."

I pause, swallowing to wet my dry throat.

"And I soaked in every word from the pastor and youth minister, from the deacons. I used to pray for all sorts of ridiculous things. "Please, God, let me improve my vault runway placement. Please Jesus, can you help Maddie win this rodeo?" I say it mockingly now, but I had no problem asking for things like I was writing a letter to Santa.

"And then something happened that made me stop trusting the church and had me questioning my beliefs. Our beloved, and I do mean *beloved* youth minister was caught molesting younger girls in our youth group."

His face morphs from shock to anger. I know the feeling. He grabs my hand and holds it tight and I love the feeling of his rough palm, so much larger than mine. It helps me feel strong enough to continue.

Bitterness seeps into my voice as I remember when my parents delivered the news—along with a deacon from the church. "My parents set us down one day when Raven and I were eleven and Maddie was nine. They asked us if Pastor Jake had ever touched us intimately and inappropriately. Had we seen him touch other girls intimately and inappropriately? And did we know what they meant by those words and the context they used them in?"

He's looking horrified now, but let's me continue without interruption.

"He didn't, by the way. He went to prison for sexually assaulting seven different girls ages twelve to fourteen over a six-year period before he was caught. When he was arrested and the news came out, our church was divided. You should have seen the way people turned on each other. Self-proclaimed Christian men and women called those girls whores and liars and Jezebels for what that man did to them when they were too young to have the maturity and knowledge to fight back. Too young to understand that their friend and leader, Pastor Jake was using them to commit sin and pedophilia and that it

Chapter 24

wasn't their fault." The more I speak, the angrier I get.

"Because surely, those people said, this was a man of God, who dedicated himself to the cross under oath. They said this kind of sin happens in the Catholic Church between priests and altar boys, not in Ascension Parish, not in our church. And I listened and I learned, and I hated them all for it, because those girls were my friends. Those horrible people were trying to make themselves feel better about their own flaws and sins, by convincing themselves that he was innocent, because the people in that church loved nothing more than to look down on others in the name of their religion."

I know it's not all Southern Baptists, or even all Christians that do this and think these ways. But the minority that aren't good like they claim to be ruined things between me and the church. Raven told me in private that she feels the same.

It's silent for a few minutes while people start filing in and I can tell that Chase is at a loss for what to say after hearing about a church that let me down by showing me that I can't trust man to speak the word of God.

I sigh, tired. "I will never follow religion again, but I am a spiritual person. I lit the candle to show my gratitude. But I honestly can't tell if it was a lie."

He looks at me with all kinds of words in his eyes, but all he says is "I lit my candle for you Lennie. Everything is going to be okay in time, I have faith in you. I hope you can find that faith in yourself."

I didn't say anything in return because I couldn't, so he put an arm over my shoulders and hugged me in the pew while I cried.

And that was enough for me in this moment.

Chapter 25

boketto
(v) the act of gazing vacantly into the distance without thinking

By the time October rolled around, I was able to start taking walks without hobbling in pain the next day. I took solitary walks around the lake to think, going longer and longer each day as the leaves change to orange and red all around.

On Monday, I think about how the team is probably working out kinks in their routines.

On Tuesday, I think about an assignment for my English Narrative and Narrative History class.

On Wednesday, I think about how I haven't had any kind of meaningful conversation with my twin lately.

On Thursday, I think about how Chase's hair fell over his eye as he helped me position myself in PT earlier, and how easy it is to be happy when I'm with him.

On Friday, I think about how lonely I am, and yet how I don't really want to spend time with my friends. I don't particularly think I'd make good company for anyone. Other than Chase.

Wash. Rinse. Repeat.

A few days before my birthday, I'm in my Great Victorian Novels class and

Chapter 25

we're continuing our dissection of Brontë's works. Professor Zhao stands at the podium, clicking his prompt to change slides on the big whiteboard screen.

"Wuthering Heights is widely regarded as one of the greatest love stories of all time. Because in this book, Emily Brontë showed her audience that love is defies not only time, but death as well. But let's explore this in a more modern viewpoint. One that didn't have a name in 1901. Toxic love. Our discussion today will not be about the ill-fated love between Catherine and Heathcliff, but what that love did to everyone around them, in the end, leaving them to die without ever being together."

He clicks from a picture of the wild moors of England to a sprawling manor that depicts Wuthering Heights, the story's namesake manor.

"The story begins when Lockwood goes to visit a lonely home in the Yorkshire moors called Wuthering Heights. He's struck by the owner Heathcliff's cold and gruff manner, his house appearing to be a physical manifestation of his personality. Lockwood is attacked by one of Heathcliff's dogs, and his injury forces him to stay and let the servants nurse him back to health."

He clicks the next slide, a picture of a spectral woman, looking into the window where a man lies in a huge bed.

"Lockwood finds a journal and begins to read about Heathcliff and a girl named Catherine, adopted siblings who escape the misery of their upbringing in each other's company. He drifts off but is awakened by a ghost outside of his window. The ghost cries out that its name is Catherine, and she's come home at last. Heathcliff runs in and begs the ghost to come to him, but then she vanishes."

I remember my thoughts reading that part. This mean, cold-hearted man became more human in my eyes at the moment. I felt his misery and his love for her, and it broke my heart a little.

"As children, Catherine becomes fond of her adopted sibling, Heathcliff. But then their father dies, and her mean brother Hindley becomes master of Wuthering Heights. He returns and resumes treating Heathcliff like a servant. Catherine is all that makes life tolerable for him.

"One day, they're exploring the moors and a dog bites Catherine. Servants take her to Thrushcross Grange, but Heathcliff is turned away on account of his dark skin and gypsy-like appearance. Catherine is pampered for weeks and returns to the manor looking more like the beautiful woman she is, and Heathcliff takes notice."

He pauses, looking around the room. We're in a half state of listening and paying attention. It's a recap for us, so I tune him out as my thoughts drift to Luca and me.

Were we toxic?

Certainly not in the way that Heathcliff and Catherine were. I went for one solid year without seeing that my boyfriend was in pain. I was blinded by my own love and overlooked his flaws and insecurities. I let him commandeer my time, and I told myself that it was because he loved me so much, like I loved him. Of course, he just wanted to be with me.

I can see now that it was a crutch for him. By keeping me close, he felt more secure in our relationship. By taking advantage of my kindness and wanting me constantly in the kitchen, he was seeking the comfort of home, of being taken care of. I lost who I was a bit, I think. Or maybe I've just found who I am on the other side, armed with a list of things I won't be allowing in any future relationships.

Professor Zhao is finishing up, so I sit up a little straighter and pay attention.

"Heathcliff dies alone in the rain. Though some people claim to have seen his ghost roaming the moors with Catherine, Wuthering Heights is finally left at peace."

Ringing silence.

"Toxic love. What made Heathcliff's love toxic? Let's start by discussing his part in all of this. Topic one: what did Catherine represent to Heathcliff?" Professor Zhao asks, calling on people as they start to raise their hands.

There was a lot that I took from the novel. Heathcliff was a product of his upbringing, but he did nothing to try and change.

Class finishes, and I wander out, lost in thought. Heathcliff loved Catherine so much, and she loved him back. Why did they let societal constraints keep them apart? It feels so confining, the way they lived their lives.

Chapter 25

And the way Heathcliff let that love burn him from the inside out, hurting everyone around him.

I'm walking along the lake when I see Raven on a bench just up ahead. I almost call out to her but stop once I take notice of who she's sitting by.

Chase. My Chase.

He puts his arm around her, and she kisses him on the cheek while taking a selfie of them with her camera. I freeze, as an unfamiliar feeling curdles in my gut like spoiled milk. They're together?

My chest fills with butterflies and suddenly I want to be anywhere other than here. I walk quickly past them, behind their bench, and let out a sigh of relief when they don't see me. When I get home, I lay down on my bed and stare at the ceiling, slowly processing what I saw.

I guess I never thought they'd date. Raven is wonderful, but she's not exactly girlfriend material right now. Those are her own words. And Chase is really chill and laid back and doesn't like partying or going wild all the time. Hell, he took me to church and talked to me about God. They just don't fit. But didn't I spend three years hoping they would get together, knowing they'd be great together? How could they not? They're both amazing and special people.

The truth about my feelings floats around on the edge of my awareness, and I wish I could shut it down. I do have feelings for Chase, of course I do. He's a great friend to me, and there isn't anything about him to dislike. He held my hand when I was struggling with my past and he hugged me while I cried. He brought me to his safe space to help me find peace and lit a prayer candle for me. He sat with me on a beach for hours and talked to me about his life while asking about mine, taking my mind off the fact that my boyfriend stayed too drunk to enjoy Spring Break with me.

I always kept that part of me tamped down tight because I knew he had feelings for Raven, and twin code is sacred to us. I just didn't think she would ever be receptive to his attraction, so it made him feel safe to have feelings about, even subconsciously.

I'm not sure at what point they went from friendly feelings to more, but I'm struck with the reality that I'm not only feeling jealousy. I've spent so much time with him for the past few months, little glances here, meaningful conversations there. I feel like a weight was just dropped on me, pressing me down and making it too hard to get out of bed.

    Because I'm in love with Chase, and he's kissing Raven.

Chapter 26

finifugal
(adj) hating endings; of someone who tries to avoid or prolong the final moments of a story, relationship, or some other journey

My birthday was on Friday, and Raven and I celebrated by having dinner and drinks with our group of friends and their boyfriends. Chase had an away game, so he wasn't there. Part of me was glad because I'm not so sure I could handle seeing him and Raven together.

I haven't asked Raven anything about their relationship. My twin knows me better than anyone, and I can never get away with a lie to her. She's too sharp for that. So, when he's coming and going, which is often, I make myself scarce. I've wished for Raven to settle and be happy with someone far too long to let my feelings show their face. I can't let my battered heart ruin things for Raven. Because if she looks in my eyes and sees my love for her boyfriend, she wouldn't hesitate to put me first. It's just her way. But I won't let her this time. I love her too much.

I tried not to notice how happy and vibrant Gabby and Cora were with their boyfriends, but I was rapidly becoming very aware of the fact that I was alone.

It wasn't until I saw Raven and Chase together that the possibility of an *us* with Chase came and left before I knew to wave goodbye.

I tried not to dwell, I did.

When we had PT, I was civil but forced myself to stay detached. His confusion at my withdrawal showed on his face for a few days, but the worst was the hurt that I read in his expression when I started being "busy" when he asked me to hang out. I don't know if that was better or worse than the cool aloofness that he treated me with after I declined his offer to start running with me to keep me company as I progressed in my physical therapy.

I think he read through my excuse when I cited a busy school schedule as the reason I chose to run when I knew he'd be at hockey practice.

He'd made Captain this year.

With all this time that I was putting into working on school in order keep to myself, I was the best student in the world. While I tried to focus on the fact that my straight As could only be a good thing, it was just another reminder that no matter how well I did this year, my degree was useless to me now.

But still, I spent all of my time in the library. It wasn't because it was easier to avoid people here. It's a beautiful place to study! Turns out, you can make yourself believe anything if you really put your mind to it.

Raven was relentless in trying to coax me out of my shell. She wanted to go to the movies, to the new coffee shop, to hockey games, to the mall.

I'm just soooo busy, sorry sissy!

I became a master in excuses and made myself feel better when Raven gave me looks of hurt by reassuring myself that she'd get Chase to take her.

This was reinforced the next day when she ran out the door, shouting "Don't forget to lock up, I'm going with Chase to the beach!"

In November?

I sincerely hope they freeze, I thought to myself with a sneer.

I turned another page in the book I was reading and forced myself to focus on the escape it provided.

* * *

"Hey Lennie Loo!" Gabby chirps, as she drops on the couch next to me. "Want some chips?" She shakes her bag of Sun Chips in my face.

Chapter 26

"No thanks," I say, glancing briefly up from my book.

"Girl, it's Friday night. Why are you reading on the couch?" Cora asks, walking into the room.

I raise an eyebrow and continue to pretend to read.

Raven walks in and settles in an armchair, turning the TV on.

"I'm surprised you're not at the library," Cora continues, smirking at me. "Did they finally kick you out?"

I turn a page.

After a moment, Gabby asks, "Wanna help me plan a little weekend trip away with Dylan? I want to surprise him and you're the best at finding hidden gems to visit," Gabby asks, trying to butter me up.

Gag. I love Gabby, but planning a trip for the love birds tops my list of "Don't wanna, can't make me."

"Why not just do a staycation in Boston, at a hotel?" I offer.

"Okay. Thanks Len," she says, disappointed. "Why don't we all grab a blanket and go see the sunset together?"

"No thanks. I've had more than enough sunsets."

"Seriously Len, what gives? Now you hate sunsets?!" Cora snaps, losing her patience with me.

"Yes, Cora. Now I hate sunsets."

She looks at me with exasperation. "Can I ask why?"

I close my book with a snap. "The truth about sunsets is that they're just a metaphor for death and endings. They're not beautiful. They're the fiery pits of hell swallowing up the past and keeping it there. They're the death of a day, an ending that you'll never be able to rewrite. I've had enough of that for a lifetime."

"Bravo, winner of the dramatically morose award goes to Lenore Landry. You'd make Edgar Allan Poe so proud." Raven snarks from her chair.

She has a point, but I'm not about to let her make it.

"Oh really," I snap "And what is that supposed to mean?"

"Lord, gimme strength," Cora whispers, exasperated.

"It *means*, that all you fucking do lately is mope around in your own little world and read! You don't go out, you don't see your teammates, and you definitely don't hang out with us anymore! Every time I try to spend time with you, you have some paper or some project or some magical fucking portal to Narnia opens in your room and you disappear again!" she yells every word. "Cora and Gabby are our best friends, and you're isolating yourself from everyone just like you did when you dumped Luca. I'm sick of it! Stop hiding from the world, Lenore! You're just making things worse for yourself!"

I throw my book to the side, chest heaving, turning to Raven. Everything that I've been holding against her comes pouring out.

"You want to talk about hiding from reality, Raven? You? That's mighty rich, coming from the one who fucked her way through campus, becoming the party girl to escape the past. The one who can't even get back on a goddamn horse. The one who caused us to fucking hydroplane because she's too afraid of dying every time the wind blows too hard to keep calm and think rationally when things go sideways!"

She looks stunned, speechless for once. I hear a voice in the back of my head saying I'm taking out my anger on her because she's with the man I love and I shut that voice down because for once, it feels good to be the loud one.

"You all feel this way?" I ask, noting that Gabby and Cora are averting their eyes. "Hello?!"

"Yes, okay!" Cora throws her arms up. "You've changed Lennie! You started school sweet and yes, maybe a little naive, but also fun and kind and interesting and adventurous! Now you hole yourself away, and we didn't do anything to you! You don't even try to participate in life anymore!"

"You have changed, since the accident and we know that you're disappointed about losing gymnastics, but we only want to see you be happy," Gabby says softly.

I snort derisively. "You all just want me to be happy, that's it? No, you want me to move on and get over my so-called disappointment because you want your sweet, agreeable friend back. You don't get it! I'm not disappointed and moping around for Christ's sake!" I stand up and face them all down.

"I'm fucking *mourning* a future that I spent a lifetime building, that was snatched away from me. I'll bet not one of you is on the same path you wanted for yourself when you were little. Raven wanted to be a ballerina, an

Chapter 26

astronaut, a veterinarian, and a movie star, all when she was 8. I set my mind on being an Olympic gymnast when I was five years old and *never once*, not even for a second did I deviate from that plan! I worked towards my future and my dreams, and I *never* changed my mind or gave up!" Like an animal backed into a corner, I keep lashing out.

"And now that it's all over, I'm just supposed to be okay with it? I'm supposed to move on and find my new happiness?" I shout the last sentence at them, and it's met with silence. What comes screaming out of my mouth next takes me by surprise as much as it does them. "How can I move on when *I don't know who I am without gymnastics*! And nobody, *nobody* understands. But yeah, I guess I'll go browse a catalog of hobbies and activities and hope one of them sticks so that I can get over the *disappointment* and get back to being your happy little friend."

My chest is heaving with sobs, and they all just stare at me with stricken faces and gaping mouths as I turn to grab my coat and run from the house.

No one chases me. And really, why would they?

I walk the first few miles in a rage, crying until my eyes run dry and my mind starts analyzing what just went down. I replay their derisive looks, their judgment. Have they even tried to console me these past few months? Do they even care, or are they just sick of being around the sad girl?

I find myself at the campus entrance and take a path to the sidewalk around the lake, seeing Solis Library and Caritas Chapel on the horizon.

Now that my initial rage has calmed down, I can't stop seeing the look of complete and utter hurt on Raven's face when I hurled those words at her. *God*, the things I said to her. I took her trauma and her anxiety and fear, and I used it to hurt one person who *never* do the same to me. We don't use each other's weakness as tools to fight with, we don't weaponize our words. That's not our way and it never has been. I let my feelings over a man that was never even mine affect how I treated her. And now that I am really looking inward, I can acknowledge what else I did.

I heard Chase talk with his friend about how he liked Raven years ago. Any other time I would have gone straight to her and dished, gushing like the schoolgirl I am. But I didn't. For some selfish reason, I kept that truth to myself. What does that say about me? Could she have been happy with him this entire time?

The further I walk from the house, the further the lead in my stomach sinks. I never gave a thought to anything other than my single-minded pursuit of the Olympic team. And who's to say that I ever would have made it. Who's to say that I would have succeeded? It wasn't just that the future was ripped away from me unwritten, it was that I had nothing left once that dream was taken from me. Like the saying goes. Never make someone your everything, because when they leave, you're left with nothing.

And I haven't even tried to see past that.

I let bitterness take root and I wallowed in self-pity. I pushed my family away, just like I did with my friends and Chase. I've ignored every attempt that my academic advisor has made to set an appointment with me. I've ignored girls from the team and my old coaches reaching out.

I've done this to myself. I sat in misery, and I got good and comfortable there.

This is all my fault.

Before I'm aware of it, I'm walking around to the back of Solis Library, following the path back along the lake. I'm getting tired, having walked at least five miles, so I go to sit and lean against the fence surrounding the HVAC system and whatever else is behind the six-foot barrier. It's white PVC, the kind they make pretty suburban fencing with, but bigger and sturdier. It's seamless, so I'm not sure how they get in and out, but I lean against it and prepare to calm my racing heart.

As I lean back, settling in to watch the sun finish its path to darkness, I notice something odd. This fence has *give*. I push my back against it and hear a rattle as it moves back and then forward.

Turning around, I examine it further and realize, this isn't just part of the fence. It's a gate. A seamless gate without a discernible handle or latch. My curiosity takes over and I examine it with my hands, trying to find any way to open it. I'm not sure if I'm even allowed to go back there, but I keep searching. Why is this gate designed to look like it's not here? Standing on my tiptoes, I reach over the top and my hand finally finds a lever.

Chapter 26

The gate gives way and I look around, expecting to see a maintenance man getting ready to yell at me for trespassing. None emerge, so I quickly rush through the gate, closing it behind me. There are plenty of streetlights around the lake for safety, so I can see everything pretty well. The fence backs up to about three feet in front of the sidewalk that lines the lake, so there wasn't a way to back up and see the full picture from that viewpoint. All you can see is the building and the top a huge and very full oak tree.

But what you can see from inside the fence is that it's not just an oak tree. It's an oak tree that has a wrought iron spiral staircase attached to it as if it grew that way. Winding stairs lead up to the second floor, but I can't see beyond the orange and yellow leaves. The fence and vantage point must be perfectly aligned to not see it from the sidewalk, because the leaves are bare for months in the winter.

I slowly make my way up the stairs that wind up the broad tree trunk and step onto the landing of a concrete balcony with wrought iron rails. It opens just enough for one person coming off the last step of the staircase.

I open the door, fumbling to the right, finding a large light switch and flipping it on.

My heart is pounding as I open the carved wooden door and step into the room.

The cozy room is about 16x16 in size, perfectly square. A window is situated to the left of the entrance door, and one other door is directly opposite from where I'm standing. A space heater that looks to be unplugged stands in the corner. Vents around the baseboards are keeping the room warm, which is a relief because I've cooled down after my walk. In another corner lies a stone fireplace, with a basket of wood next to it. I take a seat on the dark green velvet sofa and look at the rest of the furniture; a squishy-looking armchair and ottoman with a big round coffee table in the middle, stacked with books and a written sign. I'll read that after I explore.

An overhead chandelier lights the space, and it looks just as old and ornate as the rest of the room. I get up, leaving my coat on the sofa and wander along to look at the carved mahogany bookshelves that line every wall. There are old copies of *Little Women* and *Pride and Prejudice*, mixed in with Harry Potter and *The Hobbit*. There are romance novels, history texts, thrillers. Penelope Douglas, Colleen Hoover, Stephen King, Ann Rule…some familiar authors, some not. Books are stacked on top of each other, laying on their sides or lined spine side up along the shelves.

It's all beautiful chaos, and I'm still in a little bit of shock that I found this place. I venture through the other door and find myself in a closet full of cleaning supplies. When I look back at the door, it's disguised as a shelf and the door handle is hidden if you don't know where to look. I head through the closet door and find myself in an upstairs hallway, before turning back to see the placard "Janitors Closet" next to the door.

Of course, no one would think to come in here, seeking out a hidden room. I turn back, closing the closet door and shutting myself back in the secret room. Sitting back on the sofa, I grab the framed sign. The paper is yellowed, and it's clearly been typed with a typewriter.

```
Congratulations, fellow Kalon Knight.
You've found Locum Quietam. The Quiet Place. Did it take you years
to find? Perhaps a day? Oh, how I wish I could see you discovering
this special room. How did it get here you ask? Well, it started
in 1824, the year Solis Library was established. Connor Clarkson
was the headmaster of Kalon University at the time it was built.
His mother fell ill and passed away from typhus syncopalis after
visiting with her sister in Connecticut at the end of 1823. It was
dreadful, really, and Connor's father Adrian was devastated.
Instead of letting him waste away in his home where he had
secluded himself, Connor begged his father to come work at the
university as head of the janitorial staff. He finally gained
Adrian's agreement by promising to build him a second, secret
office where he could go to be alone, when he needed the solace of
silence.
And so, Connor had this room built from a secret set of blueprints
that remains lost to this day. The only ones that are known do not
include The Quiet Place. When his father passed away peacefully to
go be with his mother, Connor decided that this room should remain
for those who seek peace and solitude.
And so now I ask, dear student, that you keep the secret as well.
```

Chapter 26

```
Tell only those absolutely dearest to you, those whom you know can
keep this space safe and hidden in the spirit it was built for. I
hope you find the comfort you're looking for.
So, cozy up near the fire, grab a book from the shelf, and search
for whatever it is that you're after in the pages of a story. But
I must warn you, if you take a book, leave a book. You wouldn't
want the ghost of Adrian Clarkson to seek you out for tarnishing
his most cherished place, now, would you?

Yours in Solace,

The Quiet Keeper
```

I put the sign down carefully, lost in thought. Who wrote that? Was it Connor or someone who knew him?

I can identify with Adrian's pain in the sense that I can't stand to feel it in front of others. I'm not sure if it's the part of me that hates being vulnerable. Perhaps the part that came from my mother and doesn't like to be overly emotional, especially when those are negative emotions.

I've never been comfortable talking about my feelings or letting others know that I need help. I definitely get that pride from my father.

But no, whether those traits are hereditary or learned, I am who I am. When the hard stuff comes, I don't want to face it. I hide, avoid, deflect, deny. Anything to not face the truth and the pain and the finality head on. And instead of speaking about my pain and fears, I push everyone away so that I'll be left alone in my misery.

But that only works for so long. I can't outrun the past and I can't hold off the future.

I've been fooling myself for so long.

How many years did Connor's father hide himself away in this office, mourning his wife's death? Did he spend his last years with his son, or did he just waste away in the confines of these walls? Is that really what I want for myself?

I spy a battered copy of *Wuthering Heights* among the coffee table books, and I stare at it for a long moment.

I'm Heathcliff, holding onto Catherine so tightly, for so long, even after I knew that she would never be mine. I could see nothing else other than the one thing I planned for my future. I hurt people around me, lashed out in anger and defensiveness and *sadness* because I was hurting over losing just the *possibility* of something. Something that was never mine to begin with.

And Chase, who is possibly the sweetest man alive…he was never mine, either. Raven is full of life and love, and she's finally settling down. I'm happy for her. She deserves to be happy. And for that matter, so do Gabby and Cora. And I can kid myself that they just want me to get over it, but I know that they've been worried. They've been supportive and they've tried to help me, and it took now seeing that I didn't want their help. I didn't want anyone's help because it would force me to look to my future instead of clinging to the past.

Right now, it all feels like I'm on the outside looking in, because I was in a reality of my own making.

And for once I'm crying not because of what I lost, but what I found. I'm crying because I finally found the secret staircase, the secret room. After four years of searching, I have no one to tell.

And there is no one to blame but myself.

Chapter 27

súton

(n) twilight; the approach of death or the end of something

After I leave The Quiet Place, carefully closing the gate so that it appears one with the fence again, I walk over to Caritas Chapel. It's fully dark now, with temperatures in the thirties, and I'm regretting running out of the house with no plan and no cell phone.

I get in line with the dozens of people filing in; it must be time for Mass soon. As I enter the sanctuary, I bask in the warmth for a bit, and then head over to one of the altar tables, remembering when Chase and I lit our candles.

I want badly to pray for happiness, for the forgiveness that I need to earn. For a glimpse of the future, for a sign that it will all work out, for guidance on how to get there. Maybe that's all unspoken as I light my candle, but I know I need to do these things on my own. *Thank you for the clarity,* I send up.

I still have my legs, my health, my *life*. I still have my family, my good grades, my friends, and a working brain. There is so much that I have that I've forgotten to be grateful for, and I feel like the most pitiful fool ever for losing sight of that.

I sit in a back pew by myself, ready to take in my first Mass.

"You know, something told me I'd find you here," a familiar Boston-accented voice comes from my left.

I look up at Chase and take in the soft smile on his face.

"Raven called you?" I guessed.

"Raven called me. Scoot over," he says, and takes a seat by me.

"I left without my phone." I admit. "You're here to bring me back? Hopefully I look less pathetic than I did when I ran out in a fit."

He shakes his head at me, putting an arm over my shoulder and giving me a kiss on the head. "No Len, you look like you could use a friend."

We sit there for a few minutes in silence as people file into the church, and I let myself have this moment in his comforting embrace. He's warm and solid and smells like cedar and bergamot. He smells like home, and I give myself just this once to enjoy his embrace. A few fleeting moments to feel like he is mine as much as I am his.

"Why don't I get you home, and you and I can come to Mass if you're ever ready to take that step?"

I know that I can't avoid it forever.

So, I let him take me home.

Chase drops me off and leaves without coming inside, letting me know he's trying to give us all the privacy we need to hopefully make up. I'm prepared to beg and plead, but what I've not prepared for is to be surrounded when I walk into the door.

"Oh my God, Lennie!"

"We're so, so sorry Len, are you okay?"

"Never do that again, you had us so worried!"

And all of a sudden we're all hugging and crying, and I just feel overwhelmed with relief. We head back into the living room and someone orders pizza.

Raven looks at me with huge puppy dog eyes and says "Lennie, I am so sorry for how I treated you. I shouldn't have taken things so personally, I should have tried to help you and tried to understan-"

She's cutoff by Cora, who is identically shame-faced. "We all should have. Instead of just getting annoyed at you."

"We're so sorry that you've been hurting." Gabby chokes out while still crying.

"Stop. All of you," it's my turn to cut everyone off. This has gone on long

Chapter 27

enough.

"I'm the one who's sorry. I was hurting, yes, but that's no excuse to hide myself away. I let myself become such a miserable person. I was holding on to that dream so hard that I couldn't see the truth of things. It was never mine. I was never an Olympic gymnast. Of course, I wanted to be, but I based my plans for my entire life, my whole future on just the chance of it happening. Never did I stop to think that it wasn't guaranteed to me. It was a hard lesson to learn, and I'll admit that I didn't handle it the way I wish I would have." I scoot closer to Raven and grab her hands.

"Rae, I do not blame you *at all* for the accident, and I am so sorry that I said those things to you. I didn't mean them, and I hope you can all forgive me. I am so, *so* sorry," I end on a choked cry.

Raven wipes her eyes and I feel terrible all over again.

"Of course, I forgive you, you're my person," she says, pulling me into a hug.

My person.

And then Cora and Gabby pull us into a group hug and vow to move forward together. The lead in my stomach finally dissipates, and one more weight is lifted off my shoulders. We talk well into the night, and I finally fall into a deep sleep on the couch, surrounded by my best friends. For the first time in weeks, I'm not woken up by nightmares.

* * *

Chase and I start running together the next week and I'm able to hold my own again. I won't be learning new skills or rocking the balance beam, but my knee and ankle are finally in great shape.

We don't talk on our runs because he likes to concentrate on breathing and I think people who can talk and run are psychopaths, but it's nice to spend time with him again. He invites me and the girls to his hockey games, and I promise that we'll be there.

I still love him, but I'm trying. I know in time it will fade. I am determined to shed my inner Heathcliff. No more hiding and moping. No more coveting.

The nightmares are still coming sporadically for Raven and me. When we go home for Thanksgiving break, I decide for both of us.

"You're sure you want to go see it? Absolutely sure?" Daddy asks, wariness coloring every word. He told me after the accident that he paid the junkyard owner to keep it. He's spoken with a therapist ever since Raven's incident as a child, which severely traumatized him, and when he confided about the accident, she told him that we may need to eventually see the jeep to bring some closure. To confront it and move on.

"Yes, we're sure. We need to face it and get some closure," I say firmly. Raven is still uneasy, but she has her reasons. Reliving the past is not as easy for her, but I promised to make her face only the car crash with me. We both need to put this behind us.

Gus goes with us to the junkyard over in Geismar, one town away. We called ahead, and the owner walked us back to a huge tarp-covered pile.

I grab Raven's shaking hand and say "It's in the past. Let's leave it there."

She nods, and we take in the wreckage. Jeep Wranglers are tough—one of the reasons we were allowed to pick it out. But going against a two-ton truck going fifty miles an hour, even without the trailer attached…the Jeep had no chance. The entire passenger side is an impression of twisted, dented metal. Fire and Rescue had to cut the door off in order to get me out, so that's gone. What looks to be dried blood stands out on the light gray seats, and I force myself to see it.

I finally let my mind go back to that night. A blaring horn and the screech of brakes. Raven's cry of fear. The smell of gas and smoke. The metal twists and tears and the truck grill meets my side with a crunch of metal and shatter of glass. Shock takes hold of me at the sudden pressure. Searing pain shoots through my body as the metal rips open tissue and breaks bones. Raven screams my name like she'll never be able to see me again.

I don't cry as I remember all of this, and neither does Raven. Auguste and Daddy shed a few tears that they angrily pawed away, as though they were offensive. Gus has always been especially protective over his "Little Landrys" and I know he's torn up to see my blood on the seat and imagine my body in the twisted hunk that remains of our Jeep.

"I was afraid you wouldn't make it," he admitted sadly.

Chapter 27

"Raven called us screaming. She was almost incoherent. I've only been that scared once before in my entire life." Daddy said to me. "I'm so thankful that you surviv-" his voice breaks.

He clears his throat and gives himself a moment. "Thankful that you both survived."

"Me, too," Raven said.

And that's just it. We survived. And I intended for us to make the most of that. I'd said to Raven last night when we prepared ourselves for today "We lived. And instead of focusing on what that accident took from us, I want to take from it. I'm claiming the joy of life from it. The joy in what you have. The joy in just the knowledge that we survived to live another day and to live each day being grateful to be alive. But you already have that, so what are you taking?"

She thought for a while. "I'm taking nothing else for granted, that's what I'm taking. I don't want to look back and worry that my last words to someone were negative, and I don't want to look back and feel that my relationships were lacking from anything that was in my control."

And by the time we returned from Thanksgiving break, I was ready to tackle the question of my future head on.

* * *

"I was hoping I'd be seeing you soon, but I have to say that I'm shocked to actually see you keep an appointment," Mrs. Newbury said, peering over the top of her glasses at me. I smiled, knowing I deserved the dig.

"I know, it seems that I had to do some maturing this semester." I admit and then I spill my guts to her. I confessed my fears that I didn't know what path to take or how to get there, and in the end, she showed me what I was missing all along. I was already on the right path.

I was just too blinded by my own stubbornness to see it.

As I'm getting up to leave, she says one last thing to me. "You gave a lot to the sport and to your team, Lennie. It's time to let it give something back to you. Your education."

After I leave her office, I walk towards Lectio Hall for one of my classes. It's a little early, so I want to find a place to sit and read while I wait. It's the first day of December and large snowflakes fall in a thick curtain. It doesn't snow much before January, so it feels special to me. I love being outside on days like this, so I wore my thick wool pea coat and pom pom hat so I can sit and enjoy the peaceful snowfall.

I get a sense of deja vu when I see Raven and Chase heading over to a bench. They sit down and situate themselves, Raven holding her camera up for a selfie while Chase wraps his arm around her and kisses her while holding her cheek in his hand.

I stare at them for a beat and force the sadness down.

No room for that.

So, I hold my head up and walk quickly by them, sighing in relief to be away from the happy scene.

But a tear falls down my face before I can stop it, followed by another.

"Lennie, wait up!"

Oh no.

I quickly wipe my face and turn around to see Chase jogging up to me with a smile. He looks at my face and his smile drops.

"What's wrong?" He asks.

"Oh, nothing, just heading to class."

He looks concerned. "Are you crying?"

Another tear escaped before I could stop it.

"No." I squeak before steeling myself. "My eyes are just leaking, apparently," I try to joke. "I saw you guys but wanted to give you some privacy, it looked like you were busy. In case you were wondering why I didn't say hi." Now I'm just rambling. *Shut up Lennie.*

"Lennie. Why are you upset?" he asks, undeterred. His beautiful brown eyes narrow in concern, never leaving mine. It's disconcerting.

"I'm fine," I say. "You and Raven are a really cute couple, Chase," I say more firmly. "I'm happy that you two are together."

"Umm what?" he says, tilting his head and looking at me like I've just asked for directions to Hell.

Chapter 27

"Raven and I are not *together*."

"Oh, I saw you kissing just now. And spending time together, I-"

"I've been helping her this semester with a photography project to get volunteer credits for my scholarship."

Ringing silence fills the air between us, and I rack my skull in search of two brain cells to rub together. I didn't ask Raven about Chase to protect her own happiness, this relationship that I imagined between the two of them. I feel so stupid.

"Oh, I um…" I suddenly feel like my head is too big for my body.

"Lennie," Chase says slowly, searching my eyes intently. "Why does the thought of me and Raven dating make you cry?"

Oh hell. Death by mortification, this is how I go. It's been a great twenty-two years, thanks for the memories!

"Chase…I just, um. I-" I don't get the chance to string together more unfinished words before he cuts me off.

"Please let me be right about this," he mutters, right before grabbing my face and kissing the absolute life out of me.

At first, I freeze in shock, until the warmth from his hands and mouth register. I wrap my arms around his neck and kiss him back with everything I have. My awareness contracts to Chase and Chase only, the cold and snow forgotten. After several moments, he pulls back and looks at me. "I was worried that I would never have the chance to do that," he says, smiling softly.

"Same," I gasp out, still swooning a little, and a lot in shock.

He kisses me again lightly before pulling back to look at me.

"Is this okay?"

"Yes," I manage. Is this happening?

I look over at Raven who's sitting up on the bench, shamelessly ogling us and wave goodbye to her. She has a huge grin on her face as she waves back.

"Can we go somewhere to talk? My face is kind of frozen," Chase says, earning a laugh from me.

"I know exactly where to go," I say.

I lead him to The Quiet Place, which I only told the girls about before swearing them to secrecy. As I walk into the room ahead of Chase, I'm relieved that the space is empty, although I spy the big stack of books Gabby, Cora, Raven and I left when we visited the day after The Living Room Showdown. It looks to have been rifled through.

"Holy…" he trails off, looking around. "It really exists."

"I discovered it the night you found me at the church and gave me a ride home," I say, sitting on the coach. "I felt so alone that night because I'd pushed everyone away, every single person in my life, and I realized that I'd found this place after four years but had no one to talk to about it."

"I get it," he says, sitting beside me and grabbing my hand. "I did that for a while, too."

"When?"

"When you started dating Luca," he admits, sending a shock wave through me. "I've been into you since I saw you my freshman year."

That can't be right.

"But I didn't meet you until our Sophomore year," I say.

"True, but I saw you first. It was before classes started, in the quad. We were hanging out before our team orientation, and you and Raven walked by. I had on sunglasses, so I just stared at you. You were so beautiful. And then Dominick popped off with something dumb, and Raven shut him down. I saw you around a few times that year, but I was too shy to come up to you," Chase gives me a self-deprecating smile, shaking his head at his perceived cowardice.

"And then we saw you at the pool, and you showed Luca up and I couldn't get you off my mind. When my cousin invited me over that day you made us all gumbo before the LSU game and I showed up with Luca, I was shocked to see you. I thought, this is my in, but I wasn't quick enough. Luca asked for your number, basically put a claim on you and since we were teammates, you became 'untouchable' as bad as that sounds." I'm surprised to hear all of this, and he keeps going, which is good because I think I'll die if he doesn't.

"And you seemed happy, for the most part. When he bragged about how great of a girlfriend you were, when he asked you to make him dinner or pulled something immature, I just gritted my teeth and tried to ignore it." He's wearing his feelings all over his face, fidgeting on the couch as if those

Chapter 27

emotions are clawing their way out of his mind after being held hostage for so long, making their way to the surface in the form of rushed words and furtive glances.

"And when we went to Myrtle Beach and you sat on the beach with me and we watched the sunset together, I let myself start liking you even more. It's one of my favorite memories. Everything that came after you started PT with me just made me want you that much more. I said yes to Raven when she asked me to do the project with her because I thought I might steal more time with you. But then you became so distant that I didn't think I had a chance."

He's looking at our linked hands like he's afraid to look at my face to see my reaction.

"Chase…" I start. "I've spent the past few weeks trying to avoid you because I saw Raven kiss you on that same park bench last month. I thought you were together. I knew you always liked her, and I just thought-"

"What do you mean, you knew I always liked her?" he asks, looking up at me in confusion.

"That day when we officially met in my kitchen, I overheard you and Dylan talking about us. I don't remember word for word, but it sounded like you said you weren't attracted to me, but you did like Raven. I kind of wrote you off that day because obviously twin code beats any kind of team bro code that you hockey players have."

He shakes his head, laughing. "Oh man, we are something else. No Lennie, I've never liked Raven. She's great, like I've said before, but she doesn't do it for me. It's always been you. As a matter of fact, I joked with Raven when I was buzzed over last spring break that we should double date with you and Luca. She laughed in my face and said that I was too much of a sweetie," he says with a grin. "Pretty sure that I remember telling Dylan I was attracted to you, right before I found out that Luca asked for your number. Geez, saying it all out loud now is making me feel really childish actually."

"To say that I'm feeling childish is an understatement." I admit.

He kisses me again, and instead of going over all of the what ifs and what could have beens, I just focus on the present.

And kiss him back.

Chapter 28

ubuntu
(n) the belief that we are defined by our compassion and kindness towards others

The next few weeks flew by, while I worked out what steps I needed to take next for my future and Chase and Raven finished her selfie project.

It was a time-lapse sequence that was supposed to represent the ebbs and flows in a couple's relationship. Set in the same ten different settings, over a supposed one-year period, they took three hundred and sixty five selfies together. The park bench, the beach, our living room, his bedroom, the park and so forth, all in different seasons and with different clothes on. What changed were their expressions to the camera, and each other.

Raven said that she meant to showcase how love is so enthusiastic and hopeful at first, and then the first fight happens, and resentment starts to slowly leak in. They'll make up, fight again about the same things not changing, then drift apart. They'll get drunk one night and have wild sex, reigniting their relationship.

Then maybe one of them begins to have feelings of straying, which was depicted in one selfie at the beach with Raven looking into the camera with a forced smile and Chase looking off in the distance, presumably at another woman. Raven said that she loosely based the idea on my and Luca's demise, but I thought it was beautifully and brilliantly done.

Chapter 28

They worked hard on it, and in the end, I had really sentimental feelings when watching the five minute long video.

It's what ultimately brought Chase and I together.

Walking hand in hand with Chase down the snowy path towards Bellus Hall, I feel a deep sense of ease. It's the second Friday in December, and we're heading to meet Jared and Gabby for lunch before he and I go on a date.

I'm not sure if it's because we have years of history being friends, but this relationship feels more solid and deep than mine with Luca did at this stage.

We've been together for two weeks, but I haven't told him that I love him yet. Fear of him pulling the brakes keeps my mouth in check from spilling those three little words.

"You're going to be at the game tomorrow, right?" he asks, squeezing my hand.

"All four of us will be, actually. We're riding together with Gabby." I reply.

He's playing away at Boston College tomorrow, so we're all banding together so they have support from Kalon.

We've made signs for Jared and Chase; I can't wait for him to see.

Gabby's says, "Hey #29, if you get a hat trick tonight, I'll do that thing you like!"

Mine says "It's pucking awesome being your girl, #13!"

We're dorks, but it was fun making them.

"Are you nervous?" I ask. Boston College is tough this year, and they compete in the Frozen Four against Kalon U.

"Nah, we've got this," Chase says, nudging me and smiling down. Gosh I love his smiles. It always feels like they're only for me.

"So where are we going on our date, sir?"

"You hate surprises don't you? This is like the third time you've asked."

"I don't hate them, but I'll give you a secret about girls. We need to know how to dress or we're hopelessly anxious."

He throws his head back and laughs.

"Yeah, I guess you have way more options than men. I'll let you off the hook. Wear whatever casual thing you want, just make it comfortable."

"Alright," I nod. "I can do that."

He drops me off after lunch so I can finish studying for finals and figure out what to wear. He is a very literal person, so I decide to go full on cozy. I wear black leggings and a tank, with a lightweight cardigan topped with long, thick socks and knee high boots. My thick wool pea coat and pompom kit cap complete my outfit.

"You look adorable," he says when I open my door. He kisses me forehead and then pulls me into a warm hug.

"Ready for our date?"

"Ready!"

We drive for a few minutes, talking about something funny that happened in the locker room, and I'm surprised when he stops in front of his apartment. We've been on a few dates, and I finally got to see his apartment last week. He shares it with his best friend Jared. Chase glances over at me.

"I hope this is okay. Jared's out with Gabby for the night, and I wanted to cook for you."

"You *cook*?" I ask him astonished. He laughs a little as we get out of the truck.

"Yes I cook, ya goose. Not every man is helpless in the kitchen!"

"Well, I know that, I guess I just expected *northern* men to be," I tease. Kinda. I did really think that.

"I went home last Sunday and asked my mom to show me how to make her shepherd's pie. It's not really complicated, and it's one of my favorite things that she makes."

"I've heard the name, but I don't know what that is." I say and he stops midway to opening his apartment door. He looks at me incredulously.

"You've never had shepherd's pie? Have you seriously not been to any Irish places in Boston in *four years*?"

"Hey!" I poke him. "You never had gumbo before me!"

We move into the kitchen, and he starts getting stuff gathered to cook as I take my coat, hat, and boots off.

"Uh yeah, because gumbo comes from one specific state over a thousand miles away. Ireland is an entire country, there are Irish restaurants all over the country."

Chapter 28

He has a point.

"Alright Mr. O'Leary, I give you permission to drag me all over the country on a tour of Irish restaurants."

"Mr. O'Leary is my father, and they're called Pubs, sweets." He bats me on the forehead with the dishtowel he's holding and gets to work.

Chase and Jared's apartment is way neater and tidier than I thought a guy's apartment would be. Luca's frat house was always one step up from grimy and about six steps down from clean.

They have an open floor plan, showcased by a living room with hockey memorabilia on the walls, a typical guy black leather sofa and love seat, and like eleven thousand games stacked near their Xbox. Oh, and a cute little Christmas tree with red and gold ornaments.

Where my house is filled with girly touches like throw blankets, fresh flowers, and potted plants, a beautiful menorah for Cora, and a pretty, white Christmas tree, theirs is masculine and minimalist.

I make myself busy peeling potatoes while he browns the meat and cuts the veggies.

"Talk to me about some of your favorite spring break trips?" I ask.

He smiles at me. "You remember that?"

"What? Of course, I do Chase. That's one of my favorite memories too," I say in surprise. Did I not tell him that?

"Huh. I didn't realize. Let me think. They all stand out in their own way. A lot of them were when it was still cold and/or snowing. Like Colorado and Wyoming. I love the snow."

"Me too. I will never forget my first snowfall. It was the first night we got back after Christmas break, my freshman year. I woke Raven up at like two am or something like that to go lie on the picnic table in front of Anderson Hall. It was stunning."

"Oh, I know, I love quiet nights when it's snowing. It's a special kind of peace."

He totally gets it.

"So, there was this one day at Yellowstone. We had just seen the geyser Old Faithful go off, and we were driving somewhere else to eat lunch. A lot of the animals come out of hibernation in April, and the bison have their calves. I'd never seen a bison in person before, and they're massive. I was fourteen at the time, thinking I was this big, bad high school hockey player, but I felt tiny and weak when I saw what they could do."

"Did it gouge you?"

"No, but that's because my parents are smart and taught me animal safety during one trip to Maine." He lifts the pan to toss the browned meat. Impressive.

"But"—he pauses so as not to burn himself on the boiling water as he slides the chopped potatoes in— "the tourists who go there have no sense of self preservation. We saw black bears and grizzly bears in fields, parking lots, and roads. Wanna guess how many people we saw out of their cars, taking videos and pictures of these animals like a hundred feet away?"

My eyes go wide. "You're joking!"

"Nope. There were always a handful and I just hoped that I wouldn't have to see someone mauled by a bear or trampled by a moose. I saw some close calls. Bears coming out of hibernation are skinny, but they're still alert and they're also…hungry." He says with a wolfish smile, making me laugh.

"But that day leaving Old Faithful, I did see a full grown male bison completely ram a car door. It was too close to his mate, and they're fiercely protective. I almost pissed myself," he said with a chuckle.

"Oh my gosh, I'd be terrified. But now I also want to see a bison in real life. From afar. Very afar," I add.

"Maybe we'll see one together, love." He says, and my heart staccatos over the term of endearment.

And if I thought I knew before, I am positive now that I love him. The words beg to be freed, but I don't want to push him away by showing too much too soon.

He puts together the dish and we turn on Elf while it cooks, snuggling on the couch.

"Byeee Buddy. I hope you find your daaad," I say in Chase's ear with the narwhal voice, making him laugh. It's my favorite part of the movie.

"God I love you," he says, still chuckling. We both freeze, and he looks at

Chapter 28

me with wide eyes. "Len, I- I wasn't thinking, I didn't mean to just blurt it out like that."

I'm just staring at him in shock with my mouth hanging open like an idiot. "It's not that I don't mean it, I just, I know it's too soon, I'm sorry if that makes you feel uncom-" I decide to let him off the hook with a finger to his mouth.

"I love you too," I say, kissing him softly.

"Yeah?" His relief is written all over his face.

"Yeah."

"Well…good then," he says with a beautiful smile before wrapping me in his arms and kissing me.

What starts out slow and sweet, heats up and turns into him maneuvering me onto my back with him between my legs, on top of me. We speak between kisses.

"I've loved you for so long. Since the beach," he says, before moving his tongue with mine.

"I've loved you since the church," I respond, kissing him back until we're both breathless.

"When you lit a candle for me and held me while I cried." He takes my cardigan and tank off.

"You knew I was lonely and sad, and you spent your day with me on the beach. No one has ever made me feel like you do," he says, as I remove his t-shirt.

"I love you Lennie," he pulls my socks off.

"I love you too, Chase," I flick open the button on his jeans.

He surges back down to kiss me again and the timer goes off, making us both jump. He lets her forehead fall against my shoulder and rasps out a laugh.

"Saved by the bell?" I ask.

The look he gives me when he meets my eyes is a new Chase to take in, full of heat. "Not on your life," he says. He gets up, taking the casserole dish out of the oven and sets it on the stove. Then he takes my hand and leads me to his bed where he sits down and looks up at me.

"That has to rest, or we'll scald our mouths. I'm more interested in getting naked with you, but if you want to wait, say the word."

I bend down and get level with his eyes, my hands on his broad shoulders. "Not on your life."

Clothes finish coming off, I go under Chase, and I'm in absolute bliss as we explore each other. It's a different kind of first time. Being intimate with someone that you're already in love with is freeing, in a way. My first time I was in my head, a little afraid of the unknown, and really just ready to get it over with, which makes me a little sad to think back on. I was nineteen and in the throes of falling in love with Luca, all of the butterflies and innocence. I just wanted to check those boxes, have the experience, become a woman.

Now, here with Chase, I have none of that in the back of my mind and I can just experience the moment for what it is. We move together as one, and by the time I'm crying out, he's shuddering over me with his face pressed into my neck. We don't move for a while, and I just lay there slowly running my fingers up and down his back.

"You have no idea how nice it feels to be touched like this," he says.

"Yeah?"

"Mm hmm. It's been a really long time since I've been in a relationship, and I've never loved anyone before you. It makes this feel..."

"More meaningful?"

"Yes."

"I'm glad. I-"

I'm cut off when his stomach grumbles loudly in protest of not eating dinner yet, and we both laugh.

"Time to eat, big guy!" I pat his back and we get dressed before he dishes up the food and we sit down to watch my favorite Christmas movie, Christmas Vacation.

And this shepherd's pie?

Mouthwatering.

Chapter 29

apricity
(n) the warmth of the sun in winter

"Why are you nervous, sweets?" Chase asks as I obsessively braid my hair over and over.

We're in Chase's truck, heading to dinner at his parent's house where I'll be meeting them for the first time.

"I've only met a boyfriend's mom once in my whole life and she thought I was a hick."

More braiding.

"Len, I haven't brought anyone home in over five years. Trust me, they're going to love you. They've begged me to find a nice girl to bring home."

Faster braiding.

"Okay, change of subject. Talk to me about your meeting with your advisor. I kept meaning to find out what happened, but we ah…get off track," he says with an easy smile and a heated glance.

I smile back at him, replaying memories of us together, touching and kissing in bed last weekend. "I'm never going to be able to look my Ma in the eye again when she makes shepherd's pie," he'd said that night, making me laugh until I cried.

"Yes, actually it was amazing, and I felt like an idiot for thinking that I was finishing wasted degrees. The whole time I was working towards this year, my only thought was how to apply what I was learning to help me with transitioning to being a sports caster for network coverage of competitions and meets. And my minor was just because I love English and Literature so much. My advisor helped me see that both degrees are perfect for someone wanting to work in the literary field, specifically as an editor."

His whole face lights up in a way I've never seen, and I'm a little mystified.

"*Really*. You don't say," he says. "Now that I think about it, you'd be perfect. You read all the time and you have no problem correcting *my* grammar…" he trails off with a grin.

"I just don't see how you can mix up Y-O-U-R and Y-O-U-R-E constantly!" I say in my defense.

He just laughs it off, pulling up in front of a pretty two-story house with white siding, and both downstairs *and* upstairs railed-in porches. A big bay window juts out from the first floor. I hope has a window seat to look at the beautiful lake across the street.

"Yeah," he says as he turns the truck off. "You and my mom are going to get along just fine."

We head inside the warm house that smells like pot roast and fireplace. A staircase leads to the second floor right inside the foyer, and the wall is lined with photographs all the way up, similar to my family home.

As we walk into the front living room, I am immediately in lust. Not only is the bay window in fact, home to a beautiful window seat, but across the room there is a massive fireplace that is surrounded by built in bookshelves that are stuffed with what must be over five hundred books.

My jaw drops and stays there, and I ignore Chase's knowing laughter as I take in my new inspiration for any future house that I may own.

"Chase, is that you? Well, hello there!" A beautiful older woman with shoulder length light brown hair comes into the room and spies us. She grabs Chase in a big hug and smacks a kiss on his cheek. "Hey Ma, good to see you." he says, pulling me towards him. "This is my Lennie. My girlfriend," he adds with a proud smile and I'm a proverbial puddle on the ground.

"Well, I'd hoped that was the capacity he'd be bringing you in. I've heard

Chapter 29

your name for years," she says, pulling me into a big hug. She has to stoop down to reach me. "It's so nice to finally meet you, call me Sabrina."

"It's nice to meet you too," I say, sagging just a little in relief.

She's absolutely lovely.

Chase has her general coloring, but he must look more like his father. She's about four inches taller than me, while he towers over both of us.

"Yeah, I finally managed to make her mine," he says, putting his arm around me and kissing my temple. I hug him tightly for a few beats, feeling a warm rush of gratitude that meeting his Mom is effortless. "And you'll never guess what she wants to be when she graduates, which I just found out about five seconds ago. *An editor.*"

Her answering smile is like a kid's at Disney World.

He continues, "And weren't you just going on and on about work being so busy that you were thinking of taking on a paid intern after Christmas?" he says in leading, with a Cheshire cat smile.

"Oh, I wouldn't expect . . ."

"That's exactly what I was saying, actually," she cuts me off, grabbing my hand and leading me towards the seating area in front of the window seat. There are two love seats facing each other with a coffee table in between and she leads me over to one. None of my own mother's quiet southern hesitation. This woman is a force who knows what she wants, and I have no choice but to follow and sit with her.

"Go on and see if your father needs help," she shoos Chase off after she sits me down. "Let's talk shop, Lennie. Tell me about yourself, major, minor, your interest, and experience?"

"Well," I say, rubbing my clammy hands on my jeans as the warmth from the fire starts to heat my cold extremities.

"I'm majoring in Communications and minoring in English Literature. I've never worked in the editing or publishing world, but I read any chance I can get, any and all genres. I was an elite gymnast for fifteen years, and kind of put all of my eggs in one basket before I was injured this past summer."

I fill her in on the accident.

She looks at me with sympathetic eyes. "Yes, Chase told me about your injuries and some of what came after. He said it took you a while to come to terms with everything, and I think it's really admirable that you were able to recognize that it's time to move on. It can't have been an easy process."

"Thank you, it wasn't, but I don't expect things that are worth it to ever be easy to gain or to get over," I can say that truthfully now that I'm through the worst of it. "But I think that's life."

"Very true," she pats my hand. "Now as far as having no experience, that's my main qualification. That, and an aptitude for literature, with a good head on your shoulders. I want a blank slate, an intern that has no existing habits or tendencies that need to be trained out of them."

"Well, I am happy to apply, if you think I'd be a good fit. Ever since I spoke with my advisor and she helped me see that I could actually use my degrees for something that I love, I've finally been getting really excited for the future again," I admit.

When she pointed out that I have an ideal education to make something of myself in the literary world, it was like feeling the sunshine again after a long, cold winter.

"Alright, let's go make sure my husband hasn't burned dinner," she said, standing up.

"By the way," I say as we head towards the kitchen. "Your front room is my new favorite room ever."

"You and me both, sweetie."

I follow her into a large space, the kitchen being its own room at the back of the house, and we find Chase and his dad laughing together with beers in their hands. A small TV on one of the counters plays a Bruins hockey game. I was correct in my earlier guess. Chase is almost a carbon copy of his father, though he's a good two inches taller.

"There's the beauty, let's look at you," his dad says to me. I give him a hug and introduce myself. "Nice to meet ya sweetheart, I'm Connell O'Leary."

His Boston accent is twice as thick as Chase and Sabrina's, and it makes something ping in my heart. Since when did an accent other than my own make me feel like I was home?

As the night progresses, I hear all about "Chasey Boy" growing up, laughing

Chapter 29

uproariously at the embarrassing stories and *awwww*-ing at the sweet ones. They are full of love, and I can't wait for our families to meet.

***

Which happens one week later during Christmas.

Since this is presumably our last Christmas in Boston, Raven and I beg our parents and siblings to come spend Christmas week with us. Cora and Gabby both left last week to stay with their families, so there is room for all our family. But our parents get a hotel room again—this time because and I quote "We've had a lifetime of y'alls noise, we want some quiet now that we're done raising you heathens."

We're not *that* loud. Except yeah, we are, but I don't think I realized it until Chase came over to meet everyone on the first night. We'd just gotten everyone inside and settled. Chase helped me make a big pot of chili which he kept tasting and adding stuff to. He was fidgety and nervous… it was really cute.

Alas, he had no need to be. My loud, boisterous family all piled in the house in a flurry of coats and greetings and hugs and *holy crap it's cold here*'s and luggage and mixed French and actual flurries because it was snowing again…and I turned to see the dazed look on Chase's face while I held in my laughter.

"You did say you were always lonely as an only child," I teased, nudging him. I waved my arm at everyone taking off coats and scarves. "*Bienvenue* to the exact opposite."

He smiled so brightly at me, and it only made me love him more. He wasn't nervous anymore and I knew my family would love him because he's an amazing, genuine person, who makes others feel comfortable. He's also a man's man so I know that Daddy and my brothers will latch onto that.

After all, Cajun men are famous for being "ruff and gruff." I once saw my dad grab a water moccasin by its tail and then whip it around in a circle, knocking it's head on a tree to kill it instantly. I was awed. I had almost stepped on it, not paying attention, and he shoved me out of the way and saved me before it could strike.

I let everyone smother me and Raven for a few minutes, and then turn to introduce Chase, but see that he's already talking to my parents. Daddy is pulling him into a backslapping hug. It's a testament to Chase's size that his knees hardly even buckle.

"Good to see ya again Chase, how's ya Momma and them?" Daddy asks. Chase looks quizzically at me and I laugh.

"He means 'how's your family?'" I say out of the corner of my mouth.

I make sure to bring Allan, Auguste, and Maddie over to meet him and then I go to the kitchen to help Raven get out bowls and silverware.

Everyone makes a real effort to get to know Chase, and he makes it easy. He wants to know all about our horses ("I'm not too manly to admit that they scare the crap out of me") and the LSU football team ("Your offense is wicked good") and what other Cajun foods does he need to try ("Lennie's gumbo is my favorite food on earth"), and they just eat it up.

Daddy pulls me aside before they head out, and says "Ya done good with this one, cher. He makes you happy?"

"The happiest I've ever been."

"Then get to planning your next trip down. *Together*," he says, surprising me. I say bye to Momma and then head into the living room. Someone set up a fire in the fireplace and brought out drinks. Allan rubs his hands together, suddenly looking devious.

"Game night boys and girls," he says, excitedly.

Everyone but Chase groans in unison.

"You all hate game night?" Chase asked, confused.

"Well, my man, let's let you in on the family secret," Gus drawls. "It's well known in our house that little brother here is the worst loser on the face of the planet."

"Am not!" Allan scoffs.

"How do you fix your mouth to say those words?!" I ask. "You are a *terrible* loser."

"*And* the worst winner," Raven adds, raising her eyebrow.

"You literally flipped the coffee table when I beat you at monopoly!" Maddie helpfully points out.

"*And* when I was winning at Uno, you cheated by acting like you didn't have all of those special cards! And then you danced around the living room like an idiot!" I add.

"Okay okay, call off the firing squad. I was talking about Pictionary; you can't cheat at that. Come on, we played at a frat party one time, and it was a blast!"

"You played Pictionary at a frat party?" Chase asks incredulously. "I'm not much of a partier, but even I get wilder than that."

We all got a good laugh in before Allan pipes up. "My bad, I should have clarified. This is Dirty Pictionary."

We all groan again, and Gus says "Dude, I'm not drawing boners with my little sisters."

"Ehhhh, fair point," Allan concedes before Maddie shocks us all by yelling "Oh come on, it's not like any of us are virgins!"

"Madeline Shae!" Gus and Allan shout in unison, while Chase turns bright red, and Raven just laughs.

"Oh relax," I say, "Baby sister is almost twenty."

"Fuck it!" Gus says, "Let's play!"

Turns out, when you're playing in groups of two and getting tipsier and tipsier, Dirty Pictionary is tons of fun. Raven and I were banned from being teammates after the tenth consecutive time that we won Catchphrase in the eighth grade, so I'm on Maddie's team, Raven is with Chase, and my idiot brothers are together.

"Dammit Aug! How did you not get 'Erection'?!"

"You drew a dick that looks like a boomerang, what the hell does *your* junk look like? Is that why he's sad, he has a boomerang dick?"

"I drew a sad face because he doesn't have a boner! I drew a happy face because he *has* a boner! Soft points down, boner points up! SOFT, SAD!! BONER, HAPPY!!" He's red in the face and shouting and we're all laughing so hard at him that we're crying. Chase is literally snorting and hiccuping.

He looks over at me with a big grin and mouths "I'm so happy."

Man, oh man, I love my family.

After we finally cut Allan off from playing, we head out into the snow. It's the snowiest December on record for Boston, and there is a foot of fresh powder to play in, much to everyone's excitement. Well, with the exception of Raven.

We made snow angels, built snow men, or in my brothers' case, snow *woman*, complete with realistic giant boobs, and eventually ended the night with an epic snowball fight. We stayed up late around the fire, sharing funny stories with Chase from our childhood. When we finally crashed in my bed, he pulled me close and snuggled against my back.

"This was one of the best nights of my life," he murmured sleepily.

I couldn't agree more.

Chapter 30

metanoia

(n) the journey of changing one's mind, heart, self, or way of life

Over the next few days, we show everyone around Boston. The day before Christmas Eve, Chase and his dad take Daddy and my brothers to a Bruins game. Momma and us girls are going to bake cookies and drink wine while watching Christmas movies. We invited Sabrina, but she's visiting with her sister, Gabby's mother.

We all end up in the living room, watching Home Alone, another favorite of mine.

"You know, I always watch this movie and think back to when y'all were little. I used to imagine that we left one of you at home and it would ruin the movie for me," my Mom says.

Wine has loosened her tongue because she's normally pretty quiet and only speaks when necessary.

"Yeah right, like you'd forget one of us. If you ever didn't know where we were, you'd call in the cavalry to hunt us down." Raven jokes, snorting into her wine glass.

"No one has a tighter hold on their kids than Harry and Lynn Landry," I said, mocking something people at church used to say when we'd line into church single file and take up our entire pew.

"Well, when you have five children, you have to make sure you keep them straight. It's not easy being outnumbered," she said with a frown.

"Is that why you and Daddy were so strict?" I ask, and the wine must be loosening my tongue too, because I doubt I'd have the guts to say what comes out next. "I was so naive when I came to college. I honestly lost track of all the times I was embarrassed by my lack of experience or had to learn a hard lesson."

"Same, sister," Raven said, clinking glasses with me.

Momma looks hurt, and I feel a little guilty. "Maddie is that how you feel too," she asks.

A few beats pass before Maddie nods carefully. "It was a culture shock when I moved into the dorms and all of a sudden had freedom over my actions and whereabouts," she admits. "The first time I was invited to a party, I had to force myself not to say, 'I'm not allowed to.' It was an adjustment and at first a went a little wild because of it. I learned to reel it in and use moderation, but I wish I had more experience before college."

Well, this night took a turn. We love our mom, and I don't want her to feel like we're ganging up on her. On the other hand, what we're saying is valid.

She appears to absorb all of this before speaking.

"I've never spoken much about Maman, other than to say that she moved back from France after she divorced my father. I think it's time that I told you about my upbringing." She steels herself with a sip of wine before getting started. Oookay, this is a first. We go quiet, waiting. I've always wondered why the mystery.

"Your grand-mère, Clémence, was the most beautiful girl in Canton d'Argenteuil, which is a town just north of Paris. She met my father, your late Papaw Troy, when he was stationed in Paris during the Cold War. They had a whirlwind romance, and when he left for the states, she came with him. At the time, he was stationed in Hawaii, and they married there. I was actually born in Honolulu."

My sisters and I are listening with rapt attention. All we were told growing up was that her parents divorced, their mother abandoned all of them when she fled back to France, and Papaw Troy died ten years later of a heart attack.

Chapter 30

"We were happy for a long time, at least that I can remember. Daddy was PCSed to Alaska, and it was like another adventure. I remember us flying to California when I was five. We bought a car and drove up through California, Oregon, Washington, and then through Canada through the Yukon before getting to Alaska.

"It was like another world. Keep in mind, we arrived in summer, so we had plenty of daylight to explore. But when winter came, Daddy was shipped off to Vietnam. Maman started to get depressed. It was dark almost all day and night, and bitterly cold. She didn't work, so all she did was stay at home, drinking wine and missing France.

"When Daddy got out of the army in 1976, he moved us back to his home, in Louisiana. Ft. Polk was his home base, and after he processed out, we moved to Evangeline Parish to Daddy's hometown of Ville Platte in southwest Louisiana. Maman hated it as soon as we drove up. She loved Hawaii because who didn't, but the long, dark nights spent holed up with only me for company in Alaska had started to make her bitter and hateful." She pauses to take a sip of wine. I have never been more invested in someone's history. It's like finding a hidden compartment full of gems in an attic trunk.

"Anyway, Daddy took over his father's rice farm operation. He was gone from sunup to sundown. Maman would be drunk by the time I got off the school bus, so it fell to me to make sure supper was on the table most nights. When Daddy finally came home, she'd go from crying, to raging at him from taking her from her home in France, to cursing him for abandoning us in Alaska and to berating him for forcing her to be a farm wife.

"She eventually met some 'friends' at a bar down the road and started spending all of her time with them, drinking and partying. I was twelve at this point and starting to feel the strain of her resentment towards me, and their failure of a marriage. Daddy tried to remain at work as much as possible, and I couldn't blame him. Horses were my only source of happiness in those days. I'd go out riding and training with barrels and the dummy goat I used for practicing tying, and like Daddy, I'd stay gone as long as I could.

"Maman finally left us just before Christmas. Her note said she was taking the bus to Shreveport and flying home to Paris, and she cleaned out their checking account for the money to get there. She didn't even say goodbye to me."

A tear fell down my mom's cheek. I've ever seen my mother cry before. The wine feels like soured milk in my stomach, and I put my glass on the end table so that I can hand her a tissue. Maddie goes and sits next to Momma on the couch and gives her a side hug. She smiles and pats Maddie on the knee before continuing.

"Anyways, things got pretty bad for me after that. I had so much resentment for both of my parents, that I started taking it out on Daddy. I yelled at him that he didn't love my mother enough and that's why she left us. I ran away a few times to a friend's house down the street, causing him all sorts of stress and grief. And when I went from middle to high school, I learned that I could manipulate my father. He only wanted me to be happy, and when he discovered that giving me my way made me hug him instead of glare at him, well, he was all too happy to try and find some peace. He was so tired."

I never got to meet my grandparents, and I'm seeing them in a whole new light. I couldn't have imagined any of this. It was nothing like my happy childhood, and suddenly I'm feeling very grateful for it.

"So, in high school, I partied. I tried drugs, I slept around. I didn't care about my grades as long as I was passing, and I raised as much hell as I could. I was arrested once for underage drinking, but I manipulated my father into believing it wasn't really my fault. I still feel a lot of shame about these things to this day. It wasn't until I put myself in a really bad position that I turned things around. The crowd I ran with was partying in a field and had a huge bonfire. I was stoned and wasted and passed out near the fire. I was told that one of the seniors, I was a junior at the time, dragged me off to the edge of the woods and tried to rape me. Someone, I never found out who, came across the senior trying to take off my pants."

Imagining my mother sleeping around gives me the cringes, but imaging someone taking advantage of her while passed out has me trembling.

"That's not the worst part, but thankfully he was stopped. In the meantime, the fire caught some of the tall, dried grass and trees all around. It was January, and everything was bone dry. The fire caught and burned fast and hard, and

Chapter 30

it took an hour for the fire department to put it out. When I woke up, I was surrounded by EMTs and fire fighters, and one of my best friends was dead. She'd passed out closer to the fire and died while everyone fled and panicked. A bunch of young, inexperienced kids who thought they could drink and smoke up whenever they wanted, and that's what became of it. I almost died alone in a field, like my friend. It was the worst kind of wake-up call. I stopped partying, I got my grades up, and when that senior who tried to rape me asked me to prom at the end of my junior year, I told him to eat shit."

All three of us girls gasp out a laugh. Our mother didn't curse. She said things like *"fiddlesticks"*, *"dagnabbit"*, and I'm pretty sure I heard her say *"sheezbots!"* once.

She continues, "I spent the next eighteen or so months straightening up my act. It was the best time that I've ever had with my father. I had no way of knowing that he would die the week before I graduated college. I came home when I could, but I spent four years in Baton Rouge getting my degree and meeting your father, while Daddy worked himself to the bone to put me there. I'm so glad that I got those good months with my father, but I could have had *years*, and I will have to live with that forever."

Now all three of us girls are sniffling. This is the most I've ever heard our mom speak, and it's the most candid that she's ever been.

"I don't know what to say," Raven admits.

"I'm so sorry, Momma. I hate that you went through that," I add.

She nods in acknowledgment. "And when you girls were younger and Pastor Ja-when that *man* molested those girls, it made us even more fearful for your safety and well being. We held on that much harder."

Silence, as we all take it in.

"Did you ever hear from your Maman again?" Maddie asks.

Momma scoffs, finishing her wine. "No, we never did. Daddy did get in touch with her brother, my uncle Michel, who told us that she arrived safely. I didn't hear from her again. Not one phone call or card, and no word from her family other than to send a letter when I was twenty-seven that she died from a blood clot and was buried in a family plot. I thought a lot about going to France to meet my family and visit her grave, but I find that I'm at peace. Having your own family brings a lot into perspective. Your Daddy and I were always protective of you all for so many reasons, but my own personal reason was because I didn't want to see you make the same mistakes that I did. When you're a child, growing up, you fail to realize that you're also watching your parents grow up right alongside you. The act of learning and maturing never actually stops, if we're lucky." She puts her wine glass on the coffee table and then sits up a little straighter.

"We live and learn and make mistakes, even to this day. I don't claim to always be right, and I'm sure that we could have found a happier middle ground when it came to giving you all more freedom, but all we can do is move forward. I hope you see that I came from a place of love, and not purely the need to control you. I just wanted to keep you safe, and in my own way I'm sure that I managed to be extreme about it, but I can't bring myself to regret it because your daddy and I are so proud of who you all have become."

We don't stay up much later than that, but after we all went to bed, I find myself tossing and turning for hours. In truth, I'm torn between being thrown by the knowledge she shared, and guilt for getting things so wrong. I let so much resentment for my mother build over the years.

It was easy to villainize her. She rarely showed us physical affection. She was withdrawn at the worst of times, and aloof at the best. I never truly doubted her love for me, but I remember seeing other moms with their daughters. They showed up for practices, and they let their daughters hang all over them.

They hugged and kissed their daughters, whereas mine would send me off with a simple "Love you," and a wave. But knowing what I know now, what kind of woman would I have grown into had I lived the kind of life she did? She grew up with a cold, hateful and perpetually drunk mother and an absent father. She had no real love and affection, and when she sought out an escape from her inner demons, it didn't end well. She had no real role model or someone to lean on, apart from her father for such a short time.

Would I be uncomfortable with physical affection and emotions? She was an only child, and with everything else, it's no surprise that she's self-sufficient

Chapter 30

and self-possessed. I think I would be, too. But instead of remaining an island, she got married and had not one, but five children. We wanted for nothing. And in all fairness, while Raven may have been chomping at the bit to run wild and free, I caged myself in with my sport.

Even if I had a longer leash, I wouldn't have used it. I was too busy and too dedicated to gymnastics.

And I also know that while I resented my mother, I never truly resented my father and I feel guilt over that. My mother lived a lonely and tumultuous childhood, and then turned around and made sure that her family never suffered the same fate. She took care of us and showed us what a great mother should be.

I'll take that any day.

* * *

We go to Chase's family home for dinner on Christmas Eve and have a wonderful time. If Connell and Sabrina were shocked by our lively family, they didn't show it. The men eventually broke off and talked hockey, which my dad and brothers were now officially obsessed with, and the women sat around in the front sitting room drinking wine.

"I always wanted a daughter," Sabrina is wistfully telling us. "God gave us Chase and didn't see fit to give us another, and that's good by me. But it's so nice to sit and have girl time with you sweet women." I make a vow to bring Raven over here as often as possible so that she can have her girl time fix. It's not exactly a chore, Sabrina is great company.

She and my mom got on fabulously, a perfect example of opposites attract. The quiet southern woman, and the force of nature Bostonian who laughed out loud when she heard Daddy say, "Man alive, these yankees up here about scared me off the road!"

Christmas the next day is spent at the house in a whirlwind of wrapping paper, bows, mimosas, and the usual who-can-talk-the-loudest cacophony of voices.

Chase and I gave each other our gifts the night before. He gave me the framed picture of us kissing for the first time in the snow. Apparently, Raven saw the opportunity and wanted us to have the moment immortalized, so she took a few beautiful shots with her camera. I gave him an LSU beanie and tease him that it's because we all know that only southern schools win the football championships.

It went down in history as the best Christmas to date.

Chapter 31

dérive
(n) a spontaneous and unplanned journey where the traveler is guided by the landscape and architecture

Heading back to classes after the new year felt different than all the years before. This time, I had a purpose when I listened to my professors lecture. I had direction and a new goal, and I learned with different intentions.

I did end up getting hired as an intern with Sabrina at her publishing house, Beaux Mots. I asked her why she named it "Beautiful Words" in French, and she laughed and said, "Well it just felt fancy at the time, and Irish isn't exactly a phonetic language."

Being immersed in the editing world was exciting to me and I caught on very fast. By March, I was reading over shorter submissions, proofreading, and editing passages, and even pitched a new title for a manuscript that Sabrina loved and kept.

In addition, I accepted the offer to be a volunteer coach, though I told them I could commit to only six hours a week while I juggled my twenty-hour a week internship. I coached my group of girls on leveling up in skill, specifically bars and floor. Turns out, my weakness on bars didn't translate to my coaching abilities. By the time Spring Break rolled around, I was thriving.

In another surprising turn of events, my parents planned a co-spring break trip with Chase's parents. That April, we all visited the Grand Canyon. Being there is like nothing I've ever experienced before, and I could tell by the awed looks on everyone's faces that they felt the same. Standing on the edge of the rim and seeing the vast beauty carved by Mother Nature is amazing. Pictures can't do it justice. The scale is just so enormous that it swallows even your own sense of depth and distance.

I've never felt as small and insignificant in my life, nor have I ever felt as alive.

"I feel infinite."

Charlie had it right in The Perks of Being a Wallflower.

We spent our time in the Village, taking hikes around the south rim, and doing different tours. My favorite was the Pink Jeep Sunset tour, we all squished in together and had fun with the tour guide. He told us that the North rim is closed from December to May, and that a small group of rangers stay in the lodge during those months to maintain it. My mind immediately flashes to The Shining by Stephen King.

He also told us that he's hiked around the entire rim of the canyon, earning our respect. Some of the hikes we've been on were pretty daunting, and that's not even going down into the canyon. I was too wary of hurting my knee, so Maddie and Raven stayed back with me. We went to the El Tovar dining room and had a fancy lunch instead.

On our last evening there, Chase and I went to go watch the sunset together. We found a place away from everyone else and sat down on a big boulder to take in the show.

I've watched a lot of sunsets and even a few sunrises at this point in my life but watching them at the Grand Canyon is unmatched. Chase puts his arm around me as we settle down on our blanket. It's a breezy sixty-five degrees, perfect weather for our last night here. It's been an amazing trip, the best of my life.

"Do you think your family had fun?" he asks.

"Oh gosh, I know they did. We never traveled growing up, not outside of competitions for me and Mads. Allan and Auguste played rec football and baseball, but theirs was a local league. Travel was seen as a necessary expense

Chapter 31

for sports, but that was really it. Our mom moved around for a while when she was a child, but when her father put roots in Louisiana, that was it. And Daddy never left the state before he met my mom and starting tagging along when she did rodeos."

"Well, I'm glad that you have the travel bug. We're going to go on so many adventures together."

I smile at him, and he leans down to kiss me. "Have you heard anything about the draft? I know it's not for a while, but…"

"Yeah, actually. Now that our season is done and I have an agent, there are two teams looking closely at me. One of them is Vancouver, and the other is the New York Islanders."

"You're kidding! No Bruins?"

"Not that I'm aware of. But they already have a really solid lineup for wingers, so I'd rather be put on a team where I stand a chance of playing and not just sent down to the farm team waiting for someone to retire or get injured before getting called up."

"That makes sense. Wow. I hear Vancouver is absolutely beautiful."

"Yeah. Still planning to wait on applying for publishing houses until we find out?" He tries to sound nonchalant, but I can hear the worry in his voice.

"Chase, yes. We've spent enough time apart. I am one hundred percent willing to follow where you go. The rest will fall into place as long as you and I are together. You taught me to have faith in myself and in us. This is me showing you that."

He pulls me tight and squeezes me with gratitude.

Pondering my own words, I'm struck with the sense of lost time. My eyes well as I realize how much time we've really lost. Chase looks over and notices my despondent mood.

"Sweets? What's wrong?"

I sniffle. "I just-we've lost so much time together and I only now realized it. We could have been doing this for years, Chase, and-"

"Love, stop. We were inevitable, Lennie, whether I loved you in secret for three more minutes or three more years. You were always going to be mine because I've always been yours."

W o w.

He lifts my chin with his hand and kisses me softly. "And Lennie?" His smile is devastating. "You were worth the wait. Now let's watch this sunset."

And we did. We watched the beautiful end of our last day in Arizona. As the valley became swallowed by shadow, the jagged rocks reflected the last beams of this days sunshine, turning them to burning, brilliant shades of crimson, gold, and ocher.

It was the most breathtaking death that I've ever seen.

* * *

A few weeks later, the girls surprise me with another trip.

"Len. Lennie. Lenore!"

I slowly open my eyes, registering the sunlight filtering through the blinds. And then I look left and jump out of my skin because my psycho twin is standing over my bed like a serial killer.

"Gaaaah! What the *hell*, Raven?" I yell, hitting her with my pillow.

"Well, I've been trying to wake you up for like five minutes!"

"Maybe pick a way that's less Ted Bundy?!"

She rolls her eyes at me.

"Whatever, you grump. Get up, we have plans today!"

I glance at the clock, and groan.

Thanks for the Sunday 7am wake up Raven. Pretty sure we didn't have plans, but what the heck, I'll bite.

"And those would be?"

"We're going to Martha's Vineyard!" Gabby shrieks, as she runs into the room and jumps on the bed with me.

"What? Seriously? All of us?" I'm immediately wide awake and excited.

"Yep. So, thank your twinster for making us all get up at the crack of dawn *on the Lord's day,*" Cora gripes from the doorway, with a death grip on her coffee.

"We've all been studying for finals and not coming up for air and thought it would be nice to get out of the house and go explore a new place together,"

Chapter 31

Raven says, shrugging and looking a little embarrassed. "Like old times."

Wow. My sister is awesome, and she doesn't do it a lot. I think it's an effort to keep her bad-ass image, but she can be incredibly thoughtful.

Now that I'm done with my coaching gig and the team won their second consecutive championship, after which my heart burst purely with joy, I've basically given myself over to studying day and night.

And she's right. We've been all work and no play this close to graduation. The ending is imminent, and I think we're all feeling varying degrees of excitement, trepidation, fear of the unknown, and readiness to start the next season in our lives.

Throwing off my covers, I say "Let's do this, then!"

We take the Island Queen ferry to Martha's Vineyard, and it's like a postcard. The cliffs at the coast give way to green grass, swaying wildflowers and dune wheat, lighthouses, and picturesque buildings.

After looking at our options, we start our day out with breakfast at Rosewater Market, grabbing a sunny spot in the courtyard, and people watch while drinking coffee and tea and eating breakfast sandwiches.

Afterward, we hopped on a bus tour of the five lighthouses on the island. Turns out, you can go up in four out of the five of them. It also turns out that scaling a lighthouse is easier than it sounds. I recommend it for the amazing views, don't recommend it on account that my legs felt like wet noodles after the second one.

I didn't climb anymore after that, nor did most of the group.

We visited a few farms to look at the animals before ending up at The Grey Barn and Farm and buying our weight in cheese, baked goods, and totes to carry them in.

For lunch, we stopped at Larsen's Fish Market where Cora, the most adventurous eater of the group, tried to get us all to try fresh oysters.

"You two are making Louisianans look bad. Aren't you guys known for eating oysters?"

"Yep, sure are. I'll eat them if they're heavily steamed, but I maintain that raw oysters look like slimy vaginas."

"Ewww, Raven!" I gripe. "They do look like huge lougies, though," I admit.

"So, you just suck them down, out of the shell?" Gabby asks curiously.

"And you are from the bougiest coast in Connecticut missy, what's your excuse for never trying an oyster?"

"Because my mother says that shellfish contain heavy metals and are breeding ground for bacteria that cause vomiting, diarrhea and death, and wouldn't let them in our house," Gabby says pragmatically.

Cora just stares at her.

"Huh, okay. Moving on. Take the shell, scrape the oyster, squeeze some lemon on it, top it with some hot sauce, and then, like so." Cora swallows hers whole. "Ta-da! Delicious. Now you go."

Gabby grabs the smallest oyster, and eyes it skeptically as she follows Cora's instructions. She tips back her head, scrunches her nose, and says, "Here goes nothing," as she lets the oyster fall into her mouth.

Her eyes fly open wide, and she doesn't quite get it down her throat. She starts trying to chew it and gags, her panic showing all over her face. Gagging again and flapping her hands, she looks around frantically before apparently saying to hell with it. She spits the partially masticated oyster back on her plate and sits back with a look of utter horror on her face.

Raven and I are laughing with tears rolling down our faces, while Cora just looks at Gabby with her mouth hanging open. "Why the hell did you try to chew it?" she asks, mystified.

Gasping for air, Gabby chugs what's left of her water before snatching Raven's and drinking that too. She swishes it in her mouth several times before speaking.

"Why the *hell* did you let me put that into my mouth?!" she accuses Cora while Raven and I giggle uncontrollably. "That was the nastiest, slimiest, softest, *hunngh*" she breaks off as she gags again.

"Oh my God Gab, stop gag-*huuungh*" Cora gags, but manages to recover with a shiver. "In my defense, you were supposed to just swallow it down!"

"What's the point of food that's so disgusting you can't even chew it?!"

"Yeah, remind me never to take food recommendations from Cora," Raven says dryly.

"What, is Gabby not selling you on oysters?" I tease.

Chapter 31

We spend the rest of the day looking at pretty houses, browsing boutiques, and going in and out of museums. On the ferry back to Boston, we watch the sky start to broadcast the sun's decent on the back deck. We're beat after the day, and it strikes me that this could be our last little adventure together.

"Where do you think we'll all end up?" I ask, unwilling to accept that this is the end for us.

"I'll probably stay in Boston," Gabby starts. "Dylan found a job here. Plus, my family lives here. My brother is moving back to work with my dad after he graduates from law school next week."

"We know you'll end up where Chase does," Raven says. "I'm not sure about me. I can work anywhere with my degree. Or if I decide to play 'fuck around and find out' and just give photography a go."

"I'll be getting my masters in New York at Columbia," Cora shares, earning gasps from the three of us.

"You got in?!" I cry out.

"I confirmed with them last night after sitting on my decision for a few months, but I didn't want to make today about that," she admits. "It feels like the end and part of me didn't want to acknowledge that we may all be scattering away from Boston."

"Then let's make a pact. No matter where we end up, we will always find a way to be in each other's lives." I say firmly.

"Duh."

"It's a promise."

"Always."

Chapter 32

quatervois
(n) a crossroads, a critical decision, or a turning point in ones life

The next two weeks fly by, and before I know it, the final party of our college lives is tonight. Part of me wanted to stay in with Chase and watch a movie, but I know this is the last chance for us to say goodbye to this version of ourselves before we head into the real world as adults after graduating tomorrow.

He tells me to get ready with the girls one last time, saying he'll meet us there. I choose my outfit carefully. White skinny jeans, a tight black-and-white striped top with a boat neck and three-quarter sleeves, and camel high-heeled booties with a matching cross body clutch. I take my time doing my hair and makeup, thinking back to our first party together. Remembering how young and naive and innocent we all were. In the past four years I've watched Gabby, Cora, and Raven grow into amazing women. They're strong, kind, intelligent, and have been the greatest friends to me, even when I was at my lowest.

Because that's what good friends do, isn't it? They hold you up when your own legs can't support you and they champion around you until you believe in yourself the way that they do.

They love us in spite of our flaws, and we love them back because of it.

I walk into Raven's room, taking in her edgy bohemian look. She's added

Chapter 32

quite a few tattoos over the years, and she looks like a gypsy goddess.

"What do you think?" I ask, turning in a circle. "Too Librarian from New Hampshire?"

She laughs, shaking her head at me.

"No, you look like Lenore Landry, future bad ass editor, who's gonna marry Chase and give me lots of babies to spoil."

"Who's to say you're not gonna have babies first? I'm on track to becoming a big, serious boss lady," I tease.

"Yeah, I doubt I'll ever find a man who can keep up with me," she says, shrugging. "It's on you to carry on our superior genetics. Also, I don't want kids."

"Lord," I shake my head. "Let's just focus on getting drinks first."

We arrive at the same house from freshman year, Beta Sigma Sigma Gamma. I thought it was so mysterious and grand back then. Now I see that it's just a house, with memories and ghosts, and skeletons in the closet just like any other house.

Still, there's something poetic about ending where we began. There's a guy at the door handing out cups of beer, some new pledge, no doubt.

"No thanks," I say, trying to brush past.

"Seriously, I have to give everyone a beer," he says in a bored voice.

"No thanks, I don't want one," I say more firmly.

"Why are you being rude about it? It's my job, lady."

Lady?!

In that moment, I remember Gabby being dragged away as her arms flapped uselessly at her sides. I remember every boy and man who told me to "smile, you're prettier that way" and every time I was spoken down to or dismissed because I was being "too timid" or "emotional" or viewed as irrelevant because of being female.

Hell no, this just won't do.

I square my shoulders and look this kid square in the eye. He may have me in height, but I have him in Angry Female.

"Rejecting a drink from someone that you don't know isn't rude, *guy*, it's smart. Every pamphlet in the student union and every rapey frat house movie ever made has taught women not to trust anyone with our safety. I don't know you. I've never seen you before in my life, so if I or anyone chooses to refuse a drink, you should be a man and accept that you haven't earned an ounce of my goddamn trust and move on! I don't owe you anything, not my time, not my respect, not my manners. I'm for damn sure not gonna to let you play the 'don't be a rude girl' card so that you can save face!"

His face screws up like he's going to snap back at me, but he doesn't get the chance. At least twenty people around us break out into applause and cheers, and I let that be the last word as I breeze past him into the house.

I meet up with Chase and we end up having a lot of fun before choosing to call it an early night around midnight, closing our last chapter of college as more mature and complete people than we started.

The next day at graduation is kind of a blur, to be honest. In the blink of an eye, we're taking pictures in front of Bellus Hall with the other five thousand graduates. Only my parents made it up, since my siblings all had jobs and finals of their own.

At dinner with Chase's parents that night, talk turns to the future.

"Well, I know Raven is coming home for the summer to regroup and apply for jobs," Daddy is saying. "Lenore, have you and Chase finalized anything?"

I can tell he's hopeful that I'm returning to Louisiana.

"Yes, actually. Well, not on the job front, because I'm not planning to apply for anything until Chase has been drafted." It's a matter of what team, not *if*. He's the most developed player Kalon has had in all four years, and not only is he confident in his abilities, but his agent is also.

"I'm staying in Boston," I say, and immediately note the way my parent's shoulders droop. "I'm going to be working at Beaux Mots this summer, and Chase and I are moving in with Connell and Sabrina."

Sabrina beams at me, and I smile back.

"But we're planning to come down for a week in June and in July before the draft." Chase hastily adds.

"I know that I speak for us both when I say that we'll miss our daughter, but I don't think either of us ever expected Lenore to stay in Louisiana," Momma says with a smile. "She has too much wanderer in her for that."

Chapter 32

"You'll always have a place at home, cher," Daddy says. "You both come visit whenever you can."

* * *

When we visit the first time in June, Chase has a blast. He's never been to Louisiana, so everything was new and amazing to him. It helps that we showed him *le bon temps*. He may have traveled all over with his parents, but he clocked a lot of firsts in that trip, though he refused to ride a horse. First time seeing an alligator in the wild, first time on an air boat, first time eating crawfish, first time gagging while watching someone suck the head of the crawfish, and first time viewing the constellations.

"Just look at that. I love Boston, but you can't see the stars there, not like this," Chase breathes out, sounding awed as we lay side by side on a blanket in the back field one night.

"Yep, too much light pollution. That's one of the reasons Momma wanted to live so far out in the country. She taught us about the stars."

"Show me a constellation?"

I scan the sky, remembering the last time I did this, how hopeless I felt. I spy one of my favorite constellations, one of the easiest to spot due to its unique shape.

"There, see the one that looks like a giant fishhook?"

"Yeah."

"That's Scorpius. To some, it represents the Scorpion or Scorpio, the zodiac sign. But to the people of Hawaii, it represents Manaiklalani, the demigod Maui's magical fishhook. The legend says that he used it to create the Hawaiian Islands. To this day some people wear pendant necklaces of his fishhook as a symbol of energy, prosperity, and strength."

"I like that," he says.

I think back to that August night when I found only death and danger in the summer sky. I was searching for hope and answers and didn't find any that night. But Scorpius was in the sky that night, a shining symbol of life and fortitude, and I chose to overlook it.

I guess we see what we want to see.

* * *

September

If someone had told me at the beginning of college, or hell, even the beginning of this year, that I would be sitting at a downtown cafe in New York City with Chase, my ex-boyfriend, and Luca's girlfriend Camille, I would have called them insane.

But here we are.

Luca and Chase rekindled their friendship after running into each other at the dry cleaners. Chase was picking up his suit to prepare for pre-season media, and Luca was picking up his suits for his investment banker job.

He figured out his future after all.

We spent a few weeks slowly getting reacquainted, briefly stumbling over the awkwardness of having been a formerly intimate couple who now has different partners. I'm happy to say that it's been wonderful having Luca back in my life. He will always be the first buddy I had.

Camille is now a friend to me as well, and it's been nice to have someone in the city other than Cora. Now that it's September, she is busy again with school. And yes, in case you're wondering, Camille does spend lots of time in the kitchen cooking for Luca. It's a good thing she's a chef at a restaurant uptown, and presumably loves to cook!

Chase ended up getting drafted by the New York Islanders. It was one of the best days of his life, he said, and I basked in his happiness like it was my own.

Because of course it was.

Things moved fairly quickly after that. We got a small, and I do mean *small*, one-bedroom apartment close to the practice arena on Long Island. Sabrina and Gabby helped me apply to every entry position at publishing houses, sending out a dozen emails with my resume and a recommendation letter from Beaux Mots.

Chapter 32

When we returned from our last visit to Louisiana at the end of July, I had a few entry-level offers.

I chose the one with the smallest company, eager to get in on the ground floor of the growing publishing house. Luckily, it was on Long Island, within walking distance for the few days a week that I don't work remotely. I never did get another vehicle. I'm sure if we ever move from the city, it will be necessary, especially if we have children. For now, I'm content with this life that we're starting together, full of promise and hope.

I don't look at sunsets as endings anymore. The real truth about sunsets is that they're always followed by the sunrise. They're the ending to one day and an opening to another, an endless chance to grow and change and evolve into the people we're meant to be. Losing it all feels like a failure. But sometimes it's the only path to finding who you really are. I'm thankful for every beginning and ending that I've ever had.

After all, they lead me to this point in my life.

My sunrise.

Epilogue

veneration
(n) a deep reverence, a passionate love for something or someone on a spiritual level

Three years later

Raven

"You gonna make it?" I ask Chase, biting my lip to keep from laughing at him. It's Independence Day weekend, and Lennie and Chase flew in to spend a week at our parent's house, along with Chase's parents. It's their first time visiting Louisiana, and they're in the barn petting the horses and feeding them apples with Lennie and our mom.

"How do people do this every day?" he says, sitting on a bale of hay with his head between his knees, gripping his hair in both hands, and looking like a maniac.

"Sit up, she's going to think something's wrong with you!"

"There *is* something wrong with me, I am *actively trying not to shit my pants!*"

I can't hold it back anymore, and my loud country laugh comes flying out of my mouth.

"You're being a big baby, of course she's going to say yes to you! You're practically married already!"

He whips his head up and narrows his eyes. "Shhh, she's going to hear you!"

Epilogue

he hisses at me.

Rolling my eyes, I take some test shots of the big pond on our land, making sure to get the huge live oaks draped with Spanish moss in the frame.

"Okay, time to pull up your big boy britches."

"What are britches?" he asks, confused.

"Yankees," I say, rolling my eyes skyward. "Here she comes, it's go time!"

He takes a deep, fortifying breath before heading over to Lennie.

"Come over here with me sweets, I have something to show you."

"Ohh, are the ducks back?" she asks, looking around.

"Close, come near the water."

I let them pass me, looking down at the pictures I just took, trying to seem like I'm not paying attention. Once they go by, I sneak up behind them and find cover behind a big tree trunk. I'm close enough that I can see and hear them, but I'm far enough away to make it seem like they're all alone.

"Is there another big fish that you need me to identify?" she asks, peering into the water. They're under a big oak tree, and there's only a field lined with more huge trees beyond the pond. Long tendrils of moss wave in the gentle breeze. It's hotter than hell and as humid as a steam room, but I'll make sure these pictures convey only love and serenity.

Chase gets down on one knee and Lennie finally turns from the water, gasping when she sees him. He has the ring box in shaking hands, and she immediately brings both hands to her face.

I've shot a few freelance engagements and I swear, they do that every. single. time.

I just chuckle and snap away.

"Chase!"

She doesn't move her eyes from his face, so I'm guessing that she's missed that fact that everyone in our families has come up behind me to watch.

"Lennie, I've loved you for longer than we've officially been together. It just gets better every day. You are the most graceful person I know. You put up with ten-day road trips, my busy schedule, crazy hockey groupies, and everything in between with a smile on your face. You told me the definition of veneration once in that church in Boston, and at the time, I couldn't tell you that it was how I felt about you. How I feel about you. The veneration I have for you is unmatched. And I'm sure I had a whole grand speech planned, but I literally can't remember any of it other than I love you. Will you marry me?"

And son of a bitch, tears are even running down *my* face at that declaration.

"Yes!" she shouts, tackling him to the ground in a huge hug.

I snap away as everyone laughs and cheers and claps behind me, and I finally put the camera down and join them.

After I make them take the obligatory engagement shots, they all head inside to celebrate.

I stay out there looking at the pond, trying to will myself to get closer to the edge. Blind panic freezes me before I can take a step, seizing my muscles and sending electric shock from my stomach to the roots of my hair.

I take a step back and then another before I'm able to breathe again.

Giving one last longing look to the barn housing my sweet, sweet horses, I turn away and head back inside.

Ready for Raven's story? Read about her and Gabby's brother, Grant, in The Thing About Sunrises, available for preorder here.
https://www.amazon.com/dp/B0C9XDPQM5
Read on for a sneak peek!

Curious about Chase's first impressions of Lennie, and that fateful conversation he had with Dylan? Sign up for my newsletter here and I'll send you a bonus chapter from his POV!
https://dl.bookfunnel.com/fikihp607t

Sneak Peek: The Thing About Sunrises

(Subject to Change)

PART I - Grant

"The walls we build around us to keep sadness out also keeps out the joy."

Jim Rohn

Prologue

"He's gone."

The words that gasp from my mother's lips as my father holds her close while she sobs and sags against him register in the recesses of my brain, yet I can't make sense of them. The police officer stands in the entry way, looking like he would rather be anywhere other than a stranger's foyer in the middle of the night, carrying news of death like a harbinger from Hell.

In the background I hear my little sister Gabby start to cry out over and over, "NO NO NO NO!" though her words barely penetrate the buzzing in my ears.

Impossible. I just saw him hours ago. Real and healthy, and *alive*. This can't be true. My older brother, the person who I most looked up to in life, is never coming home.

Stolen from us in the middle of the night.

Gavin died alone in the dark on his way back from dinner with friends, celebrating his graduation from law school that day, only to fall victim to icy asphalt and winding roads.

The next weekend at his funeral, my parents have fallen victim to shock and grief, and I numbed myself with scotch before I gave his eulogy. I spoke of his kindness, his strength, how people always knew where they stood with him, because he was honest.

An open book.

How he planned to dedicate his life to fighting for justice alongside our father at his law firm, and eventually me, working to advocate for victims' rights and being their voice in the courtroom.

It was my father's dream to have The Ellis Firm transform to Ellis and Sons, and Gavin and I eagerly worked towards the path of helping him realize that dream. Working alongside his sons, fighting the good fight is all he's ever wanted, and I will start law school in the fall as planned.

We may have lost Gavin, but my father won't lose his dream. I plan on filling those impossibly big shoes that Gavin left behind with everything I've got.

Chapter 1

Seven Years Later

"Dude, you don't understand. She wanted it, man! She showed up all legs for days, tits overflowing, and then wanted to act coy. We met on fucking Tinder for Christ's sake, it's not like she's some nun! This bitch is in it for a payoff, Graham!"

"It's Grant, actually," I say, dryly.

I sit back and rub my eyes, which does nothing to get the grit out. I'm starting to regret those last few scotches from last night. Attempting to will away the pounding at my temples, I take a deep breath and hold up a hand.

"Once again Mr. Jacobs, I must insist that you refrain from using wording that can implicate guilt or perceived sexual intentions, and I can assure you that calling your accuser a bitch and disparaging her appearance doesn't paint you in a noble light."

Christ, this guy is a piece of work.

Accused of sexually assaulting his date for the night after he went from being demanding to physical, a miss Lyla Huntington maintains that following their dinner date, she was able to flee his vehicle after he aggressively groped her.

The guy reeks of alcohol even after sleeping overnight at the county jail where I'm meeting with him. Daddy has some big bucks and called in the best criminal defense lawyer in Boston.

Yours truly, as my father is currently working a convoluted homicide case.

Chapter 1

I don't envy him in the slightest, though right now I think I'd rather be going over tedious forensics and blood splatter evidence than spending one more second with this spoiled little shit.

And yet, my brain is already working around a defense for this man, viewing the angles, recalling loopholes in the law, creating a loose outline in my mind's eye for how I'm going to fight these charges.

I didn't get my professional reputation as a bulldog for playing it safe in the courtroom, after all.

A few hours later, after knocking back some extra strength Tylenol with a scotch chaser, I'm heading to Del Friscos with my best friend Jace to meet up with some friends from law school for dinner and much needed drinks. Jace works in civil law at a firm in the Seaport District, where he lives in a high rise close to the steakhouse, so I ubered to his apartment before walking with him to dinner. Jace's the smartest guy I know, though why he went into civil law is beyond me. His brain has corporate lawyer written all over it, but he's also the most compassionate man I know, and he claims that he's found his niche.

"Tell me again about this guy you're dating. Brandon?" I start as we step out of his building. I immediately start sweating. It's a hot day for it being April and I'm regretting not changing out of my suit and tie before coming over.

"Braydon, and he's great actually, I'd love for you two to meet soon. We've been taking it slow for a while, but he wants me to meet his mom next weekend."

"Glad to hear it, man."

"Any special lady you have your eyes set on, Grant?" he asks coyly, the jackass knowingly pushing my buttons.

I snort. "Yeah, sure. Her name is Easy and I met her at the bar the other night. Put her in a cab afterward and never looked back."

"When are you going to stop with these one night stands, man? Doesn't it feel empty?"

I sent him a withering glance. He knows better than most why I find my escape from the day at the end of a bottle of scotch and no-strings release with a bar hopper. Is it the healthiest of coping mechanisms? Maybe not, but I'm not about to start pulling at that thread, especially after the day I've had.

I followed my interview with Mr. She-Wanted-It with a meeting confirming defense strategy for a one Mrs. Horowitz who is accused of trying to hire a murderer for her husband. The wench had the audacity to actually make a pass at me when I saw her alone in the hall afterwards, so let's just say that I'm not in the best frame of mind right now.
Especially towards women.

We make it to the restaurant where the guys are already seated, and our buddy Tanner picks up in the middle of his thoughts as though our arrival is a brief interlude to his monologue.

"She blew my mind, dude," he says dreamily. "I never thought I'd be going back for repeats, but she's a wildcat." God, this guy. He's been gushing about some chick that's tied him up in knots. Literally, she tied him up like some kind of grade b porn dominatrix and he looks so dazed and blissed out that I'm starting to wonder if he's stoned. Ironically, this is the man who is running for election in the next few years for District Attorney. The voters would weep if they could hear him now. Or roll their eyes, in the case of this voter.

"Hey guys, not to steal Tanner's pervy thunder, but I asked you all here because I have some news."

Thank you Damian for that much needed change of topic. I can always count on him to be levelheaded and mature. Which fits since he works in tax law.

"I'm going ask Nikolette to marry me this weekend."

That was enormously short lived relief.

"Right on brother!" Tanner claps him on the back while I take a bitter sip of my drink.

"Hell yeah," Jace offers.

"God, what is with everyone wanting to wife up lately," I grumble, the scotch loosening my tongue just enough to let me forget friendship etiquette. My cousin, who is like a little brother to me, just called last week to let me know he proposed to his girlfriend of three years and asked me to be the best man.

Don't get me wrong, Lennie is great. I met her when they stayed a few

Chapter 1

weeks at my family's home in Connecticut last summer. She's a sweet girl, but Chase is an NHL player. I told him he should be spending his younger years playing the field and sowing his oats, and he cheerfully told me to fuck off. Once I spent time with Lennie I could see how right they are for each other, but a piece of me thinks settling down this young is a mistake.

Back to the present and everyone is glaring at me for being the insensitive jerk that I am, and a small lick of shame flares in my gut as I realize that I not only spoke out loud, but probably just shit all over Damian's parade.

"Sorry man. Long day and I'm feeling especially bastardy. If you're happy, I'm happy for you." I do actually like Nikolette, she's feisty and a lot of fun to be around.

"All good, brother." Yeah, Damian is nice like that, the most easy going one of us all.

Tanner starts up some funny story of about a wedding reception fiasco and I tune him out, thinking back on the events of today. I can't get past the tainted feeling of that woman hitting on me.

"I'd love to take you out for a drink to thank you for how hard you've worked for me. Or maybe I can cook you dinner and we can test out the thread count of my sheets." She purrs while putting her hand on my arm.

I made an excuse about not dating clients (true) and got the hell out of there. What about me made her think I'd even entertain screwing her? Does she see just how slimy of a defense attorney bastard I am and think like I have no morals or standards at all?

Is this who I've become?

I'm lost in reflection and self-loathing when I'm jostled by Damian jumping out of his chair next to me. I smell something floral and mouthwatering and look to my left to see a beautiful woman I've never met before. She has long, dark shiny hair and is dressed in a flowy, bohemian looking dress with a wide belt.

Come to think of it, she looks vaguely familiar. Am I drunk already?

Then I look closer and notice some kind of sparkly chain that connects to a necklace and encircles her breasts. That, and arms full of tattoos. Just the sort of woman my mother would shiver at because tattoos and body jewelry "screams trashy and cheap" and I hate that I'm instantly attracted to her.

I come back to reality to hear Damian gushing at her. "You look great, I'm glad to see that your color is back! The last time I saw you, you looked like you were going to waste away, girl."

"I know, that was the sickest I've ever been in my life. Thank God for Nik, she took really good care of me. It's good to see you, I'm just meeting some friends here for dinner."

That accent. Southern, sweet Jesus.

He turns towards us, putting his arm around her. "Guys, this is a good friend of mine and Ni-"

I snort, taking in her petite form, tamping down on the attraction that I should not be feeling for this chick. "Let me guess, she's your hairdresser." I say snidely, knocking back my third (fourth?) scotch and vaguely registering alarm bells in the back of my fuzzy brain.

She whips her head towards me and glares in contempt, which deep down I know I earned. Her green eyes are striking, gleaming like gemstones as they narrow on me in repulsion.

"Actually, Mr. Suit, I'm a Senior Financial Analyst," she scathingly replies, raising her eyebrow. "What is it that you do for a living? Wait! Let me guess." She taps her finger on her full mouth for a second, looking pensive. "I've got it." She points to me with a shit-eating grin.

"Vacuum cleaner salesman."

My mouth falls open and next to me, my former best friend snorts into his beer while every other fucker at this table laughs at my expense. I hope they all develop hemorrhoids overnight.

"Raven! Over here girl!" a woman shouts from a few tables down.

"Give Niki a squeeze from me okay? Great to see you Damian!" she starts to head towards her table.

She looks back at me and bites out, "Oh and it was SO lovely to meet you, Mr. Salesman." And then she has the audacity to salute me before turning on her heel and walking off without a second glance behind, leaving me embarrassed, chastised, and dumbfounded.

Chapter 1

Thank you for reading the sneak peak of The Thing About Sunrises. I am so excited for you to get your hands on Grant and Raven's beautiful story! You can preorder here. https://www.amazon.com/dp/B0C9XDPQM5

Acknowledgments

Who would have thought that at 37 years old, I'd be trying something new and writing my first author's note. Certainly not me.

This book started with an idea for one scene, the pool scene when Lennie shows up Luca. As I started writing and gave myself over to the process, the characters didn't fit the mold I put them in. They morphed into who they were meant to be, transforming the story from the rom-com it was intended to into a story that showcased different types of love and the strength it takes to change and grow and learn to stand on two feet and approve of who you see in the mirror.

It was at first titled Veneration, then changed to The Truth About Sunsets when it became less about the love story, and more about the journey that it took to get there.

I want to thank my husband Michael for inspiring me to write about love and for picking up my slack while I did it. I want to thank my children, my parents, and all of my siblings and their spouses for inspiring me to write about family. I especially want to thank my sister Codi for being a beta reader and giving me great guidance throughout the entire process. You're the best at giving gentle, honest advice!

And thank you to my mom who encouraged me throughout the process and proudly proclaims to be my biggest fan!

I want to thank my three best friends, Lisa, Jess, and Fatima for inspiring me to write about friendship, and a special thank you to Fatima who I must have exchanged a million texts with while I was writing this book. Thanks for the great advice!

Thank you to Leslie Ann Tuttle for the first developmental edit of this novel, and for helping me shape it from its conception to execution!

And I want to thank my favorite gymnasts, Nastia Liukin, Shawn Johnson, and Simone Biles, for inspiring me to write about gymnastics, and for giving girls a goal to work towards, and a dream to fight for. I hope that I did the sport justice.

Thank you to my friends Brooke Meyer and Karen Condon for helping me this former Southern Baptist learn a little about Catholicism. And I want to thank the city of Boston for existing and giving me so much to fall in love with. I look forward to many more trips and many more new experiences.

Thank you to everyone who beta-read this novel, and a very special thank you to the world's best beta reader, Ayesha Abdul Ghaffer. Your suggestions and edits were so helpful and perfect!

A big thanks to Grey's PR for helping spread the word about my first book!

And lastly, thank you to all gymnasts for working hard and being you. It was a privilege to research my favorite sport, and I am amazed and awed by everything I found. Your hard work and dedication made me want to tell this story.

I guess gymnastics gives something back after all.

About the Author

Lacey Lorraine has been writing since she was a child, be it essays, short stories, blog posts, or journal entries. As an Army Brat, she has lived all over, including Alaska and Bahrain, and it shaped her love for travel and adventure. After a lifetime of being a voracious reader, she finally took the plunge and became an author, and it has been the most difficult and rewarding journey of her life. Currently, she is married to her high school sweetheart and they live in Florida with their children and pets…and Lacey's thousand-book collection.

You can connect with me on:
- http://laceylorraine.com
- https://twitter.com/Lace_Writes
- https://www.facebook.com/authorlaceylorraine
- https://www.instagram.com/authorlaceylorraine
- https://www.facebook.com/groups/705985018205792